A CHILDREN'S HISTORY OF INDIA

SUBHADRA SEN GUPTA has written over thirty books for children including mysteries, adventures, ghost stories, comic books and books on history. To her surprise, the Bal Sahitya Akademi thinks she is doing a good job and has given her the Bal Sahitya Puraskar in 2014. Right now she is waiting for a time machine so that she can travel to the past and join Emperor Akbar for lunch. She loves to travel, flirt with cats and chat with auto-rickshaw drivers. If you want to discuss anything under the sun with her, email her at subhadrasg @gmail.com.

PRIYANKAR GUPTA graduated from the National Institute of Design, specializing in animation film design. He has worked with various publishing companies across the world as an illustrator for children's/YA books.

A CHILDREN'S HISTORY OF INDIA

SUBHADRA SEN GUPTA

illustrated by Priyankar Gupta

Published by
Rupa Publications India Pvt. Ltd. 2015
7/16, Ansari Road, Daryaganj
New Delhi 110002

Sales centres:

Allahabad Bengaluru Chennai
Hyderabad Jaipur Kathmandu
Kolkata Mumbai

ISBN: 978-81-291-3697-8

Third impression 2016

10 9 8 7 6 5 4 3

Printed by Replika Press Pvt. Ltd, India

This book is a small offering to all the teachers who made history come alive and made me fall in love with the subject. Most of all, it is for Dr Narayani Gupta, teacher, mentor and friend.

And for my friend, Natasha Raina Kanwar, who is forever waiting for a magnum opus.

CONTENTS

SECTION ONE

ANCIENT INDIA

SECTION TWO

MEDIEVAL INDIA

SECTION THREE

BRITISH PERIOD

SECTION FOUR

INDEPENDENT INDIA

Section One

ANCIENT INDIA

(2600 BCE–1200 CE)

1
A LAND CALLED JAMBUDVIPA

~ The Landscape ~ The Monsoons ~ Discovering the Past ~ Time before History ~

In the beginning, they called the land Jambudvipa, the land of the rose apple. A land of plenty, with the soaring snow-capped mountain ranges of the Himalayas in the north and the tumultuous waters of the Indian Ocean in the south. A land covered by a network of ever-flowing rivers, bringing the promise of fertile soil, and generous harvests. The wave-lashed coastal regions of the peninsula encouraged adventure and trade and the forests were filled with the bounties of nature. It was a land that welcomed people, encouraged them to weave cloth and mould pottery, to dance and sing, to experiment with spices and live off the soil.

This generous land would one day be named India, after a river, the Indus. And from the time of the Aryans, we call our country Bharatvarsha, after an Aryan tribe, the Bharatas. However, its earliest inhabitants named it after a fruit—the jambu—the rose apple or jamun. So since ancient times, India was Jambudvipa, or the island of the rose apple.

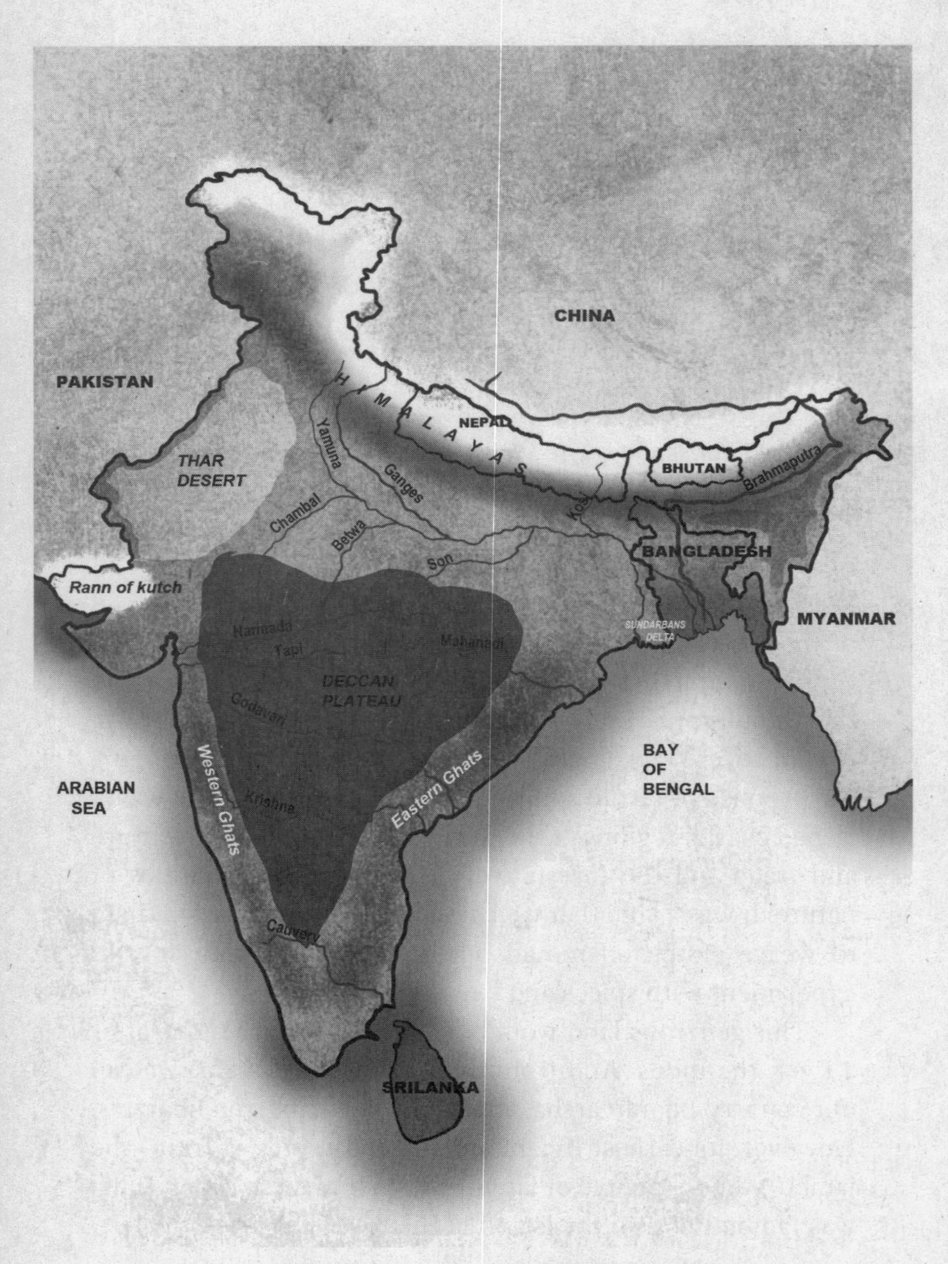

The Indian subcontinent. The land once called Jambudvipa. Today, we call it India and Bharat.

The Landscape

India is so big that it has every kind of landscape imaginable—mountains, plains, deserts, plateaus, deltas and coasts. Its climate ranges from the icy winters of Ladakh to the tropical summers of Kerala. And all these geographical features have played an important part in our history.

Let's first study the physical map of modern India. The Himalayan mountain range stands like a snowy crown in the north, separating India from the rest of Asia. This range, an immense 2,400 kilometres long, has several romantic names steeped in history and legend—Karakoram, Hindu Kush, Pir Panjal—and peaks like the Everest, the Annapurna and the Kangchenjunga. During ancient times, when invading armies moved only by land, these mountains acted like the ramparts of a fortress, discouraging attacks and allowing India to live in comparative peace. Of course, there were mountain passes like the Khyber and the Bolan in the north-west; these were mostly used by traders to take our goods as far as Europe but they also let in invaders—from Alexander in the third century BCE to Babur in the sixteenth century.

Rivers are at the heart of our civilization. The Himalayas are the source of three mighty rivers—the Indus, the Ganga and the Brahmaputra, that have spread their network through tributaries across the land from Punjab to Assam. The Indus flows out of Tibet, curves south into north India and then flows into the Arabian Sea in today's Pakistan. The Ganga rises in a glacial cave in Uttarakhand and then moves east towards the Bay of Bengal, creating one of the world's biggest and most fertile alluvial plains. The Indo-Gangetic plain is at the heart of India's civilization and has seen some of the most

The ice-capped mountain ranges of the mighty Himalayas.

important events in our history—from the Buddha standing at its banks in Varanasi to the rise and fall of the famous city of Pataliputra.

The mighty Brahmaputra also starts its journey in Tibet but turns east and flows through Arunachal Pradesh and Assam, only to turn west into modern Bangladesh, where it meets the Padma, a tributary of the Ganga. Here, the many streams of the Ganga and Brahmaputra flow into the Bay of Bengal, creating a delta criss-crossed by streams that has been coveted over centuries by different invaders for its fertile soil.

Similarly, in the south, the great kingdoms rose and fell by the rivers, like the fabulous city of Vijayanagar that stood by the Tungabhadra. The Narmada and the Godavari brought life to central India; and the rice, spice and cotton fields of the Deccan were fed by the waters of the Krishna and the Kaveri.

Cotton was grown and then woven into brightly coloured fabrics that were loaded on to ships that voyaged to Arabia and Mozambique, Java and Bali. Along with items of trade, traders carried with them the rich heritage of our culture.

The many ports along the western and eastern coasts, like Kaveripattinam, Bharuch and Kochi, saw many Arab, Malay and Chinese traders. Soon enough, the cotton and spices that we were famous for brought the Portuguese, the French and the English to our shores. They were not interested in peaceful trade but came to destroy, conquer and colonize the country and changed India's history forever.

Indians and Geography

The ancient Indians were never very keen to draw accurate maps. In the Puranas, they described the world as a flat disc with a mythical mountain called Meru at the centre, surrounded by seas and seven islands or dvipas. These seas were said to be made not just of water but also milk, treacle, butter and ghee!

The Monsoons

Another mighty force of history races across the sky in the form of rain-laden clouds. The monsoon winds rise up in the Indian Ocean during summer and then, like clockwork, they move north, up the Indian landmass, bringing rain. One branch comes up from the Arabian Sea, the other from the Bay of Bengal and as they collide with the Himalayas, they pour their life-giving rain all across the land. They water the wheat fields of Punjab, the paddy fields of Bengal and the forests of Madhya Pradesh. By autumn, the same winds move in the opposite direction, raining on Tamil Nadu and Kerala.

When Arab sailors discovered how these winds moved like clockwork across the oceans they used them to sail to and back from India. So it was the monsoon winds that first brought Arab, and then European, trading ships to our ports.

The magic of the monsoon rains—varsha—is an integral part of our culture, as the whole land looks up anxiously to the sky for those first grey cumulonimbus clouds. Kalidasa would compose a paean, a song of praise, to the clouds in *Meghdutam*. We dance and sing and celebrate its arrival with colourful festivals. Rabindranath Tagore writes,

> *Lightning darts through the clouds, ripping them,*
> *Dotting the sky with sharp, crooked smiles.*

Indra's Thunder

In ancient times, Indians prayed to Lord Indra, the god of thunder and lightning to bring rain. Our myths say that every summer Indra rides out on his celestial elephant Airavata to battle Vritra, the demon of drought.

Discovering the Past

India is an ancient land, and that is why we have so much history to study in school! For example, the cities of the

Harappan civilization were built nearly 5,000 years ago. Also, since the land is so vast, kingdoms have risen and fallen all across it, sometimes at the same time, and that can be very confusing. For example, while the Tughlaqs were ruling in Delhi, there were the kings of Vijayanagar and the Bahmani sultans ruling in the south and other small kingdoms elsewhere. So how do historians and archaeologists discover what happened so long ago and also keep track of so many confusing, simultaneous events?

For very ancient times, for which we have little information available in writing, it all depends on what the archaeologists tell us. They are a little like detectives, piecing together a portrait of the past. They dig at historical sites, preserve old monuments and study what they find. They also learn to read ancient scripts and study inscriptions carved on rocks, pillars, on the walls of temples and on copper tablets. During their excavations, they unearth pottery, metal tools, remains of houses, jewellery and even toys and weapons and this gives us an idea of how people lived in the past. For example, for the Harappan cities, where we have still not managed to understand their script, all our knowledge has come from the work of archaeologists.

In later periods, coins give us names and dates of kings and palm-leaf manuscripts provide information about the events of the time. Among manuscripts there are religious texts like the Vedas and Upanishads, stories like the Puranas and Jatakas, political texts like the *Arthashastra*, and poems, plays and memoirs.

Historians gather all these sources of information and piece together the history of a place and a time. This history is not just about kings, battles and dates, it is also about how ordinary people lived—the houses they lived in, the food they ate, the clothes they wore and what the children studied in school. History is also our literature, music, dance, painting, architecture and sculpture. The word 'history' says it all—it is the story of our past.

Time before History

There is a period considered as *pre-history,* when people lived a primitive life mainly as nomads. This period is called the Stone Age. The first people were hunter-gatherers—they lived in caves, hunted wild animals and gathered fruits and leaves for food. Then they learned to make primitive stone tools and discovered how to make fire. The primary record we have of their lives are the paintings on the walls of certain caves—vivid sketches of stick-figure humans hunting and dancing, working and playing, and paintings of several kinds of animals.

> ### Bhimbetka
>
> *The finest Stone Age cave paintings can be seen at Bhimbetka in Madhya Pradesh. They are painted in red, green, white and ochre colours that the painter must have made by grinding coloured rocks and minerals and mixing them with gum.*

Then humans took a giant leap when they learnt to grow crops and invented the wheel. As they had to take care of the crops they planted, they stopped wandering and started living in villages. From villages grew towns and cities, which then progressed into kingdoms. India's history really begins from

Stone Age paintings on the walls of caves in Bhimbetka, Madhya Pradesh.

the first cities that came up around the Indus, marking the beginnings of one of the oldest civilizations of the world—the Harappan civilization.

2
A CITY NAMED HARAPPA
(2600 BCE–1500 BCE)

~ What is a Civilization? ~ Discovering the First Cities ~ City Planning ~ Daily Life ~ Religion ~ Crafts and Trade ~ The Mysterious Seals ~ The Cities Begin to Die ~

For 5,000 years, we forgot about Harappa and Mohenjo-daro. We knew that we belonged to an ancient civilization because we had very old literature like the Vedas and the Upanishads, but no one was very interested in putting a date to them. If today we can claim to be one of the oldest civilizations in the world, a contemporary of ancient Mesopotamia and Egypt, we have to thank a group of Englishmen for that.

In the nineteenth century, when India was under British rule, these men came to India as soldiers, engineers and bureaucrats and they fell in love with the country. They learnt Indian languages and they restored not just our monuments but also much of our literature, painting and sculpture. Today we know about Harappa because of men like William Jones, the scholar who founded the Asiatic Society; Alexander Cunningham, the archaeologist who laid the foundation of the Archaeological Survey of India; James Prinsep, who cracked the Brahmi script of Ashoka; and

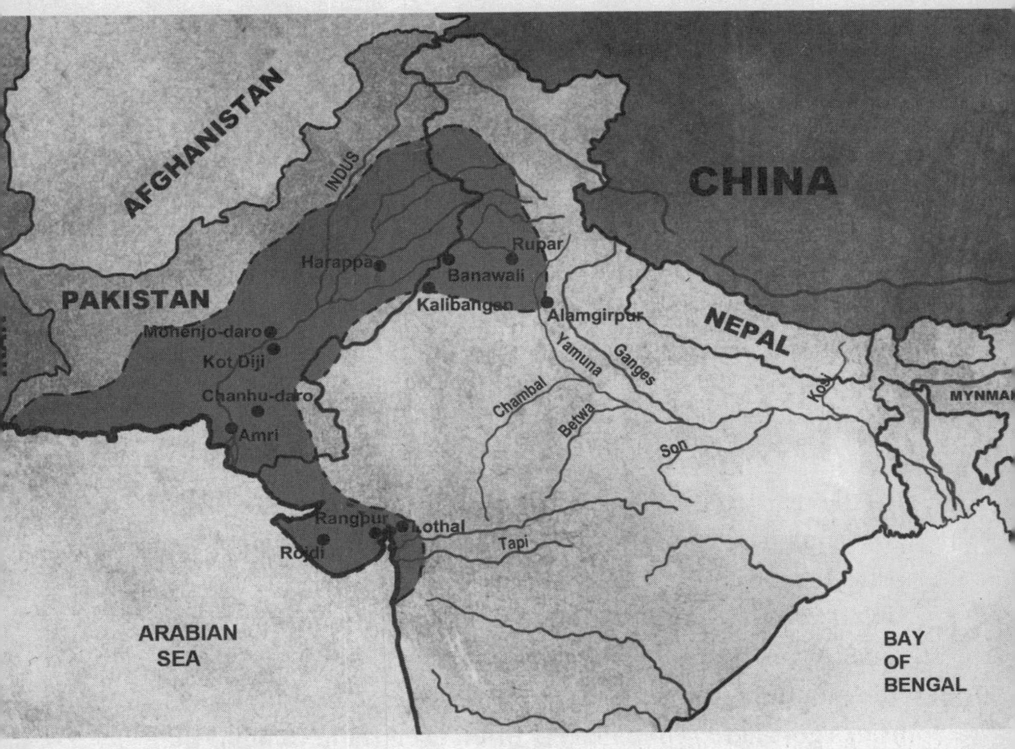

The area where remains of the Harappan civilization have been found.

Mortimer Wheeler, who rescued the hidden civilization of Harappa.

What is a Civilization?

Harappa is called the first civilization in India, but what does that exactly mean? The earliest civilizations in the world rose by the banks of rivers—the Nile in Egypt, the Tigris and Euphrates in Iraq (called the Mesopotamian or Sumerian civilization) and the Indus in India. A civilization begins when people start living in cities and they no longer survive only by agriculture. The villages around a city supply the food while the city people are craftsmen, soldiers, administrators and traders, all ruled by a king. Cities begin to trade with other cities and gradually develop a coinage. A civilization also means that there is a written language, there are palaces, forts and temples, and its people have developed their own culture through literature, sculpture, painting, music, dance, crafts and religious rituals. Cities are always interesting places, changing and evolving in exciting ways.

Discovering the First Cities

In the early years of the twentieth century, the British government decided to build a railway line in the western province of Sindh, a desert region. There, the British engineers found mysterious piles of bricks and huge mounds covered in sand. At one place, the local people called it Mohenjo-daro or 'the mound of the dead' but no one had a clue about how the bricks got there. The villagers often used them to build their houses and the railway engineers also helped themselves to some to lay the tracks. They were unaware of the fact that the bricks were over 4,000 years old and belonged to the first cities of India!

Luckily, the archaeologists arrived soon after in 1920 CE. They chanced upon one of the oldest civilizations in the world, one that had flourished by the banks of the Indus River as far back as 2,600 BCE. Initially, it was called the Indus Valley civilization but now we call it the Harappan civilization after the first city to be discovered. This is because, a century later, we came to know that the civilization was not just limited to the banks of the Indus—remains of settlements have been found as far away as Jammu and Haryana.

In the team working at the Indus Valley sites were two

young Indian archaeologists—D.R. Sahni and R.D. Bannerji as well as the Englishmen Mortimer Wheeler and John Marshall. And what they unearthed were not just pottery or sculpture but *entire* cities with roads, houses and water pools made entirely of bricks. Today, over 1,000 Harappan sites have been discovered. Among the important ones Harappa, Mohenjo-daro and Chanhu-daro are in Pakistan. The ones in India include Kalibangan (Rajasthan), Rupar (Punjab), Lothal and Dholavira (Gujarat).

The First Sighting

Alexander Cunningham had seen the brick mounds in the 1870s, nearly fifty years earlier. He found ancient pottery and a tiny square seal engraved with the image of a bull, with some words in an unknown script. He thought the seal was foreign and soon forgot all about it!

City Planning

What amazed the archaeologists was the layout of the cities—they were identical, which meant they were planned. They all had broad central avenues bisecting at right angles going north-south and east-west, with narrow lanes leading off from them, exactly like the streets of modern New York. The main streets were as wide as a two-lane highway, so they were designed for quite a lot of traffic. At one end was a higher area protected by a wall, like a fortress, that must have housed the government or the nobility and archaeologists call it the Citadel.

As more Harappan sites were discovered, archaeologists realized that the bricks were made in the same sizes and the houses were built in the same design. The houses had rooms around an open courtyard and some houses, probably belonging to wealthier people, had a second storey. The windows did not open out into the lanes, so if you were walking along a lane you would just see blank brick walls on both sides. Strangely there were no palaces, temples or pyramids to be found.

Sanitation was very important in the Harappan civilization, as most of the houses had a bathroom and Mohenjo-daro even had a swimming pool. Called the Great Bath, this pool had steps leading down to the water. The floor was lined with tar to make it waterproof and it had sophisticated piping so that the water could be changed regularly. Perhaps the most amazing thing was that all these cities had brilliantly designed underground sewer systems that are absolutely essential for any modern city. In fact, most 'modern' Indian cities did not have one till the twentieth century! The giant pipes were made of bricks and there were manholes for cleaning them. There were also large garbage

Dating Harappa

Since no one has yet cracked the Harappan script, how did they fix on a date for the Harappan cities? It was through the Harappan seals that were found in Mesopotamian cities by archaeologists excavating in modern Iraq. They concluded that Harappa and Mesopotamia must have traded with each other. As we can read the Sumerian script of Mesopotamia, we can date these cities.

cans on the streets that were cleared regularly.

Daily Life

Historians have pieced together a portrait of the life of the Harappan people from what they have found at these sites—pottery, jewellery, toys, terracotta figurines, carvings on the seals, remnants of grains, bones of animals and even dice from board games. Today the Sind region is a dry and arid land but at that time, the area was richly forested—wild animals like lions, deer, rabbits and peacocks are shown on the seals. The people had domesticated the cow and the bull, and knew of elephants, camels and pigs.

The land was fertile and the villages around the cities supplied them with grains and vegetables. They ate wheat, barley, rice, chickpeas, peas, melons, dates, berries, coconut,

Terracotta figurine and toys from Harappa.

bananas, pomegranate and garlic, all cooked in mustard and sesame seed oil. Also on the menu were mutton, beef, pork, fowl, fish, turtle and occasionally the meat of the gharial, the crocodile with the long snout.

Fragments of woven cotton have also been found at the site—the men and women probably wrapped one strip of cloth at the waist like a skirt and another like a shawl over the upper body. Women did dress up, with pretty bangles, earrings and necklaces made of beads, gold and silver. Make-up boxes have also been found at these sites, with remains of kohl and face paint in red and green. Terracotta toys like animals and carts with moving wheels, rattles, birds, whistles and monkeys that run up and down a stick have been unearthed.

Religion

What was puzzling to archaeologists was that, unlike most ancient cities, the Harappans had no palaces, mausoleums or temples. Historians have to speculate about who the rulers were and what the religion of the people was. Traditionally, in India, temples have a bathing pool, so historians think the Great Bath may have been part of a temple complex. The cities may have been ruled by a theocracy of priests and the images of the deities in the temples may not have survived because they were made of wood.

Female clay figures with a fan-shaped headdress have been found, who might have been a mother goddess figure. Then there is the image of a naked man sitting in a cross-legged posture wearing a buffalo horn headdress, found on one of the seals. He is surrounded by animals and has people standing before him like devotees. He could be an earlier form of the god Shiva, who is also called Pashupati, the lord of animals. If we could only read the line of script on these seals, we would have an answer to all these questions.

Crafts and Trade

The cities were centres for crafts; there were potters, wood carvers, metal workers, basket makers, jewellers and textile weavers. Plates, bowls, glasses and storage jars were

Bust of a man wearing a diadem and a flowered dress.

> ### *A Priest and a Dancer*
>
> *Two sculptures found at the Harappan sites have fascinated historians. One is a stone sculpture of a bearded man, wearing a flowered robe and a diadem, who has the grim, arrogant look of a priest or king. The other is a tiny bronze statuette of a pert young girl with an elaborate hairdo, wearing an arm full of bangles and a flirtatious smile. Historians call her the Dancing Girl because she stands as if she is tapping her foot to music.*

made on the potter's wheel and painted in black and red patterns. The Harappans did not know the use of iron, so tools were made of copper and bronze. The jewellery, especially, was surprisingly sophisticated, made with gold, silver and beads. Historians have found a beautiful gold necklace with a row of leaf-shaped pendants that would be trendy even today! There is also evidence of a jeweller's workshop, strewn with beads. Kalibangan was probably a centre for making bangles as many were found around this site.

The Harappans probably traded by sea with Mesopotamia from the port of Lothal, sending textiles, jewellery and pottery. They also traded by land, importing precious stone and metals from Afghanistan and jade from China.

The Mysterious Seals

Today, all we have are the finds of the archaeologists, the rest of the answers lie in the seals. The rectangular seals that have been found at these sites are made of a stone called steatite, or soapstone, and are the size of large postage stamps. There is a line of pictorial script on top and a picture below and these pictures say a lot about the life of the people. Many of these seals depict animals—the most beautiful of them is a profile portrait of a hump-backed bull with carved horns and generous dewlaps. Also seen are rhinoceros, deer and a one-horned antelope.

So far, at least five hundred symbols of the Harappan script have been found, almost all on seals. For a whole century, we have failed to decipher the script, not even computer programmes have helped. Even the uses of the seals are a mystery. Were they some sort of stamps to be put on bags for trade? Or were they identity cards to be carried by official or the symbols of families? No one knows.

Mohenjo-daro or Meluhha?

We don't know the original names of the Harappan cities. The Mesopotamians mention trading with three places to their east—Meluhha, Dilmun and Makan. Maybe Mohenjo-daro was once called Meluhha?

The Cities Begin to Die

Around 1500 BCE, the cities of the Harappan civilization began to disintegrate. Historians have argued about the many reasons why this could have happened. The Indus may have changed course or may be because one of its biggest tributaries, the Ghagghar had dried up. The Harappan civilization was river-based. There may have been natural disasters like a long drought or earthquakes, or even floods, which could have destroyed these cities. Some even think that Harappa could be the first example of the negative effects of deforestation, as they cut down forests for wood to make bricks.

Also, around this time, a new people were entering India from the west and they may have attacked these cities, forcing people to flee and abandon their homes. Historians at one time thought there was an Aryan invasion, where the Harappan people lost in a war. Now it is thought that the nomadic Aryan tribes entered India in waves from Afghanistan, mainly in search of pastures for their herds of cattle and came into conflict with the Harappans. Unlike the Harappans, they were a warlike people—they knew the use of iron and so had better weapons. Plus they had horse-drawn chariots that gave them an advantage during battles.

The Dholavira Signboard

The largest carving of the script has been found at Dholavira. It is not a seal but a big rectangular piece of stone with one line of script that the archaeologists call a 'signboard'. Do you think it was the signboard of a shop saying 'Finest Pottery' or 'Fresh Fish'?

The Harappans were a peaceful people, as proven by the few weapons found at the sites. Probably all these factors combined and led to the end of the Harappan civilization that had lasted for 1,000 years. The cities would crumble in the sun and be forgotten for two millenniums.

Elsewhere in the World

The other early civilizations at this time were Mesopotamia in Iraq and the Shang dynasty in China. The Minoan civilization also flourished in the island of Crete in Greece. The Pharaohs were ruling in Egypt around the same time and building the great pyramids!

On the Net

Google 'Harappa' and you'll find many websites and a huge selection of images. The best website for this is www.harappa.com which has lovely photographs and a walkthrough. Also check out the video called 'Indus Valley Civilization' on Youtube. It is a fantastic animated film made at IIT Kanpur, and imagines daily life in the Harappan cities.

3
THE POETS OF THE VEDAS
(1500 BCE–500 BCE)

~ Where did the Aryans Come From? ~ The Vedas ~ A Pantheon of Deities ~ Worshipping the Gods ~ The Ramayana and the Mahabharata ~ Daily Life of the People ~ The Beginnings of the Varna or Caste System ~

With the decline of the cities of Harappa, a new chapter begins in the course of our history. Now starts the story of the Indo-Aryan people, on a journey of discovery across North India. It is the story of a people who lived closer to nature; it is a story of open spaces and hymns to powerful gods, of cattle wars and elaborate religious rituals and the chanting of sacred rites before a fire.

The nomadic Aryans were always on the move and so they did not build cities. They lived in homes made of perishable material like wood, earth and thatch so, years later, all that enthusiastic archaeologists could find was a meagre hoard of pottery and tools. But what we do have is a rich treasury of literature composed over 3,000 years ago. We have the magical words of poets speaking to us from across the span of time, singing to us in unforgettable verses. Whatever we know about the history of the Indo-Aryans is because of one of the oldest literature in the world—the magnificent Vedas.

Where Did the Aryans Come From?

The word arya means 'kinsman' or 'companion'. Historians think that the original home of the Aryans was somewhere in Central Asia. They were tribes of nomadic people moving from place to place with their herds of cattle in search of new pastures. Some tribes migrated towards Europe, others moved first into Iran and then entered India through Afghanistan around the time when the Harappan cities were in decline.

At one time historians thought the Aryans invaded India and attacked and wiped out the Harappan cities but they no longer think so. The tribes entered India around 1500 BCE in many waves and gradually occupied the land, but there is no evidence of an invasion. The verses in the Vedas mention battles and the destruction of cities, so the Aryans might have come into conflict with the Harappans as they moved across North India, but they did not occupy their cities. Instead, they moved on eastwards, leaving these already-declining cities behind them. That is how the plains round rivers like the Ganga and Yamuna were soon occupied by the Aryans.

Sapta Sindhu

In the early verses of the Rig Veda, the land is called Sapta Sindhu, or the land of the seven rivers. These were the Indus, and its five tributaries Jhelum, Chenab, Beas, Ravi and Sutlej, and the seventh river, Saraswati. The Ganga, however, is not mentioned.

The Indo-Aryans first settled in the Punjab area and then gradually moved eastward along the fertile plains of the Ganga and the Yamuna. Here they began to clear forests to grow crops and then started to live in villages. It was the next stage of their civilization as they progressed from being nomads to farmers. Soon they were living in villages and would later build towns and cities.

The Vedas

The Aryans did not have temples with images of gods in them. Instead, they prayed to their gods by building altars in the open air and sacrificing animals while the poet-priests sang verses of praise in the religious ceremony called yajna. These verses or shlokas are our oldest literature, and would one day be collected in the Rig Veda and the three Vedas that followed—the Sama Veda, with mantras and melodies; the Atharva Veda, with charms and magic spells; and the Yajur Veda, with the rules of rituals. What is amazing is that, in the early years, the Aryans had no written script and so these verses were preserved by memorizing them. This is called an oral tradition, where generations of priests learnt

> *Women, the Makers of Civilization*
>
> *Anthropologists and historians say that the shift from nomadic to village life happened because women began to plant crops that needed tending. This happened first in Mesopotamia (modern Iraq). So it is women who started the process of civilization.*

these hymns by heart till they were finally written down centuries later.

The word veda means 'knowledge' and vidya means 'learning'. Many consider the Rig Veda to be among the oldest texts in the world, probably composed between 1,200 to 1,000 BCE, although the oldest written manuscript that we have is only from the eleventh century CE. Older manuscripts, written on fragile palm leaves did not survive. The Rig Veda has ten 'mandalas' or books, containing 1,028 verses and the oldest sections were composed by the families of sages or rishis like Vishwamitra, Vashistha, Bharadwaja and Atri. Most of the verses are in praise of gods such as Indra, Agni, Varuna and Surya. Only a few goddesses like Prithvi, Ushas and Aranyani get mentioned. The other three Vedas are a mix of prayers, incantations for sacrifices and even mighty curses and magic spells. So these ancient rishis even cursed in Sanskrit!

A god of the Aryans.

Later sacred texts include the Brahmanas, the Aryanakas and the Upanishads. There is one Vedic shloka that many of you know. It is the Gayatri Mantra, written in praise of the sun God Surya and goes, '*Om bhur bhuvasva, tat savitur...*' So when you sing it, you are welcoming a new day with a song just like a Vedic sage!

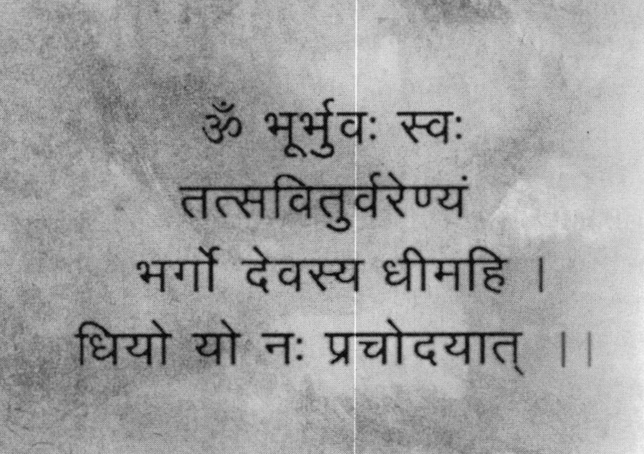

The Gayatri Mantra in praise of the sun god Surya.

A Pantheon of Deities

Many things about nature must have puzzled the Aryans. Where does the sun come from and where does it vanish at night? Why do we have rain, thunder and lightning? How do crops grow? So they began to worship nature and their gods were the various aspects of nature.

> **Hymns and Funny Poems**
>
> *All the poems in the Vedas were not solemn prayers. There is a funny rhyme about frogs croaking in the rainy season, poems by angry lovers and one hilarious lament by a gambler who has lost everything.*

There was Surya, the sun god; Varuna, the sky god; Agni, the god of fire; Vayu, the god of the winds; Indra, the god of thunder and rain; Prithvi, the earth goddess; and Aryanani, the goddess of the forest. Indra, who was also the commander of the celestial army, has the maximum number of verses addressed to him. Varuna is sort of a judge, watching the humans from the sky, and most of the Vedic poems beg for his kindness. Some of the most lyrical verses are addressed to Usha, the beautiful goddess of dawn.

The most mysterious god was Soma, who was associated with a divine drink that made the drinker think he was immortal. This was because it was made by crushing a plant that gave the drinker hallucinations! What exactly was soma, the drink? Scholars can't agree. Some think it was a Himalayan plant, others speculate it was the fly agaric mushroom that produces hallucinations. Maybe it was bhang, ginseng or opium. Whatever it was, it was hard to find and the soma ceremonies gradually died out. Soma was very popular with the priests, who sang its praises with great enthusiasm.

What is interesting is that, over the centuries, most of these Vedic deities have been forgotten by the people. We no longer worship Indra or Varuna. The three most popular deities today–Vishnu, Shiva and the Devi are not mentioned much in the Vedas.

Agni

The most important god at a yajna was Agni, the fire god. And one shloka in his praise says, 'Great Agni, though your essence is just one, your forms are three. As fire you blaze here on earth. As lightning you flash across the sky. In the heavens you flame as the golden sun.'

Worshipping the Gods

The religious rituals of the Aryans—yajnas—were performed

in the hope of pleasing the powerful gods. Brahmin priests were crucial to the ceremony as they claimed to be the only ones who knew how to make the gods listen to their prayers. The ceremony consisted of a sacred fire being built in an altar and the priests droning away at mantras as they poured ghee, milk and curd into the fire. An animal would be sacrificed and offered to the gods and then there would be a big feast.

Later, when kingdoms appeared, three sacrifices became popular with kings who wanted to show off their power. They were the Ashwamedha or the horse sacrifice, the Rajasuya and the Vajpeya. In the Mahabharata, Yudhisthir would perform the Ashvamedha sacrifice by letting a horse roam free as an excuse to conquer other kingdoms and then sacrificing the poor horse! These yajnas often went on for months, with an army of Brahmin priests, hundreds of guests and huge expenses.

The Ramayana and the Mahabharata

During later Vedic times, when we had kings and battles, there was an interesting bunch of men who kept the history of the period alive. They were called the sutas and were bards, balladeers and travelling storytellers. Many of them would work as charioteers during battles and, after seeing all the action, head out with their bag of heroic tales. They also narrated stories about the bravery of their patrons during yajna ceremonies. Everyone in a village became very excited when a suta came to visit.

Our greatest epics from the Vedic period—the Ramayana and the Mahabharata were kept alive by these sutas. They travelled from village to village telling the story of the

Ramayana—how a prince of Ayodhya was banished to the forest by his cruel stepmother and then battled Ravana, the king of Lanka to rescue his wife Sita, or the story of the Mahabharata—how the cousins, Pandavas and Kauravas, battled at Kurukshetra for the throne of Hastinapur, probably sometime between 1,400 BCE and 800 BCE. With every telling, these bards added their own bits to the story so that it became longer and more complicated. That is how the Mahabharata has *one lakh stanzas*, eight times the combined length of the Iliad and the Odyssey, the two most well-known Greek epics.

While the epics had many poetic embellishment and showed the vivid imagination of the sutas, they do give us some information on the period, even though they are not always historically accurate. We discover the names of Aryan tribes, the names of kings and kingdoms and also learn of the culture and religion of the time. The Mahabharata even tells us what the Pandavas had at a picnic by the Yamuna River—roasted meat!

Daily Life of the People

The Aryans were divided into several tribes, called janas. Each tribe would settle in a group of villages and they fought with each other all the time. As the Aryans' wealth was in their cattle, most of these battles began when one tribe raided the herd of another. Over thirty warring tribes are mentioned in early writings and the dominant ones were the Puru, the Kuru, the Bharata, the Yadu, the Turvasha, the Anu and the Druhyu. If some of these names sound familiar, it is because they would all fight in the great battle of Kurukshetra, as described in the Mahabharata.

Each tribe had a chieftain called the rajan and it was his job to protect the tribe. Each tribe had two assemblies of members, called the sabha and the samiti, which took decisions on all important matters. The sabha was probably a smaller gathering of seniors and the samiti was a general assembly.

People lived in families pretty much like ours. The boys helped their fathers with farming or making pottery; the girls helped around the house. Only the Brahmin and a few Kshatriya boys went to school. The girls had some freedom but were still not valued as much as boys. They did move around freely, did not veil themselves; there were no child marriages and widows were allowed to remarry. Old texts also mention girls who chose their own husbands.

The Beginnings of the Varna or Caste System

This was also the time when the varna or caste system began to appear in Vedic society. In the beginning, varna was a social division and was just meant to indicate a man's profession. The priests, teachers and physicians were the Brahmins, the warriors were

Girl Power

Some women did act independently. Gargi, Visvavara, Apala and Ghosha were sages who wrote hymns. Gargi once argued so fiercely with the sage Yajnyavalkya that he lost his temper and threatened to curse her. Vishpala, Mudgalini and Vadhrimati became warriors. But such women were rare.

called rajanya or Kshatriyas, the farmers, craftsmen and traders were the Vaishyas and the Shudras were the labourers. It was only in later Vedic periods that these varnas or castes became rigid and once you were born into a caste you could not move freely from one caste to another. Later, these social divisions got even more complicated with sub-divisions based on the jati or tribe and gotra or clan. You were supposed to marry within your jati but outside your gotra and some Hindus still believe in this archaic system.

In the early times, the caste system was much more flexible and people were free to change their professions and marry into other castes. There is an old hymn where the writer says that he is a poet, his father is a physician and his mother grinds corn. So, unlike what people believe today, our caste system was not hereditary. Also there was social mixing among the Aryans and the non-Aryans as well as marriages between the two—the heroes of the Mahabharata are shown marrying non-Aryans: Arjuna married the Naga princess Ulupi, Bhima married the asura

Devas and Asuras

The Indo-Aryans called their enemies asuras and their gods devas. It was the opposite in Iranian mythology where the ahuras were the gods and the devas like Indra were the demons! One doesn't really know how this reversal of names happened. In Hindu mythology the asuras fought the gods in heaven, the rakshasas fought them on earth. So Ram, an avatar of Vishnu fights Ravana, the rakshasa king of Lanka.

princess Hidimba and Krishna's queen Jambavati was also a tribal princess.

There was also another group that the Aryans called the dasas, who may have been the original inhabitants of the land. Initially, the Aryan tribes were often at war with the dasas; the word dasa later came to mean 'slave'.

Elsewhere in the World

Meanwhile, in Egypt, famous pharaohs like Ramesses II and Tutankhamun ruled. The early Mayan culture was also developing in Central America. The Mycenaean civilization was flourishing in ancient Greece. The first written script in China also appeared around this time, carved on bones.

On the Net

Check out www.indoaryans.org to read more about the Vedas.

4

THE RISE OF MAGADHA (500 BCE–321 BCE)

~ Rise of Kingdoms ~ New Ideas, New Thoughts ~ The Buddha and Mahavira ~ Bimbisara and Ajatasatru ~ Trading by Land and Sea ~ Invasion of Alexander

Over the centuries the Aryans gradually moved eastward until they were living across the Indo-gangetic plains of North India. They first lived in villages and then towns and cities sprang up. Soon powerful warriors conquered the land and built their own kingdoms. Around the sixth century BCE, there was a lot happening in India. Kingdoms were rising and falling and kings were battling each other. There were ambitious princes snatching the throne from their fathers and others walking away from their royal lives, seeking answers to philosophical questions. Great thinkers like Gautama Buddha and Vardhamana Mahavira were starting to preach in and around the land. And a young king from far-off Greece called Alexander came charging across Asia to conquer a legendary land called India. Two thousand five hundred years ago, these were exciting times!

By this time, we have several sources of historical information. There are the Vedic texts like the Brahmanas, the Upanishads and the Puranas, Buddhist texts like the Jataka tales, as well as the Jain religious texts. The Jatakas and the Puranas tell us many fascinating stories about the people of the time—a weaver in Varanasi, a courtesan in Vaishali or a rich merchant of Ujjaini. Finally, there are the writings of Greek historians and army generals who visited India during the invasion of Alexander.

Rise of Kingdoms

The Aryans had discovered iron and they used iron axes and scythes to clear out the forests and settle in villages all across modern Uttar Pradesh and Bihar. Gradually, the small clusters of villages with a tribal chieftain grew into kingdoms. The use of iron-tipped ploughs led to bigger harvests and hammers and chisels helped the craftsmen make their goods—like metalware and wood crafts—faster and better. Coins began to be used instead of the older system of barter and that helped in trade. A thousand years after Harappa, India was once again transforming into an urban civilization.

These kingdoms were called janapadas, meaning 'the footsteps of the tribe'; the big ones were called mahajanapadas and the books say there were sixteen of them. Soon,

Alexander's Misconception

When Alexander headed for India, the great Greek conqueror thought the world was flat and ended in India and that there was an endless ocean beyond. He planned to arrive at the edge of India and take a ship and sail home to Greece!

towns appeared and kings built capital cities with houses, roads and palaces surrounded by a fortified wall. Archaeologists have excavated some of these cities at Koshambi, Hastinapur and Ujjaini and found the remains of palaces, temples, houses and walls.

Some of these kingdoms were monarchies, that is, they were ruled by a king. Others like the Licchavis of Vrijji or the Mallas of Kusinagar were republics and were ruled by a group of tribal chieftains. Of course, these were not republics the way we think of the word, where everyone has a vote. Instead, in a system called an oligarchy, only the tribal chiefs met and voted about important matters; the common people had no say at all. However, these 'republics' did not last and were conquered by larger kingdoms like Kosala and Magadha. Interestingly, many of the most powerful kings, like Prasenajit of Kosala or Bimbisara of Magadha, were not Kshatriyas, or warriors.

By now, we had well-organized kingdoms with a proper administration that collected taxes and so the kings were rich men with large armies. Most of the taxes, called bhaga, came from the farmers, who gave a share of their crops to the king; the craftsmen, who paid a share of their earnings, and the merchants, who gave a share from their sales. In return, the king promised to protect them against attacks, build towns where farmers and craftsmen could sell their produce and wares,

Mahajanapadas

In some lists, the sixteen kingdoms are Magadha, Kashi, Kosala, Vatsa, Chedi, Anga, Vrijji, Malla, Panchala, Matsya, Avanti, Kuru, Assaka, Surasena, Kamboja and Gandhara.

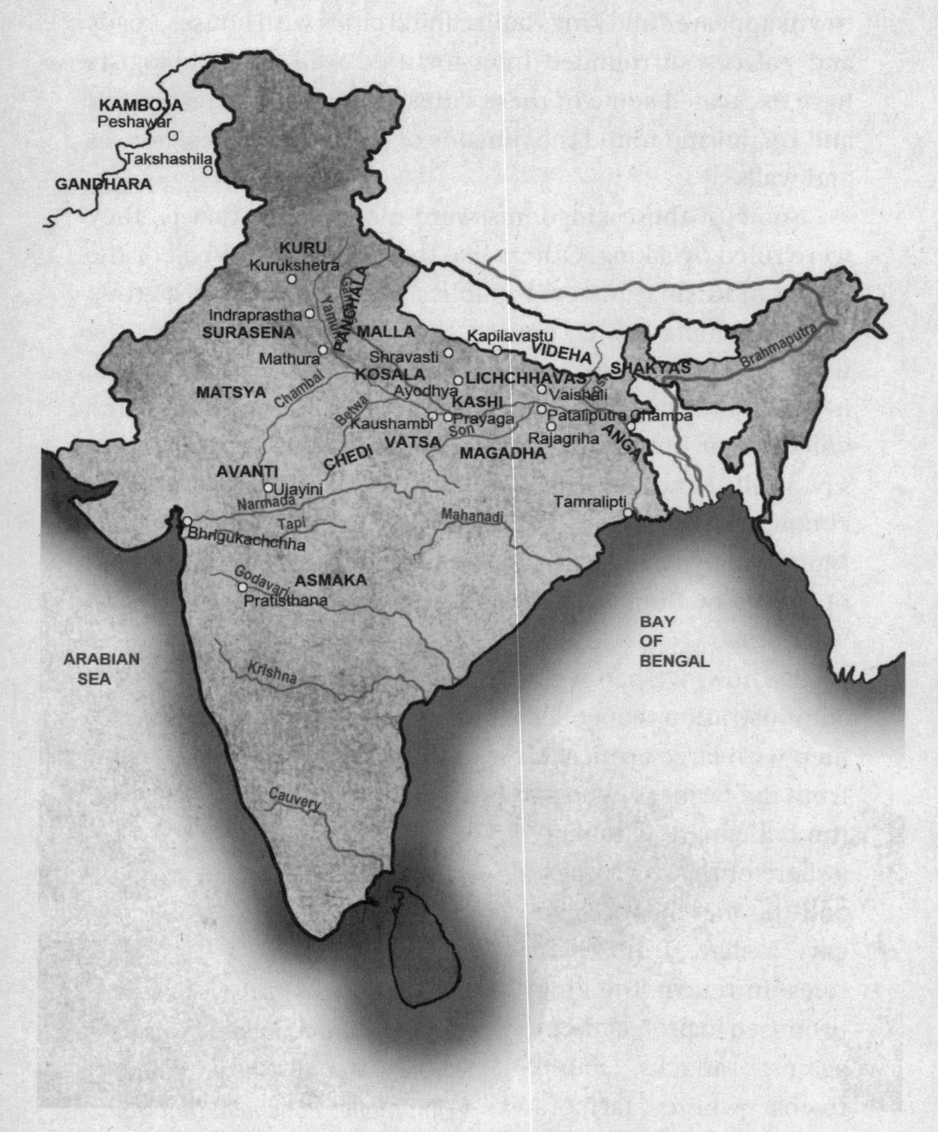

The Mahajanapadas spread from the north-west to the east.

build roads to encourage trade and ensure proper law, order and justice. Many towns came up around this time, such as Ujjayini, Kaushambi, Champa, Vaishali, Ayodhya, Tamralipti, but the most magnificent of all was the city of Pataliputra (modern Patna), that would be the capital of kingdoms like those of the Nandas and the Mauryas for 1,000 years.

New Ideas, New Thoughts

This was also a time when many great thinkers and philosophers emerged, all writing and debating their ideas. Most interestingly, people actually liked to listen to them! These scholars were also teachers or gurus and had schools called ashramas or gurukulas, where they taught students. Towns even had special assembly halls for debates called kautuhala shalas, that is, halls for arousing curiosity!

Scholars would be invited to a town to debate their theories and ideas, people would crowd in to listen and the winner of the debate would be given rewards, usually cows or land. Scholars and intellectuals were encouraged to think freely, question and criticize everything, even what the Brahmin priests, who were still very powerful, were saying. Every kind of opinion was encouraged and we even had atheists who denied the existence of god and were called nastikas.

Among the first thinkers were the rishis or sages who wrote the Upanishads. What is interesting is that many of them were non-Brahmins, especially Kshatriyas, and they were quite critical of the way Brahmins refused to share their knowledge about the Vedas and made people perform expensive religious rituals. Incidentally, both the Buddha and Mahavira were also Kshatriyas. The Brahmins claimed to have answers to everything because only they knew the Vedas but these scholars speculated about deeper philosophical questions beyond what was said in the ancient texts.

These thinkers were seeking answers to many questions about life. Why should society be divided into castes? What makes the Brahmins superior to everyone else? Why do we need expensive religious rituals? Isn't an animal sacrifice immoral because it is taking a life? If God is for everyone, shouldn't we be able to pray to him directly without needing priests to make him listen to our prayers? The Brahmins, of course, felt threatened by these thinkers, since this affected their livelihood, and tried to prove that only they could make the gods hear us. So you can be sure there were lots of angry debates at the kautuhala shalas. It was a very intellectually stimulating time for the people of India.

Four Ashramas

At this time, Brahmins taught people about the four ashramas or stages of Hindu life—Brahmacharya, or the student life, when a person was educated; Grihasta, or the household life, when he got married and raised a family; Vanprastha, or the retired life, when he lived in a forest and spent his time meditating; and Sanyas, or the renounced life, when he became a sadhu or ascetic.

The Buddha and Mahavira

The teachings of two thinker-philosophers have lasted the

test of time and are now a part of our lives—Gautama Buddha, who founded Buddhism, and Vardhamana Mahavira, who founded Jainism. And both of them wandered the dusty paths of the Ganga valley, preaching and building a family of disciples. They rejected the caste system and were against priests, animal sacrifices and religious rituals. They preached in the spoken language of the people which was Pali, a dialect in which the Buddhist canons were written. This meant that everyone understood what they were saying because they were not chanting in Sanskrit, which was no longer spoken by the people. What is even more extraordinary is that they lived at the same time and knew about each other.

Upanishads

The word Upanishad means 'to sit near'. It meant to sit before a guru to gain knowledge. There are eleven main books of the Upanishads, some of which are the Katha, the Mundaka and the Kena Upanishads.

Siddhartha Gautama was born probably in 566 BCE in Lumbini in modern Nepal. He was the son of Suddhodana, a chieftain of the Sakya clan of Kapilavastu. The Buddhist chronicles say that when Siddhartha was born, a sage predicted that he would become a wandering monk. So his father tried to stop Siddhartha from seeing anything disturbing that might lead him to renounce his royal life. But one day, Siddhartha saw an old man, a sick man and a funeral and was moved by the pain and suffering in the world; he wanted to discover the true meaning of life and death. He left his family and wandered from place to place seeking an answer to what

Gautama Buddha

causes sorrow or dukkha and how we can face the sorrows in our lives.

Siddhartha met many teachers but none of their answers pleased him. Then, meditating under a peepul tree at a place called Uruvela, a small village beside the river Niranjana, he discovered the answer himself; he was 'enlightened'. The answer lay in what are called the Four Noble Truths, that tell us why we face sorrows and the Eight-Fold Path, that teaches us how to face them. The path really teaches us to live a moral life. The Four Noble Truths are: The world is full of suffering. The main cause of suffering is desire. To end suffering we have to end our desires. To end our desires we have to follow the eight-fold path. The Eight-Fold Path is having the right thoughts, beliefs, speech, action, livelihood, effort, memory and meditation.

Now Siddhartha was the enlightened one or the Buddha and he would spend the rest of his life walking from place to place spreading his teachings. The followers of his teachings came to be known as Buddhists. Today, Buddhists from across the world visit Uruvela, or modern Bodh Gaya in Bihar, to visit the Buddha's place of enlightenment and his teachings have brought peace and wisdom to millions of people.

Vardhamana Mahavira was born in 540 BCE in Vaishali and his mother was a Licchavi princess. He, too, left his home in search of truth and, after wandering for twelve years, he gained enlightenment and preached for the rest of his life. Mahavira's followers called him Jina, or 'the great conqueror' and they came to be called Jains. The Jains believe that Mahavira was the last in a line of twenty-four teachers, called tirthankaras, and their teachings form the basis of Jain faith. At the core of Jainism is ahimsa or non-violence towards every form of life as Jains believe all living things have a soul. Jains are strict vegetarians and do not harm any living things.

Vardhamana Mahavira

Mahavira was against rituals and preached a simple way of life that followed the philosophy of the three jewels or triratnas of right belief, right knowledge and right action. Later, the Jains came to be divided into two main sects, the Shvetambaras, whose monks wear white, and the Digambaras, or 'sky clad', whose monks don't wear any clothes at all and follow very strict rules of ahimsa.

Bimbisara and Ajatasatru

Magadha became the most powerful of the mahajanapadas

because of its great king Bimbisara (545 BCE-493 BCE), who ruled from Rajgriha, its capital. He was the first king to realize the advantage of having a standing army ever ready to defend the kingdom. He ruled in a fertile land that produced big harvests and where there was much trade along the roads and river, so he grew rich from taxes. Magadha also had large deposits of iron ore that was used for making tools and weapons. Bimbisara conquered some of the nearby smaller kingdoms and with the powerful ones he built alliances, often through marriages. He married Mahakoshala, the sister of Prasenajit, the powerful king of Kosala; Chellana, a Licchavi princess; Khema, a Madra; and Vasava of Videha.

Now we start reading stories of royal intrigue and the battles of power. When Bimbisara became old, he was imprisoned by his son Ajatasatru (493 BCE-462 BCE) and the impatient prince took over the throne. Bimbisara was a follower of the Buddha and so the Buddha hurried to Rajgriha to intervene but Ajatasatru refused to listen to him. When Bimbisara died in prison, his queen Mahakoshala, Ajatasatru's mother, killed herself. This made Prasenajit very angry; he attacked Magadha and defeated Ajatasatru. Later, he forgave his nephew and gave his daughter's hand in marriage to him.

Ajatasatru was a great general. He invented a giant catapult that used stone balls and a chariot called rathamusala, that had sharp blades attached to its wheels to cut down enemy soldiers! He extended his father's kingdom even further and laid the foundation of the new capital of Pataliputra by building a fortress by the banks of the Ganga. His son Udayi built the city. Two later dynasties, the Shishunagas and the Nandas, would rule Magadha from here. Then Pataliputra would become the legendary capital of the Mauryas, who built the first Indian empire, and would be the home of a great king called Ashoka.

Trading by Land and Sea

By now merchants were travelling to other kingdoms and even sending goods across the seas. Pottery, metalware, textiles, precious stones, rice and spices were taken by road in caravans of bullock carts and by river on boats. A Jataka story mentions a caravan of 1,000 bullock carts travelling down a highway!

The pottery of Magadha or the woven cottons of Varanasi were sold at high prices in far-off provinces like Taxila or sent to distant lands by ships from the port of Tamralipti. Soon, some of the richest people in a town were the merchants and the craftsmen. They, of course, did not like the fact that, according to the old caste system, the Brahmins and Kshatriyas claimed to be superior to them. They were attracted by the teachings of the Buddha and Mahavira, who

> *Amrapali*
>
> *The Buddha was staying in a mango grove in Vaishali that belonged to Amrapali and accepted an invitation to her home. Many noblemen offered her money to let them invite the Buddha instead but she refused. She donated the mango grove to the Buddhist sangha and later became a nun. We have one of the poems she wrote in a Buddhist scripture called Therigatha, 'Verses of the Elder Nuns', which contains a collection of short poems from the early followers of Buddhism.*

rejected the caste system, and many, therefore, embraced the new religions.

The Buddha welcomed everyone into his fold, irrespective of caste or wealth. Among his disciples were Upali, a barber, who belonged to the lowest caste, and Sunita, a sweeper woman. Others were Anathapindika, the richest man in the town of Sravasti, who build the first Buddhist monastery or vihara and Amrapali, the famous courtesan of Vaishali.

Invasion of Alexander

During this time, a Greek army from far-off Europe invaded India and surprised everyone. Alexander, the king of the tiny Greek kingdom of Macedonia, took on the huge Persian empire in modern day Iran and defeated the Persian king Darius III. Then after crossing Persia and modern Afghanistan, he entered India in 326 BCE. Ambhi, the king of Taxila, promptly surrendered to him. The Greeks next came into conflict with an Indian king the Greeks called Porus. His Indian name must have been Puru or Paurava, and he ruled over the kingdom of Paurava, between the Jhelum and the Chenab rivers. When invited to meet Alexander, he sent back the message that he would be happy to meet Alexander but only on the battlefield.

It was going to be a battle between giants and the Greeks were worried. Their horses were getting scared before the elephants that the Indian king used and Porus also had a battalion of archers, who used giant bows. They would stand in a row with the bows resting on the ground and used long, iron-tipped arrows that could pierce armour. The Greeks then decided to build a bridge of boats to cross the Jhelum

River, that was in full spate as the monsoon had started. The rains proved an advantage for the Greeks because Porus's archers could not rest their giant bows on the muddy ground. Then the Greeks attacked the elephants, which ran amuck and killed many of Porus's soldiers.

After a fierce battle, Porus was finally defeated. The old man had nine wounds on his body. When he was brought before Alexander, the Greek king asked Porus, 'How would you like to be treated?' Porus replied proudly, 'Like a king!' Alexander was very impressed with his answer and his dignity, even in defeat, and the two men became friends. Porus was given back his kingdom. We get this story from Greek historians who admired Porus's courage but, oddly enough, no Indian book mentions either him or Alexander. Alexander's invasion opened the land trade routes to the Middle East, Egypt and Europe. His historians give us much information on India and help us fix some dates in Indian history. When Alexander decided to return to Greece, he left his generals as governors of the land he had conquered. So many small Greek kingdoms survived in the north-west, in Afghanistan and Punjab, for centuries and they influenced our art and coinage.

Alexander then moved eastward, planning to cross the subcontinent, but his soldiers, tired after years of fighting, rebelled. So, very reluctantly, Alexander decided to go back. He never reached Greece but died in Babylon in 323 BCE and his empire was divided up among his generals. When he died, Alexander was only thirty-three years old.

Elsewhere in the World

Alexander's empire was divided among his three generals: Antigonus got the Greek areas, Seleucus Nicator got the Middle East and Persia, Ptolemy got Egypt and declared himself the pharaoh. Queen Cleopatra was his descendent and so she was of pure Greek blood, not an Egyptian.

Two contemporaries of the Buddha and Mahavira were the philosophers Confucius in China and Zarathustra in Persia.

On the Net

Google Alexander and check out the map showing his journey across the two continents.

5
THE MAGNIFICENT MAURYAS
(321 BCE–185 BCE)

~ Chandragupta and Chanakya ~ Running an Empire ~ Megasthenes ~ Bindusara ~ Ashoka the Great ~ Ashoka's Dhamma ~ Pillars and Stupas ~ Living in a City ~ Trading with the World ~

Legends say that while he was camped in India, Alexander met a young warrior named Chandragupta, who wanted his help in defeating the mighty Magadha kingdom, ruled by the Nanda dynasty of Pataliputra. The Greek conqueror was not impressed by Chandragupta and refused and, soon after, Alexander headed home because his battle-weary soldiers refused to go any further. One of the reasons for their reluctance may have been their fear of facing the huge army of Dhana Nanda, that, as reported by the Roman historian Curtius, had 20,000 horses, 2 lakh foot soldiers, 2,000 four-horse chariots and 3,000 elephants. It would have been a much tougher battle than fighting Porus.

Even though Alexander had refused to help him, Chandragupta did not give up his fight and his road to the throne of Magadha is quite an extraordinary story. Within a couple of years, Chandragupta Maurya had become the founder of the Mauryan empire, the first empire in India that spanned a large part of the Indian subcontinent, and his grandson was King Ashoka, one of the greatest kings the world has ever seen.

Historians have gathered the story of the Mauryas from books like Kautilya's *Arthashastra*, excerpts from Greek ambassador to Chandragupta's court Megasthenes's *Indika*, Buddhist and Jain chronicles and the edicts of Ashoka, inscribed on pillars and rocks. Greek and Roman historians mention an Indian king called Sandrocottos of Palibothra, who signed a treaty with Seleucus Nicator. It was their funny way of spelling Chandragupta of Pataliputra.

Chandragupta and Chanakya

There are many stories about Chandragupta's beginning and no one really knows the truth but one fact is clear—he was not of royal blood. He grew up very poor and even the title he took—Maurya—has no noble history. The Jain books say he grew up in a village of peacock tamers (mayura poshaka) and so his name came from mayura, a peacock. Others say he took his mother's name, a low-caste woman named Mura. Buddhist texts say he belonged to the Kshatriya caste of Moriyas, a clan of Sakyas, but when his father died young, the boy and his mother came to live in a village near Pataliputra where he was brought up first by a cowherd and then a hunter.

Meanwhile, interesting things were happening at the court of Dhana Nanda, who was a miserly king and hated by his subjects. He taxed his subjects ruthlessly and there were rumours that he had buried his fabulous treasures in a cave in the bed of the Ganga. At his court there was a scholarly

Brahmin named Chanakya who somehow angered the king and was publicly humiliated and forced to flee from the city. Chanakya vowed revenge and may have even escaped with some of the king's treasures.

The next part of the tale is probably a story dreamed up by storytellers. Chanakya came to a small village and saw some boys playing there. One boy, in particular, caught his eye. They had created a make-belief royal court and this boy, in torn clothes and dusty feet, was playing the king. Chanakya was impressed by the boy's quick wit and intelligence. He offered to take the boy as his pupil and took him to Taxila, far away in the north. There, young Chandragupta not only received a proper education but also trained as a warrior. One day, Chanakya's young protégé was going to avenge his guru's humiliation.

This was the time when Alexander invaded India and Ambhi, the king of Taxila surrendered and invited the Greeks to his city. So it is possible that Chandragupta went to meet the Greek king here, though he failed to win his support. Then, watching Alexander defeat Porus, he learnt how a much smaller army can defeat a larger one by the clever use of military strategy. It was a lesson he would put to use two years later when he attacked Pataliputra.

Initially, Chandragupta's campaign was an utter failure and his small army lost every battle. Then one day a disheartened Chandragupta got a lesson in military strategy from a simple village woman. The woman had given her son a plate of hot rice to eat. When the boy burnt his fingers she said to him that he should first eat from the edges where the rice had cooled and not from the middle where it was the hottest. Chandragupta now knew what he had to do to win. Instead of besieging the fortified and well-guarded Pataliputra in the heart of the Magadha kingdom, he now began at the edges, first conquering the border areas and moving inwards till one day he finally captured Pataliputra. Dhana Nanda was banished from the kingdom and Chanakya had his revenge.

Chandragupta Maurya ascended the throne of Magadha in 321 BCE and ruled for twenty-four years. Chanakya became his chief adviser and put to practise many of the theories about governance and taxation he had talked about in the *Arthashastra*. Soon after winning the throne, Chandragupta came into conflict with the Greek general Seleucus Nicator, whose share of Alexander's conquests included the western Punjab region.

Their armies met at the Indus River in 305 BCE and, though we have no details, it is probable that Chandragupta won because Seleucus withdrew, leaving him with land till Kandahar in Afghanistan. According to the treaty, all Chandragupta gave in return was five hundred elephants. The treaty mentions a marriage alliance and historians wonder if Chandragupta also married a daughter of Seleucus. The two kings kept in touch and a Greek ambassador named Megasthenes arrived at Pataliputra soon after.

Arthashastra

Chanakya wrote the famous political treatise called Arthashastra *that gives us much of our information about Mauryan India. Chanakya was called by different names—Vishnugupta and Kautilya among others.*

Exactly why do we call Chandragupta's kingdom an empire? It is because an empire is *much* larger than a kingdom, with many provinces and people of different races living in it. By the time of Ashoka, the Mauryan empire extended from Bengal in the east to Afghanistan in the west and from Kashmir in the north to Karnataka in the south. We know this because Ashoka's rock inscriptions, pillars and stupas have been found at all these places.

Interestingly, this was also the time when the Roman empire was rising in Europe and the Mauryans traded with Rome just as they did with kingdoms in the Middle East and Egypt, ruled by the Greek descendents of Alexander's general Ptolemy, and with Burma and China in the east. Pataliputra had a separate department to take care of foreigners. So it is possible that people from many countries visited it. We know of two more Greek ambassadors who visited the Mauryan kingdom: Deimachus of Syria during the reign of Bindusara and Dionysius of Egypt during the time of Ashoka, though neither of them left a record of their visit.

Running an Empire

Imagine trying to run such a huge empire 2,000 years ago! The Mauryan administration was very well-organized; taxes were collected efficiently and the king became very rich. The empire was divided into provinces, often ruled by princes, and the provinces were divided into districts. There was also a proper bureaucracy with officers called mahamatyas managing different departments. There was a standing army with a commander-in-chief and battalions were stationed in each of the provinces.

The first ever census in India was carried out by the Mauryas, who listed the number of families, their caste and occupation in the empire. The tax from land, called bhaga, was the main source of income and so the land in every village was surveyed and farmers had to pay anything from one-fourth to one-sixth of their produce, which was enforced very strictly. The next source of income was from trade. By then, India was trading with Rome, Egypt, China, Sri Lanka and craftsmen and merchants were becoming very prosperous. These taxes helped pay for the standing army, the salaries of government officers, for building roads and, of course, for maintaining the luxurious life of the royal family.

Megasthenes

Relations between Seleucus and Chandragupta must have been quite close because soon after the battle, the former sent an ambassador to Magadha. Megasthenes stayed in India for many years and later wrote a book about his experiences called *Indika*. Sadly the book is lost and all we have are excerpts quoted by Greek and Roman historians like Diodorus, Strabo and Arrian. It is in these excerpts that, for the first time, we get a vivid description of life in Pataliputra—not just the life of the king but also of the people. Megasthenes writes about Chandragupta:

'The occasions on which the emperor appears in public are celebrated with grand royal processions. He is carried in a golden palanquin. His guards ride elephants decorated with gold and silver. Some of the guards carry trees on which live birds, including a flock of trained parrots, circle about the head of the emperor. The king is normally surrounded by armed women. He is afraid that someone may try to kill him. He has special servants to taste the food before he eats. He never sleeps in the same bedroom for two nights.'

Bindusara (297 BCE–273 BCE)

After twenty-four years as king, Chandragupta became a Jain monk and his son Bindusara became king. Accompanied by the monk Bhadrabahu, Chandragupta travelled to the south, where he meditated in a cave and then starved himself in a ritual Jain death called sallekhana. Even today, at the Jain holy site of Shravanabelagola in Karnataka, there is a hill called Chandragiri, a cave named after Bhadrabahu, and a temple called Chandragupta Basadi.

We know very little about Bindusara, Chandragupta's son, except that he ruled for twenty-six years and seemed to have carried on with his father's policy of conquests. One of his titles was amitraghata or 'slayer of enemies' and ancient Tibetan texts say he conquered the 'land between the seas', which could mean the Deccan peninsula.

Tribal People

The Mauryans did not find it easy to control the tribals living in forests and usually left them alone. Chanakya mentions that the people of the forest provided timber, metals, honey, animal skin and elephants and were often employed as soldiers, spies and assassins.

Bindusara continued to keep in touch with the Greek kings who ruled in the Middle East and Egypt. He is said to have written to Antiochus I of Syria requesting that he sent sweet wine, dried figs and a philosopher. Antiochus replied that he'd be happy to send the wine and figs but in Greece a philosopher couldn't be sold!

Ashoka the Great (268 BCE–232 BCE)

When Bindusara died in 273 BCE, everyone expected that his eldest son Susima would become king but his younger son, Ashoka, the governor of Ujjaini, had other ideas. He was supported by Bindusara's chief minister Radhagupta and, after a long struggle in which Susima died, Ashoka finally became king. His early years were like that of any other king—making conquests, running the empire, and living the luxurious life. Ashoka was an ambitious warrior and a true heir of Chandragupta, but then, in 262 BCE, something happened that changed not just Ashoka's life, but the course of Indian history.

In ancient times, a king had to go on conquering land because more land meant more tribute and taxes. By the time Ashoka came to the throne there was only one kingdom that was left to conquer—Kalinga (modern Odisha). If Kalinga fell, the Mauryan empire would have covered most of North and Central India. Kalinga was also important because it had many ports on the Bay of Bengal, and would make trading with the Far East easier.

In 262 BCE, Ashoka invaded Kalinga, fought and won a fierce battle, by the end of which both sides had lost thousands of soldiers. But as Ashoka stood on the battlefield, surrounded by terrible scenes of bloodshed, he asked himself, for the first time, if victory in battle was worth the price in lost and ruined lives. Then, in the only instance in the history of the world, a *victorious* king decided he would not fight another war of conquest again. In one of his inscriptions, Ashoka admits that

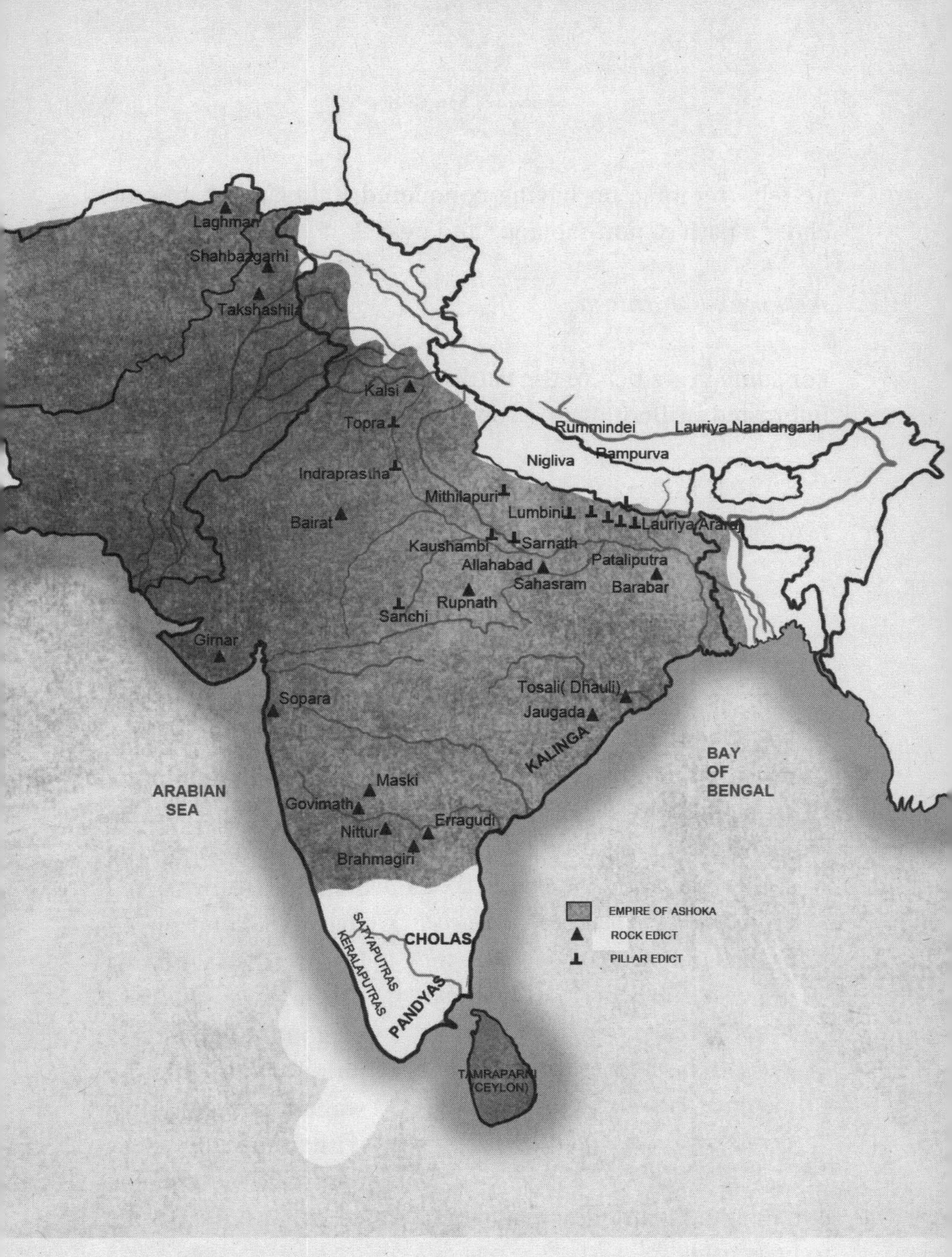

The Mauryan empire during the reign of Ashoka, showing locations of pillars and rock edicts.

he felt, 'remorse on having conquered Kalinga and now he chose a path of non-violence and peace'.

Ashoka's Dhamma

For some years before the battle at Kalinga, Ashoka had been interested in Buddhism, probably also because his first wife Mahadevi was a Buddhist. The tragedy of Kalinga finally changed him. It even changed his attitude towards his people and his role as a king. He chose a new way of living for everyone that he called dhamma and it was inspired by the teachings of the Buddha. He instructed that rocks and pillars be inscribed with this dhamma or 'the laws of good conduct and moral living' and he wanted people to live with 'non-injury, self-control, equable conduct and gentleness'. Imagine a fierce king asking people to be gentle!

Discovering Ashoka

Ashoka had been forgotten until the nineteenth century, till James Prinsep deciphered the strange inscriptions found on pillars and rocks, written in the Brahmi script and the Prakrit language. The Brahmi script was an ancient script that was no longer used by people as it had been replaced by the Devanagri script that we use today to write Sanskrit and Hindi. Prakrit, like Pali, was a dialect spoken by people. Suddenly the great king was speaking to us across a span of 2,000 years!

What is even more interesting is that Ashoka was not

just preaching to people, he was also changing himself. From a warlike king he now became a king who cared for the happiness of his subjects. 'All men are my children and, just as I desire for my children that they may obtain every kind of welfare and happiness both in this and the next world, so do I desire for all men,' was his new belief.

In accordance with this new belief, Ashoka did much for the welfare of his subjects. He built roads and planted shady trees along them; he built inns for travellers. Wells were dug, there were free hospitals for people and animals and gardens were planted to grow medicinal herbs. The king went on tours every year to meet his subjects and listen to their problems.

In Ashoka's kingdom, the war drum, the bherigosha, now fell silent and the drum of dhamma, the dhammagosha was now heard everywhere. However, this did not mean he became a weak king. He gave up the policy of conquest and offered his friendship to other kingdoms instead, but he also kept his army ready to defend his empire against any attack. Ashoka ran an efficient empire for thirty-six years. He made it clear that in his kingdom all religions were to be respected and his dhamma was more code of conduct and not a religion.

Ashoka was the first Indian king to realize that ruling over such a diverse nation as India—with so many different languages, cultures and religions—needed a policy of religious tolerance. It was important that people learnt to live peacefully together. The next ruler to realize this was the Mughal king Akbar who, of course, had not heard of Ashoka. Two modern leaders who admired Ashoka greatly were Mahatma Gandhi and Jawaharlal Nehru.

In 253 BCE, a great religious gathering of Buddhist monks was held at Pataliputra where it was decided that monks

would be sent to other countries to spread the teachings of the Buddha. Among the places mentioned were Burma, Afghanistan, the Greek kingdoms of West Asia and Sri Lanka. The most famous of these missions was the one led by Queen Mahadevi's son Mahendra to Tamraparni, or modern Sri Lanka. Mahendra carried with him a sapling of the sacred Bodhi tree under which the Buddha has gained enlightenment and soon converted King Tissa of Lanka to Buddhism. Later Ashoka's daughter and Mahendra's sister Sanghamitra went there to preach to the royal women.

If today Buddhism is a world religion it is because of Ashoka's efforts to spread the words of the Buddha. Later when the religion more or less vanished from India it continued to flourish in Tibet, Burma, China and Japan.

Pillars and Stupas

Ashoka's royal proclamations on dhamma were carved on rocks and sandstone pillars all across the Mauryan empire. As most of the people could not read, officials were told to read them out at regular intervals. The text is similar in most of these edicts and they start with these words, '*Devanampiya piyadasi raja hevam aha...*' or 'The beloved of the gods, Piyadasi raja declares...'

Dhamma

What is the dhamma or dharma as preached by Ashoka? It is to speak the truth; respect other religions; obey your elders; follow the path of ahimsa; give to the poor; be kind to all, especially servants and slaves, and live together peacefully.

Devanampiya (beloved of the gods) and Piyadasi (of pleasing looks) were titles of Ashoka and, in these edicts, he speaks in a gentle, thoughtful, and surprisingly modest voice for a powerful king.

So far archaeologists have found fourteen rock edicts and seven pillar edicts written in Prakrit, Sanskrit, Aramaic and Greek. During Ashoka's reign, stone was used for building in India for the first time and the pillars were given such a brilliant polish that they still gleam in the sun. Ashoka also built Buddhist monasteries, called viharas, all across his kingdom and established pillars with carved figures on top at places where the Buddha had visited. The Buddha gained nirvana in 543 BCE at Kushinagar and he was cremated there. The ashes from the funeral pyre or the relics of the Buddha had been buried in eight stupas. Now, these were opened up and the relics distributed into many more stupas. One such stupa is at Sanchi, near Bhopal. Sadly, very little of Pataliputra remains, but while digging for a sewer system in Patna, some of the logs of the walls of the city and

An Ashokan pillar.

stone pillars of a hall were discovered.

Ashoka died in 232 BCE and was succeeded by his grandson Dasaratha. After him, the Mauryan dynasty weakened and, in 185 BCE, the last Mauryan king Brihadratha was assassinated by his commander-in-chief Pushyamitra Sunga, who began the Sunga dynasty.

Living in a City

In the writings of Megasthenes and Chanakya, we get a portrait of what life was like in a Mauryan city. The most glamorous of them was, of course, Pataliputra, one of the greatest cities of the ancient world. Among the other cities were Ujjayini (modern Ujjain), Takshashila (modern Taxila) and Varanasi, which were also centres of learning.

Pataliputra stood by the banks of the Ganga and was protected by a wall made of logs of wood and a deep moat. At night, the moat bridges were raised and no one could enter the city except the spies who came to report to the king. They knew of secret passages below the walls.

The city had palaces, bazaars, inns, monasteries,

Greek Kings

One of Ashoka's edicts mentions the Greek kings ruling in West Asia, Greece and Egypt during Ashoka's time—Seleucus's grandson, Antiochus II Theos of Syria, Ptolemy II Philadelphus of Egypt, Antigonus Gonatas of Macedonia, Magas of Cyrene and Alexander of Corinth. Of course, the Prakrit inscription calls them Amtiyoge, Tulamaye, Antekine, Maka and Alikyasudale!

parks and bathing tanks—much like our modern cities! The royal palace, surrounded by a wall and guarded by soldiers, stood at the heart of the city, with the mansions of the nobility surrounding it. Craftsmen had separate areas allotted to them and they had many different kinds of workshops. There were weavers, dyers, potters, basket makers, blacksmiths and carpenters, stone and ivory carvers, garland makers and jewellers. The craftsmen were organized into guilds called shrenis and these were powerful organizations respected by the king.

> *Lion Capital and Chakra*
>
> *Two Ashokan sculptures are symbols of the republic of India—the Ashoka Chakra at the centre of our national flag and the Lion Capital that has four lions who represent the spreading of the message of dhamma to the four corners of the world.*

Trading with the World

By now, India was trading with many countries and Mauryan punch-marked coins made trading easier. The two main trade routes were the Dakshinapatha, that connected Pataliputra with the ports of Gujarat, and the land route, or Uttarapatha, that went from the eastern port of Tamralipti north up to Taxila. From here it connected with the Silk Route that went from China to the Middle East and then on to Rome. Our trade with the Roman empire kept growing and soon some of the richest people in the cities were merchants.

Archaeologists excavating at the ancient port of

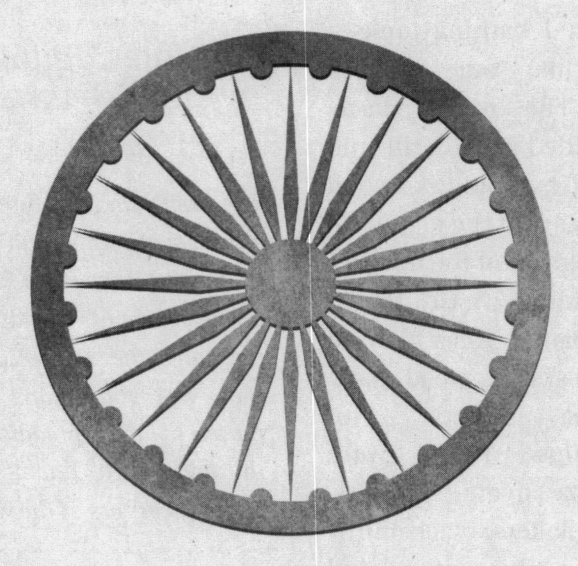

The Ashoka Chakra.

Arikamedu, near Puducherry, have unearthed Roman gold coins and amphorae jars. These jars were used to carry wine and oils, so by Ashoka's time, Indians were already enjoying Roman wines and olive oil! Trading was a dangerous job because of highway robbers, and traders usually moved in a huge caravan of carts and only travelled during the day. The biggest exports from India were textiles, jewellery, pearls, sandalwood, spices and the pottery of Magadha, called Black Polished Ware, that was highly prized everywhere.

Elsewhere in the World

In China, Emperor Shih Huang-ti of the Chin dynasty began to build a wall to stop invasions from the north. Additions were made for 2,000 years and this wall became what we now know as the Great Wall of China.

Museum Visit

The museums at Delhi, Kolkata, Sarnath and Patna have Mauryan carvings, pottery and coins. At the entrance of the National Museum in Delhi, there is a wonderful replica of Ashoka's rock edict at Girnar. At Patna, there is a full size stone figure of a woman holding a fly-whisk, called the Didargunj Yakshi, which is the finest example of Mauryan sculpture. In Kolkata, check out the carved panels from the stupa at Amravati.

6
KINGDOMS, CULTURE AND TRADE (200 BCE–300 CE)

~ The Indo-Greeks ~ The Sakas ~ The Pahlavas ~ The Kushans ~ The Satavahanas ~ The Cholas ~ The Pandyas ~ The Cheras ~ Sangam Literature ~Trade and Culture ~ Religion and Art ~

When an empire declines, a slew of small kingdoms spring up in its place. That is exactly what happened at the end of the Mauryan empire. A line of weak kings followed Ashoka, and the provinces began to break away as local chieftains asserted their power. After assassinating the last Mauryan king, Brihadratha, Pushyamitra Sunga began to rule at Pataliputra in 185 BCE. By then the great Mauryan empire had shrunk to just the region of Magadha.

The next five hundred years would be a very confusing time in Indian history, with many kingdoms, big and small, rising and falling. The borders kept changing all across India. Historians call this a time of 'murky obscurity' and 'trackless wilderness', since sometimes we know nothing about a king except his name on a coin.

Many of these kings belonged to foreign tribes like the Greeks, the Sakas (Scythians), the Pahlavas (Parthians) and the Kushans (Yueh-chi). A lot of them were nomadic tribes of

Central Asia that were pushed out by other tribes and entered India. At the same time, kingdoms began to appear south of the Vindhyas, ruled by Indian dynasties like the Satavahanas in the Deccan and the Cholas, Pandyas and Cheras in the southern region called Tamilakam. So anyone trying to draw a political map of the country at this time would have had a very difficult time indeed!

One would think that such a time of political upheavals would have made life difficult for the common people but, surprisingly, this was a period when people became prosperous since trade continued to flourish. There was much progress in literature, art and architecture and the religions flourished in monasteries and temples. As a matter of fact, this was the time when the foundations of the rich cultural age of the Guptas were laid.

The turn of the first millennium was an interesting time in India and we find much information about this time in Hindu texts like Patanjali's *Mahabhashya* and *Manusmriti*; Buddhist texts like *Divyavadana*, the Jataka tales and *Milinda Panha*; and the amazing Sangam literature of South India. Another interesting source is a book written by an anonymous Greek sailor called *Periplus of the Erythraean Sea*. He wrote it as a sort of guide book for sailors travelling along the Arabian Sea and it is full of details about ships, ports and trade. Finally we have a treasure trove of coins, sculpture and paintings that tell us a lot about the history and life of the time.

The Indo-Greeks

After Alexander went back in 323 BCE, some of his soldiers did not leave with him and parts of Persia and Afghanistan saw small kingdoms ruled by Greek generals. Two Greek kings, Demetrius II and Menander I, entered India and conquered land up to Punjab. Demetrius's capital was at Sakal (modern Sialkot). Menander is famous for becoming a Buddhist and having long conversations with a Buddhist monk which were collected in *Milinda Panha*.

These Greek kings left no written history but they were very enthusiastic about issuing silver coins. Often one side of the coins had their portrait. There seemed to have been many Greek kings during this time but often all we know about a Greek ruler is his name from a coin and how he looked—hook-nosed or weak-chinned, and the many kinds of helmets they liked wearing, all posed in a regal profile.

> *Q & A*
>
> *The Buddhist text called* Milinda Panha *is in a very interesting question and answer format. It has questions about Buddhism asked by the Indo-Greek King Menander I (Milinda). The Buddhist monk Nagasena replies to them.*

The Sakas/Scythians

The tribes of Sakas came from the Caucasus, the region at the border of Europe and Asia, and entered India in the first century BCE, building kingdoms in Western India. These Saka rulers called themselves Satraps and two famous ones were Nahapana and Rudradaman. We know about Rudradaman because he chose to inscribe his exploits on a large rock in Girnar in Gujarat, just below an Ashokan inscription, which he probably could not read. The Sakas fought other kingdoms like the Satavahanas of the Deccan, whom they defeated, but they were kept in check by the more powerful Kushans.

The Pahlavas/Parthians

The Pahlavas were a tribe from North Iran who occupied the Gandhara region in western Pakistan but they were soon conquered by the Kushans. The only interesting thing about the Pahlavas is a king called Gondophares I, because St Thomas, a disciple of Jesus Christ, visited his court and converted him to Christianity. Later St Thomas would land in Kerala, introduce Christianity to India and die in Madras (Chennai). Today, a church stands at the spot where St Thomas was assassinated.

Coins

We learnt to mint good quality coins from the Greeks. The Mauryan coins just had a design punch-marked on a piece of metal. The Greek coins were round or square, had the profile of the king and his name on one side and the image of a deity on the other.

The Kushans/Yueh-chi

The Kushans belonged to the Yueh-chi tribe of China, who were driven out of their homeland by the Huns. The Great Wall of China was built to stop these marauding Huns from entering mainland China. The Kushans first settled in Afghanistan in the first century CE, defeated the Indo-Greeks, the Sakas and the Pahlavas and kept moving east till they reached Varanasi. Their kingdom included Punjab, Kashmir, parts of Rajasthan and eastern Uttar Pradesh.

The greatest Kushan king was Kanishka, whose headless image was found in Mathura. What you notice is that in the image, he is wearing a heavy ankle-length coat, carrying a lethal sword and has really large hands and feet! He came to power in 78 CE and the official Saka Era starts from then. It is a bit confusing because it is called the Saka Era when Kanishka was, in fact, a Kushan! Historians are not too sure how this happened but it may be because the Saka rulers of Ujjayini adopted the calendar at Kanishka's death.

Kanishka ruled from Purushapura (modern Peshawar) and was a Buddhist. He built a giant stupa at Peshawar, which has now vanished; the Chinese traveller Xuanzang, or Hsuan Tsang, saw it in the fifth century. During Kanishka's reign, the Fourth Buddhist Council was held at Kashmir and it is here that the Buddhist faith split into two sects—Theravada (Hinayana) and Mahayana. Today, Sri Lanka and Myanmar still

The Two Schools of Buddhism

The Theravada school treats the Buddha as a great teacher and a human being. The Mahayana school believes that he was a reincarnation of god and worships his images in temples.

follow the Theravada school while China, Tibet and Japan chose the Mahayana way.

The Satavahanas/Andhras

The dynasty that flourished in the Deccan for the longest time after the Mauryas was called the Satavahanas. They ruled from the first century BCE to 220 CE from their capital at Pratisthana (modern Paithan). The greatest ruler of them all was Gautamiputra Satakarni (106–130 CE), who extended the kingdom to most of the Deccan, including parts of modern Gujarat, Andhra Pradesh, Madhya Pradesh and Orissa. The Satavahanas encouraged trade with other countries and grew very prosperous. Though they were Hindus themselves, the kings were generous patrons of art and architecture for all religions. The famous gateways of the Buddhist stupa at Sanchi were built at this time.

> **Asvagosha**
>
> *Not just goods but books, too, travelled along trade routes. The works of the playwright Asvaghosha were lost in India, but manuscripts were found in the town of Turfan, on the Silk Route, near the Gobi Desert in China!*

The Cholas

Around this time, several kingdoms began to appear in the south. One such was the kingdom of the Cholas. They had existed even at the time of Ashoka, who mentions the dynasty in one of his inscriptions. The Chola king Karikala ruled in the Tamil Nadu region with his capital at Uraiyur. He was often at war with the neighbouring Pandya and Chera kingdoms and even invaded Sri Lanka. He built the legendary port of Puhar at the mouth of the Kaveri River on the east coast. After his death, Chola power declined till the ninth century CE.

The Pandyas

The Pandyas ruled in the Madurai region of Tamil Nadu and, according to Megasthenes, the Pandya kingdom was founded by a woman who maintained a large army. The Pandyas were often at war with the neighbouring Cholas and Cheras and one king, Nedunchezhiyan, defeated both kingdoms. He was a great patron of art and literature and one of the legendary Sangam assemblies of literature was held at Madurai during his reign. At these assemblies, poets and philosophers gathered for recitations and debates.

The Cheras

The Cheras ruled over modern Kerala from their capital at Vanji and are also mentioned by Ashoka in an inscription. The Chera king Nedum Cheralathan was often at war with the Cholas and the Pandyas and is said to have captured a Roman trading fleet off the Malabar Coast. The Chera rulers encouraged trade and during their reign, Arab traders took Indian goods to Egypt and Rome across the Arabian Sea.

Sangam Literature

The word sangam means 'assembly' and, at this time, a remarkable amount of poetry was written and collected in Tamil Nadu that is collectively called Sangam literature. Legends say that there were great literary assemblies organized by the Pandyan kings between 100 CE to 250 CE at Madurai where poets and balladeers of the land came to recite their creations. These poems were then collected into eight anthologies and ten long poems. This collection consists of over 12,000 poems by 473 poets, including some women. Some poems are as short as three lines and others as long as eight hundred lines.

What is remarkable is that, unlike the poetry of the north, like the Rig Veda which is connected to religious rituals, these are purely secular poems about people and their lives. As the poet A.K. Ramanujan, who translated them says, they are 'poems of love and war'. So they portray the time with colour and vivacity, and are a rich source of information about the society and culture of the times.

Trade and Culture

Trade flourished during this period, not just between different regions but also with other countries. Trade was a major source of income for the kings and just as Kanishka encouraged trade along the northern Silk Route, the Satavahanas

Grammar

During the Sangam period, the first work on Tamil grammar, called Tolkappiyam, *was also produced.*

Headless image of the Kushan king, Kanishka.

developed the highway called Dakshinapatha, that led to the ports of Gujarat, and took Indian goods across the Arabian Sea as far as Rome and Egypt. The Cheras of Kerala also began trading with Europe and Africa. The Cholas began to build ports on the eastern coast like Puhar (also called Kaveripattinam) that had trading links to the Far East, Burma, China and Indonesia.

What did India send to the world? It was an exotic list of silk and cotton textiles as well as spices, precious stones, jewellery, tortoise shell, ivory, teak and sandalwood. There were also peacocks and monkeys in the cargo, which were kept as pets by the rich women of Rome! As India did not buy very many Western goods, very often the payment was made in gold and that made kings and merchants very rich. The kings would then build temples and palaces like the Brihadishwara Temple at Thanjavur built by the Chola king Raja Raja.

Religion and Art

During this period, mainly because of the influence of Buddhism and Jainism, Hinduism began to change. There was less emphasis on rituals and sacrifices and the old Vedic gods like Indra and Varuna vanished as Shiva and Vishnu began to be worshipped more. Buddhism spread to other countries during the reign of Kanishka. Now there were monasteries along the Silk Route in Central Asia and China. In Afghanistan, huge statues of the Buddha were carved on a hill at Bamiyan, which were later destroyed by the Taliban in 2001.

Some of the finest Buddhist art and architecture was produced at this time. Till the Mauryan times, the only stone carvings were on pillars, but now it took the form of very finely carved sculpture. Some of the best sculpture of these times can be seen around the stupas of Sanchi, Bharhut and Amravati. But these were not just religious creations; they also depicted the daily lives of the people. We can learn much about the layout of the cities, the homes and clothes of people of the time through these stunning works of art.

Till now, the Buddha used to be depicted in art by a symbol—like the Bodhi tree or feet—but now, his images began to be made and placed in prayer halls. There were two main schools of sculpture at Gandhara and Mathura and the main theme was Buddhist. At Gandhara, which was often part of the Indo-Greek kingdoms, there was a definite influence of the styles of Greece and Rome. So, here, the Buddha is seen wearing a pleated toga-like garment, has European features and, at times, even sports a moustache!

In Mathura, the sculptures were done on red sandstone with white flecks and the images here, of the Buddha and the Jain tirthankaras, have a sublime beauty.

Elsewhere in the World

Jesus Christ was born at Bethlehem in Palestine. The Roman empire was at its zenith and around the time Pataliputra declined in India, Rome became the most famous city in the world.

On the Net

Read more about how the Roman empire came up at www.bbc.co.uk/schools/romans.

7

THE GOLDEN GUPTAS (300 CE–500 CE)

~ Chandragupta I ~ Samudragupta ~ Chandragupta II Vikramaditya ~ How Did the Guptas Rule? ~ Life and Times ~ Trading with the World ~ Gods, Goddesses and Demons ~ Building in Stone ~ Kalidasa and Others ~ Looking up to the Stars ~ Decline ~

After the Mauryas, the next dynasty that could claim to have created an empire was the Guptas. In the fourth century CE, their kingdom, though not as big as the Mauryas, did cover most of North and Central India. Indian historians often call the Gupta period the 'Golden Age' of Indian history because at this time, India was a vibrant civilization where trade and commerce flourished and people lived in peace and prosperity. The kings ensured law and order and provided a stable government. This led to a surge of creativity in architecture, sculpture, painting and literature as well as many new discoveries in science.

By now, there are various sources with the help of which historians have been able to recreate the history of the period. There are sacred books like the Puranas and the epics, Ramayana and Mahabharata, which take their final shape during this period. There is also literature of the period—the works of Kalidasa, Vishakhadutta and Vatsayana. We also have inscriptions such as the one in praise of Samudragupta, carved on an Ashokan pillar in Allahabad, as well as a large hoard of gold and silver coins. There is also the beautiful sculptures and the incomparable mural paintings of the Ajanta caves. And, most interestingly, there are the traveller's tales, the finest being the writing of the Chinese pilgrim Faxian or, as we popularly call him, Fa-Hien.

Chandragupta I (321 CE–335 CE)

Two people with the title of raja—Srigupta and Ghatotkacha—are mentioned in the Puranas as the early kings of the Gupta dynasty. They may have been local chieftains of the Kushan kings. In those days, even small chieftains called themselves rajas. It was Ghatotkacha's son, Chandragupta, who was the first important ruler of the Guptas. He married a princess of the Licchavi tribe called Kumaradevi and it must have been an important marriage

Another Chandragupta?

To make things kind of confusing, we have three Chandraguptas in ancient India belonging to two dynasties. The Mauryan king Chandragupta Maurya ascended the throne around 321 BCE. Exactly 600 years later, another Chandragupta from the Gupta dynasty became king, around 321 CE. His grandson was another Chandragupta, who had the additional title of Vikramaditya. And all three of them ruled from Pataliputra. Go figure!

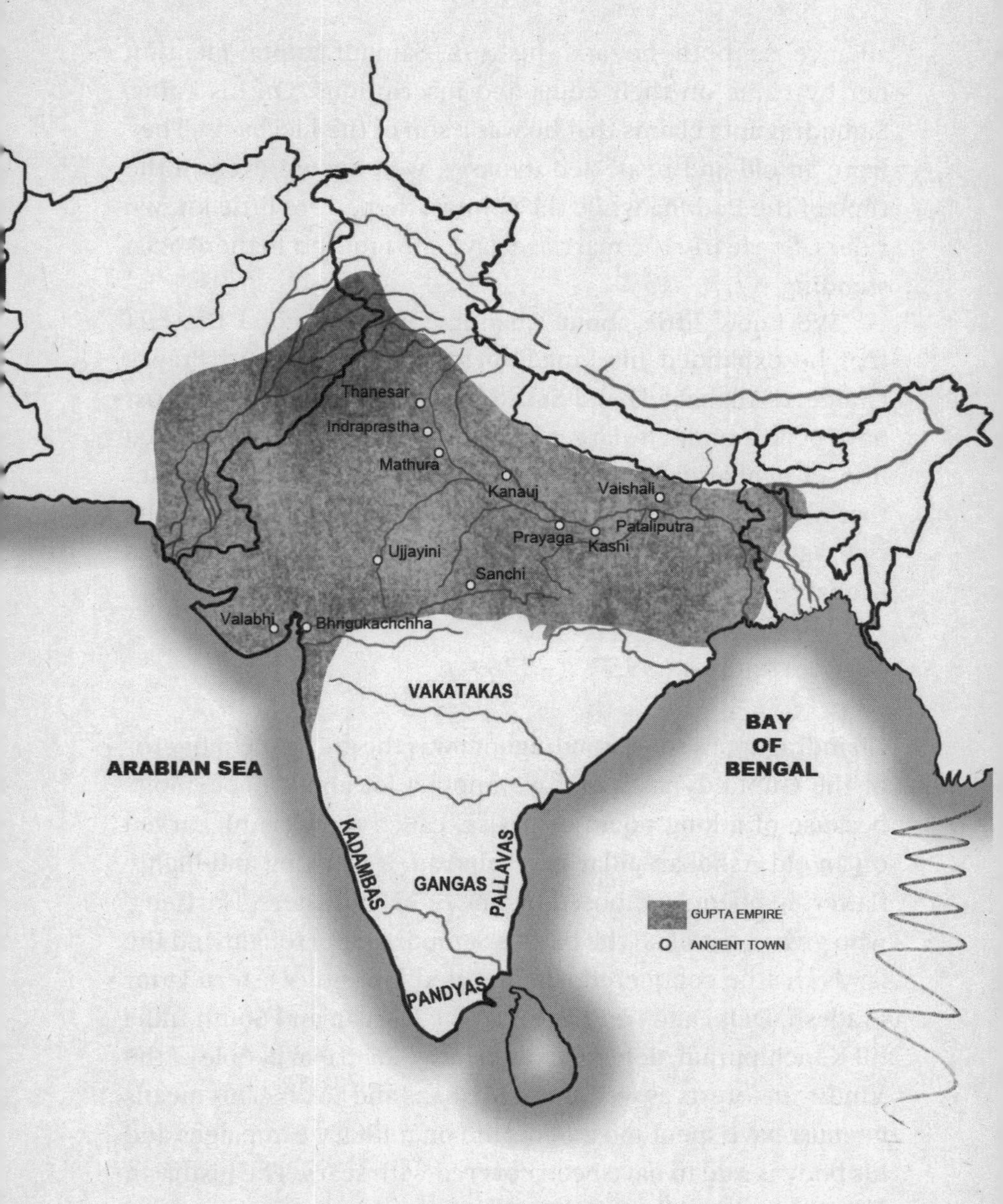

The empire of the Guptas.

alliance as both he and his son Samudragupta mention her by name on their coins and inscriptions. On his coins, Samudragupta claims that he was a son of the Licchavis. They were an old and respected dynasty, well known even in the time of the Buddha while the Guptas, then, were little known rulers. So clearly the marriage gave the family a higher social standing.

We know little about Chandragupta I beyond the fact that he expanded his kingdom from Pataliputra to Prayag (modern Allahabad) and Saketa (modern Ayodhya). It must have been among the larger kingdoms of the time, as he called himself maharajadhiraja, 'lord of the lords'. This also meant that he ruled over the mineral rich regions of Bihar and the rich agricultural land of eastern Uttar Pradesh, which was probably what made his kingdom very prosperous.

Samudragupta (335 CE–375 CE)

Chandragupta's son Samudragupta was the greatest conqueror of the Gupta dynasty and we know a lot about his exploits because of a long poem of praise, called a prasasthi, carved on an old Ashokan pillar in Allahabad. It is a long and highly flattering poem, composed by one of his ministers, Harisena, who gives a list of all the battles Samudragupta fought and the lands that he conquered. He defeated kings of western Uttar Pradesh, Delhi and went as far as the Deccan and South India till Kanchipuram, defeating on the way the tribal people of the Vindhyan forests as well as the Kushans and Sakas. This means he must have spent most of his life on military campaigns and his body is said to have been covered with scars. The historian Vincent Smith calls him the 'Napoleon of India'.

The kingdom Samudragupta controlled extended roughly from Bengal to Delhi. All his neighbouring kings acknowledged his sovereignty and sent him tributes. He also had contact with the king of Lanka, who took his permission to build a guest house for Buddhist pilgrims in Bodh Gaya. His court poet Harisena mentions that Samudragupta was a caring ruler, a patron of the arts, and was himself a poet and musician. His coins not only show him wielding a sword and a battle axe but also playing the musical instrument veena. He must have been an interesting man: a battle-scarred veteran who was a caring king, a connoisseur of music and poetry and was tolerant of all religions.

Chandragupta II Vikramaditya (375 CE–415 CE)

The Gupta empire reached its zenith during the reign of Samudragupta's son Chandragupta II, who took the title of 'vikramaditya'. He extended the kingdom up to Gujarat by defeating the Sakas. This also meant that the Guptas now controlled the highly lucrative trade from the western ports of Bharuch, Cambay and Sopara.

Chandragupta II was a good ruler with an efficient administration, so there was peace in the land and the people

The Allahabad Pillar

The Ashokan pillar in Allahabad is like a diary of the ages. Not only does it have inscriptions by Ashoka and later by Samudragupta's minister Harisena but also by the Mughal king Jahangir. So there are inscriptions on the pillar in three different scripts!

prospered. Chandragupta II's empire now went as far as Gujarat and eastern Afghanistan in the west and Bengal in the east. In the north, it included modern Punjab and Rajasthan. He had defeated many of the kings of the Deccan, but instead of annexing their land, he made them his allies, who sent him tribute. He also had marriage alliances—he married his daughter Prabhavati to the powerful Vakataka king Rudrasena II. When Rudrasena died, young Prabhavati became the regent of her infant son and the Vakataka kingdom became virtually a part of the Gupta empire.

Legends say that Chandragupta II presided over a glittering court; among his talented courtiers were the navaratnas or 'nine jewels'. One of them was the famous poet-playwright Kalidasa. The next Indian king to have a legendary group of 'nine jewels' would be the Mughal emperor Akbar.

This was also the time when the Chinese monk Fa-Hien walked on foot from China to India in search of sacred Buddhist books and, in his records of his travels, he draws a portrait of a peaceful and prosperous land with a cultured and civilized people.

Fa-Hien

He travelled within India from 405 CE to 411 CE on a fifteen-year journey on foot, visiting Buddhist monasteries, and wrote an account of his travels after returning to China. He learnt Pali and Sanskrit and translated sacred Buddhist works into Chinese. He describes many places like Pataliputra and talks of the life of the people there but, oddly enough, he does not mention the name of the king.

How Did the Guptas Rule?

The king was at the heart of the whole administrative set-up. He was helped by the royal princes, a council of ministers and a bureaucracy. The empire was divided into provinces and districts, with the princes as governors of provinces. Unlike the Mauryas, who ran a tight, centrally controlled administration where officials were paid a salary, the Guptas allowed much more freedom to their officials. These officials were often given land grants, from which they got rent, instead of a salary. But this meant that the farmers were at the mercy of these landowners and it often led to their exploitation. Also many of these administrative posts were made hereditary and that led to inefficiency.

Life and Times

Fa-Hien's account and the descriptions of writers like Kalidasa give us a portrait of life and times in the Gupta period. Most of the people lived in villages but there were also many prosperous towns that nurtured a rich cultural life. The plays, stories and poems of this period describe the lives of the rich citizens. These citizens were called nagarikas, who led a very cultured, though rather lazy, life. They

Grand Titles

Unlike the Mauryas, who remained mere rajas, the Gupta kings liked to give themselves pompous titles. They were maharaja-dhiraja, parameshvara, paramabhattaraka, paramadvaita, chakravarti and, of course, vikramaditya.

dressed in muslin, put on perfume and wore flower garlands in their hair. Every evening, they would saunter to the theatre to enjoy performances by singers and dancers. They themselves composed poetry, painted and played musical instruments.

However, society at this time was also beginning to become more rigid in matters of caste and the condition of women was getting worse. Buddhism had encouraged a more equal society without caste and given more freedom to women. As the influence of Buddhism waned and Hinduism became the main religion, Brahmins began to control society more and more with their inhuman rules about the caste system. The lower castes were treated very badly while the chandalas, the supposedly 'untouchables', were forced to live outside towns and villages in terrible conditions.

Women had no freedom and were treated like possessions. Till the Vedic times, they were allowed to study but now the Brahmins declared that women were so defiled, they could not touch the sacred books and so they were no longer educated. Girls were married off at an early age and forced to stay at home, running the household and bringing up children. They could not go out alone. The condition of widows was pathetic

Ajanta

The mural paintings on the cave walls of Ajanta give us a good idea about the clothes and jewellery worn by people in the Gupta period. You can even study the patterns woven and embroidered on the textiles and the intricate designs of the jewellery worn by a goddess or a princess, all in glorious colour!

and this is the time when the first instances of widows committing sati—burning themselves on the funeral pyres of their husbands—come up. The oldest memorial to a sati can be dated to the sixth century.

Painting of Avalokitesvara at Ajanta.

Trading with the World

Trade prospered in the early part of the Gupta age, both within the kingdom and also with the world, especially with the Roman empire. Ships left the ports of Tamralipta, and Puhar, or Kaveripattinam, on the Bay of Bengal for Suvarnabhumi (Myanmar), Yavadvipa (Java) and Kamboja (Cambodia). The western ports of Bharuch, Sopara and Kalyan on the Arabian Sea were connected to Arabia, Iran, Egypt and then on to Rome. We sent to the world our famous textiles, spices, pearls, ivory, perfume, indigo, sandalwood and precious stones. In fact, the Roman empire exported such large amounts of Indian spices and textiles that some Roman senators were worried it would bankrupt their government!

However, by the time of the later Guptas, many factors gradually led to a decline in trade. One was the collapse of the Roman empire; another was the invasion of Central Asian tribes like the Huns. Then there was the waning influence of

Buddhism, which had always encouraged enterprise and had been the religion of the merchant class. Hinduism treated merchants as a lower caste and disapproved of travel—the Brahmins declared that you would lose your caste if you crossed the seas. Towns and cities now began to die and by the time the Chinese pilgrim, Hsuan Tsang visited the great city of Pataliputra in the seventh century, he said it had shrunk to the size of a village.

Gods, Goddesses and Demons

The main religions of the people were Hinduism, Buddhism and Jainism. The Gupta kings were Hindus and worshippers of Lord Vishnu, and Garuda, the half-human half-bird vahana of Vishnu, was their royal emblem. Samudragupta is said to have performed the ashvamedha sacrifice. However the personal beliefs of the kings did not influence royal policy and the Guptas were tolerant of all religions. Buddhist and Jain monasteries flourished and some of the finest Buddhist and Jain art and literature was produced during this time.

By now, Vedic sacrificial rituals were dying out and there was a growing popularity of the religious belief called Bhakti. In Bhakti, one prayed directly to the gods without the need for priests, animal sacrifices or elaborate religious rituals. Many temples were built for gods like Shiva, Vishnu and the goddess Devi. They were popular deities who did not demand expensive and cruel sacrifices and instead were worshipped with flowers and fruits, the waving of lamps and incense and the chanting of mantras—what is called puja. The old Aryan-Vedic pantheon of Indra, Surya and Varuna, who demanded sacrifices, no longer held sway and soon became minor gods banished to the corners of temples.

During the rule of the early Gupta kings, Buddhism was still an important religion and there were many monasteries across the kingdom. The famous Buddhist university at Nalanda in Bihar was patronized by the Guptas and scholars came from many other lands to study there. Indian monks like Kumarajiva and Bodhidharma travelled to China carrying the teachings of the Buddha.

However, by the time of the later Guptas, Buddhism was in decline. One reason was that its primary patrons were merchants and now, they were finding it hard to carry on trade. Another reason was that in Mahayana Buddhism, the Buddha had been transformed into a god whose image was to be worshipped, and many felt that it was no longer any different from Hinduism. Another reason might be that barbaric Hun invaders like Mihirkula destroyed monasteries and killed thousands of monks across Afghanistan and India.

Building in Stone

The only architecture made in stone during the Mauryan times was the Ashokan pillars, but now, small temples made completely with stone started to be built. These were simple structures with a single room with a flat roof, which was the sanctum where the

> **Bodhisattvas**
>
> *A bodhisattva is the Buddha in an earlier birth. Bodhisattvas were also worshipped and there were many in the Buddhist pantheon like Amitava, Avalokitesvara, Padmapani, Manjushri, Maitreya, Vajrapani and there was even a goddess, Tara.*

image of the god was placed, and a porch with pillars outside. Unlike later Hindu temples, that were covered with intricate carvings and sculpture, only the door lintels of these early stone temples had some carvings. The sculpture studios in Mathura began to produce images of gods and goddesses and these were also carved on rocks and in caves.

Kalidasa and Others

This was a time when literature, especially in Sanskrit, flourished, with the poetry and dramas of Kalidasa, Sudraka and Vishakhadutta. Kalidasa probably lived in Ujjayini during the reign of Chandragupta II and, fortunately, many of his works have survived. His plays and lyrical poems are considered among the finest in the world. The most beautiful is *Meghduta*, where a demi-god, a yaksha, sends a message to the yakshi he loves using a cloud as a messenger. He tells the cloud the route to follow across the land and through these verses, Kalidasa describes the beauty of the Indian landscape in unforgettable verse.

Kalidasa

The works of Kalidasa include the plays Abhijnanasakuntalam, *the famous story of Shakuntala, daughter of the sage Vishwamitra, and Dushyanta, king of Hastinapur;* Malavikagnimitra *and* Vikramorvashiya. *His lyrical poems include* Kumarasambhava, Raghuvamsa, Meghduta *and* Ritusamahara. *They all have such long names, don't they?*

Among the others, Sudraka wrote the play *Mrichhakatika* and Vishakhadutta wrote *Mudrarakshasa* and *Devichandraguptam*. Panini produced a book on Sanskrit grammar called the *Ashtadhyayi* and the Panchantantra stories were written by Vishnugupta. This was the time when the epics Ramayana and Mahabharata took their final form and many of the Puranas were also written.

Looking up to the Stars

During this time, great progress was made in astronomy, mathematics, medicine and even metallurgy. Indians created the numeral system that is used around the world today—the one that includes the zero—and they also worked out the decimal system. These numerals were taken to Europe by the Arabs, who called it hindusat. And, if you think about it, we wouldn't have had computers without the zero!

The great astronomer and mathematician Aryabhata worked out that the earth moved on its axis and explained that a lunar eclipse was a natural phenomenon and *not* the demon Rahu swallowing up the moon. A mathematical prodigy, he worked out the exact length of one year, the radius of the earth, the formula to calculate the area of a triangle and the value of the pi.

Iron Pillar

The iron pillar that stands within the Qutub Complex at Mehrauli in Delhi is the finest example of ancient metallurgy. It has an inscription about a king Chandra and even though it has been out in the open, it has not rusted in sixteen centuries!

Varahamihira was another great mathematician who wrote the *Brihat Samhita*, an encyclopaedia of science. The physicians Charaka, Dhanvantri and Sushruta wrote books on medicine and surgery that included instructions on surgical procedures and how to build and run hospitals. Even veterinary science saw the book *Hastyayurveda*, on how to take care of elephants!

Decline

Chandragupta II was followed by his son Kumaragupta and grandson Skandagupta, who were the last of the powerful Gupta kings. This was the time when the Huns began to appear from Central Asia and invaded India. Skandagupta defeated the Huns successfully but gradually, these invasions weakened the dynasty. Later, weaker kings allowed their provincial governors to break away and establish their own kingdoms and the Gupta kingdom kept on shrinking. Soon, like in the aftermath of the Mauryas, North India was divided into a number of small kingdoms perpetually at war with each other.

Elsewhere in the World

In 467 CE, the Roman empire came to an end. One of the causes was the attack by Attila the Hun, who destroyed the city of Rome. The Huns were also, at least partially, responsible for the decline of the Gupta empire.

About this time, Islam was beginning to spread in Arabia through the teachings of Prophet Muhammad (570 CE–632 CE).

Museum Visit

Some of the finest Gupta sculptures can be found at the museums in Sarnath, Mathura and the National Museum in Delhi.

8
SOUTHERN SUNRISE
(500 CE–1200 CE)

~ The Chalukyas of Vatapi ~ The Pallavas of Kanchipuram ~ The Pandyas of Madurai ~ The Cholas of Thanjavur ~ Temple Towns ~ Sculpture and Architecture ~ Songs of the Saints ~ Trade Winds ~ Decline of the Southern Dynasties ~

Around the sixth century CE, first the Satavahanas, who had gained power after the Mauryas, declined in the Deccan and then the Guptas rose and fell in the north. This led to the rise of a number of new kingdoms in the Deccan and the south that left their imprint on the history of our country. Many were small and vanished soon after they rose but a few lasted longer, and contributed significantly to the life, economy and culture of the region. These dynasties ruled over large kingdoms and patronized art and architecture and led to a magnificent period of prosperity in the history of South India.

Of the many kingdoms, the four most interesting and influential were the Chalukyas, the Pallavas, the Cholas and the Pandyas, who battled for supremacy in the region. By now, there are many sources of information available to us—the rich literature in Sanskrit, Tamil and Kannada, inscriptions on the walls of temples and copper plate grants, sculpture and paintings—so we know quite a lot about this period.

Many of these dynasties, such as the Cholas, had been around for centuries as a small feudatory, and now rose to prominence under powerful kings. As a matter of fact, in one of his rock inscriptions, Ashoka mentions the Cholas as far back as the third century BCE. As the north once again entered a time of confusion after the decline of the Guptas, the Deccan and the south rose into prominence. These dynasties grew rich through trade and became generous patrons of art and architecture.

Deccan

The word Deccan comes from the Sanskrit word dakshina, meaning south. But which area exactly is the Deccan and where does the deep south begin? The Vindhyan mountain range bisects the Indian subcontinent and south of it is the Deccan plateau region of Madhya Pradesh, Maharashtra and Andhra Pradesh. Moving south beyond the Kaveri River into Karnataka, Tamil Nadu and Kerala is South India.

During this time, we see great innovation in the architecture of temples, a profusion of rich literature in both Sanskrit and the regional languages, the growing popularity of poetry of the mystical Bhakti saints, and the start of a cultural life around temple towns, with dancers, singers, weavers and craftsmen all creating a unique religious and cultural environment that lives on even today. The south was rising to majestic power.

The Chalukyas of Vatapi

The Chalukya kingdom rose between the Vindhyan mountains and the Krishna River in modern Karnataka. They ruled from their capital city of Vatapi (modern Badami). The most famous of the Chalukyan kings was Pulakeshin II (608 CE–642 CE), who was a contemporary of King Harsha in the north. We know of the exploits of this conqueror because of a eulogy, a poem of praise, by his court poet Ravikirti, carved on the walls of a Jain temple in Aihole. In this long poem, Ravikirti boasts that he is as great a poet as Kalidasa and, interestingly, this is the oldest mention of the famous poet and playwright.

Ravikirti tells us that Harshavardhana, the king of Kanauj, after conquering most of North India, invaded the south but he was defeated by Pulakeshin II by the bank of the Narmada River. However, the greatest enemy of the Chalukyas were the Pallavas and Pulakeshin also defeated the Pallava king Mahendravarman I. But Mahendravarman's son Narasimhavarman I defeated the Chalukyas and Pulakeshin II died in battle. The Pallavas then occupied Vatapi. Later, Pulakeshin's son Vikramaditya I captured and occupied the Pallava capital of Kanchipuram for a while. And so it went on, one battle after another with no final victory.

Pulakeshin II is also said to have sent an embassy to the court of the Persian king Khosrau II. The Chalukyas grew rich through trade as the land route to the western ports was through their kingdom. They called themselves 'lords of the dakshinapatha' and their main port was Revatidvipa, (modern Goa). They were great patrons of architecture, art and literature and built beautiful temples; some of them still survive at Pattadakal and Aihole in Karnataka. This was also the time when the caves at Ajanta were painted with murals. No one knows exactly when these man-made caves began to be painted but Buddhist monks worked on them for centuries. Historians give dates roughly from 200 BCE to 650 CE.

After Pulakeshin II, the Chalukya power declined, though different branches of the dynasties, called the Eastern and Western Chalukyas, survived for some time after. The Chinese pilgrim Hsuan Tsang, who travelled through the kingdom of Harsha, also visited the Chalukya region and has left a description of the countryside and the life of the people.

The Pallavas of Kanchipuram

The Pallava dynasty built its kingdom from their capital at Kanchipuram and the region they ruled was called Tondaimandalam, in modern Tamil Nadu. All information we have about the Pallavas shows them being at constant war with their neighbouring kingdoms of the Chalukyas, the Cheras and the Pandyas.

The two greatest Pallava kings were Mahendravarman I (590 CE-630 CE) and his son Narasimhavarman I (630 CE-668 CE). Mahendravarman I

So Many Kingdoms!

The political history of this period is very confusing, with so many kingdoms, big and small, rising and falling across the south that it is hard to keep track. Among the big ones there were the Chalukyas, the Vakatakas, the Pallavas, the Pandyas, the Cheras, the Cholas, the Hoysalas, the Gangas, the Kadambas, the Kalachuris, the Yadavas and the Rashtrakutas!

was defeated by Pulakeshin II in battle and, in retaliation, Narasimhavarman I occupied the Chalukyan capital of Vatapi. Narasimhavarman also invaded and conquered Sri Lanka. The Pallavas built ports along the Coromandel Coast and there was prosperous trade with the countries of the south-east—Burma, Malaysia and the Indonesian islands of Java and Sumatra—during their time.

Who *were* the Pallavas? Historians have speculated about the origins of the Pallavas for a long time. Some felt, because of the similarity in their names, that they were a branch of the Pahlavas or Parthians who were ruling in the north. The more probable explanation is that they were a local tribe. The word pallava in Sanskrit means 'creeper' and the Tamil word for it is tondai; the Pallava land was called Tondainadu or Tondaimandalam.

The Pallavas were great builders and constructed many beautiful temples at their capital, Kanchipuram. Mahendravarman I was a great patron of the arts—he himself was a musician and a poet and also wrote humorous plays. He liked unusual titles, among them were chetthakari (temple builder), mattavilas (addicted to enjoyment), chitrakarappuli (tiger among painters) and vichitrachitta (myriad minded).

Mahendravarman I was also keen to develop sea trade and began building the port of Mamallapuram (modern Mahabalipuram) near Chennai around this time. His son Narasimhavarman I continued with the development of the port, and as he was called mahamalla, the great wrestler or warrior, the port was named after him. He is said to have had a grand total of 250 titles!

A later Pallava king Narasimhavarman II (695 CE-728 CE), also called Rajasimha, built the Shore Temple that still

The shore temple at Mamallapuram in Tamil Nadu.

stands beside the ocean at Mamallapuram, and nearby are the shrines called the five Rathas, carved out of gigantic rocks. He also built the Kailasanatha Temple in Kanchipuram, which is the first temple designed in what came to be known as the Dravida style of architecture. Till this time temples were mostly built in wood and brick but the Pallava shrines were built all in stone, with a high spire, and the walls and pillars were covered in carvings. This became the basic structure that all later southern temples would follow.

The Pandyas of Madurai

The Pandya dynasty ruled around Madurai in southern Tamil Nadu and they were often at war with their neighbours, the

Pallavas. The kings were, like the rest, great patrons of art and literature and their capital city, Madurai, was one of the greatest cultural centres of the period. In earlier times, poets and singers gathered here for the legendary literary assemblies called Sangams, while painters and sculptors worked on building beautiful temples. Many of the books written in this time have descriptions of the glittering city life of Madurai. The Italian traveller Marco Polo visited the city and wrote an account of his experiences there. Even today, the fabulous Meenakshi Temple, built during the rule of the Pandyas, stands at the heart of the city, a jewel of temple architecture.

The Cholas of Thanjavur

The Cholas rose to power as the Pallavas and the Pandyas were on the decline in the south and their kingdom would ultimately cover most of South India. There had been Chola chieftains and minor kings in the region for centuries, but the foundations of an empire were laid by King Vijayalaya in the ninth century CE when he defeated the last Pallava king and established his capital at Thanjavur. Later, King Parantaka extended the empire by conquering parts of the Pandya kingdom. By the tenth century, the Cholas ruled over most of South India and they had a well-organized bureaucracy, a standing army and a navy. The Cholas were one of the longest surviving dynasties of India and they would remain in power till the thirteenth century.

The greatest of the Chola kings were Raja Raja I (985 CE-1016 CE) and his son Rajendra (1016 CE-1044 CE). Raja Raja defeated the Pandyas of Madurai and the Cheras of Kerala and conquered parts of Deccan and the Mysore region. He even invaded Sri Lanka and conquered the Maldives islands. Raja Raja recognized the value of a strong navy; as merchants were trading with the countries of the Far East, a powerful Chola navy was required to guard trading ships. The Cholas made sure they monopolized the trade along the coastal areas of Tamil Nadu, Kerala, Sri Lanka and the Maldives. This made them fabulously rich and they used this wealth to build magnificent temples. The most famous of them is the legendary Brihadishwara Temple at Thanjavur built by Raja Raja and the Gangaikonda Cholapuram Temple built by his son Rajendra.

Rajendra Chola was a great conqueror. He headed north on his campaigns, defeating the Western Chalukyas and the Palas of Bengal and reached as far as the Ganga River. He was given the title of gangaikondachola or 'the Chola who conquered the Ganga'. He then began building a new capital near Thanjavur that he named Gongaikondacholapuram and built a temple to rival his father's Brihadishwara shrine. Here he built a huge temple tank for which water from the Ganga was brought in hundreds of vessels.

Hello China!

The Cholas sent an embassy to the court of the Sung kings of China in 1015 CE and a Chinese court record says they offered the following gifts: glassware, camphor, brocades, pearls, rhino horns, ivory, incense, rose water, asafoetida, borax, plum flower and cloves. In return they were given 81,800 strings of copper coins called 'cash'!

Another of his ambitious campaigns was a naval attack on the south-east Asian kingdom of Srivijaya, in the Malay Peninsula, and Sumatra region. Indian merchants were being harassed by the Srivijaya ships and Rajendra Chola sent his navy and defeated them.

After the rule of a long line of kings, the Chola dynasty finally declined in the thirteenth century.

Temple Towns

One the greatest gift to posterity of the southern dynasties is its art and architecture. The magnificent temples of Kanchipuram, Madurai, Thanjavur, Chidambaram and Srirangam were all built during the rule of the Pallavas, the Pandyas and the Cholas. Pilgrims came from far-off places to visit these temples and soon, people began to settle down around these places of worship. The main street and bazaar lead off from the temple gateway, where craftsmen opened their workshops, and soon, a town grew around the area, with a soaring gateway and the spire of the temple at its heart. There were festivals and processions, daily pujas

Cholamandalam

The Chola region was called Cholamandalam; when the British arrived, they simplified the name to Coromandel. Even today India's eastern coast, from Orissa to Tamil Nadu, is called the Coromandel Coast. Interestingly, the ancient Chola port of Puhar, or Kaveripattinam, may have been swept away by a tsunami in the second century CE.

and special rituals that have continued for centuries. A temple town is a uniquely colourful world even today.

These temples offered many kinds of employment to people—priests, stone carvers, flower sellers, weavers, jewellers, guards, cleaners, cooks, dancers and musicians. Shops around the temple sold textiles, jewellery, brass utensils, garlands, fruits—and everything else needed for the puja. The temple authorities would invite poets and singers to perform: religious teachers would lecture and debate in the mandapam halls. Temple dancers called devadasis would dance during the religious ceremonies. Temples had schools, debating societies, poetry, dance and music performances—it was, in itself, a complete and vibrant cultural world.

Brihadishwara Temple

The spire of this big temple is 65 metres high and the black stone Shivalingam in the sanctum is 3.6 metres tall. The walls are covered in inscriptions that give us a lot of information. According to one such inscription, Raja Raja Chola gifted not just gold and jewellery but also a number of villages for the running of the temple. There is a list of 600 employees that includes priests, temple dancers, singers, attendants, etc., who served the temple but nowhere do we find the names of the stone carvers who built it!

Fortunately, unlike in the north, the southern temple towns did not face the destructive invasions of Muslim conquerors like Mahmud of Ghazni, the Sultans of Delhi or the Mughal emperor Aurangzeb and so, some of the finest examples of ancient Indian architecture and sculpture have survived. Even today, life in these towns are centred around these temples and in Kanchipuram or Madurai, the skyline is dominated by a series of towering pyramidal gopuram gateways, ornamental structures that are seen at the entrance of the temple complex, that are intricately carved and painted in dazzling neon colours.

Sculpture and Architecture

In the beginning, we built stone temples by cutting through rocks to create caves and then by gradually cutting and carving the stone. But a change in temple architecture began with the Pallavas. At Mamallapuram, we can see both the rock-cut cave temples, built by Mahendravarman I, and a free-standing stone temple, built by Narasimhavarman II.

The art of building free-standing temples began with the Shore Temple at Mamallapuram that stands at the edge of the ocean with walls worn smooth by the salty sea breeze. Then followed

> **Dravida and Nagara**
>
> *The temple design of the south is called Dravida and that of the north is called Nagara. The biggest difference is that the temple spire of Dravida temples is pyramidal while the Nagara spire has more of a curved bell shape. Also, northern temples usually do not have carved mandapam halls or the stunning gopuram gateways seen in their counterparts in the south.*

the magnificent Kailasanatha Temple at Kanchipuram, with a soaring spire and walls and pillars covered in sculptures, and the Dravida style of temple architecture began to take shape. The Chalukyas, the Pandyas and the Cholas followed with more temples that continued with a similar architectural pattern.

Soon the temples got bigger and more elaborate until we get them with a multitude of courtyards, rows of gopurams and many shrines. Even today a temple precinct has a unique, lively, colourful life full of pilgrims, tourists, garland and fruit sellers, busy priests and happy children, the clang of temple bells, the loud chanting of mantras and the fragrance of incense floating in the air. The general structure that a southern temple follows is this: One enters the temple through a high gopuram gateway which leads into a courtyard with another gopuram, usually leading to a second courtyard with many small shrines. The main shrine, called the garbha griha, stands in the middle of the central courtyard and the image of the main deity is kept here. The image is usually carved in stone or metal and stands covered in flowers, clad in rich silks and jewels, glittering in the light of tall oil lamps. Over this shrine is the tall spire called the shikhara. The garbha griha and shikhara are together called the vimana, or the chariot of the god.

The many halls built along the courtyards are called mandapam and these have various purposes. For example, the mahamandapam in front of the main sanctum is where devotees gather to watch religious ceremonies. The natya mandap holds dance performances and the bhoga mandap is for distributing food to people. Then there is an amman shrine, that has the image of the consort of the main deity. A Shiva temple will have an amman shrine of Goddess Parvati; where Lord Vishnu is the main deity, the amman shrine would be a temple to Goddess Lakshmi.

What makes these temples so fascinating is that they are covered in extraordinary sculpture. Walls, pillars and ceilings teem with figures of gods, goddesses, demons, prancing horses, caparisoned elephants, marching soldiers, dancers and musicians—it is like watching a portrait of the period carved in stone. At the Shiva temple at Chidambaram, for instance, the walls are carved with all the dance mudras used in Bharatanatyam.

The Chola period also saw the creation of one of the classics of Indian sculpture—the delicately moulded, elegant figures of deities in sinuous poses, called Chola bronzes. These are still created in Swamimalai by a complex technique called the lost wax process. The image is first carved in wax, which is then covered in a clay moulding. Molten metal is then poured into the clay. The wax melts away and once the clay mould is broken, the bronze image is magically revealed.

Songs of the Saints

At this time, there was a significant change in the way people prayed to their gods and it began in the temples of the south. The old Vedic ways of religious ceremonies and yajnas conducted by Brahmin priests had convinced people that they could communicate with their deities through these elaborate and expensive religious ceremonies. But gradually, a quiet revolution began as more and more people decided it was time they prayed directly to their gods by doing a puja and there was a deity waiting for them in the sanctum of the temples.

This revolution began with poet-philosophers who wrote poetry about how the gods belonged to everyone—people did not need priests or expensive rituals for their prayers to be answered. Their songs said that people should pray directly to their deities at the temples and all they needed was a heart full of prayers and a handful of flowers to perform their own pujas.

This popular belief came to be known as Bhakti, which signified faith and complete devotion to god. The two deities that were the most popular with people were Shiva and Vishnu and now, temples were built for them as the old Vedic gods like Indra, Varuna and Surya were no longer worshipped. The poet-saints who sang in praise of Shiva were called nayanmars or nayanars, and those worshipping Vishnu were the alvars or azhwars. Most importantly, their poetry was in Tamil, the language of the people, and not Sanskrit, so that everyone could understand them. Tradition says that there were twelve alvars and sixty-three nayanmars and even today their images are worshipped and their songs are sung every day in the temples.

These poet-teachers believed that everyone was

Nataraja

The most famous Chola bronze figure is of Lord Shiva as Nataraja, the lord of dance. Nataraja is shown surrounded by a circle of flames, one leg bent at the knee and the two front hands curved in a dance mudra. The third hand holds a flame and the fourth a small drum, the damaru, and his hair flares out around his head as if he is swirling in a divine tandava. He stands on a dwarf called Apasmara or 'ignorance'.

Chola bronze image of Nataraja, lord of dance.

born equal. Many of them came from the lower castes, who were often refused entry into temples by Brahmins. Among the nayanmars were Sambandar, Appar and Sundarar and the alvar poets included Nammalvar and Tiruppan. They came from all stratas of society—a cowherd, a weaver, a washerman, a potter, a toddy maker, a hunter, a fisherman and even a highway robber. A few were women like Andal and Mahadevi Akka.

Bhakti was a people's movement, led by poets and singers, and it quickly spread across the land. There were soon poet-saints like Tukaram and Eknath writing in Marathi; Tulsidas, Mirabai and Surdas in Hindi; and Chaitanya in Bengali, all singing of the joy of their loving devotion to god. Later, there would be more poems in a similar vein—the dohas, or poems of Kabir, who was a weaver, and the songs of Guru Nanak, which would form the foundation of Sikhism. And it all began in the temples of the south.

Trade Winds

When the Pallava and the Chola ships sailed east, they also carried India's culture and religion with them. The ports of Mamallapuram, Nagapattinam and Kaveripattinam were constantly busy with ships unloading goods and traders coming in from China, Persia, Malaya, Burma, Portugal and Arabia to export and import goods.

India's biggest export was its many-hued textiles. Indian designs would influence those across the world—the Indonesian batik patterns began in India, so did the chintz of England. India also exported precious stones, ivory, ebony, amber, coral, perfumes, rice, pulses and spices. In return, it bought Arab horses, Chinese silk and elephants from Burma.

A Song to Shiva

The poet Sambandar describes Shiva in this way—
'The serpent is his ear stud, he rides the bull
He is crowned with the pure white crescent
He is smeared with the ashes of destroyed forests
He is decked with a garland of full blossoming flowers.'

One interesting result of this trade was that we learnt to chew paan! The habit came from Malaysia and it soon entered our temple rituals where the betel leaf and areca nuts were offered to the deity.

The Cholas were trading in the east with the Srivijaya empire of the Malayan archipalego and the Tang dynasty of China. In the west, they had contacts with the Persian empire and the Abbasid sultans of Baghdad. In the eighth century there was a Hindu temple at Canton in China. Indian architecture also influenced the building of monuments like Angkor Vat in Cambodia and Borobudur in Indonesia. Even today, there are Hindus living in the island of Bali and the classical dances of Thailand and Bali often depict stories from the Ramayana. The Khmer kings of Cambodia took the title of 'varman' like the Pallava kings and their temples had carvings of the Buddha, sinuous apsaras and the faces of Hindu deities.

Decline of the Southern Dynasties

The main reason for the decline of the southern dynasties was their endless wars with each other. The Pallavas were responsible for the decline of the Chalukyas and they themselves vanished because of the Cholas. At the same time, in the north, the first Muslim kingdom had been established in Delhi and soon the armies of the Delhi sultans were swooping into the south looking for plunder. These armies would just come to collect gold and jewels and would then leave and the southern kingdoms would soon recover. However this constant state of war led to the gradual decline of the great southern dynasties. But in the fourteenth century, there was a revival when the magnificent Vijayanagar empire rose to power by the banks of the Tungabhadra River.

Elsewhere in the World

In Europe, the Crusades were taking place (1096 CE-1281 CE). The Christian kings sent their armies to free the Holy Land of Palestine from the Muslims. In China, during the reign of the Sung dynasty, they developed the art of block printing, and began using gun powder and the magnetic compass.

Museum Visit

If you live in Chennai, go and see the beautiful Chola bronzes at the museum. Visit any temple down south and you will see the different design elements of its famous temple architecture.

9
A KING AND A PILGRIM
(600 CE–700 CE)

~ Thaneshwar and Gaur ~ Harshavardhana Becomes King ~ Administration ~ Hsuan Tsang in India ~ Harsha's Religion ~ Harsha: Patron of Arts ~ Embassies to China ~

After the decline of the Guptas, North India splintered into many kingdoms. There were the Maukharis of Kanauj, the Pushyabhutis of Thaneshwar, the Chalukyas of North Deccan and King Shashanka of Bengal. But the greatest of the kings to rule North India after the Guptas was Harshavardhana of Thaneshwar and Kanauj.

By now we have literature, biographies and travelogues providing us with the history of the period. The most important of the sources we have for this period is *Harshacharita*, a biography of Harshavardhana written by Banabhatta, his court poet. There is the account of the Chinese pilgrim Hsuan Tsang. There are also inscriptions and coins that tell us of the history of the times.

Thaneshwar and Gaur

The two most powerful kings battling for supremacy in North India were King Prabhakarvardhana of Thaneshwar and King Sasanka of Gaur. Prabhakarvardhana ruled over Punjab and a large part of Madhya Pradesh. Sasanka was the king of Bengal; he had conquered Bihar and Orissa and was threatening to attack Kanauj and Assam. The conflicting ambitions of the two kings led them to ally with other kings. Prabhakarvardhana married his daughter Rajyashri to Grahavarmana, the Maukhari king of Kanauj, who was opposed to Bengal. Sasanka allied himself with Devagupta, the king of Malava, who was fighting Thaneshwar.

In 604 CE, Prabhakarvardhana died and was succeeded on the throne by his eldest son Rajyavardhana. Sasanka took advantage of the situation and invaded Kanauj. Grahavarmana was killed defending his kingdom and his queen Rajyashri was put in prison. Hearing this, her brother Rajyavardhana marched out to face Sasanka and was killed in battle by Sasanka's ally, the king of Malava. With the death of three kings within such a short time, there was a great crisis in the royal families of both Kanauj and Thaneshwar. Sasanka was hovering to swoop in again and both Kanauj and Thaneshwar needed a great military leader. This was when Harsha stepped in.

Harsha's Contemporaries

When Harsha came to the throne of Thaneshwar (modern Punjab and Haryana), the other neighbouring kingdoms were Kanauj (in modern Uttar Pradesh), Gaur (in modern Bengal), Kamarupa (in modern Assam), Chalukyas (in the Deccan), the Pallavas, the Pandyas and the Cholas (all in Tamil Nadu), the Cheras (Kerala) and Kalinga (in modern Orissa).

Harshavardhana Becomes King (606 CE–647 CE)

Harsha was the younger brother of Rajyavardhana of Thaneshwar. When he came to the throne after the sudden deaths of both his father and his brother, he was only sixteen years old. But this young king faced the challenges in front of him with remarkable courage and military genius. He swore vengeance against Sasanka but, first, he had to rescue his sister. As he began his search, news came that Rajyashri had been set free and had retired to a forest in the Vindhya mountains. Harsha managed to rescue her just as she was about to walk into a fire and end her life.

Harsha now entered into an alliance with Bhaskaravarmana, the king of Kamarupa, and then went after and defeated Sasanka, who eventually retreated to Gaur. Sasanka's ambitions were thwarted, although he continued to rule in the east. After Sasanka's death, much of his kingdom was taken over by Harsha's ally Bhaskarvarmana. Then, for six years, Harsha led a relentless campaign of conquest that gave him an empire that stretched from Gujarat to Bengal and Punjab to Central India, the biggest empire since the Guptas. However his foray south of the Narmada River failed as he was defeated by the Chalukyan king Pulakeshin.

Administration

As his sister Rajyashri had no children, the Pushyabhuti kingdom of Thaneshwar and the Maukhari kingdom of Kanauj were unified under the control of Harsha. His next act was to shift his capital to Kanauj as it was in a much more central location and made it easier for him to run his kingdom. This was also the time when the Hun tribes were invading India through the mountain passes in the north-west and Thaneshwar had always been threatened by Hun attacks. Kanauj now replaced Pataliputra as the principal city in the region and both Banabhatta and Hsuan Tsang described it as a magnificent metropolis full of beautiful mansions, palaces and having a rich cultural life.

Hsuan Tsang describes Harsha as being a tolerant, energetic and generous man and a very hard-working king: 'His rule was just and humane. He forgets to eat and drink in the accomplishment of good works.'

The great Chinese traveller and monk, Hsuan Tsang.

Harsha continued with the system of administration that had been established by the Guptas and the people were taxed lightly. He travelled constantly to supervise the work of the kingdom and, like Ashoka, he built rest houses and hospitals and supported many religious orders.

However Harsha's kingdom was not as prosperous as that of the Guptas and peace and order was not as well maintained. Hsuan Tsang himself was robbed twice on the highways and he witnessed an attempt on Harsha's life by Brahmins, who were angry at his favouring the Buddhists. Just a few centuries earlier when Fa-Hien had travelled in the same region during the reign of Chandragupta II, he had described a happy and prosperous people and mentioned the peace and order maintained by the rulers.

Hsuan Tsang in India

Hsuan Tsang was a Buddhist monk from China. In 630 CE, he decided to travel to India in search of original Buddhist texts. He was welcomed at Kanauj by Harsha and they became good friends. His writing is full of praise for the king who he describes as being tolerant, generous and hard-working. When Hsuan Tsang left, Harsha gave him an elephant, 3,000 gold coins and 10,000 silver pieces and soldiers to guard his books and images, though, unfortunately, some of his books were swept away in a flood on the Indus.

At Nalanda, one of our oldest universities, Hsuan Tsang studied under a famous scholar called Silabhadra and stayed there for two years. He learnt Sanskrit and Pali and collected many original manuscripts to take back to China. His writings show that he loved Nalanda and he described the place in this way:

> **Many Spellings**
>
> *One name has so many confusing spellings! Hsuan Tsang, Hiuen-tsiang, Hsuien-tsang, Tang-sanzang, Tang Seng, Yuan Chwang, Xuanzang, and so on. Pick any that you can spell easily!*

'An azure pool winds around the monasteries, adorned with the full-blown cups of the blue lotus; the dazzling red flowers of the lovely kanaka hang here and there and outside, groves of mango trees offer their gentle shade.'

Hsuan Tsang wanted to go to Sri Lanka next. He travelled south as far as Kanchipuram, which was also a great centre of Buddhism. Here he heard that there was a civil war raging in Sri Lanka and so, he turned back and headed north again. He stayed for a while with his royal friend Harsha and joined him at a religious festival at Prayag, which he describes in his writings.

All on Foot

Hsuan Tsang travelled for seventeen years, all on foot! He crossed the Gobi Desert, made his way through the Silk Route and entered Afghanistan, which had many Buddhist monasteries. He visited Samarkand, saw the Buddha images at Bamiyan, and finally entered India. He visited Kashmir, Punjab and then settled at the University of Nalanda in Bihar. He returned to China in 647 CE with twenty horseloads of manuscripts and spent the rest of his life translating them. He wrote his memoirs, Si-Yu-Ki: Buddhist Records of the Western World, *which gives a personal account of his travels.*

Harsha's Religion

Harsha was initially a worshipper of Lord Shiva but later he became very partial to Buddhism, and this may have been because of the influence of his good friend Hsuan Tsang. His sister Rajyashri had also become a Buddhist. However, he was a tolerant king, and all religions were allowed to flourish in his kingdom. Every five years, Harsha held a religious assembly at Prayag, where scholars of all religions were invited for debates and discussions.

Hsuan Tsang attended one of these assemblies and describes, maybe with some exaggeration, gorgeous processions of prancing horses and caparisoned elephants, dancers and musicians, golden images of the Buddha being carried in chariots and the king scattering pearls, gold and silver flowers among the people. Harsha was known for his generosity, and at Prayag he would distribute all his belongings to the poor until he had nothing left and would have to beg for a set of clothes from one of his noblemen!

Schools of Buddhism

By this time, Buddhism was divided into three main schools of thought. The Theravada (Hinayana) school was the oldest and it believed that the Buddha was a human being and a great teacher. In the Mahayana school, the Buddha was worshipped as a god and his image is placed in temples, called viharas. Vajrayana was a mix of Buddhism and Tantric practices—they used mantras, and gods and goddesses like Avalokiteshvara, Maitreya and Tara were also worshipped.

Harsha organized the fifth Buddhist Council at Kanauj in 641 CE, where Hsuan Tsang was an honoured guest. By now, the Mahayana and Vajrayana schools of Buddhism had become more popular than the original Theravada sect and many scholars held discussions about them. Harsha also donated the revenue of a hundred villages to Nalanda University. Buddhism encouraged

A Chinese Buddha image.

scholarship and other universities besides Nalanda, like Vikramashila, Odantapura and Somapuri, were also teaching Buddhist scriptures. Apart from Buddhism, ancient Sanskrit texts like the Vedas and Upanishads were also taught at all these universities, as well as logic, grammar, mathematics and medicine.

Harsha: Patron of Arts

Harsha reigned over a magnificent court of poets, dramatists and philosophers. He was not just a patron of literature

> **Harshacharita**
>
> Harshacharita *by Banabhatta, is the first biography of an Indian king. It began a useful tradition since after this, many such charitas, or stories, of kings were written by royal poets, making the job of historians much easier!*

but a writer himself. He wrote three Sanskrit plays and a book on grammar. The plays were *Nagananda, Ratnavali* and *Priyadarshika,* the last two being romantic comedies, and all three have survived. Harsha also played the lute and enjoyed the company of artists. The most famous in his court were, of course, Banabhatta who wrote the books *Harshacharita* and *Kadambari,* and the grammarian Bhartrihari.

Harshacharita primarily deals with the dramatic story of Harsha ascending the throne after the death of his brother, rescuing his sister and taking vengeance on the evil Sasanka. The rest of the story of Harsha's reign has to be gathered from the writings of Hsuan Tsang.

Embassies to China

At this time China was ruled by the Tang dynasty and there was close contact between the two countries. After meeting Hsuan Tsang, Harsha sent an embassy to China in 641 CE and soon, a Chinese embassy arrived in Kanauj. There must have been regular contact between the two kings since one ambassador by the name of Wang Xuance came to India three times and wrote of his travels.

Harsha died in 648 CE after a reign of forty-one years and

it seems he did not leave an heir because the kingdom was usurped by his minister Arunasva. Then, as it happens when a strong king passes away, the kingdom soon collapsed and a time of chaos prevailed.

Elsewhere in the World

Christianity had now spread to Europe while Islam began to spread in the Middle East. In Central America, the Mayan civilization was at its zenith. It covered Mexico, Guatemala, Belize, Honduras, El Salvador and the Yucatan Peninsula. This was also when the majestic Mayan stepped pyramids were built in Yucatan.

On the Net

Google Hsuan Tsang and track his amazing journey across China and India, especially the Silk Route along which he travelled to Afghanistan. Buddhism reached China via this famous route.

WHAT HAPPENED AND WHEN

Dates in history can be very confusing, especially because BCE time moves backwards and CE moves forward. Also at one time they were called BC and AD, now they are BCE and CE. Originally, the dating was BC and AD as dictated by the Roman Catholic Church to dates before and after the birth of Jesus Christ. Now it is called the Common Era. So BC has become BCE and AD is CE. And when your history goes back 5,000 years, it's easy to get dates and events muddled up! Here's a list of when things happened in Ancient India to help you get things straight:

Before the Common Era (BCE)

2600 BCE-1500 BCE—Harappan Civilization
1500 BCE-500 BCE—Composition of the Vedas
600 BCE—Rise of Kingdoms and Republics
500 BCE-321 BCE—Rise of Magadha
560 BCE-467 BCE—Life of Vardhamana Mahavira
556 BCE-468 BCE—Life of Gautama Buddha
327 BCE-325 BCE—Invasion of Alexander of Macedon
321 BCE—Chandragupta establishes the Maurya dynasty
315 BCE-305 BCE—Megasthenes in India
268 BCE-231 BCE—Reign of Ashoka
250 BCE—Third Buddhist Council at Pataliputra

185 BCE—End of the Mauryan rule; Sungas take over
180 BCE-165 BCE—Rule of Indo-Greek kings in north-west India
50 BCE—Rise of the Satavahanas in the Deccan

Common Era (CE)

78 CE—Reign of Kanishka of the Kushan dynasty
319 CE-335 CE—Reign of Chandragupta I of the Gupta dynasty
335 CE-375 CE—Reign of Samudragupta
375 CE-415 CE—Reign of Chandragupta II Vikramaditya
405 CE-411 CE—Visit of Fa-Hien
455 CE—Skandagupta faces invasion of the Hunas
476 CE—550 CE Aryabhata, the astronomer
505 CE—587 CE Varahamihira the astronomer
543 CE-566 CE—Rise of the Chalukyas under Pulakeshin
574 CE-660 CE—Rise of the Pallavas
606 CE-647 CE—Reign of Harshvardhana of Kanauj
630 CE-643 CE—Hsuan Tsang visits India
680 CE-720 CE—Reign of Narasimhavarman II of the Pallava dynasty
899 CE-1300 CE—Rise of the Chola dynasty
985 CE-1014 CE—Reign of Raja Raja I Chola

Section Two

MEDIEVAL INDIA

(1200 CE–1750 CE)

1
THE ARRIVAL OF THE MUSLIMS
(1200 CE–1300 CE)

~ Age of the Three Empires ~ Kingdoms Galore ~ Mahmud of Ghazni ~ The Rajputs ~ Muhammad of Ghur ~ The Delhi Sultanate ~ The Slave or Mamluk Dynasty ~

Muslims had been living peacefully in India long before the dramatic arrival of the Turk and Afghan invaders. For centuries, Arab traders in their dhows, or sailing vessels, followed the monsoon breezes and headed to India, anchoring at the ports of the western coast. They were welcomed by people from the kingdoms of Malabar to Sindh and allowed to settle and practise their religion. These lively ports had a vibrant population of Hindus, Muslims, Jews, Armenians and Christians, all of whom lived amicably together.

The first Muslim kingdom was established in the Indian subcontinent in the eighth century by Muhammad bin Qasim in Sindh and Multan, but as the Arabs never came into the Ganga valley, they were never a threat to the kingdoms of north India. The north-west region had seen the invasion of many tribes—the Sakas, the Kushans, the Huns—and so the Indian kings did not take the presence of the Arabs as a serious threat. It was only with the invasion of Mahmud of Ghazni that these kingdoms would get a taste of an aggressive Muslim conqueror. India was at the cusp of some very interesting changes.

By now, we have myriad historical sources to choose from. There are palaces, fortresses, mausoleums, temples and mosques built by the kings that survive till today. We have not just literature but also royal histories, royal orders and official correspondence and a rich hoard of coins. There are histories written by witnesses like Kalhana, Ziauddin Barani, Muhammad Qasim Firishta and Amir Khusro. One of the richest sources is, of course, the writings of travellers from all across the world. Among them were the legendary Al-Biruni, Ibn-Battuta, Ralph Fitch, Francoise Bernier, Niccolao Manucci and Jean-Baptiste Tavernier, all gossipy observers who tell wonderfully colourful tales.

Al-Biruni (970 CE-1048 CE)

This famous Persian traveller came to India during the invasions of Mahmud of Ghazni and writes about a Hindu festival: 'When the sun marches in Libra, it is called Dibali. Then people bathe, dress festively... In the night they light a great number of lamps in every place so that the air is perfectly clear.' Clear air on Diwali night? Looks like they weren't bursting crackers in the eleventh century!

Age of the Three Empires

After the death of Harshavardhana in 648 CE, his capital, the city of Kanauj, remained the symbol of imperial power and was coveted by three powerful dynasties—the Gurjara-Pratiharas of Western India, the Rashtrakutas of the Deccan and the Palas of Bengal. Kanauj was of great strategic importance, as whoever controlled it also controlled the rich and fertile Ganga plains. The city was so battered by two centuries of conflict that it never rose again and this state of constant warfare also weakened the three dynasties.

In many ways, the fate of North India reflects the history of Kanauj—exhausted by war and at the mercy of petty, arrogant and ambitious kings, none of whom had the ability to unite the region under one banner. And because they were so busy with their battles, none of them noticed the growing threat from the kings of Afghanistan. The Gurjara-Pratihara kingdom had been the bulwark against invasions from the north-west but by the tenth century, they were badly weakened and the Chauhans, who replaced them, were never as strong.

Kingdoms Galore

It would be a nightmare to try to draw a map of India in the tenth and eleventh centuries–kingdoms were forever rising and falling and perpetually shifting borders. In the north there were the Chalukyas (Gujarat), the Chandelas (Bundelkhand), the Gurjara-Pratiharas (Ujjain), the Kalachuris (Jabalpur), the Paramaras (Malwa), the Gahadvalas (Kanauj), the Chauhans (Ajmer), the Gangas (Orissa), the Palas and the Senas (Bengal).

Moving southwards there was another line of the Chalukyas (Badami), the Rashtrakutas (Deccan), the

Yadavas (Devagiri), the Kakatiyas (Warangal), the Hoysalas (Dwarasamudra), the Pallavas (Kanchipuram), the Cholas (Thanjavur), the Pandyas (Madurai) and the Cheras (Kerala). One historian counted nearly *thirty* dynasties rising and fading within a century!

Mahmud of Ghazni (997 CE-1030 CE)

India was like a ripe fruit waiting to be plucked by a determined conqueror. For Mahmud, the king of Ghazni in Afghanistan, the prospect of rich treasures to be looted from Hindu temples and the zeal of converting people to Islam made the idea of an invasion very attractive. Mahmud had no plans of establishing a kingdom in India; he only wanted riches and, with it, the titles of 'ghazi', a religious warrior, and 'butshikan', or the destroyer of images. More than the death and destruction that he spread across the land, what Mahmud showed to later invaders was that India could be conquered easily from the north-west.

Between 1000 CE and 1026 CE, Mahmud of Ghazni invaded India *seventeen* times, going as far east as Mathura and Kanauj, killing and destroying all the way. Mahmud's main aim was to loot temple treasures but he also destroyed them to prove his religious credentials as a 'warrior' of Islam. The most devastating of these attacks was the one on the Somnath temple in Gujarat, where he stripped the temple of its gold, silver and jewels. He also took away several Indian craftsmen as prisoners. Then, with his loot, Mahmud built the magnificent city of Ghazni, filling it with mosques, libraries, seminaries and his own mausoleum.

The Rajputs

The word rajput comes from the Sanskrit word rajaputra, or the sons of kings. At this time, a number of small kingdoms arose, ruled by kings who called themselves Rajputs. Most of them claimed they were Kshatriyas who were descended from the sun (suryavanshi), the moon (chandravanshi) or the sacred fire (agni kula). Each dynasty then added legendary heroes like Rama and Krishna to their family trees! There was also a legend that these tribes had risen from the sacred fire of a yajna on Mount Abu. Historians feel that these kings were originally from Central Asian tribes like the Shakas, Hunas and Kushan, who had settled in western India and now claimed to be Kshatriyas.

Among these Rajput kings were the Tomaras of Delhi, the Solankis of Gujarat, the Gahadvalas of Kanauj, the Paramaras

Prithviraj Chauhan

The poem 'Prithviraj Raso' by Chand Bardai is about Prithviraj and Sanyogita, the daughter of King Jaichandra, of the Gahadvalas of Kanauj. The Chauhans and the Gahadvalas were always at war and so Prithviraj was not invited to Sanyogita's swayamvar ceremony, where she would choose her husband. Instead, an image of Prithviraj was placed at the door in the uniform of a guard to insult him. Sanyogita put the garland around the neck of the image and Prithviraj appeared and swept her away on his horse. It is a romantic story, but it's probably not true!

of Malwa, the Chandelas of Bundelkhand and the Chauhans of Ajmer. They all ruled small kingdoms and were perpetually at war with each other. Now, in case of an invasion from Central Asia or Afghanistan, the Chauhans were the first on their way. In the last years of the twelfth century, the Chauhan king was young Prithviraj Chauhan, who would pay the greatest price for this lack of unity among the Rajput kingdoms.

Muhammad of Ghur

Like Ghazni, Ghur was a small kingdom in Afghanistan with an ambitious king who looked towards India for conquest. After the death of Mahmud of Ghazni, Muizzudin Muhammad, the king of Ghur, conquered Ghazni and then invaded India. But there was one big difference between the two men—Mahmud had only come to loot, Muhammad of Ghur had plans to stay.

Muhammad of Ghur led a number of expeditions into India, starting from 1175 CE, when he was defeated by the ruler of Gujarat. On his next attack, he conquered Punjab. Then, in 1191 CE, Prithviraj Chauhan, the ruler of Ajmer, and Muhammad of Ghur faced each other on the fields of Tarain and Muhammad was defeated. He was badly injured and would have fallen to his death if a soldier had not sprung on to the saddle of his horse and carried him away.

But Prithviraj made a serious tactical mistake—he did not chase the Ghur army out of India or kill Muhammad, but let him retreat. He would pay a huge price for this foolhardy act of chivalry. Next year, Muhammad of Ghur was back and at the Second Battle of Tarain in 1192 CE, Prithviraj was defeated and captured. Some of the Rajput kings did come to his help but Jaichandra of Kanauj stayed away. The victory at Tarain paved the way for a Muslim dominion in North India.

Soon the Ghurid army had conquered Delhi and then moved on to defeat Jaichandra and occupy Kanauj. Then, Muhammad of Ghur's generals swept across the plains of the Ganga till Bihar and now, Ghur had a kingdom in India. Muhammad put his most trusted general Qutub-ud-din Aibak in charge in Delhi and returned to Ghur.

Thus began the rule of the sultans of Delhi, who introduced a new culture and religion that would change both the political and social landscape of India.

The Delhi Sultanate

The period from 1206 CE-1526 CE is called the Delhi Sultanate, when five Muslim dynasties occupied the throne of Delhi—the Slave or Mamluk dynasty (1206 CE-1290 CE), the Khaljis (1290 CE-1320 CE), the Tughlaqs (1320 CE-1414 CE), the Sayyids (1414 CE-1451 CE) and the Lodis (1451 CE-1526 CE). The last Lodi king, Ibrahim Lodi, would be defeated by Babur, the king of Kabul, who would then establish the Mughal empire.

What Happened to Prithviraj?

Prithviraj was allowed to rule Ajmer as a vassal of Muhammad for a while until he was executed for rebellion. Coins have been found that say 'Prithvirajadeva' on one side and 'Sri Muhammad Sam' on the other. One of the names of Muhammad Ghur was Muhammad bin Sam.

The Slave or Mamluk Dynasty

When Muhammad of Ghur died in 1206 CE, his deputy in Delhi, Qutub-ud-din Aibak, declared himself the sultan and began what is called the Slave or Mamluk dynasty. The Arabic word mamluk means 'owned' and what is remarkable is that three of the kings of this dynasty—Qutub-ud-din, Iltutmish and Balban—were originally slaves. In those days, prisoners of war were made slaves but the system of slavery was a rather fluid one. The more able and talented of the slaves were often freed and some, like Aibak, rose to positions of power.

Qutubuddin Aibak (1206 CE-1210 CE) only managed to rule for four years after he rose to power. He died after falling from his horse while playing chaugan, a form of polo. He was succeeded by Shams-ud-din Iltutmish (1211 CE-1236 CE), a former slave of Aibak, who became the king's son-in-law. He was the ruler who laid the foundation of the kingdom by establishing a proper system of administration and a court with its own etiquette and norms.

Slaves to Kings

Muhammad of Ghur had no sons but he had a trusted group of freed slaves. Three of them, Tajuddin Yildiz, Nasiruddin Qabacha and Qutub-ud-din Aibak, divided up his empire after his death and Aibak got the Indian region.

Many able men now began to arrive from other Muslim countries and were given posts in the government—they became the new nobility. Iltutmish expanded the kingdom towards Bengal and made sure that the north-west borders were protected against a Mongol invasion. Qutub-ud-din had started building a tower of victory and a mosque in Delhi that Iltutmish completed. We now know them as the Qutub Minar and the Quwwat-ul-Islam mosque, the oldest mosque in India.

The Qutub Minar in Delhi.

Iltutmish was a very unusual king for his time. He rejected his unworthy sons and chose his daughter Razia as his heir apparent. The nobles, of course, did not approve of his appointing a woman as the head of the kingdom, since it had never been done before! After his death in 1236 CE, the nobles went against the dead king's wishes and put one of his sons Ruknuddin Firoz on the throne. Firoz turned out to be a wastrel who was highly unpopular and Razia managed to gather the support of the people to become the new sultan of Delhi.

The reign of Razia Sultan (1238-1240 CE), is one of the most interesting interludes in the rule of the Mamluk kings. A woman sultan in medieval times was unheard of and when the nobility failed to control her, they were instantly up in arms against her rule. Battling rebellious nobles and court conspiracies with great courage, Razia managed to rule for three years. She was indeed a remarkable woman—she assumed the title of 'sultan' not 'sultana', the usual name given to a woman of her rank, which traditionally meant 'king's wife'. She was also a remarkable ruler—she sat in court with her face uncovered, wore male attire and led her army in battle. She was popular with the people but the nobles would not stop opposing her. Finally, in 1240 CE, she died, under somewhat mysterious circumstances, while fighting a rebellion.

The next king of the Mamluk dynasty was Nasiruddin Mahmud (1246 CE-1266 CE), another son of Iltutmish. But the real power lay in the hands of a nobleman called Ghiyas-ud-din Balban (1266 CE-1287 CE). Balban was another former slave who had married his daughter to the young sultan and, after the death of Nasiruddin, he occupied the throne. He was the last of the Mamluk sultans and, like Iltutmish, he strengthened the army and did much to consolidate the hold of the sultans over a large part of North India. Balban also strengthened the borders in the north-west against the danger of a Mongol invasion.

Razia and Shazia

In Bulbuli Khana in Chandni Chowk in Delhi there is an open enclosure with two graves that locals say are of Razia Sultan and her sister Shazia. However, there are no records of this and history does not mention any sister.

Balban has been described in historical records as a

ruthlessly efficient man who finally managed to rein in the troublesome nobles and even had them prostrating themselves before him in court. Even the faintest sign of rebellion was instantly suppressed and the grim sultan sat in an austere assembly protected by a band of fierce armed guards. There was little laughter or celebration as 'the Sultan was himself a paragon of severity and harshness'. The nobles, now cowed into obedience, must have regretted their rebellions against the more civilized Razia.

Who Were the Mongols?

The Mongols were nomadic tribes that swept out of Mongolia to invade China and then India. Round this time, the great conqueror Chenghiz Khan was leading his Mongol army across Asia, spreading death and destruction everywhere. He built the largest empire in history—stretching from China to the Middle East. Babur, the founder of the Mughal empire, was also a descendent of Chenghiz Khan.

At the death of Balban, there was no natural heir and two factions of nobles fought for power. The faction supporting the Khaljis triumphed and Jalal-ud-din Khalji came to the throne. Thus ended the first Muslim dynasty to rule from Delhi. It had lasted less than a century.

The Mongol conqueror Chenghiz Khan.

Elsewhere in the World

Chenghiz Khan was conquering kingdoms from China to the Middle East. In Europe, the Crusades—military expeditions to free the Holy Land (Palestine) from Muslim rulers—were still going on. The Crusades went on intermittently from the eleventh to the thirteenth century. The Khmer rulers of Cambodia were building the great temple of Angkor Vat.

Walkabout

If you are in Delhi, visit the Qutub Minar and the Quwwat ul-Islam Mosque in the Qutub complex. These are the oldest Sultanate buildings in India.

2

THE DELHI SULTANATES (1300 CE–1526 CE)

~ The Khalji Dynasty ~ The Tughlaq Dynasty ~ Invasion of Timur ~ The Sayyid Dynasty ~ The Lodi Dynasty ~ The Sultan and His Nobility ~ Administration and Land Grants ~

At the death of Balban in 1287 CE, the Slave or Mamluk dynasty ended, but four more dynasties would follow. By the time Babur invaded India in 1526 CE, the sultans had ruled for three centuries and Muslim culture had become a part of Indian life. Some of the best sources of information about this period are from royal historians like Zia-ud-din Barani, who wrote *Tarikh-i-Firoz Shahi*, and the writings of the scholar and poet Amir Khusro. Also, there are the writings of travellers like the Moroccon Ibn Batuta and the Italian Marco Polo. Batuta lived in Delhi for eight years and was appointed as a qazi (judge) by Muhammad bin Tughlaq.

The Khalji Dynasty

At the death of Balban, various powerful cliques among the noblemen battled for the throne of the Mamluks and the faction led by the Khalji clan triumphed. Jalal-ud-din Firuz

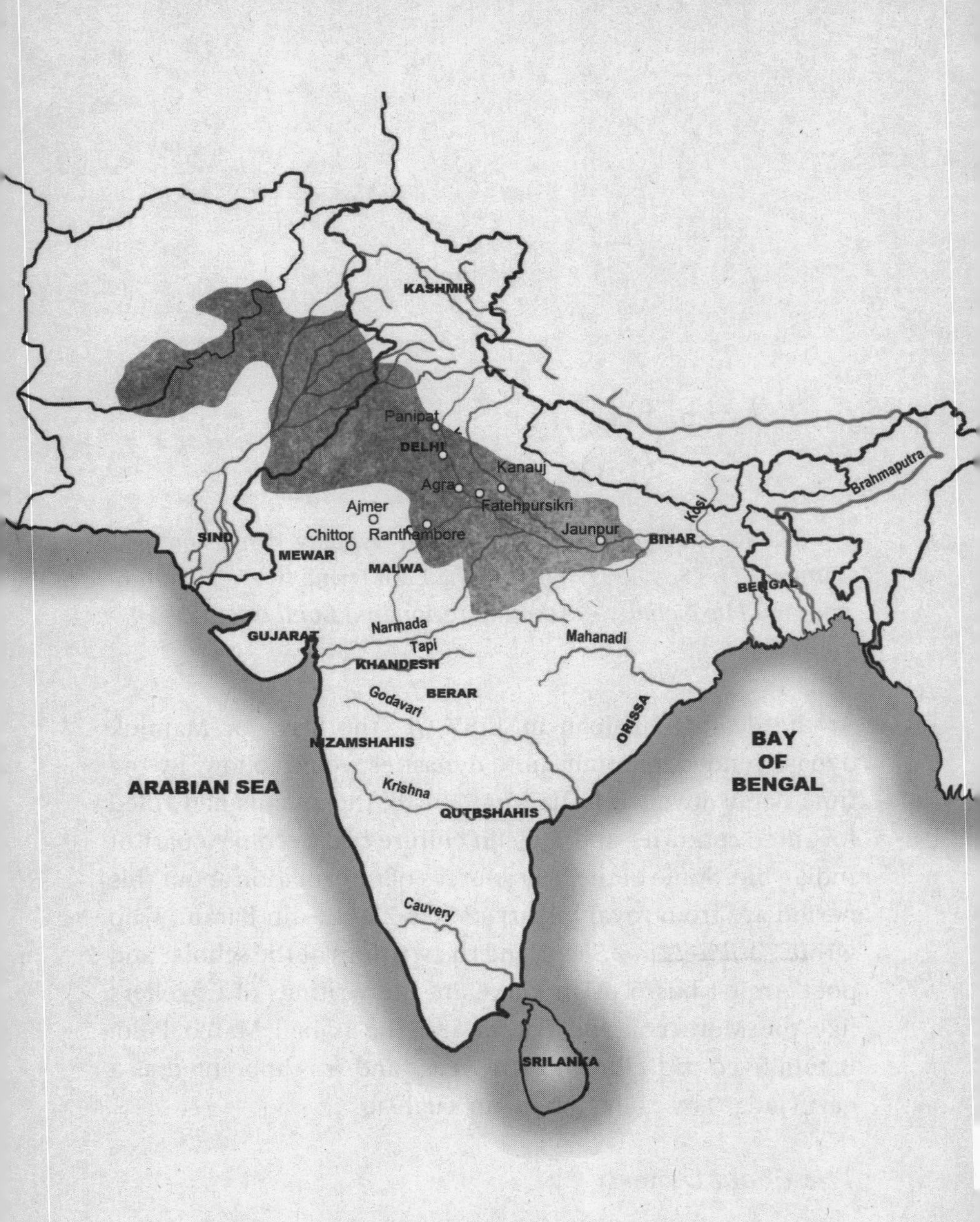

India in 1526 CE during the invasion of Babur.

Khalji (1290 CE-1296 CE) was the new sultan of Delhi and he was a surprisingly kind and gentle man. It is said that when he discovered conspiracies being hatched by his courtiers to unseat him, he magnanimously forgave them! But these qualities were hardly ideal for a sultan occupying an alien country who had to also control a band of troublesome noblemen.

One man watching from the sidelines was the sultan's nephew and son-in-law Ali Gurshap, the ambitious governor of the province of Kara. He went off on a secret military expedition to the Deccan and looted the kingdom of Devagiri. When the sultan objected, Gurshap acted very contrite and invited his uncle to visit him at Kara, promising to hand over the treasures. When the old sultan arrived there, trustingly without any guards, he was assassinated.

Immediately afterwards, Gurshap took over the throne, killed the sons of Jalaluddin and took the title of Alauddin Khalji (1296 CE-1316 CE). He began to expand his kingdom and found an equally ruthless deputy to carry out his plans of conquest. This deputy was a slave called Malik

Amir Khusro

Born in 1325 CE *to Turkish parents, Amir Khusro became a popular poet, using a language that was a mix of Persian and Hindi that he called Hindawi, an early version of Hindustani. He also wrote about the Khalji and Tughlaq rulers. He composed many ragas and hymns in praise of the Sufi saint Sheikh Nizamuddin Auliya. Khusro's grave is close to the dargah of the saint in Delhi and his songs are sung there even today.*

Kafur, who led campaigns into South India right up to the Pandya kingdom of Madurai. He came back with an enormous loot of gold, jewels, horses, elephants and slaves. After the invasion, the defeated southern kings were allowed to rule as long as they sent regular tribute to Delhi.

Unlike Jalal-ud-din, Alauddin was a tough and efficient ruler who managed to control the unruly nobility. With tributes arriving from many kingdoms he became very rich. But he was also a very miserly man who wanted to have a large army but did not want to pay his soldiers a good salary. So he came up with the plan of fixing the prices of goods like food grains, sugar or cooking oil—prices of food items were kept very low and any shopkeeper charging extra was punished.

Kafur's Loot

Ziad-ud-din Barani writes that the haul from the south consisted of 612 elephants and 20,000 horses. Rows of loaded camels brought back 96,000 mans of gold (about 241 tonnes) and countless boxes of jewels and pearls.

Alauddin was a suspicious, humourless man, and trusted no one. He forbade social gatherings in people's houses because he thought they would plot against him. He taxed the nobility heavily and fixed the salary of soldiers so low that they were always at the edge of penury. He had spies reporting to him constantly and punishment for breaking the law was swift and severe. In his last days, the powerful sultan, now old and ill, became a puppet in the hands of his trusted deputy, Malik Kafur, who imprisoned Alauddin's son Khizr

Khan. After the sultan's death, he tried to play kingmaker until he was killed by his soldiers.

The Tughlaq Dynasty

After a time of confusion post Alauddin's death, Ghazi Malik, the governor of Dipalpur, came to the throne as Ghiyas-ud-din Tughlaq (1320-1325 CE). He was a well-liked king who began to build the fortress of Tughlaqabad after he came to power.

When the Mongols invaded the north-western borders in 1325 CE, Ghiyas-ud-din succeeded in keeping them away. On his return to Delhi, he was welcomed by his son Fakhruddin Jauna before a wooden pavilion that had been built for the victory celebrations. As the sultan sat inside, the elephants came marching by and the victory celebrations started. But, suddenly, the pavilion collapsed, killing Ghiyas-ud-din inside. Some sources say

Padmini of Chittor

On one his conquests, Alauddin laid siege on the Rajput fortress of Chittor (modern Chitaurgarh). Legends say he wanted to capture the queen of Chittor, Rani Padmini, who was a famous beauty. The Rajputs fought with great courage but they were outnumbered. As the Rajput warriors came out in one final, suicidal attack, the women of the court, led by Padmini, walked into the fire in a ritual suicide called jauhar. *The Padmini-Alauddin story was told much later by the poet Malik Muhammad Jayasi and is probably not true.*

that it was, in fact, Jauna who was responsible for his father's death—the traveller Ibn Batuta accuses Jauna of murdering his father. Ziauddin Barani, however, is silent about it, but then he was the royal historian who could not risk angering Jauna, who was famous for his bad temper.

Prince Jauna now took the title of Muhammad bin Tughlaq (1325 CE-1351 CE). His eccentric schemes and unpredictable behaviour has fascinated people for centuries, for which he was known as 'the mad king'. He was a highly educated and intelligent man but had a violent temper that could turn very cruel and he never won the love of his subjects. He was surprisingly tolerant in some matters, however, and gave jobs to men according to their ability—including the poor and the Hindus. This, of course, did not please the nobility and the religious leaders, called the ulema, who wanted all the well-paid government jobs.

Muhammad bin Tughlaq experimented with many policies, some of which were good in theory, but somehow never worked in practice. First, he decided to shift his capital from Delhi to Daulatabad (previously known as Devagiri). It was a sensible plan in theory, since Daulatabad was more central and less threatened by the Mongols. But instead of shifting

Cities of Delhi

Each dynasty of the Sultanate liked to build a new capital city! After the city built around the Qutub Minar by the Slave kings, Alauddin built a new capital in Delhi that he called Siri. Later, the Tughlaqs built the fortress of Tughlaqabad, the city of Jahanpanah and the palace complex of Feroz Shah Kotla.

The dargah of Sheikh Nizamuddin Auliya in Delhi.

The Saint and the Sultan

When Ghiyas-ud-din was building his fortress at Tughlaqabad, the Sufi saint Sheikh Nizamuddin Auliya was building a baoli (water tank) at his seminary and the labourers preferred to do his work over the sultan's. A furious sultan ordered them to stay away but they disobeyed him. Sheikh Nizamuddin Auliya then predicted that one day, the fortress the sultan was so proud of would be abandoned: 'Ya basey gujar, ya rahey ujaar.' *(It will be the home of gypsies or it will be ruined.) Several centuries later, he has been proved correct. Today, Tughlaqabad is a desolate ruin while the dargah of Nizamuddin swarms with devotees of every religion swaying to the rhythm of the devotional quawwalis.*

only the court and the government offices, the sultan ordered all the *citizens* of Delhi to move! Of course, people protested about leaving their homes, but they were forced to leave by the sultan's soldiers and they suffered severely on the long journey. After all this, Muhammad discovered that it was impossible to manage the kingdom from his new capital. So, a few years later, the capricious sultan ordered everyone back to Delhi again, causing many more deaths on the way.

In 1329 CE, Muhammad bin Tughlaq decided to introduce a token currency of copper coins. Each coin would be valued as one silver tanka. It was a good idea, since this could then save the silver reserves in the treasury. Unfortunately, there were no controls or checks in place for the manufacturing of the coins and soon, people were forging them by the hundreds. This led to the value of the coins plunging to nothing. The sultan was then forced to exchange the copper coins for silver and the historian Barani writes that, for years, heaps of copper coins lay rusting in the sun at Tughlaqabad.

Then Muhammad decided to raise the taxes on farms in the doab region,the fertile area between the two rivers Ganga and Jamuna. In protest, the farmers burnt the standing crop and abandoned their fields and this led to a terrible famine in Delhi. When Muhammad bin Tughlaq finally died in 1351 CE, it was said that his death liberated not only the sultan from his people but also the people from him.

Muhammad was succeeded by his cousin Feroz Shah Tughlaq (1351 CE-1388 CE) and in a reign of thirty-seven years, Feroz brought peace to the troubled land. He tried to please the nobility and the ulema by giving them land grants called iqta, that were made hereditary. This meant that at the death of a nobleman, the land grant would be inherited by his son. Firoz Shah also ruled strictly according to Islamic laws to please the ulema. This made these courtiers very ambitious and later, it led to courtiers becoming more powerful than the sultan.

Feroz was a cultured man and enjoyed literature. He was also the first sultan to build canals, tanks, wells, hospitals and rest houses for the welfare of his people. He founded many towns like Jaunpur, Firozpur, Firozabad and Hisar, that still survive today. These towns became centres of crafts and industry and gave employment to people. He established schools and colleges called madrasas where he had Sanskrit books translated into Persian and Arabic.

Tughlaq Today

Muhammad bin Tughlaq continues to fascinate people even today. Playwright Girish Karnad wrote a famous play, Tughlaq, *about this complicated, unpredictable but oddly likeable man.*

Feroz transported an Ashokan pillar from Meerut to Delhi and placed it inside his palace complex at Feroz Shah Kotla. Barani describes how the pillar was wrapped in cotton and transported by boat across the Jamuna. One of Feroz's madrasas still stands beside a lake in Hauz Khas in Delhi.

The area controlled by the Sultanate was at its biggest during the reign of Muhammad bin Tughlaq but it was hard to control far-off regions. Feroz did not go on military expeditions like his predecessors and so the regions in the south soon broke away and the kings stopped sending tribute. This was the time when the Vijayanagar empire began to rise, which would eventually spread across South India. During the later reign of the Sayyids and Lodis, the Sultanate was reduced to the region around Delhi and parts of Rajasthan.

Invasion of Timur

In 1398 CE, a decade after the death of Feroz Shah Tughlaq, the Sultanate faced a most devastating attack by the Turkish-Mongol conqueror Timur. He entered Delhi and, for three days, his soldiers ransacked the city and massacred the citizens. He went back with a huge booty as well as many Indian craftsmen, who were forced to build the monuments in Samarkand. The Tughlaq dynasty could not survive this invasion. Delhi was left in ruins and took decades to recover.

> *Timur*
> *(1336 CE-1405 CE)*
>
> *One of the most brutal conquerors in history, Timur rose from the Uzbekistan-Tajikistan region of Central Asia. His army overran regions from China to Syria, which he plundered while killing thousands of people. At his death, his empire broke up into small kingdoms. Babur, the founder of the Mughal dynasty, traced his ancestry to two conquerors–Chenghiz Khan and Timur.*

The Sayyid Dynasty (1414 CE-1451 CE)

Timur had only come to plunder in India and, when he left, he appointed a nobleman named Khizr Khan as his governor.

Khizr soon declared himself the sultan of Delhi and started the Sayyid dynasty. The Sayyids had four kings and the sultans could achieve very little as they were busy trying to control their rebellious noblemen. The kingdom began to shrink as provinces like Bengal and Malwa broke free under powerful governors who, at times, even invaded Delhi!

The Lodi Dynasty (1451 CE-1526 CE)

The next sultan to start a new dynasty was Bahlul Khan Lodi. By then, most of the provinces had broken away and he struggled to keep the kingdom together. His son, Sikandar Lodi, was an efficient king but his only memorable act was the founding of the city of Agra.

The last Lodi king was Ibrahim Lodi, who decided to replace some officials in his court with younger and more loyal men. The displaced nobles were, of course, displeased and they then invited Babur, the king of Kabul, to invade India. In 1526 CE, at the First Battle of Panipat, Ibrahim Lodi was defeated and killed, Babur occupied Delhi and Agra, and thus began a new dynasty that would become famous across the world—the Mughals.

The Sultan and His Nobility

The position of the Delhi sultan was rather different from that of a Hindu raja since they were aliens ruling over a conquered land. So they were dependent on the nobility, the men who had come with them, to keep them in power and to the ulema to give them religious legitimacy. This meant that a powerful clique of noblemen and ulema controlled all government posts and Hindus were excluded. The problem with this system was that the nobility began to form cliques and fought with each other for power, thus weakening the Sultanate. Every sultan struggled to control these ambitious men. Razia died fighting them and Muhammad bin Tughlaq tried to defy them—he made an attempt to find men based on merit and even appointed a barber, a cook and a gardener to high positions. The only sultans who could keep these nobles in check were Balban and Allauddin Khalji.

Administration and Land Grants

The administration of the Sultanate was headed by the wazir (prime minister), who kept a record of revenue and expenditure and people appointed in governmental positions. The qazi was the chief judge and advisor on religious matters. The bakshi was the paymaster of the army and the ariz-i-mumalik was in charge of the army. There were four government departments: diwan-i-wizarat (finance); diwan-i-risalat (religious affairs); diwan-i-arz (military affairs) and diwan-i-insha (royal correspondence).

Turks, Afghans and Persian noblemen dominated the administration and even Hindu converts were rarely appointed to high positions. These officials were given hereditary land grants, iqta, instead of a salary and they, in turn, collected revenue from farmers to pay for their own expenses as well as to maintain soldiers and horses for the sultan's army. This system weakened the sultanate as the larger landowners often refused to obey the sultan and the farmers were often exploited.

Elsewhere in the World

The Renaissance began in Europe and there was a wonderful growth in architecture, literature, sculpture, painting and the sciences. In Peru, the Inca civilization built the city of Machu Picchu. In England, King John signed the Magna Carta that protected the rights of the people against the powers of the king.

On the Net

Read more about Timur and his conquests. Also check out the Renaissance and the Magna Carta, and see how Western civilization was now progressing faster than the east towards democracy, which promised a better life for people.

3
NEW KINGDOMS RISE
(1336 CE–1565 CE)

~ The Rise of Vijayanagar ~ Krishnadeva Raya ~ The Bahmani Dynasty ~ The Deccan Sultanates ~ Other Regional Powers ~ Arrival of the Portuguese ~

During the reign of Muhammad bin Tughlaq, the armies of the Sultanate reached as far south as Tamil Nadu. However, it was difficult to control far-off regions from Delhi in those days. What usually happened was that local kings acknowledged the supremacy of Delhi and sent regular tributes but, in fact, ruled independently. The threat being held over these vassal kings was that if they did not obey, the sultan would come marching back and destroy their kingdom.

But these kings were always looking for an opportunity to assert their independence, searching for the moment the centre became weak, so that they could break free. This is exactly what happened after the death of Feroz Shah Tughlaq and the invasion of Timur, which devastated Delhi for many years.

So while the later Tughlaqs, and the weak Sayyids and Lodis, were on the throne in Delhi, the great Hindu kingdom of Vijayanagar rose by the banks of the Tungabhadra River,

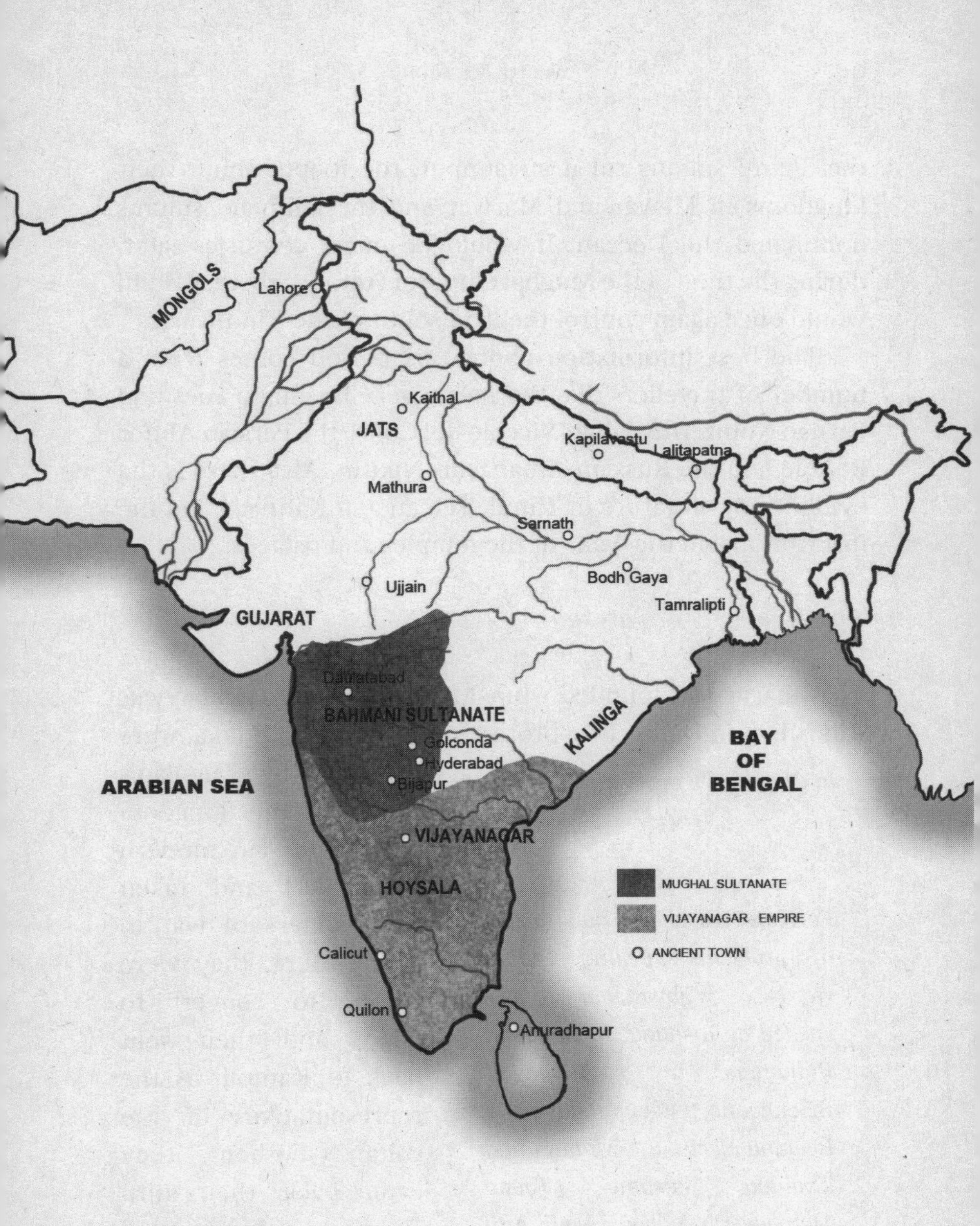

The Vijayanagar empire and the Bahmani Sultanate.

the Sharqi sultans ruled at Jaunpur, the Rajputs built their kingdoms in Mewar and Marwar and the Bahmani sultans dominated the Deccan. It would be many centuries later, during the time of the Mughal emperor Aurangzeb, that Delhi would once again control the land south of the Vindhyas.

The best information about this period comes from a number of travellers like the Portuguese Domingo Paes and Fernao Nuniz, the Italian Niccolo dei Conti, the Persian Abdur Razzaq and the Russian Athanasius Nikitin. Also there is the evidence of literature in Tamil, Telugu and Kannada and the inscriptions on the walls of the temples and palaces.

The Rise of Vijayanagar

Vijayanagar was founded while Muhammad bin Tughlaq was still ruling in Delhi. Two brothers, Harihara and Bukka, were captured by Tughlaq's army in the kingdom of Kampili (in modern Karnataka) and taken as prisoners of war to Delhi. Here, they were forced to convert to Islam and then sent back to Kampili as the representatives of the sultan. When they came back, their guru Vidyaranya reconverted them to Hinduism and inspired them to break

Spelling

Foreign travellers had a lot of problems spelling Indian words. Vijayanagar was spelled as Bisnaga, Bichenagar, Bidjanagar, Bisnagar, Bizenegalia, Visajanagar and Beejanugger! Muhammad Tughlaq became Togao Memede; Ydallcao was Adil Khan and poor Nizam-ul-Mulk became Ozemelluco!

free from the chains of the sultans. The brothers began the Sangama dynasty and founded the city of Vijayanagar, the City of Victory, which became famous across the world.

Harihara became the first king in 1336 CE and he was followed on the throne by his brother Bukka in 1356 CE. The Vijayanagar empire lasted 230 years and their kings were called 'raya'. The three main dynasties of the time were the Sangama (1336 CE-1485 CE), the Saluva (1485 CE-1505 CE) and the Tuluva (1505 CE-1565 CE). Among its greatest kings were Deva Raya II, Saluva Narsimha, Achyuta Raya and the greatest—Krishnadeva Raya.

The magnificent city of Vijayanagar rose by the banks of the Tungabhadra River and it was the most powerful Hindu kingdom of medieval times. It defied the Muslim powers for two centuries and, at its zenith, Vijayanagar ruled over all of peninsular India, from the Arabian Sea to the Bay of Bengal and through trade and tribute it grew fabulously wealthy. Travellers have left descriptions of magnificent celebrations with parades of prancing horses, caparisoned elephants and marching soldiers all led by musicians and dancing courtesans, clad in silks and jewels. Vijayanagar has been described by travellers as a magnificent city of palaces, temples and arcades. Today the ruins of Vijayanagar lie scattered around the village of Hampi in Karnataka. Vijayanagar was always at war with its neighbours and managed to survive for two centuries through clever diplomacy and military might. The kings were great warriors who faced the opposition of the Gajapati kings of Odisha, the Bahmani sultans of Golconda and later, the sultanates of Bijapur and Ahmednagar.

Vijayanagar, under the generous patronage of their kings, saw a great flowering of architecture, sculpture, literature,

The Vitthala temple, Vijayanagar, built by Krishnadeva Raya.

dance and music. Its famous bazaars glittered with shops selling everything from textiles and jewellery to spices and metal ware. The kings built temples all across South India that were covered with the most exquisite sculpture. One can see the finest examples at temples like Virupaksha and Vitthala in Hampi, Karnataka. In fact, many of the South Indian temples we see today were built or expanded by the kings of Vijayanagar. Those eye-catching gopura gateways soaring to the sky, teeming with images, was a creation of its architects.

Krishnadeva Raya

Vijayanagar's greatest king was Krishnadeva Raya (1509 CE-1529 CE). During his reign, Vijayanagar dominated the southern peninsula and the city was the main centre of commerce and culture in the south.

Krishnadeva Raya was a military genius and never lost a battle. He defeated the king of Odisha and the sultan of Golconda and his army defeated and occupied Bijapur. He conquered the Raichur Doab, a very fertile area between the two rivers Krishna and Tungabhadra, which had always been coveted by both Vijayangara and the Bahmani sultans of Golconda. He was an efficient king who improved agriculture by building canals, dams and water tanks. He encouraged trade and, during his reign, Vijayanagar became a centre of commerce with traders coming to its busy bazaars from across the globe.

Krishnadeva Raya was also a patron of the arts and a poet. Only two of his poems have survived. He was also a remarkably tolerant man who employed Muslims in his army and they were allowed to take their oath on the Quran. He was the one who built one of the most beautiful temples at Hampi—the incomparable shrine to Vitthala. He was ruthless in battle but, unlike the sultans, he never sacked an occupied city or massacred a defeated army. Warrior, statesman, poet, builder, Krishnadeva Raya was

Tenali and Others

Krishnadeva Raya had eight talented courtiers called the 'astadiggajas', which literally meant 'eight elephants'. Among them were the poet Allasani Peddana and the poet and humorist Tenali Ramakrishna. We know him as Tenali Raman, whose clever stories still make us laugh.

truly an enlightened king.

During his reign, Vijayanagar controlled all of South India and the empire was fabulously rich. This meant that it faced the envy of the other southern kingdoms. Sadly, Krishnadeva Raya was followed by a number of weak kings and the royal family was divided by intrigue and power struggles. In 1565 CE, at the Battle of Talikota, Vijayanagar was defeated by a confederacy of southern sultanates of Bijapur, Golconda and Ahmednagar. The city was destroyed, the palaces and temples were set on fire and its people massacred. The people who survived the devastation fled and Vijayanagar never rose again. Today, the ruins of the city lie around the river by the village of Hampi in Karnataka.

> *Images*
>
> *If you wonder what Krishnadeva Raya looked like, in one of the ante rooms of the Venkateswara Temple at Tirumala-Tirupati, there are the metal images of Krishnadeva Raya and his queens Chhina Devi and Tirumale Devi. Once after a famous victory at Udayagiri, Krishnadeva Raya covered the image of Lord Venkateswara with 30,000 gold coins.*

The Bahmani Dynasty (1347 CE-1527 CE)

While the Tughlaqs ruled in Delhi and Harihara Raya in Vijayanagar, a new power rose in North Deccan that was the Bahmani kingdom. It was founded by Ala-ud-din Hasan who ascended the throne in 1347 CE with the title of

Ala-ud-din Bahman Shah. The Bahmani kingdom lasted for 180 years with their capital first in Gulbarga and then later in Golconda. The kingdom stood north of the Krishna River; south of it was the Vijayanagar empire with the Raichur Doab in between and the two kingdoms battled endlessly over this fertile patch of land. The ones who suffered the most in this endless state of war were, of course, the people of this region.

The Bahmani dynasty survived for nearly three centuries but it was weakened by the battles between different groups of the nobility. There were two factions of nobles—the Dakhani and the Pardesi—and they were always scheming against each other. The Dakhani, or Deccani, were of local origin while the Pardesis were men who had arrived from Persia, Turkey and Afghanistan seeking positions at court. Many of the sultans found it impossible to control the two factions.

One of the most powerful sultans in the dynasty was the sultan Firoz Shah Bahmani (1397 CE-1422 CE). Firoz Shah conquered the Raichur Doab by defeating Deva Raya I of Vijayanagar. The Raya paid a tribute of 10 lakh gold coins, pearls and elephants and one of his daughters was married to the Bahmani sultan. Firoz Shah came to Vijayanagar to marry the princess in a grand ceremony.

Hasan Gangu

Ala-ud-din Hasan was an Afghan adventurer who rose in the service of a Brahmin named Gangu, and was also called Hasan Gangu. The Mughal historian Firishta says that the word 'bahmani' comes from Brahmin.

Unfortunately, this did not end the conflict between the two kingdoms.

Firoz Shah was a cultured man who patronized artists and scholars and soon his court became a centre of culture in the Deccan. He also included Hindus in the administration and many Brahmins managed his revenue department. In the court at Golconda, a new multi-racial culture began to emerge—it was a unique blend of Muslim and South Indian traditions and can be seen even today in Hyderabad.

Another powerful man of the Bahmani dynasty was Mahmud Gawan who was the prime minister of the sultan Muhammad Shah III. He was successful in controlling the warring nobles and created a powerful kingdom. Mahmud was a Persian who became a trusted minister and he was the real ruler for the eighteen years of his sultan's reign. He was not just an efficient administrator but also a patron of the arts and built a madrasa in Bidar, where students from across the country came to study. Gawan fell victim to court intrigue and in 1481 CE, at the age of seventy, he was executed by the sultan.

Firoz Shah Bahmani

He was a man of many talents and was interested in botany, astronomy, geometry and logic. He was a poet and calligraphist and also built an observatory in Daulatabad. He spoke Persian, Arabic, Turkish, Telugu, Kannada and Marathi. He had a large harem with women from many regions and it was said that he conversed with them in their own language!

The Deccan Sultanates

By the sixteenth century, the Bahmani dynasty had become very weak and powerful governors of provinces broke away and formed their own kingdoms. These were the Nizam Shahis of Ahmadnagar, the Adil Shahis of Bijapur, the Qutub Shahis of Golconda, the Imad Shahis of Berar and the Barid Shahis of Bidar. It was a confederacy of these sultanates that defeated the Vijayanagar army at Talikota in 1565 CE.

The Mughals, when they came to power, attempted to conquer these Sultanates. Akbar annexed Ahmednagar and Aurangzeb occupied Bijapur and Golconda. Strangely, this ambition to capture the Deccan Sultanates became one of the causes of the decline of the Mughal empire. Aurangzeb camped for twenty years fighting an endless war in the Deccan, leading to a decline in the administration of the north. Ironically, after his long and hard conquest, the empire became so large and unwieldy that his descendants found it impossible to control it.

Other Regional Powers

By the time of the Sayyids and Lodis in Delhi, there were many small, independent kingdoms in North India. In Rajasthan, there were the Marwars under Rao Jodha and Mewar was ruled by Rana Kumbha. Malik Sarwar began the Sharqi dynasty in Jaunpur and the Ilyas Shahi and Hussain Shahi sultans ruled in Bengal. Malwa became independent under Hushang Shah, Gujarat under Muzaffar Shah, and Khandesh under Malik Raja. Kashmir was ruled by the famous Zain-ul-Abidin, who was an enlightened and tolerant king. Most of these kingdoms would be annexed by the Mughals in the sixteenth century.

Arrival of the Portuguese

In 1498 CE, two ships captained by Vasco da Gama of Portugal landed at the port of Calicut in Kerala. Till now, the traders between India and Europe had to travel up the Red Sea and then by land across Egypt or the Middle East. Both these routes were controlled by the Turks and the European powers were looking for a new route to obtain pepper and textiles of India. Vasco da Gama had finally discovered the sea route from Europe by going round the Cape of Good Hope in Africa.

Vasco da Gama landed at Kozhikode, the capital of the kingdom of Calicut in Kerala ruled by Samudri Raja, whom the Portuguese called Zamorin. When Zamorin welcomed Gama and let him trade in spices, few could have realized that a new naval power had arrived in India. The profits of this trade were huge. On this first trip, Gama made sixty times the cost of his voyage!

Portugal then decided to dominate the trade in this region. They arrived with ships armed with guns and had soon

Columbus and da Gama

Both Christopher Columbus and Vasco da Gama left Europe in search of a direct sea route to India. In 1492 CE, Columbus decided to sail west and landed in North America, which he claimed was India! Gama sailed east in 1498 CE, went round the continent of Africa and then he employed two Gujarati men to guide his ships across the Arabian Sea.

pushed away the Arabs traders who had been trading peacefully there for centuries. They also built a fortress at the port of Goa and traded with Vijayanagar and the Bahmani sultanate. One of their most prized exports was Arab horses that were needed by Indian armies.

Vasco da Gama

The arrival of the Portuguese paved the way for other European powers to come to the ports of India for trade. This resulted in the coming of the French and the British and led to the colonization of India.

Elsewhere in the World

One of the most powerful empires of the time was the Ottoman empire, which ruled over modern Turkey, the Middle East and parts of Eastern Europe.

On the Net

Check out the Janissaries, an elite corps of slaves who served as the royal guards of the Ottoman sultans and were famed for their strict discipline and their unique uniforms—their headgear, in particular!

4
LIFE UNDER THE SULTANS
(Thirteenth to Sixteenth Century)

~ Changes in Society ~ New Thoughts in Religion ~ Language and Literature ~ Architecture ~

During the rule of the sultans in Delhi, many Muslim immigrants from foreign lands came and settled in India. These people arrived from Persia, Turkey, Arabia and Afghanistan, seeking work at the sultan's court. Many were escaping the Mongol invasions. They settled in India and soon became a part of the population.

They brought with them a new religion, a different culture and a new way of living. Everything from clothing, food and language, architecture and religious beliefs was touched by a new and fresh wave of change. Both Hindus and Muslims influenced each other and, in spite of some suspicion and conflict, what evolved was a civilization that was uniquely Indian.

Changes in Society

Most of the new immigrants settled first in Delhi and then in other important towns. Towns became cosmopolitan places where people in strange clothes speaking in strange languages were now seen on the streets. Mosques began to come up and now the sound of the azaan echoed alongside temple bells. Food shops began serving exotic dishes, the bazaars sold goods from far-off lands and craftsmen learnt new crafts.

Food Platter

There were delicious new dishes on the menu! The Muslim baked khamiri roti and the Hindu fried puri were combined to make the parantha. Indian spices transformed meat dishes and we got the korma and kalia. The kabab platter appeared and desserts with rice and milk moved from payasam to phirni. The halwa came from Turkey, the jalebi and coffee from Arabia and laddus and barfis were now stuffed with dried fruits from Afghanistan.

With a sultan on the throne, the nobility changed completely as all the important government posts were now held by Muslims. The titles of the officials also changed. The prime minister was now called the wazir; the chief judge was the qazi; the paymaster was the bakshi; and the head of the army was the ariz-i-mamalik. Hindus held local government posts and continued to be influential through trade—some of the richest merchants were Hindus.

The life of the poor, however, changed little as they continued to struggle to survive. The peasants were at the mercy of the landowners, who extracted the maximum revenue they could and during famines they faced even greater misery. Rich families often employed slaves and cities had slave markets where human beings were sold like goods. The number of slaves you owned was a sign of your wealth and it is said that Sultan Feroz Shah Tughlaq owned *two lakh* slaves!

Over the years, women had slowly been losing their rights, but now, with the Muslims, the tradition of purdah put them in seclusion and made matters worse. Poor women had to go out to work but those belonging to better-off families were confined to their homes and only went out when accompanied by men. The only place where travellers mention women moving about freely is in Vijayanagar. Few women were educated as all they were allowed to do was run a home. Both Muslim and Hindu men took many wives and the Hindu widow was not allowed to remarry. There were also growing incidents of sati, where Hindu widows were burnt on the funeral pyre of their husbands.

Paper and the Spinning Wheel

Arabs learnt the craft of manufacturing paper from the Chinese and introduced it to India. This made it easier to produce handwritten books. The spinning wheel also began to be used around this time and speeded up the work of weaving cotton.

New Thoughts in Religion

During the sultanate period, two religious movements became popular—the Hindu Bhakti and the Islamic Sufi. At the same time, Buddhism, which had been in decline over the past few centuries, finally vanished from the land. Many of the famous Buddhist monasteries of Taxila and Sarnath were destroyed by Mongol armies and monks were either killed or displaced.

Scholarship, scientific progress or technological development began to slow down. Earlier there had been centuries of political unrest and now the sultans did not encourage scholarship. Brahmin scholars became fearful and hid their books and the centres of Buddhist learning all vanished. This became an intellectually dark age when there was little progress in scientific thought, mathematics or technology.

Alongside the fall of Buddhism in the country, there was a growing rise in Sufi and Bhakti saints. Many of them were philosopher-poets, who sang of their love of God and spread the spirit of tolerance among people. With their poetry and teachings, they built bridges between different religious communities. People of every faith were welcome in the dargahs of Sufi saints and Bhakti poets like Kabir and Nanak. They sang that there was only one God and all religions were the same.

> ## *Nalanda*
>
> *One of the saddest events of this time was the burning of the famous universities of Nalanda and Vikramshila by Iltutmish's general Bakhtiyar Khalji. Their world famous libraries, with huge collections of manuscripts, were all destroyed.*

Sufi saints like Moinuddin Chishti and Nizamuddin Auliya opened seminaries where people were taught to live simply, donate to the poor and worship God through prayers and devotional music. The Bhakti poets like the alvar and Nayanmar saints from the south, Kabir, Mirabai and Guru

Nanak preached love of humanity and equality of all. They opposed the caste system, rejected the supremacy of the Brahmin priesthood and said that one could pray directly to God without the need for religious rituals. Both Sufi and Bhakti poets said that God was one, everyone was born equal and people of every faith were the same.

Language and Literature

It is because of the poets of the Bhakti and Sufi movements that literature flourished during this time. At a time when priests controlled all forms of worship and the caste system kept people of lower castes from entering temples, these poets gave God back to the people. They said everyone was born equal and many of them were themselves from lower castes, a few were women. Even today, their hymns are sung in temples. They said to reach God you do not need priests or expensive religious rituals. God listens to everyone and all

Guru Nanak

Guru Nanak, the wandering teacher, was a wonderful poet who set his poems to the music of the ragas. He was born a Brahmin and his constant companion during his travels was the rubab player Mardana, a Muslim. His lyrical, wise poems have been collected in the Guru Granth Sahib, the sacred text of Sikhism. There is a saying about him, 'Guru Nanak Shah faqir; Hindu ka guru, Mussalman ka pir.' *(Guru Nanak is a true saint. He is a guru to Hindus and a pir to Muslims.)*

you need is a handful of flowers and a heart full of love and devotion. Poetry in the form of devotional music and prayers became popular with people of all religions. For example, the sage Ramananda of Varanasi chose his disciples from all castes. Among them were–Ravidas a cobbler, Kabir a weaver, Sena a barber and Sadhana a butcher. They were all considered untouchables by the Brahmins and were not allowed to enter temples.

Guru Nanak

Bhakti began in the south in the seventh century and had travelled to the north by the twelfth century. It began with the growing popularity of alvar poets like Appar, Andal and Tiruppan, who sang in praise of Vishnu. The nayanar poets like Basavanna and Mahadevi Akka worshipped Shiva through verse. Their verses were in regional languages like Tamil or Kannada instead of Sanskrit so everyone could understand them.

Kabir

In a doha, or poem, translated by Rabindranath Tagore, Kabir says, 'Hari is in the east; Allah is in the west. Look within your heart, for there you will find both Karim and Ram. All the men and women of the world are His living forms. Kabir is the child of Allah and of Ram. He is my guru, he is my pir.'

There were also the Marathi verses of Namdev and Tukaram; Chaitanya's poems and songs in Bengali; the Avadhi dohas of Kabir and Surdas; Nanak's verses in Punjabi and Mirabai's in Rajasthani.

The greatest of the Sufi poets was Amir Khusro. He was a devotee of Sheikh Nizamuddin Auliya in Delhi and his verses were in his praise. For Sufis, devotion to God has an element of ecstasy expressed through sama—the singing of devotional songs. Khusro also developed the musical style of qawwali, in which songs are sung by a singer and a chorus. He used a language that was a mix of Hindi and Persian and he called it Hindawi, from which we would have Urdu and Hindustani.

Architecture

Initially, the sultans converted existing temples and monasteries into mosques. The Quwwat-ul-Islam mosque

The arch now began to be used in architecture.

in Delhi was originally a Vishnu temple and the Adhai Din ka Jhopra in Ajmer was a monastery. But gradually, new styles of architecture were introduced—arches, minarets and domes appeared on mosques, fortresses and palaces. Arabs had learnt the design of the arch and the dome from Roman architects.

Basavanna

The Bhakti poets questioned religious practices. Here's Basavanna asking about idol worship, 'How can I feel right about gods you sell in your need? And gods you bury for fear of thieves?'

Sculpture did not depict the human figure as it was not allowed in Islam and focused instead on geometric and floral designs and the calligraphy of verses from the Quran. As the actual work was still done by Hindu craftsmen, gradually there was a beautiful synthesis of Hindu and Islamic motifs that can be seen today in the building of the Qutub Minar complex at Tughlaqabad and in the Lodi monuments of Delhi. Architecture in regional kingdoms like Jaunpur, Golconda, Vijayanagar, Bijapur, were all developing their own unique architectural styles as well.

Every aspect of people's lives—religious practices, social customs, clothes, cuisine, art and literature was touched by change and, in many ways, the meeting of the ancient Indian and younger, and more vigorous, Islamic culture was a positive union. New writers and historians, musicians and artists, craftsmen and chefs made life richer and more colourful.

Elsewhere in the World

As India sank into a period of no scientific or technological progress, Europe was taking great strides in knowledge. This period, called the Rennaisance or rebirth, saw great progress in science, technology, art and architecture. The invention of the movable type by Gutenberg in 1440 CE meant that books could be produced cheaply and quickly and it led to the spread of education.

Walkabout

To see the finest collection of Sultanate buildings, visit the Qutab Minar complex in Delhi which has a victory tower, mosque and mausoleums.

5

ENTER THE MUGHALS

(1526 CE–1556 CE)

~ Zahir-ud-din Babur ~ Battles at Panipat and Khanwa ~ Nasir-ud-din Humayun ~ Sher Shah Sur ~ Return of Humayun ~ Foundations of a Great Dynasty ~

He was named Babur, meaning tiger, and he built a kingdom with the ferocity of one. With the arrival of Zahir-ud-din Babur began the tumultuous reign of the Mughals that became a legend across the world. The Mughals were among the longest surviving dynasties in India, ruling from 1526 CE to 1858 CE, a total of 332 years!

The Mughals were among the richest and most dazzling dynasty of their time and their vivid, colourful histories were carried back by travellers across the world. For the first two centuries, they were the epitome of grandeur and power, with the first six kings—Babur, Humayun, Akbar, Jahangir, Shah Jahan and Aurangzeb being truly great monarchs. In his heyday, Shah Jahan, the emperor who sat on the magnificent Peacock Throne, was the 'Great Mogul' that travellers came to see. Clearly, the Mughals liked to put up quite a show!

A dynasty is not called great only because of its longevity, its greatness lies in how they influence and transform the life of the people. The Mughal kings were not just conquerors, they were also patrons of the arts—they built some of the finest palaces, fortresses and mausoleums in India—they encouraged trade and ran an efficient administration. What finally evolved was a Mughal culture that blended Hindu and Muslim traditions and that was also genuinely Indian. By now, we have many sources of information. There are royal biographies like Akbar's *Ain-i-Akbari* and *Akbarnama*, and the group of works documenting Shah Jahan's life known as the Padshahnama. There is also Babur's autobiography, *Baburnama*; Gulbadan Begum's memoir of her brother called *Humayunnama* and Jahangir'sautobiography, *Tuzuk-i-Jahangiri*. The writings of travellers like Niccolo Manucci, Francois Bernier, Jean Baptiste Tavernier, Ralph Fitch and Thomas Coryat also shed light on the period.

There is also a rich visual record of the times in the form of miniature paintings of the era. Not only do we know how Akbar or Aurangzeb looked but also the clothes they

Reigns of the Great Mughals

Zahir-ud-din Muhammad Babur (1526 CE-1530 CE)

Nasir-ud-din Muhammad Humayun (1530 CE-1540 CE, 1555 CE-1556 CE)

Jalal-ud-din Muhammad Akbar (1556 CE-1605 CE)

Nur-ud-din Muhammad Jahangir (1605 CE-1627 CE)

Shihab-ud-din Muhammad Shah Jahan (1628 CE-1657 CE)

Muhi-ud-din Muhammad Aurangzeb (1658 CE-1707 CE)

wore, the food they ate, the furniture and carpets in the palaces, the life of the people on the street, the battle and the hunts—all through the Mughal miniatures, which projected the glamorous lives of the royal family and nobility to the world.

Zahir-ud-din Babur (1526 CE-1530 CE)

Babur had the lineage of two great conquerors, even though he was the king of the tiny kingdom of Ferghana, near Tashkent in today's Uzbekistan. From his mother's side he was descended from the great Mongol Chenghiz Khan and from his father's side from the Chagatai Turk, Timur, who destroyed Delhi in 1398 CE.

Babur was only eleven when he succeeded his father to the throne of Ferghana and his greatest ambition was to conquer the city of Samarkand, the legendary capital of Timur. Battling other claimants, he won and lost it and, in the attempt, ended up losing Ferghana. For years, he wandered with his army as a nomad, robbing villages to survive. Finally in 1504 CE, he captured Kabul and once again had a kingdom to rule. A true adventurer, he now looked to the east for more lands to conquer and India, with its tempting riches,

Timuriya or Mughal?

The dynasty Babur founded is called Mughal, the Persian word for Mongol. However, Babur thought the Mongols were barbarians and preferred to trace his ancestry to Timur and the family called themselves Timuriya.

beckoned. He led a few small raids into India till he got the chance he was looking for. Sultan Ibrahim Lodi was so unpopular that some of the nobility invited Babur to invade and he, of course, seized the opportunity.

Battles at Panipat and Khanwa

The First Battle of Panipat proves the dictum that it is the general who makes the difference in a war. The armies of Babur and Ibrahim Lodi met on 21 April 1526 CE on the fields of Panipat and, at first sight, it looked like a very unequal battle. The Lodi army rolled in with one lakh soldiers and a thousand elephants. Babur had just 25,000 soldiers including horsemen and gunmen and no elephants. But the crucial advantage that Babur had was that he was using matchlock guns while the Lodi army was still armed with swords and spears. Also Babur had an army of experienced, battle-hardened soldiers and he was a great military strategist.

At Panipat, Babur's battle strategy was built around his artillery. He created a barrier by tying wagons together, with a ditch in front, and placed his gunmen behind them. The horsemen were experienced at sweeping around, trapping the enemy in the middle and making lightning attacks at the enemy's flanks and rear. Then, as

Guns at Panipat

Cannons and matchlock muskets were used at Panipat and then Khanwa for the first time in India and created havoc among the enemy. Babur had a Turkish artillery man named Ustad Ali, who made the first cannons in India.

the two armies faced each other, Babur waited for Ibrahim to lose his patience and make the first move.

When the Lodi king finally attacked, his men were surrounded from the sides and rear by Babur's cavalry, while the artillery was shooting bullets at men armed with just swords and spears. The elephants stampeded, the surviving soldiers fled and by the afternoon it was all over. The battle had lasted only five hours, Ibrahim Lodi was dead and Babur immediately began marching towards Delhi.

Babur sent his son Humayun to Agra to capture the Lodi treasury. The king of Gwalior had joined Ibrahim Lodi's army at Panipat where he was killed. At Agra, Humayun found the royal family of Gwalior, who had taken refuge in the fort. Begging for his protection, they presented him with a huge diamond which was probably the famous Kohinoor. Humayun gave it to his father who

Journey of the Kohinoor

The diamond was given to Humayun by the royal family of Gwalior and he, in turn, gave it to Shah Tahmasp of Persia. The Shah gifted it to the Sultan of Golconda and it was back with the Mughals by the time of Shah Jahan's reign. Nadir Shah took it from the Mughals and he named it the Kohinoor, 'mountain of light'. Later, it passed into the hands of the king of Afghanistan, who gave it to Maharaja Ranjit Singh of Punjab. It was taken from Ranjit Singh's son Dalip Singh by the British and presented to Queen Victoria. It is now kept at the Tower of London. And you can be sure it will stay there forever!

promptly gave it back to him. Babur wrote in the *Baburnama,* that the diamond was worth 'two and a half day's food for the whole world'!

Babur made Agra his capital and now faced an opposition far more formidable than Ibrahim Lodi. Rana Sangram Singh, popularly known as Rana Sanga, was the legendary warrior king of Mewar and the undisputed leader of the Rajputs. He had expected Babur to gather his loot and withdraw from India, like Timur had done before him, but it looked like Babur planned to stay. So the Rana gathered together an army of Rajput kings and marched towards Agra.

On 17 March 1527 CE, the two armies met at Khanwa on the outskirts of Agra and a fierce battle raged all day. Again, Babur had the advantage of gunmen and by sunset he had won a great victory. Rana Sanga retreated from Khanwa and died within a few months. Babur had been quite anxious before the battle as he had heard of the valour of the Rajputs and is supposed to have said that the Rajputs knew how to fight but not how to win. Khanwa

Warrior-Poet

Babur was a unique king at a time when rulers were known only for their qualities as warriors. He was a tough fighter but he also loved books, enjoyed nature and laid out many gardens. He also kept a diary that he later organized into a memoir called the Baburnama, *which is written with surprising frankness. He wrote poetry and observed the world around him with the eye of a naturalist and in the* Baburnama *he described the flora and fauna of India in great detail.*

was where Babur really won his Indian kingdom. However, he did not live long enough to consolidate his victories and died four years later in 1530 CE, and was succeeded by his son Humayun.

Nasir-ud-din Humayun (1530 CE-1540 CE, 1555 CE-1556 CE)

If Babur won his kingdom, his son Humayun did his best to lose it! Humayun's biggest problems were his three half-brothers, Kamran, Askari and Hindal, who were given parts of the kingdom to govern. But each of them wanted to be king. So they were always rebelling against Humayun, who was a sentimental man and would keep forgiving them. Also, there was trouble from Afghan noblemen who had been loyal to the old Lodi dynasty. The most dangerous of them was Sher

The Mughal king Humayun.

Khan, who was already behaving like an independent ruler in Bihar and Bengal and soon began to march towards Delhi.

Sher Khan defeated Humayun in two battles: at Chausa (1539 CE) and Kanuaj (1540 CE) and then occupied Delhi. As Humayun wandered in the deserts of Rajasthan, being harassed by his unrepentant brothers, Sher Khan occupied Humayun's half-built fortress of Din Panah and declared himself king as Sher Shah Sur. It was during these years of wandering that Humayun's wife, Hamida Bano, gave birth to a son. Humayun's eldest son was born in October 1542 CE, at Umarkot and named Jalal-ud-din Muhammad Akbar. In spite of such an obscure beginning, he would one day recover all the land that his father had lost and finally lay the foundation of an empire.

Sher Shah Sur (1540 CE-1545 CE)

Meanwhile, Sher Shah built new palaces and a mosque at the citadel of Din Panah. He was already in his fifties but he was a great military leader and also an efficient ruler. Babur had only managed to conquer the land but it was Sher Shah who, in a short reign of just five years, laid the foundation of an administrative system that would later be expanded by Akbar. Sher Shah divided the kingdom into provinces called *sarkars* and *parganas* and toured them to make sure the officials were doing their work. He got the land surveyed and taxes were fixed at one-third of the crops, according to the yield of the land.

Sher Shah also organized the standing army: soldiers were paid regular salaries, horses were branded so that they could not be sold and records were kept of all the soldiers. One brilliant measure was the building of a highway connecting the east to the north-west, which helped in trade and travel. He also introduced a silver coin, the rupia, which was used for a long time. A peaceful, well-administered kingdom and safe roads meant the growth of trade and Akbar would shrewdly carry on with the same policy.

Sher Shah Sur was a great king but unfortunately he died in an accident and his successor Islam Shah could not control the kingdom. Meanwhile, Humayun who was wandering aimlessly in Central Asia, managed to get the support of Shah Tahmasp of Persia after he had presented him with the Kohinoor diamond. He first captured Kabul from his brother Kamran and then defeated Islam Shah and recovered Delhi in 1555 CE.

Chausa

At the Battle of Chausa, Humayun escaped with the help of a water carrier named Nizam. He inflated his leather water bag and Humayun used it to swim across the Ganga. In return, Nizam was allowed to sit on the throne at Delhi for one day!

Return of Humayun

So, after fifteen years of exile, the Mughals were back in India. Humayun occupied Din Panah again and soon his family arrived from Kabul. At this point, the Mughal kingdom really included only the Lahore-Delhi-Agra belt. If he wanted a proper kingdom, Humayun would soon have to start going on expeditions to conquer more land. Fortunately, by this time the problem of Humayun's brothers was finally solved. The most troublesome one, Kamran, had been blinded and sent off to Mecca, where he died. Askari also died on the way to Arabia and Hindal, who had finally joined Humayun against the other two, died in battle.

The man who helped Humayun defeat the Afghans was his general Bairam Khan, who would later stand by the side of young Akbar. Unfortunately the hapless Humayun did not get much time to enjoy his moment of triumph. The following year, he fell from the stairs of his library and died of his injuries. His son Akbar, who was away in the Punjab on a military expedition, was just thirteen when he took over the throne. It looked like the Mughal kingdom was in jeopardy again.

Purana Qila in Delhi.

Foundations of a Great Dynasty

There have been many long-lived dynasties in India; the Cholas, for example, existed even longer than the Mughals. What makes the Mughals so great then? It started with Babur, his greatness was in his character and his attitude to kingship, which he passed on to later kings, especially Akbar, who idolized him. The real founder of the dynasty was Akbar. Luckily Akbar had a long reign of nearly fifty years and had the time to establish a proper empire.

Just like his grandfather, Akbar was a humane king and had Babur's tolerant spirit that made him reach out to the Hindus as well. He was also a successful general like Babur and built up the empire through relentless campaigns of conquests. With it he combined the ability to set in place an efficient administration that ran the empire smoothly and ensured peace that let people prosper. He collected taxes efficiently, which made the family very rich. The foundation of this great dynasty was laid first by Babur and then by Akbar.

The Grand Trunk Road

The highway connecting Bengal with Punjab that was built by Sher Shah Sur is now called the Grand Trunk Road, which, even today, throngs with trucks and buses. Sher Shah built roadside inns along the highway called serais which became centres of trade and later grew into towns. The Mughals maintained this road very carefully.

Elsewhere in the World

Henry VIII, King of England, started the Reformation around this time, where he defied the Pope, rejected the Roman Catholic Church and became the head of the Church of England.

In Royal Prussia, Renaissance astronomer Nicolaus Copernicus discovered that the earth moved around the sun, instead of the sun going around the earth, as was popularly believed.

On the Net

Check out another great dynasty that was dazzling the world at the same time as the Mughals: the Tudors of England!

6

AKBAR BUILDS AN EMPIRE

(1556 CE–1605 CE)

~ Bairam Khan to the Rescue ~ The Second Battle of Panipat ~ Building an Empire ~ Enter Jodh Bai ~ Akbar's Religion ~ Running an Empire ~ Flowering of Culture ~

When he became king at thirteen, no one could have imagined that one day Jalal-ud-din Muhammad Akbar would be called 'the Great'. In a long reign of nearly fifty years, Akbar earned his title.

When Akbar inherited the kingdom from Humayun, the Mughal 'empire' included only Lahore, Delhi and Agra, and Akbar was surrounded by enemies. But eventually, he succeeded in building an empire that covered all of North India and parts of the Deccan, becoming the undisputed emperor of the country.

Akbar was a humane and tolerant king who presided over a dazzling court of highly talented men. Legends say that he had nine jewels, or the navaratna, in his court. Among those mentioned in historical records are the historian Abul Fazl; the poets Faizi, Abdur Rahim and Birbal; the Rajput general Man Singh; the finance minister Todar Mal; and the singers Tansen and Baz Bahadur.

It is in the writings of the royal historian Abul Fazl, in the two official histories *Ain-i-Akbari* and *Akbarnama*, that we get a portrait of this magnificent monarch. Visitors were fascinated by Akbar and many of them, like the Portuguese Jesuit priest Father Anthony Monserrate and the English traveller Ralph Fitch, wrote about him. We also have as sources the illustrated manuscripts produced by the miniature painting studio that Akbar set up at Fatehpur Sikri.

Bairam Khan to the Rescue

One of the few wise things that Humayun had done was to make his trusted general Bairam Khan the guardian of his son. If the kingdom survived despite Humayun's death and Akbar's young age it was because of the loyalty, courage and statesmanship of Bairam Khan. He could easily have usurped the throne but instead he became regent and made sure Akbar's kingdom was safe.

The situation was not favourable for the boy king when he came to the throne, with three

Coronation

When Humayun died, Akbar was on a military campaign in the Punjab with Bairam Khan, one of his father's trusted generals. So, till he was back in Delhi, a mullah named Bekasi, who resembled Humayun, was made to sit at a window in the royal palace to make the people believe that the king was still alive. Akbar was hurriedly crowned on a stone platform in a garden and it still stands in the middle of wheat fields near Kalanaur in Gurdaspur district.

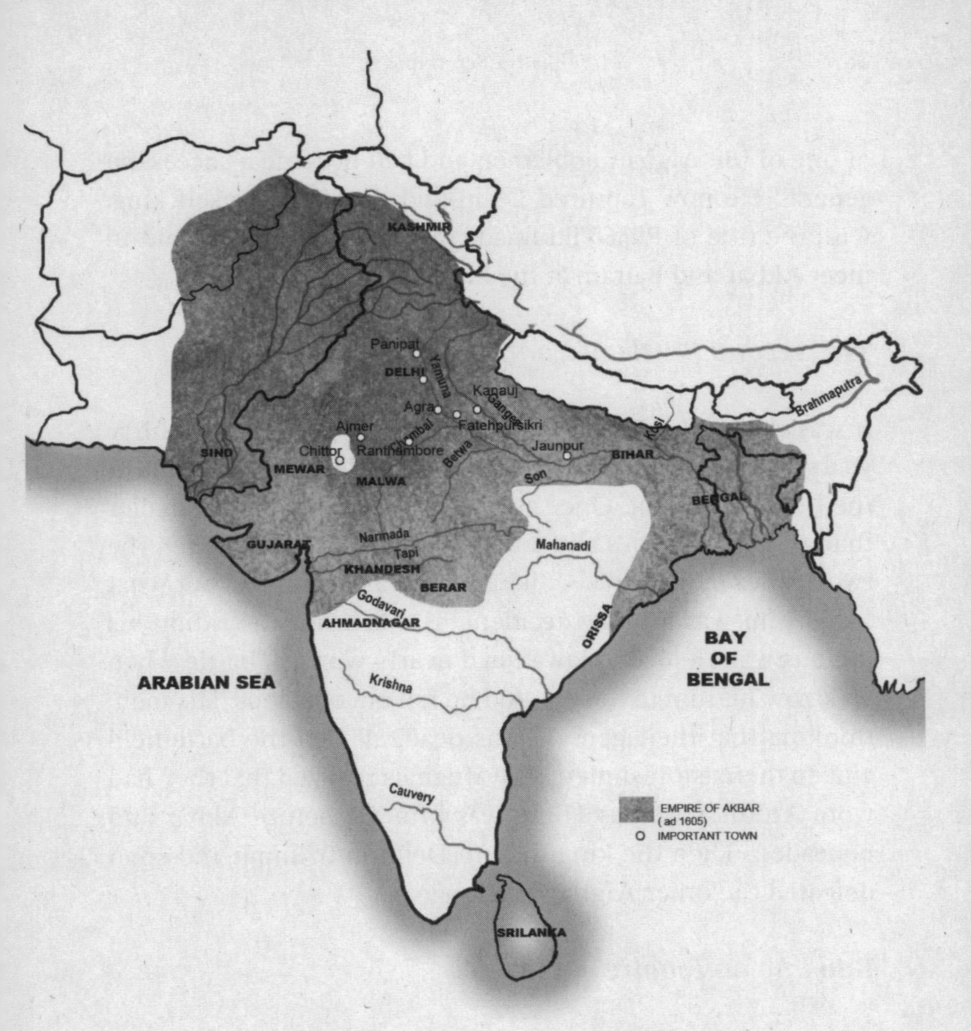

Mughal empire during the reign of Akbar.

Afghan noblemen, all claiming the throne of Sher Shah Sur, ready to march against Akbar. The Mughal army was small and battle-weary and many felt that he should withdraw to Kabul and return later to claim Delhi. But Bairam Khan and Akbar chose to stay and fight. Interestingly, their most dangerous opponent was not the Afghans but a former Hindu trader from Rewari named Himu. He had risen to become the chief adviser of one of the Afghan noblemen and had become a successful general. He now captured Delhi and declared himself king, with the title of Raja Vikramaditya. Then he marched out to meet Akbar and Bairam at the head of a huge army.

The Second Battle of Panipat

It was a remarkable coincidence. In 1556 CE, exactly thirty years after his grandfather, Akbar was going to meet Himu at the field of Panipat. Once again, his army was much smaller than the opposition's and a kingdom was at stake. When the two armies met, it looked like Akbar was in trouble, but what saved him was a lucky accident. Himu, who was riding his famous war elephant Hawai, had nearly won the battle when an arrow hit him in the eye and he fell unconscious. His men, thinking that their general was dead, all fled the battlefield and, to their astonishment, the Mughals realized that they had won. An unconscious Himu was brought before Akbar and beheaded. Then the king rode to Delhi in triumph and soon defeated the other Afghan challengers.

Building an Empire

His first victory at Panipat may have been a fortunate one but later Akbar would evolve into a brave warrior and an inspired military leader who never lost a battle in his life. He spent a large part of his reign on campaigns that ultimately led to an empire that covered nearly the whole of India. On his death in 1605 CE, it stretched from Bengal in the east to Kabul in the west; Kashmir in the north to the Deccan in the south. Babur would have been very proud of him.

Mughal emperor Akbar.

Akbar's Gujarat campaign shows the military genius of the man. In those days, military campaigns were slow affairs because most of the army marched on foot. So, usually, the opposition knew that Akbar was coming and had time to prepare. So when Akbar headed out of his new capital city of Fatehpur Sikri for Gujarat, the sultan of Gujarat expected him to arrive some weeks later. However Akbar, using a team of fast camels, covered 800 kilometres in eleven days and thus the sultan surrendered. Akbar also had clever tactics for laying siege to a fort using cannons and in this way captured Ranthambhor and Chittor, two Rajput forts that were believed to be impregnable.

Enter Jodh Bai

Akbar was the first Muslim king to realize that to establish a long lasting empire in India he had to gain the support of the majority of the population—the Hindus. It also helped that he was born in India and felt no emotional bond to another homeland. Gaining the support of the Hindus was a shrewd political move but it came from a king who was genuinely tolerant and humane. Until then, senior government posts were all held by Muslims but now Hindus were inducted into the army and bureaucracy and so became part of the nobility. In Akbar's kingdom, ability, not race or religion, was valued and that is what made him such a great monarch.

When he was twenty, Akbar married a Rajput princess, the daughter of Raja Bihari Mal of Amber (modern Jaipur) and soon afterwards, other Rajput princesses entered the Mughal harem. Earlier, many sultans like Alauddin Khalji had married Hindu princesses but the women had always been forced to convert to Islam. Akbar allowed his Hindu wives to practise their own religion, and built separate palaces for them with their own temples and kitchens. Then he joined in enthusiastically in their festivals, playing Holi and lighting lamps at Diwali. He loved wearing a dhoti and grew his hair long, wore a Rajput style turban and put a teeka on his forehead. It was his eldest son Salim, son of the princess of Amber, who was the heir apparent and later became king as Jahangir.

Akbar wanted to be a real king to his Hindu subjects. At that time,

Who was Jodh Bai?

Oral tradition says that the princess of Amber was called Jodh Bai but none of the royal histories give her name. She is referred to as 'the daughter of Raja Bihari Mal' and later, as the mother of the heir apparent, Jahangir, by her Mughal title of 'Mariam-uz-Zamani'. Some modern historians say that only a princess of Jodhpur would be called Jodh Bai and that her name was Harka Bai. No one really knows for sure.

Hindus had to pay a tax called jizya, so that they could practise their religion. Akbar abolished this tax and also the taxes taken from Hindu pilgrims. He gave grants of land to scholars of all religions and helped build and repair temples. His marriage alliances led to Rajput kings joining the Mughal court. So the Rajputs, who could have otherwise given him a lot of trouble, became his allies instead. This new Rajput nobility also helped Akbar to control the ambitious noblemen from Persia and Afghanistan. Many of the Rajputs, like Raja Man Singh, were successful generals; Raja Todar Mal became Akbar's finance minister and created a revenue system that lasted for centuries; Raja Birbal was among Akbar's closest friends.

Akbar's Religion

Akbar had a surprisingly spiritual side to his character. He was energetic and ambitious but also thoughtful and curious about philosophy and religion. In this, he resembled another great king, Ashoka of the Mauryan dynasty. Akbar realized that to rule a country with many religions, a king had to respect all faiths and treat everyone equally

Sheikh Salim Chishti

Akbar was twenty-six years old and he had no son. Then he met the Sufi saint Sheikh Salim Chishti, who said he would have three sons and the prediction came true. Akbar built his new city of Fatehpur Sikri around the seminary of the saint and named his eldest son Salim. Even today, the dargah of Sheikh Salim Chishti is filled with pilgrims who pray to Akbar's favourite saint.

and, because of this, he was loved by all his subjects.

Akbar built a palace in Fatehpur Sikri called the Ibadat Khana where he gathered scholars from all religions to hold discussions and debates. Muslim mullahs, Christian Jesuits, Buddhist and Jain monks, Zoroastrian and Brahmin priests and even atheists would all gather and debate on religion. Akbar was most influenced by the humane philosophy of Abul Fazl's father, the Sufi Sheikh Mubarak, who taught of Sulh-i-Kul, a gentle faith talking of universal tolerance and peace. Listening to the debates in the Ibadat Khana, Akbar became convinced that all religions spoke of the truth and there was one God.

Akbar was a practising Muslim; he went regularly to the mosque but he also played Holi with Hindus, worshipped the fire like Parsis, prayed to the sun, allowed Jesuit priests to teach his sons and listened to Tansen singing a dhrupad to Lord Shiva. Then he announced a new faith which he called Din-i-Ilahi, or divine faith, that was a mix of the things he had liked in all the religions. Akbar was, of course, its head priest and chief philosopher, and preached at the mosque. He had created a religion that he hoped would unite his empire but he never forced anyone to join it. However, Din-i-Ilahi did not spread

Discovering Daswant

Akbar used to wander around in disguise to meet his subjects. Once while walking around in Agra he discovered a boy drawing on the walls of his hut and took him to the tasvirkhana. Daswant was the son of a poor palki bearer and later became a famous painter.

beyond a few of his friends, like Birbal and Abul Fazl, and died with its creator.

Running an Empire

Conquering land was just the start of the challenge of building an empire. Then followed the hard work of setting up an administration that kept law and order, a revenue system that collected taxes, an economic policy that encouraged trade and the maintaining of a standing army. Akbar understood this very well and he had the energy and efficiency to set up a well-run empire.

Akbar was a very busy and hard-working king who met his subjects every day in the palace called the diwan-i-am (Hall of Public Audience). For hours, he would sit and listen to his subjects' complaints and requests. He was his own prime minister and had officers heading different

The Panch Mahal at Fatehpur Sikri in Agra.

departments. The wazir headed the revenue department and the bakshi handled army affairs. The Khan-i-Khanan took care of the needs of the royal family, the qazi headed the justice department and the sadr-i-sadr kept records of grants and donations. The king met his officials every day at the diwan-i-khas (Hall of Private Audience) to listen to their reports and also to welcome ambassadors from other kingdoms who arrived bearing gifts.

The army officers, who were all noblemen, were called mansabdars and they had to maintain a fixed number of soldiers and horses and for that they received a salary, often in the form of a land grant. They would collect the tax from the land, keep their allowance and send the rest to the king. The mansabdari ranks ranged from five to five thousand and only the royal princes had mansabs over that. However once the mansabdar died, his property became state property again. Akbar also had a personal army of

Akbar the Man

Akbar was a really interesting man. A brave warrior who fought with reckless courage; he loved sports, especially riding wild elephants, playing polo and hunting. At the same time, even though he could barely read, he was interested in books, paintings and music. He loved to learn and would sit with stone carvers and carpet weavers to learn their crafts. He was very hard-working, sleeping for just three hours a day and eating just one meal. He was curious about all religions and was genuinely tolerant. He loved the company of people and his best friends were Abul Fazl and Birbal.

loyal soldiers called ahadis, who guarded the king and his family and were often from Rajput families famous for their loyalty.

Flowering of Culture

Akbar was interested in many things, not just the job of running an empire. He invited the singers Tansen and Baz Bahadur to come and join his court. Tansen would create the raga darbari for Akbar who called him 'Mian'. There were great writers and poets like Faizi, Abdur Rahim and Birbal in his court. At Fatehpur Sikri, Akbar set up a studio for miniature painters called the tasvirkhana. Also there were workshops called karkhanas that produced carpets, rugs, jewellery, textiles, metalware and woodwork that were used by the royal family and courtiers.

Humayun brought two miniature painters, Abdus Samad and Mir Sayyid Ali from Persia and they established the first studio in India. Later, many Indian painters like Mukund, Basawan and Daswant, joined and they created a beautiful blend of Persian and Indian styles. These Mughal miniatures were used for illustrating manuscripts.

Akbar was barely literate; everything had to be read out to him. But he still loved books and had over 20,000 books in his library. He got Sanskrit books like the Mahabharata and Ramayana translated into Persian and then these manuscripts were handwritten using beautiful calligraphy and illustrated with paintings in jewelled colours. The most beautiful Akbari manuscript is Abul Fazl's *Akbarnama*.

Akbar was a passionate builder who encouraged the blending of Islamic and Hindu designs to create a unique architectural style. He first built Agra Fort and then a new city at Fatehpur Sikri that he filled with palaces, a mosque, a Sufi shrine and a majestic gateway. He also built forts at Lahore and Allahabad as well as the elegant Humayun's Tomb in Delhi. Later, his grandson Shah Jahan would build the Taj Mahal in the same design as the Humayun's Tomb.

Warrior and lover of books, a liberal man who respected all religions, a patron of the arts, a tough ruler, yet loved by his subjects, Akbar was a humane king who built an empire that would become famous across the world. The Mughal historian Haidar said at his birth, he was 'the child of a Sunni father and a Shia mother, born in Hindustan in the land of Sufism, at the house of a Hindu.' Jalaluddin Akbar, then, was a true Indian king.

Elsewhere in the World

Another great monarch ruling at this time was Queen Elizabeth I, the Tudor queen of England. Her reign was also a time of progress and saw a flowering of culture. Elizabeth sent an ambassador to the court of Akbar.

On the Net

The lives of both Akbar and Queen Elizabeth have been made into films: Jodha Akbar *directed by Ashutosh Gowariker and two films on Elizabeth directed by Shekhar Kapoor. Check them out on IMDB if you haven't seen them already!*

7

THE MAGNIFICENT MUGHALS (1605 CE–1658 CE)

~ Nur-ud-din Jahangir ~ Empress Nur Jahan ~ Arrival of the Europeans ~Shihab-ud-din Shah Jahan ~ Shah Jahan, the Builder ~ Brothers at War ~

The last years of Akbar's reign were darkened by tragedy. First there was the death of his sons Murad in 1599 CE and Daniyal in 1604 CE and also of his friends Birbal and Abul Fazl. Then there was his disappointment with his eldest son, Salim, who was not too interested in the work of the empire. He rebelled against his father and declared himself king and Akbar was reconciled with his surviving son only before his death in 1605 CE. Salim ascended the throne at Agra with the title of Jahangir, meaning 'the seizer of the world'. He would rule for twenty-two years and, to everyone's surprise, he was not such a disaster as a king.

Like his great-grandfather Babur, Jahangir dictated his own biography, *Tuzuk-i-Jahangiri*, a remarkably frank and honest book where he is open about his own failings like his addiction to wine and opium. There are also the writings of travellers: by this time the Mughals were so famous that ambassadors, traders and travellers from across the world were arriving to their courts. Among them were Sir Thomas Roe, Francois Bernier, Jean Baptiste Tavernier, Niccolo Manucci and Thomas Coryat, who not only describe the land and the people in great detail but also include a lot of fascinating bazaar gossip about the royal family. And, of course, we have the vibrantly coloured miniature paintings and a rich hoard of Mughal coins.

Nur-ud-din Jahangir (1605 CE–1627 CE)

Akbar had made sure his descendants had an easy time and there was peace during the reign of Jahangir. He was no warrior and hardly made any effort to extend the empire. He had no new ideas about administration either. However, he was a highly cultured man and he cared for his subjects. Akbar had established such an efficiently run empire that he had to just let it move along smoothly. Jahangir's reign was really an extension of his father's rule with peace and prosperity in the kingdom.

Jahangir was a liberal king like his father and he continued Akbar's policy of religious tolerance. The religious debates that Akbar had started at the Ibadat

Salim in Trouble

In 1602 CE, when Salim declared himself king at Allahabad, Akbar sent Abul Fazl to reason with him. Salim had him assassinated on the way by the ruler of Orchha. Akbar was so furious he nearly disinherited his son until his aunt Gulbadan Begum and wife Salima Sultan brought Salim to Agra and forced him to fall at his father's feet and beg for forgiveness.

Khana in Fatehpur Sikri were continued and one of Jahangir's favourite spiritual guides was a Hindu ascetic named Jadrup, who lived in a cave.

Mughal emperor Jahangir.

Jahangir also continued to maintain good relations with the Rajputs. He himself was, of course, the son of a Rajput princess and he married others like Man Bai, the mother of his son Khusrau and Jagat Gosaini, the mother of Khurram. Jahangir was known for his love of justice and had a golden 'chain of justice' with bells installed outside the palace. People seeking his help could pull the chain and appeal directly to the king.

Empress Nur Jahan

She was born Mehr-un-Nissa, the daughter of Itmad-ud-Daula, a Persian official working for Akbar. She was the widow of a nobleman named Sher Afghan and was a lady-in-waiting of Akbar's widow Ruquaiya Begum in the royal harem. Jahangir,

Painters

Jahangir had a creative bent of mind and was an excellent judge of miniature paintings. During his reign, the painters in the tasvirkhana created some of the finest paintings in the Mughal style. He encouraged them to draw from life and there are exquisite studies of birds and animals that are classics today.

who was already king, fell in love with her and married her in 1611 CE when she was in her thirties. He first gave her the title of Nur Mahal and then Nur Jahan.

A very intelligent woman, Nur Jahan was a woman of many talents and soon became involved in the running of the empire. She was a poet, who also designed fabrics and carpets; she went hunting, shooting tigers from the howdah of an elephant; owned a ship that traded with Arabia and was an energetic ruler. She is the only Mughal queen who is referred to as an empress, who signed royal orders and had coins issued in her name.

The Mughal empire was saved by Jahangir's youngest queen. He was not too interested in the work of governance or in conquests and he was also often ill—the result of years of heavy drinking. So during his last years, the real power lay in the hands of a team of four—Nur Jahan, her father Itmad-ud-Daula who was the chief minister, her brother Asaf Khan and Prince Khurram, who had married Asaf Khan's daughter Arjumand Banu. Jahangir rarely went on military campaigns and it was Khurram who led most of them. Nur Jahan approved all the royal orders and even though she was in purdah, she met officials while

Arjumand Banu and Khurram

Nur Jahan married her niece Arjumand Banu to Jahangir's most talented son, Prince Khurram. Later Khurram became king as Shah Jahan and Arjumand Banu was given the title of Mumtaz Mahal. It was after her death that Shah Jahan built the marble Taj Mahal as her mausoleum.

sitting behind a screen and decisions were taken by the four together.

In the final days of Jahangir's reign, Khurram and Nur Jahan fell apart and she supported the claim of another son of Jahangir's, Prince Shahryar. She had married Ladli Begum, her daughter by her first marriage, to him. When Jahangir died there was a sharp conflict for the throne but Khurram, supported by Asaf Khan, triumphed and ascended the throne as Shah Jahan. Nur Jahan withdrew from public life and went to live in Lahore where she built the mausoleum of Jahangir and her own.

Arrival of the Europeans

In 1615 CE, Sir Thomas Roe landed at Surat as the first official ambassador to India from the court of King James I of England and spent three years in the Mughal court. He came with the request that the East India Company, be allowed to trade in India. He was given permission for this by Jahangir, which made the Portuguese, who had already started trading in India, very unhappy. For Jahangir, this was not an important event and he would have been very surprised to

> ### *Khurram as King*
>
> *The Mughals had no tradition of the eldest son becoming king, so all the sons fought for the throne. When Khurram became king, he killed every other claimant including two brothers, two cousins and two nephews. Later, as Shah Jahan, he would watch three of his four sons die battling for the throne.*

discover that within 150 years, the East India Company would colonize a large part of India and one day replace the Mughals. Roe also wrote a diary that gives us a lot of information about Jahangir and colourful descriptions of the ceremonies at his court.

The European trading companies, like the Portuguese, the English, the Dutch and the French, began by setting up trading posts along the coasts. Gradually, they brought in soldiers to guard these trading posts and began to interfere in the political affairs of the area. They had well-trained armies equipped with the latest guns and by the time of the Mughal kings after Aurangzeb, they were creating their own colonies. As long as the Mughals were strong, they were kept under control but by the latter half of the eighteenth century, there were new centres of powers in India and they were European.

Roe Meets a Traveller

Sir Thomas Roe was travelling to Ajmer to meet Jahangir. On the way he met Thomas Coryat, an eccentric Englishman who had walked from England to India. Coryat wrote of his travels and said that the road between Lahore, Delhi and Agra was the best he had walked on.

Shihab-ud-din Shah Jahan (1628 CE–1657 CE)

For years Prince Khurram had helped in the work of the empire and had also led many successful military expeditions. So when he took the throne as Shah Jahan, he was an experienced and efficient king. He suppressed a number of revolts like those of Bundelkhand and Ahmednagar and signed peace treaties with Bijapur and Golconda, who agreed to pay a big annual tribute to him. However, his expedition to recover Kandahar from Persia failed and he did little to extend the boundaries of the empire. This meant that taxes and tributes did not grow like they did during the time of Akbar.

Mughal emperor Shah Jahan.

Another big change was that Shah Jahan did not continue with the policy of liberal tolerance of other religions like Akbar and Jahangir. This was surprising because both his grand mother and mother were Rajput princesses. His prosecution of other religions was not as planned like his son Aurangzeb, but he was keen to please the mullahs in his court and so temples and churches were destroyed and Hindus were not allowed to build new temples. Fortunately, this was balanced by his eldest son Dara Shikoh's liberal attitude and his interest in the philosophy of other faiths.

Unlike his father, Shah Jahan was also suspicious of the Europeans trading in India and kept them in check, making sure they paid their taxes and that they did not set up too many trading posts. The Portuguese were the most aggressive, so Shah Jahan attacked Portuguese settlements in Bengal, defeated their army and brought many prisoners of war back to Agra.

Shah Jahan, the Builder

Shah Jahan was passionate about architecture and is remembered the most for his building projects. His favourite queen Mumtaz Mahal died young and he built the sublime Taj Mahal in her memory. The mausoleum was built all in marble and then decorated with semi-precious stones.

When the king decided to shift his capital from Agra to Delhi, he began work on a new city called Shah Jahanabad. Here, he built bazaars, mosques and many beautiful palaces within the sandstone Red Fort. Shah Jahan loved pomp and ceremony and his magnificent court, opulent marble palaces and his famous Peacock Throne made him the 'Great Mogul' of European writings.

During Shah Jahan's reign the income of the empire was at its highest but so were the expenses, since he spent huge amounts on his building projects. The royal family lived in unbelievable luxury. For example, after becoming queen, Mumtaz Mahal's personal allowance was *six lakh rupees* a year which, in those days, was an unbelievably large amount! Also, unlike the efficient Akbar

Shah Jahan's Children

Shah Jahan had seven children; four sons, Dara Shikoh, Shah Shuja, Aurangzeb and Murad Bakhsh, and three daughters, Jahanara, Roshanara and Gauharara. Dara and Jahanara were scholars who were tolerant and generous and loved by the people. Aurangzeb was a brilliant military commander and an efficient governor but also rigid and intolerant.

who made sure the economy was healthy, the empire's income was raised by forcing poor farmers to pay more in taxes. Little was done to improve either trade or agriculture. So the ordinary people of the empire were very poor while the king and the nobility lived flashy, luxurious lives.

Brothers at War

Shah Jahan's bloody path to the throne was repeated when he fell ill in 1657 CE and his four sons, Dara Shikoh, Shah Shuja, Murad Bakhsh and Aurangzeb, went to war for the throne. Aurangzeb laid siege of the fort at Agra where Shah Jahan was living and he watched helplessly as Aurangzeb captured the throne. Dara was executed, Murad was treacherously killed and Shah Shuja vanished while trying to escape. Shah Jahan spent the last eight years of his life as a prisoner in the Agra Fort, where his daughter Jahanara was his only companion.

Despite the dazzle of Shah Jahan's reign, the

The Peacock Throne

The peacock throne was a square seat on four legs with four slim pillars in each corner holding up a canopy and was made using 1,150 kg of gold! Every inch of the throne was covered with precious jewels—diamonds, rubies and emeralds. The canopy had a fringe of pearls and two peacocks, set with turquoise and sapphires, were placed on top. In 1739 CE, the Persian conqueror Nadir Shah took it away and it was broken up after his death by his courtiers, who divided up the gold and jewels.

decline of the Mughals began at this time and Aurangzeb's rule did little to stop it.

Elsewhere in the World

The Romanovs came to power in 1613 CE and they were the last dynasty to rule in Russia. In 1682 CE the British astronomer Edmund Halley sighted the comet that was named after him. It flies past the earth every 76 years. William Shakespeare was writing his famous plays around this time.

Museum Visit

In Delhi, visit the museum inside the Red Fort to see a great collection of Mughal artefacts—clothes, furniture, arms and armour. The museum is in the palace where Princess Jahanara used to stay.

8
AN EMPEROR AND HIS ENEMIES
(1658 CE–1707 CE)

~ Muhi-ud-din Aurangzeb ~ Ruling in the North ~ Aurangzeb's Religion ~ Battling in the Deccan ~ Revolts ~ Rise of the Sikhs ~ Rise of the Marathas ~ Aurangzeb in the South ~ Later Mughals ~ Kings after Aurangzeb ~ Last Days of the Mughals ~ Why Did the Mughal Empire Decline? ~

The last years of Shah Jahan's reign saw the tragic battle between his two most talented sons—Dara Shikoh and Aurangzeb. Looking at the characters of the two princes it seems as if the qualities of the great Akbar had been divided between his two great-grandsons.

Dara was a scholar with the same tolerant and liberal spirit and eclectic mind as Akbar. He was a generous and convivial man who was very popular with people, but he was also indolent and inexperienced. Shah Jahan had always kept Dara by his side at the court in Delhi and that meant that he never led the army into battle and had very little experience of running a government.

However, from the time he was a teenager, Aurangzeb had been a military general and had been made the governor of the Deccan. He was a shrewd, battle-hardened man with great

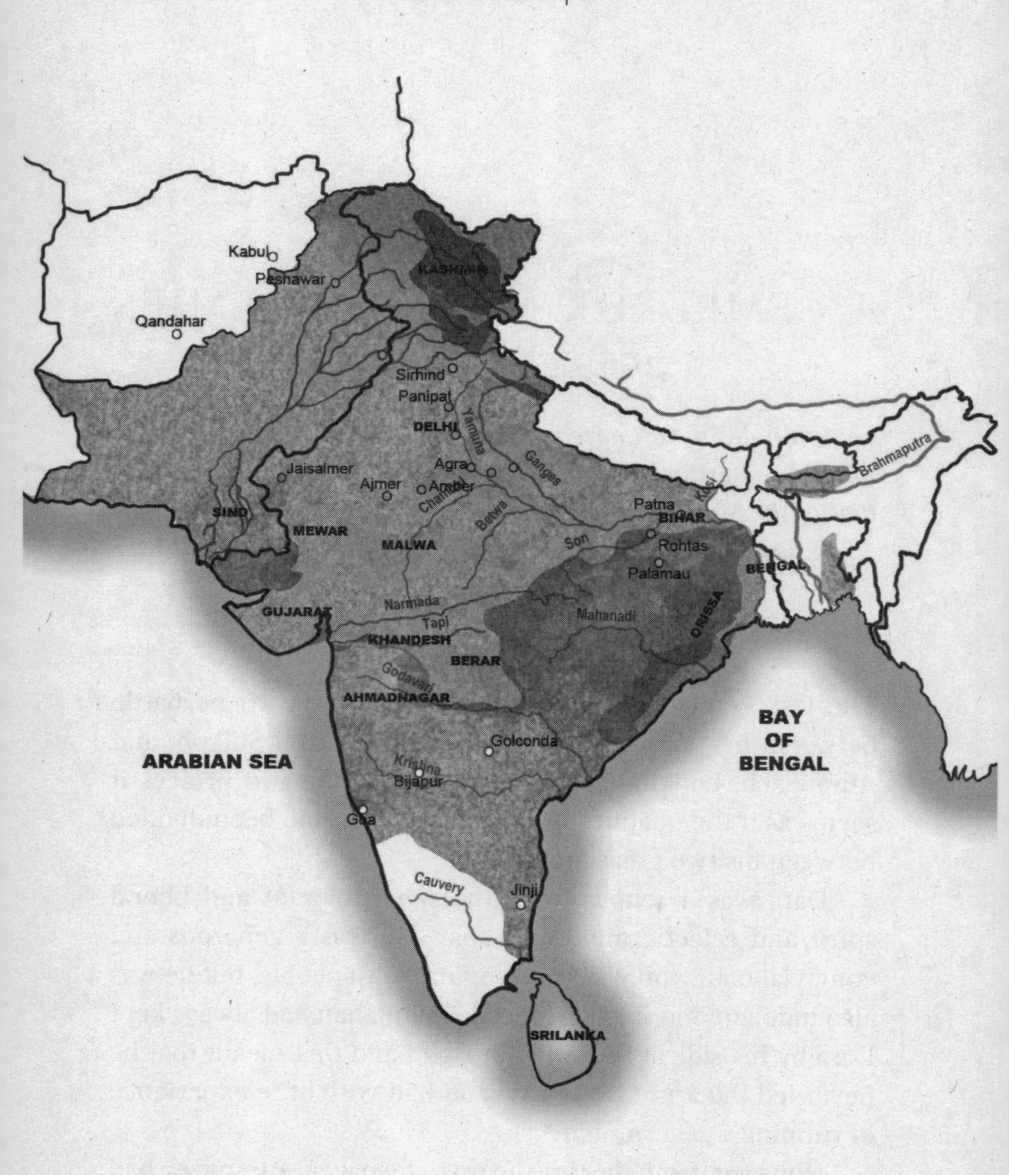

India under Aurangzeb.

administrative abilities. At the same time, he was intolerant of other religions, rigid in his beliefs and wanted the empire to be an Islamic state. Aurangzeb extended the borders of the empire because of his strengths as an administrator and general but, at the same time, he laid the seeds of its decline because he trusted few people and did not train his sons for kingship.

Muhi-ud-din Aurangzeb (1658 CE-1707 CE)

When he ascended the throne, Aurangzeb took the title of alamgir, 'world seizer'—clearly, he planned to rule over an empire that was even larger than that of his forefathers. In one way, he was unique as a Mughal king. He ruled in Delhi while his father was still alive and languished as a prisoner in the fort at Agra. He was also very different in character from the other Mughals, who were all colourful, larger-than-life characters. Aurangzeb was a reserved, humourless man with few interests, who worked very hard and lived so simply that people called him a 'zinda pir', a living saint.

In his portraits, he is usually shown clad in white and wearing few jewels. He was an orthodox, austere man who sewed prayer caps

Long Reigns

The two longest reigns among the Mughals are that of Akbar and Aurangzeb, both for forty-nine years. However the character of their reigns was in complete contrast to each other. Akbar's rule was a time of unity and prosperity while Aurangzeb ruled over a rebellious and angry empire full of discontent.

and copied the Quran to pay for his personal expenses. This saintly image that he projected hid a shrewd, cunning and ruthless mind. He used his religious image with great cleverness and so, even his most cruel acts were always garbed in religious reasons.

Aurangzeb had plotted for years to become king and, along the way, he had fooled his brothers Shuja and Murad into helping him. He had also not thought twice about putting Dara and Murad to death. The Mughals had no rule of succession, so all the sons began to fight when a king died and every such battle for the throne weakened the empire and was a cause of its decline. Both Shah Jahan and Aurangzeb had killed their brothers and nephews to reach the throne. This made Aurangzeb very suspicious of his own sons and he is the only Mughal king to have imprisoned not just his father but three sons, a daughter and a number of nephews. The fortress at Gwalior was the prison of choice for these unfortunate members of the royal family.

Children in Prison

The only crime of Aurangzeb's daughter Zeb-un-Nissa was that she had written letters to her brother Akbar when he had rebelled against their father. For this, she was imprisoned. Aurangzeb's eldest son, Muazzam, spent twelve years in prison and was so afraid of his father he would begin to shake in fear if any letter arrived from Aurangzeb.

Ruling in the North

If Akbar knew the art of pleasing his subjects, Aurangzeb was a master at antagonizing them.

He spent the first twenty-two years of his reign in Delhi and then shifted to the Deccan in 1680 CE. Here he led a nomadic life, wandering up and down the countryside trying to conquer the Deccan sultanates and battle with the Maratha king Shivaji.

Mughal emperor Aurangzeb.

It was during his reign in Delhi that Aurangzeb began to reveal his true attitude towards other religions, especially Hinduism and Sikhism. The orthodox courtiers and the Muslim priesthood were favoured by the king and he was anxious to please them. This, naturally, made the Hindu nobility like the Rajputs, who had served the Mughals loyally, very unhappy.

Akbar had removed the jizya tax from non-Muslims. Aurangzeb imposed it again and gave the money to the Muslim priesthood. This made him extremely unpopular with his subjects, especially the poor, who found the tax a big burden and resented such discrimination. Hindu traders also had to pay higher excise duties than Muslims and, in legal cases, Muslims were favoured by the qazis. Puritanical orders were also being issued—like the banning of everything from liquor to music. This led to the end of the Mughal image of being just and liberal kings.

Humayun always travelled with his library and Akbar built a pool where Tansen sang. Aurangzeb was very different from the earlier Mughal kings who were all cultured men. He disapproved of music and stopped musical performances in the palace. He disliked books, did not allow an official history of his reign to be written and closed the tasvirkhana. He stopped the tradition of jharokha darshan, started by Akbar, where the king showed himself at a window to his subjects. This was because Aurangzeb believed only God had the right to be viewed like that. A censor, called a muhtasib, was appointed to make sure shops did not sell liquor or cannabis and even measured the length of the beard of Muslim men and the dresses they wore! When one courtier appeared in court in a fashionably long robe, the king ordered it to be cut to the correct length right there!

Aurangzeb's Religion

Akbar had strived to be a true Indian king, but Aurangzeb made himself an alien occupier and the people never forgave him for that. As a true imperialist, Akbar had recognized the fact that the only way he could keep his subjects happy and united was through respecting all religions. Aurangzeb, instead, chose to follow the orthodox mullahs and decided to alienate the Hindus by turning them into second-class citizens. For the first time in the rule of the Mughals there was now a systematic persecution of Hindus not seen in any Mughal reign before.

Many temples were destroyed and Hindus were not allowed to build new ones or even repair existing shrines; they also had to pay a pilgrim tax when they visited a holy town. Two of the most sacred of the Hindu shrines, the Vishwanath Temple at Varanasi and the Kesava Deo temple at Mathura were demolished.

Battling in the Deccan

The earlier Mughal kings had led expeditions to the south and returned to Agra or Delhi. They recognized the fact that the Deccan could not be controlled from Delhi. So, as long as the Deccan sultans paid tribute, they were mostly left alone. However, Aurangzeb wanted to annex the Deccan and shifted there in 1681 CE for that purpose. Twenty-six years later, he died at Daulatabad (in modern Maharashtra) in 1707 CE without ever seeing Delhi again. The last years of his life were spent wandering around the Deccan with his huge army like a nomad warrior while the north began to break apart.

Aurangzeb had two main objectives in mind when he first arrived in the Deccan. First, he wanted to destroy the wily Maratha king Shivaji, who was a constant thorn in his side. Also, he wanted to conquer the Deccan sultanates of Bijapur and Golconda and extend the Mughal empire into the peninsula. What he did not anticipate was that one could never control the Deccan from Delhi.

Revolts

Aurangzeb's subjects were not happy. First there was the re-imposition of the jizya, then the raising of the land tax from one-third to half of the produce. Soon, the provinces were up in arms. The Jats rose in the Agra-Mathura region, the Rohillas in the east, the Satnamis and Bundelas in Central India. Many of the Rajput kings, who had earlier been friendly towards the Mughals, now began to revolt and try to rule independently and one of the fiercest opponents of Aurangzeb were the Sikhs of Punjab.

The alienation of the Rajputs was to be a great loss to the Mughal empire. They were good generals and efficient administrators who had been loyal vassals since the time of Akbar. Now, they found that only Muslims were chosen for most of the important posts and there were no marriage alliances between the Mughals and the Rajputs. When Raja Jaswant Singh of Marwar died, Aurangzeb interfered in the succession, trying to put his chosen candidate on the throne. The Mughal army also invaded Marwar and destroyed temples, which earned Aurangzeb the wrath of many Rajput clans. Akbar had made the Rajputs his allies, now Aurangzeb made them enemies again.

Rise of the Sikhs

The teachings of Guru Nanak and other gurus were very popular in Punjab and till the time of Akbar there was amity between the Mughals and the Sikhs. The first conflict took place when Jahangir suspected Guru Arjan Dev of supporting his rebellious son Khusro and had him executed. Later, Aurangzeb was unhappy with the growing popularity of Guru Tegh Bahadur and in 1675 CE, ordered his death. This led to the peaceful Sikh sect to pick up arms. Under Tegh Bahadur's son, the tenth guru Gobind Singh, the Sikhs built a military brotherhood called the Khalsa. The Sikhs would rebel often and raid Mughal provinces and would ultimately establish a Sikh kingdom in the eighteenth century.

Rise of the Marathas

At this time, a new power was rising in the craggy hills of the Western Ghats. Shivaji Bhonsle, a land owner, and his loyal band of followers, began to build a kingdom. A military genius, Shivaji used the hilly terrain to wage a guerrilla warfare that first defeated the armies of Bijapur and then challenged the Mughals. He conquered the area around Pune and then captured the forts built in the hills of the Western Ghats and was soon levying his own taxes on the region.

Shivaji was the son of the Maratha chieftain Shahji Bhonsle, a trusted courtier of the Nizam Shahi rulers of Ahmednagar, and his wife Jijabai. Shivaji lived with his mother at the family estate of Pune while Shahji lived with his second wife, Tukabai, and their son Vyankoji. Both sons would go on to establish kingdoms—Vyankoji would found the kingdom of Tanjore and Shivaji would lead the Marathas to power in the Pune-Satara region.

Shivaji grew up under the guardianship of Dadaji Kondadev, an administrator loyal to his father, Shahji. Soon, Shivaji began building up his own army. He first conquered areas in the Konkan region that were a part of the Bijapur kingdom and, very cleverly, repaired and garrisoned forts in the hilly region that became his refuge. He was a shrewd and fearless fighter and when Bijapur sent the general Afzal Khan to confront him, Shivaji retreated to the Pratapgarh Fort. When the siege became a stalemate, he agreed to meet Afzal Khan alone. No one knows who attacked first but Shivaji was wearing tiger claws hidden in the palm of his hand and killed the Bijapuri general; then the Marathas destroyed the Bijapur camp.

Shivaji Bhonsle, the great Maratha king.

Shivaji extended his kingdom up the Konkan coast and even built a navy. Soon he was challenging the Mughals. Aurangzeb sent his uncle Shaista Khan to tackle him and a giant Mughal army rolled into the Deccan to destroy Shivaji. It was a very unequal battle between a behemoth and Shivaji's small band of fighters; he had to withdraw and Shaista Khan occupied Shivaji's capital at Pune. Then one night in 1663 CE, a few Maratha soldiers entered Pune in the guise of a wedding party and attacked Shaista Khan's residence. Shaista was injured but managed to escape. However his wife and a son were killed. After this, the Maratha army swooped into the rich port of Surat and plundered the Mughal treasury.

This was a great blow to Aurangzeb's prestige. He now sent Mirza Raja Jai Singh, another senior general, down south. Jai Singh convinced Shivaji to negotiate with the Mughals. Shivaji agreed to surrender some of his forts and travel to Agra to formally offer his allegiance to Aurangzeb. He was promised that, in return, Aurangzeb would acknowledge him as an independent ruler. But when Shivaji arrived at the court in Agra, he was not given the respect he expected as a king, and was made to stand among the minor courtiers. Feeling insulted, he protested and left the court. He was put under house arrest by a suspicious Aurangzeb but he managed to escape and returned to the Deccan.

In 1674 CE, Shivaji defiantly crowned himself king, taking the title of chhatrapati, and established a Hindu kingdom. After the debacle at Delhi, the Mughals left him alone and he ruled till his death in 1680 CE. With Shivaji, the Marathas became an important centre of power in the Deccan and would later play a crucial role in the history of India.

The Great Escape

While under house arrest, Shivaji escaped with typical audacity. Every day, he began sending out large baskets full of sweets to be distributed among people. Soon the guards stopped checking them and one day Shivaji escaped hidden in a basket. Then, disguised as a sadhu, he cleverly travelled north while the Mughals went to search for him in the south. Taking a detour through Bundelkhand, he suddenly appeared before Jijabai a month later.

Aurangzeb in the South

Once he reached the Deccan, Aurangzeb conquered the kingdom of Bijapur in 1686 CE and Golconda in 1687 CE. Then he captured and executed Shivaji's son Sambhaji in 1689 CE and *his* son, Shahuji, was sent as a prisoner to Delhi. He expected the south to be peaceful from then on but he had not reckoned with the fighting spirit of the Marathas.

The Maratha chieftains were masters of guerrilla warfare; they would lead surprise attacks, appearing suddenly to kill and plunder the Mughal army and then vanish into the hills. The Mughal army was a huge, unwieldy machine blundering around in hilly tracts that were foreign to them, while the Marathas knew the terrain intimately and moved on swift horses, making them impossible to catch. The Mughals would capture a Maratha fort and the moment they had moved on, the Marathas would swoop in and take it back again. Aurangzeb, who was in his eighties by then, spent his last years dragging his weary forces across the region trying to catch an enemy he could never see.

When Aurangzeb died in 1707 CE at the age of eighty-nine at Daulatabad, the boundaries of the Mughal empire was at its widest. Few would have believed that the seeds of the decline of the magnificent Mughals had been laid during his reign.

The empire had become too large and unwieldy to be controlled from Delhi and soon the provinces began to break away under independent kings. Aurangzeb's bigoted and insensitive handling of religion had also succeeded in antagonizing a large section of his subjects: the Hindus, the Sikhs, the Marathas, the Jats...the list of the enemies of the Mughals only kept growing. Then the series of weak kings who followed Aurangzeb signalled the end of days for the mighty Mughals.

Later Mughals (1707 CE–1748 CE)

The reign of the kings who followed Aurangzeb can be divided into two sections. From 1707 CE to 1748 CE, the Mughals were in decline but Delhi was still the main centre of power in the north. After 1748 CE, the Mughal empire existed only in name. The main reason for the decline was a series of weak kings and the growing power of the nobility that fought with each other and weakened the centre even further. The noblemen would support different members of the royal family and kings were often deposed and even killed. This created an atmosphere of uncertainty with kings sometimes lasting for only a few months at the throne.

Sisters

During the battle for the throne, Aurangzeb was supported by his sister Roshanara while Jahanara favoured Dara Shikoh. Even though Jahanara chose to live in Agra with the imprisoned Shah Jahan, she remained Aurangzeb's favourite sister. At Shah Jahan's death, Aurangzeb persuaded her to return to Delhi and made her the head of his harem with the title of Padshah Begum. Both Aurangzeb and Jahanara have very simple graves that are not covered in marble, his in Daultabad and hers in the dargah of the Sufi saint Sheikh Nizamuddin Auliya in Delhi.

Soon powerful regional governors quietly broke away and ruled independently, among them were the nawabs of Awadh and Bengal, the nizam of Hyderabad and the Rajput and Maratha chieftains. They all paid lip service to Delhi but ruled as independent kings and this meant that the revenue reaching Delhi was drastically reduced. In all this endless battles for power, the real victims were the poor who often faced the exploitative demands of more than one ruler and the Maratha soldiers would lead plundering attacks to ravage villages.

Kings after Aurangzeb

Aurangzeb's son Muazzam ascended the throne as Bahadur Shah I (1707 CE-1712 CE), and tried to appease angry allies like the Rajputs. He released Shivaji's grandson Shahuji, who had been imprisoned by Aurangzeb, and offered his friendship to the Sikhs. However, he was an old man by the time he came to the throne and only ruled for five years. Bahadur Shah I was succeeded by Jahandar Shah (1712 CE-1713 CE), who ruled only for a year, and was overthrown by his nephew Farrukhsiyar (1713 CE-1719 CE).

Farrukhsiyar was a puppet in the hands of his two generals: the Sayyid brothers, Abdullah Khan and Hussain Ali Khan, who ultimately had him killed. The Sayyid brothers then put two more puppets on the throne till Muhammad Shah I (1720 CE-1748 CE) became king. Muhammad Shah I managed to strip the Sayyid brothers of their power and his long reign could have revived the kingdom but he spent too much of his time enjoying the last fruits of the Mughal empire and failed to do anything substantial.

Sensing the weakness of the Mughals, there were invasions from the north-west. First Nadir Shah, the king of Iran, invaded in 1739 CE, stealing, among other things, the fabled Kohinoor and the peacock throne of Shah Jahan, and then Ahmad Shah Abdali, the king of Afghanistan, led many invasions into India. In 1761 CE, Abdali was met by a combined army of Mughal and Maratha forces at the Third Battle of Panipat; the Mughals were defeated and they never recovered from this debacle.

Last Days of the Mughals (1748 CE-1857 CE)

Within fifty years of Aurangzeb's death, the Mughal empire was reduced to only the kingdom of Delhi. The kings now were only emperors in name: it was said, 'the kingdom of Shah Alam was from Dilli to Palam'. As the empire shrank, the revenue shrank as well, until there was nothing available for maintaining an army or running an efficient administration. The nobility was divided into cliques and much too busy conspiring against each other to run the country or lead the army. The army was equipped with outdated weapons and

So Many Kings!

There were twelve kings after Aurangzeb and the list gets longer if you count the men who sat on the throne for a few months. Among them were:
Bahadur Shah I (1707 CE-1712 CE)
Jahandar Shah (1712 CE-1713 CE)
Farrukhsiyar (1713 CE-1719 CE)
Rafi-ud-Darajat (1719 CE)
Shah Jahan II (1719 CE)
Muhammad Shah (1719 CE-1748 CE)
Ahmad Shah (1748 CE-1754 CE)
Alamgir II (1754 CE-1759 CE)
Shah Jahan III (1759 CE)
Shah Alam (1759 CE-1806 CE)
Akbar Shah II (1806 CE-1837 CE)
Bahadur Shah Zafar II (1837 CE-1858 CE)

the kings were inept generals who failed before invaders like Nadir Shah and Ahmad Shah Abdali. The country entered a time of chaos and confusion as regional powers battled with each other. The Europeans seized this opportunity and began to set up pockets of power all across India. The Marathas now moved to the north and began to interfere in the government at Delhi. The Mughal kings were just figureheads who were formally acknowledged by powerful local rulers and were puppets in the hands of their noblemen in Delhi. India was on its way to becoming a colony of the East India Company.

The last Mughal king Bahadur Shah II spent his final days as a pensioner of the English. After the Uprising of 1857 CE, he was exiled to Burma and died in Rangoon. Thus the magnificent dynasty of Babur and Akbar came to an end with a sad whimper.

Why Did the Mughal Empire Decline?

There is no single reason for the decline of the Mughal empire but it mostly began with the reign of Aurangzeb. The map of the empire at his death looked very impressive when, in fact, it had become too big to be managed efficiently from Delhi. Also Aurangzeb's lengthy campaign in the south was very expensive and emptied the treasury. His policy towards the Marathas and Rajputs left them feeling alienated. His policy towards Hindus and other non-Muslim groups also led to the decline of popularity of the Mughal rule.

One of the biggest causes of the decline was that the kings became weak and the nobility became too powerful. So groups of noblemen battled for power, played kingmaker and, at times, went off to establish independent kingdoms like those of Awadh, Bengal and Hyderabad. The revenue from these rich provinces also did not reach Delhi, which meant that farmers were forced to pay even higher taxes leading to a great deal of dissatisfaction among them. Trade went down as craftsmen could not send their goods to distant markets because of a lack of law and order. It also meant that the Mughal kings did not have enough money to pay and maintain a standing army. So when they had to face invaders like Nadir Shah, they were ill-equipped, badly trained and full of soldiers who felt little loyalty to their king. It is hard to imagine the descendants of Akbar reaching such a state but the later Mughals were quite poor and often could not pay salaries or their bills.

Elsewhere in the World

The Romanov dynasty came to power in Russia in 1613 CE and they would have seventeen tsars who would rule till 1917 CE. In China, the Ming dynasty was replaced in 1644 CE, by the Manchu (Qing) dynasty.

Fort Visit

For anyone living in Maharashtra, Shivaji's fortresses are worth a visit. There is his capital Raigarh as well as Pratapgarh, Panhala and the island fortress of Gingee.

9

LIVING IN MUGHAL TIMES

(Sixteenth to Eighteenth Century)

~ City and Village ~ The Rich and Poor Divide ~ Women ~ Tribal People ~ Trade ~ Education and Technology ~ Architecture ~ Painting ~ Music ~

The first six kings of the Mughal dynasty, from Babur to Aurangzeb, came to be known as the Great Mughals and they gave the country nearly two centuries of good administration and peace. By the time of Aurangzeb, the empire covered most of the Indian subcontinent and included parts of Afghanistan till Kabul. Trade flourished, there was the growth of towns and cities and the kings were often patrons of art and architecture. We know a lot about the life of the people during this time, beautifully depicted in the miniature paintings and described in detail in books and accounts of travellers.

The world was fascinated by the stories of the glamorous lives that the Mughals led. European kingdoms sent their ambassadors here, begging permission to trade in India. Christian missionaries arrived from Portugal and Spain hoping to convert the rich in India to their faith. Adventurers and explorers headed to the Mughal empire from Europe and the Middle East seeking their fortune. Fortunately many of them left their memoirs, which give us a wonderfully detailed portrait of the times.

City and Village

During this period, many new roads were built. They were very well-maintained and caravanserais, inns where travellers could rest on their journey, were built at regular intervals. Soon craftsmen settled around these serais and small markets sprang up as people from nearby villages brought their crops and handmade goods to sell. Mosques and temples, bazaars and homes came up and, gradually,these caravanserais grew into small towns. Some of them would go on to become cities.

What did they grow in the villages? Vegetables like spinach, cabbage, peas, onions, garlic, carrots and lemons. Fruits like bananas, melons, apples, grapes, oranges, coconuts and mangoes. Spices like pepper, cardamom, ginger, cloves, saffron, nutmeg and cinnamon. Paan was very popular and tobacco arrived from Europe at the time of Jahangir. Sugarcane was made into sugar. Cotton was an important crop as India had the biggest textile industry in the world. Tea was

Population Survey

Todar Mal, Akbar's finance minister, did a survey of the kingdom in 1581 CE and found that there were 120 large towns or sheher and 3,200 small towns or qasbas. Each qasba had up to a thousand villages around them. Historians calculate that the total population during Akbar's reign was around 180 million.

still unknown in the country.

The life of the poor changed little during Mughal times. Villages were huddles of thatched huts with ponds, mango and banana groves, surrounded by fields. Farmers tilled the land with a bullock pulling a wooden plough. In rice growing areas, rows of women would bend over the muddy earth planting rice saplings. A few irrigation canals were built to help with irrigation but the kings did little to help the farmers. Peasants had very few possessions, lived in huts and were always at the mercy of droughts and famines. Villages were run by jagirdars appointed by the king and they were only interested in collecting the maximum taxes from the farmers. No one, the king or the landowner, really cared for the welfare of the villagers.

It was the cities that grew during this period because the rich lived there—the noblemen, the rich merchants and the important officials. They lived in extravagant luxury in huge mansions called havelis, with many servants and slaves and stables full of horses and elephants. There was no tradition of planning a city; it generally grew in a haphazard manner around a citadel built by the king. There were narrow, serpentine lanes with the havelis near the centre of the city while the poor huddled in huts at the outskirts.

Cities were surrounded by stone and rubble boundary walls that were pierced by gateways. These gates were closed at dusk and soldiers marched along the top of the wall at night, guarding the city. These towns and cities were centres of trade with busy bazaars selling textiles, jewellery, pottery, metalware, wood crafts and food stuffs. The bazaars of Delhi and Agra dazzled visitors with a variety of goods and many Indian crafts were exported to Europe.

The cities were not a pretty sight as they had no proper sanitation, garbage collection or traffic control. Water came from wells or had to be carried from the river. The streets were dusty and bumpy with a noisy traffic of horses, bullock carts, palanquins, and even camels and elephants! As a matter of fact Shah Jahan's new city in Delhi, Shajahanabad, was the first time a city was planned with a central avenue, with separate areas for markets and specific areas allocated to different kinds of crafts and trade.

The Rich and Poor Divide

People in Europe were dazzled by stories of the extravagant lives of the royal family and the nobility but the poorest people in the world also lived in India at the same time. There was a stark and shocking contrast between the lives of the rich and poor. The poor lived in thatched huts, often a single windowless room with the floor of bare earth. They had few clothes, slept on mats or string cots and their kitchens only had a few earthen pots. They probably had enough to eat because food was generally cheap, but during famines or war people died by the thousands.

The rich lived in mansions hidden behind

Postal Service

The kings set up post stops called dak chowkis along the roads where post runners or harkaras were stationed. A letter carried by a runner or a horseman would reach a dak chowki and another runner would take over. Of course, this was only for the royal mail; there was no postal system for the common people.

high walls with luxuriously furnished rooms, dozens of servants, gardens and ponds. The noblemen were always trying to imitate the extravagant lives of the royal family and were often in debt because of their high expenses. All these noblemen had jagirs, country estates that were their main sources of income, but all their money was wasted on expensive living and not invested in improving trade or agriculture.

While on the surface, the extravagant, opulent lives of the rich in the cities dazzled visitors, there was no real interest in developing science, agriculture or trade. At a time when Europe was racing ahead in art, science and technology, the Mughal empire was mired in wasteful extravagance that would one day lead to the colonization of the country. Most of the wealth was used by the kings and the nobility on flashy living and very little was spent for the welfare of the people. Shah Jahan spent more on the peacock throne than on building canals to improve agriculture.

Women

The status of women continued to deteriorate during this period. Most of the women were illiterate, they were married very young and spent their lives in the kitchen and back rooms of homes. No one welcomed the birth of a daughter.

The custom of purdah was very strictly imposed on Muslims women but Hindu women, especially in the south, moved about more freely. The English traveller Ralph Fitch writes of watching Brahmin women walking down the street singing as they headed to the Yamuna River. The women of poor families who had to go to work did not follow the purdah system.

Men often had many wives and sati, where a Hindu widow was burnt on her husband's funeral pyre, was common. Akbar tried to raise the age of marriage of girls and ban sati but he was not successful. Muslim women were better educated, they had inheritance rights, could re-marry and there was no system of sati.

The Mughals gave a lot of respect to senior family women, often taking their advice on matters of the court. The royal women were educated and princesses like Jahanara, daughter of Shah Jahan, and Zeb-un-nissa, daughter of Aurangzeb, were scholars and poets. The royal women also had the right to read all important royal orders before putting the stamp on them, as Nur Jahan did during Jahangir's reign. However they also lived in strict purdah in the haramsara, guarded by soldiers and were never allowed to walk around freely.

The Problems of Purdah

The English traveller Edward Terry writes about the wife of a Muslim nobleman, who had to jump out of the howdah of a mad elephant to save herself. Her husband divorced her because she had revealed her face to strangers.

Tribal People

There were one group of Mughal subjects about whom we know very little. These were the many tribal communities living across the empire. In Central India there were the Gonds and the Mundas; in the east there were the Santhals;

in the north-east were the Khasis, the Nagas and the Ahoms. Across the land, in the north-west, there were the powerful Baluchi tribe and the Khokhars and Ghakars in the Punjab. In the south, there were the Todas, the Koragas, the Maravars, the Badagas and the Vetars.

These tribes usually lived in remote jungles or in high mountainous regions and, as they did not maintain written records, we know very little of their history. Tribal society was different in that they had no caste system and they often did not follow any of the mainstream religions. Their society was more equal and they lived closer to nature. Most of them led nomadic lives, moving with their animals in search of fresh pastures, and they sold the products of the forest—wood, honey, lac, silk, fruits, herbs, etc. The Banjaras of Rajasthan, for instance, moved across the kingdom as travelling traders, carrying goods like foodgrains, handlooms and handicrafts from the villages to the cities.

Some of these tribes became very powerful and set up kingdoms. The Ahoms had their kingdom in present day Assam with their capital at Garhgaon (modern Guwahati). The Gonds in Central India also built a kingdom that the Mughals called Garha-Katanga. One famous Gond ruler was Rani Durgavati, who ruled as the regent of her minor son. In 1565 CE, she defied the army sent by Akbar and died fighting.

Trade

The Mughals never developed a navy and most of the trade was left in the hands of Arabs. From India, the biggest exports were textiles and spices. The spice trade was a very profitable one with pepper, cinnamon and nutmeg taken by ship till the

Red Sea and then overland to Venice. By land, it was via the Silk Route across Central Asia, Persia, the Middle East and then into Europe. Some of the famous ports of the time were Masulipatnam and Nagapattinam in the south-east and Surat, Dewal, Cambay and Bharuch in the west. These were rich towns full of sailors and traders from Arabia, China, Armenia and Europe.

During the rule of the later Mughals, as the power of Delhi weakened, the Portuguese became very powerful along the Indian coast. Till then, trade had been a peaceful occupation but now, they arrived with ships armed with guns and soon began controlling the seas and pushing out the Arabs. The other European powers, the English, the French and the Dutch, followed soon after and the battle to control trade moved into the hands of these aggressive European powers.

Education and Technology

Except for Akbar, none of the other Mughals took much interest in education and the result was that, for centuries, children studied the same old and outdated subjects. The majority of the people were illiterate and the Brahmins refused to teach boys of lower castes. In this way, India fell behind in education and technology. Only boys went to school and the schools themselves were run by the priesthood, so most of the emphasis was on memorizing religious texts. The Islamic schools were called maktabs and were attached to mosques; the Hindu ones were the tols, where classes were held at the temples. For higher education there were the madrasas for Muslims and the gurukulas for Hindus.

The subjects taught to senior students were theology and

some mathematics, literature, accountancy, law, logic and astrology. Medicine was taught according to the Ayurvedic and Unani schools and they were unaware of progress in the West. There were no science subjects, and not even geography, in the syllabus. It is rumoured that when Sir Thomas Roe presented a modern atlas to Jahangir, he apparently gave it back as he wasn't interested in the rest of the world! Teaching was by rote and the quality of education was not very high. Most subjects were taught in dead languages like Sanskrit or Persian, not languages that were actually spoken by the people and most students

> ### *Exports and Imports*
>
> *India exported spices, textiles, sandalwood, saffron, indigo, sugar, rice and precious stones. It imported Arab horses, gold, silver, lead, ivory, saffron and quick silver. India still had the advantage in trade and often payment was in gold and not goods. The Mughals set up a mint at Surat to handle all the gold arriving by ship.*

Mughal coins

just wanted to learn enough to get a job in the government.

By this time printing had been invented in Europe and, books were being printed in large quantities, making them easy to buy, and thus making information accessible but it would be introduced in India much later by the British. The Mughals had no interest in new technologies and no one was interested in machines as labour was very cheap. There were no proper colleges or universities,professional teachers or a proper examination system. No laboratories, no tradition of scientific research and no factories. For all the glitter of the royal court, when it came to progress in education and technology, India had entered the dark ages.

Sawai Jai Singh

One remarkable astronomer was Sawai Jai Singh, the king of Jaipur. He built observatories in Delhi, Jaipur, Varanasi and Ujjain to study the stars and produced highly accurate readings. However he was unaware of Copernicus' theory that the earth and other planets revolved around the sun!

Architecture

Mughal architecture was a magnificent symbol of the power and grandeur of the empire and the two kings who gave it its style and character were Akbar and his grandson Shah Jahan.

Babur enjoyed laying out elaborate landscaped gardens, set with fountains and flower beds. Only one, Aram Bagh in Agra, has survived. Humayun started the fortress of Dinpanah in Delhi but never completed it. So it was with Akbar that architecture took on a true Mughal character. Akbar began with a tomb for his father and Humayun's Tomb in Delhi introduced the Persian double dome and set the mausoleum in a traditional char bagh garden. This tradition of building a mausoleum in a garden would reach its zenith in Taj Mahal.

Akbar built fortresses in Agra, Lahore and Allahabad but his greatest gift to posterity is the city of Fatehpur Sikri. It was designed as a twin city to Agra and was planned as the cultural centre of his growing empire. At the heart of the city is the dargah of Sheikh Salim Chishti, a jewel-like marble creation glowing at the centre of the courtyard of the royal mosque. Built primarily in red sandstone, the palaces of Fatehpur Sikri reflect Akbar's attitude towards his people—the design of the buildings and the decorative sculpture are a blend of Indian and Islamic motifs. The styles of Gujarat, Bengal and the Deccan mix with those of Persia and Turkey to create an

The Taj Mahal, built by Shah Jahan at Agra.

elegant synthesis that is now considered uniquely Mughal.

Shah Jahan, on the other hand, liked to build in marble. He first demolished most of the Akbari buildings inside the Agra Fort to build new palaces and then moved on to the new city of Shahjahanabad in Delhi. The Taj Mahal was the finest of his creations.

The Taj Mahal took sixteen years to build and employed 20,000 people. It was built in marble and then the walls were embellished with *pietra dura* work, where semi-precious stones were inlaid in the marble in exquisite designs of flowers and vines, geometric patterns and calligraphy.

Painting

Paper arrived in India in the thirteenth century and soon manuscripts with delicate calligraphy and illustrations were being produced. These manuscripts were works of art—a Mughal manuscript had pages of calligraphy illustrated by miniature paintings. The royal histories of Akbar and Shah Jahan were all made into sumptuous manuscripts covered with delicate, hand-

Jewels for the Taj

Shah Jahan got the purest white marble from Makrana in Rajasthan; yellow marble from the banks of the Narmada River; crystal from China; lapis lazuli and sapphires from Sri Lanka; jasper from Punjab; carnelian from Baghdad; turquoise from Tibet; agates from Yemen; corals from the Red Sea; garnets from Bundelkhand, jade from Kashgar; onyx and amethyst from Persia. The grave was surrounded by a solid gold screen.

Mughal miniature painting.

drawn borders and miniature paintings.

Among the Mughals it was Jahangir who was a true connoisseur of miniature paintings and during his reign the artists began to try newer ideas like paintings of birds and animals and true-to-life portraits. These manuscripts and albums preserve an image of the time. In Abul Fazl's *Akbarnama*, you see paintings of the king at court, soldiers going to war or the work of palaces being built.

When Aurangzeb closed the tasvirkhana, the artists migrated to the courts of Rajput kings and the rulers of hill states and created new schools of miniature paintings.

Music

Many miniature paintings show dancers whirling away before a king, accompanied by singers and musicians. Abul Fazl lists thirty-six musicians at Akbar's court, of which the most famous singer was, of course, Tansen. He not only sang classical music but also composed many new ragas like Mian ki Todi and Darbari Kanada that was created for Akbar. The king of Malwa, Baz Bahadur was a famous singer and once Malwa had been annexed to the Mughal empire, he was welcomed to Akbar's court as a singer. The royal women were patrons of music and dance as well. There was also a royal band called naubat that woke up the king with music and marked the time of the day. Today, Tansen's tomb stands next to the dargah of Mohammad Ghaus in Gwalior and is still visited by musicians.

Since most of the art,

Tansen

Legends say Tansen was born as Ramtanu Mishra in a poor Brahmin family and received musical training from Swami Haridas of Mathura. Later, he became a follower of the Sufi preacher Muhammad Ghaus, converted to Islam and married his daughter. The Raja of Rewa gave him the title of Tansen and Akbar affectionately called him 'mian'. At his first performance in Akbar's court, he was presented with two lakh rupees! It is believed that the last request of the dying Sheikh Salim Chishti was to listen to Tansen sing.

architecture and music of this era were supported by royal patronage, the slow decline of the Mughal empire meant that these arts too died gradually in Delhi and Agra. The artists then moved to the courts of the provincial kingdoms like those of the Rajputs and the nawabs of Lucknow and Hyderabad.

Elsewhere in the World

This was a period of great cultural and scientific progress in Europe and it was called the Renaissance. There were great painters like Michelangelo, Raphael and Leonardo da Vinci; wonderful writers, poets and playwrights like Shakespeare, Petrarch and Cervantes.

Activity

Create a Mughal manuscript in class. Take any Indian story and write it by hand in your best handwriting. Then those who fancy themselves as artists can draw small illustrations and decorate the pages with pretty borders. Check out images of Mughal manuscripts on the Internet for some inspiration!

WHAT HAPPENED AND WHEN

998 CE-1030 CE–Invasions by Mahmud of Ghazni
1192 CE–Prithviraj Chauhan defeated by Muhammad of Ghur at Tarain
1206 CE–Qutub-ud-din Aibak establishes the Sultanate of Delhi
1210 CE-1236 CE—Reign of Iltutmish
1236 CE-1240 CE—Reign of Razia Sultan
1266 CE-1287 CE—Reign of Ghiyas-ud-din Balban
1290 CE-1296 CE—Reign of Jalal-ud-din Firuz Khalji
1296 CE-1316 CE—Reign of Ala-ud-din Khalji
1320 CE-1325 CE—Reign of Ghiyas-ud-din Tughlaq
1325 CE-1351 CE—Reign of Muhammad bin Tughlaq
1327 CE—Shift of capital from Delhi to Daulatabad
1332 CE—Traveller Ibn Batuta arrives in India
1336 CE-1565 CE—The Vijayanagar empire rises in South India
1347 CE—Bahmani Sultanate established in the Deccan
1351 CE-1388 CE—Reign of Firoz Shah Bahmani
1398 CE– Invasion of Timur
1451 CE-1489 CE—Reign of Bahlul Lodi
1489 CE-1517 CE—Reign of Sikander Lodi
1517 CE-1526 CE—Reign of Ibrahim Lodi
1440 CE-1515 CE—Life of Bhakti saint Kabir
1469 CE-1539 CE—Life of Guru Nanak, first Sikh Guru

1498 CE—Vasco da Gama lands in India
1526 CE—First Battle of Panipat; Ibrahim Lodi defeated by Babur
1526 CE—1530 CE–Reign of Babur
1530 CE—1542 CE, 1555 CE-1556 CE–Reign of Humayun
1542 CE—Reign of Sher Shah Sur
1556 CE—Second Battle of Panipat; Akbar defeats Himu
1556 CE—1605 CE–Reign of Akbar
1562 CE—Akbar marries Jodha Bai
1564 CE—Abolition of jizya
1571CE—Akbar starts building Fatehpur Sikri
1600 CE—The East India Company is founded
1605 CE—1627 CE–Reign of Jahangir
1611 CE—Jahangir marries Nur Jahan
1615 CE—Sir Thomas Roe gets permission for the English to trade in India
1628 CE-1657 CE—Reign of Shah Jahan
1631 CE—Death of Mumtaz Mahal
1648 CE—Foundation of the city of Shahjahanabad is built
1630 CE—1680 CE–Life of Shivaji
1658 CE—1707 CE–Reign of Aurangzeb
1666 CE—Death of Shah Jahan
1675 CE—Execution of Guru Tegh Bahadur
1679 CE—Jizya re-imposed
1707 CE—1712 CE–Reign of Bahadur Shah I
1713 CE—1719 CE–Reign of Farrukhsiyar
1739 CE—Invasion of Nadir Shah
1761 CE—Third Battle of Panipat; Ahmad Shah Abdali defeats the Mughals and the Marathas
1803 CE—Shah Alam II surrenders Delhi to the English

Section Three

BRITISH PERIOD

(1750 CE–1947 CE)

1

THE EAST INDIA COMPANIES

(1700 CE–1820 CE)

~ Arrival of European Trading Companies ~ Anglo-French Rivalry ~ The English in Bengal ~ Battle of Plassey ~ Battle of Buxar ~ Wars with Mysore ~ The Maratha Challenge ~ Taking over Punjab ~ Why Did the Company Succeed? ~

In the middle of the eighteenth century, as the Mughal empire was taking its last shaky breath, there were many powers battling to step into the vacuum. The biggest challengers were, of course, the Marathas, who had reached as far as Delhi by the time, and often played puppet masters to weak Mughal kings. But the other challenger to the Mughals were not Indian but European—the trading companies of Europe now began to use their armies to grab land from a dying empire.

The English, the French, the Dutch and the Portuguese had come to India to trade but, realizing the weakness of the Indian powers of the time, they made a bid to colonize the country. The first to try were the Portuguese, who already had a colony in Goa by the sixteenth century, but the final winner was a bit of a surprise—the English East India Company.

By the eighteenth century, there is, of course, an

abundance of material for historians. The Mughals started the tradition of keeping official records and so there are a lot of government documents, as well as books by historians and the writings of travellers. Later, during the rule of the British, there are records of meetings, legislative sessions, judicial orders, surveys and reports. As printing became popular in India, there came a treasure trove of newspapers, journals and books, not just in English but also in many Indian languages, which give us a detailed account of the events of this period. Fortunately for us, the British government started the system of preserving these old papers in what is now known as the National Archives, so information about this period is abundant.

There are two main streams of history during this period—first the establishment of a colonial government in India, initially under the East India Company and then the British government. The second is of the rise of Indian nationalism and the struggle for freedom. It makes this period a complex historical story but it is also a thrilling tale, full of exciting events, sweeping social changes, and a cast of magnificent characters.

Arrival of European Trading Companies

The Portuguese explorer Vasco da Gama landed in India in 1498 CE, even before the arrival of Babur. So, by the time of Aurangzeb, European traders had been present in India for over two centuries. Earlier, the trade between India and Europe was through two major routes—by land, along the Silk Route, across Asia and by sea, via the ports of the western coast to the Persian Gulf and the Red Sea, and then by land across the Middle East to Italy. But these routes were primarily monopolized by the Arabs in the Asian section and the Italians in Europe, since the first port in Europe was Venice. So, while the Arabs and the Italians became very prosperous, other countries in Western Europe, like Spain, Portugal, France and England, were keen to find a new sea route to Asia.

Vasco da Gama discovered a direct sea route to India by going down the continent of Africa, round the Cape of Good Hope at the southernmost tip of Africa and then sailing north along the eastern coast to enter the Indian Ocean. This meant that West European countries were now no longer dependent on Venice for goods from India, China and the spice islands of Indonesia. Portugal arrived first via this route and the French, Dutch and English soon followed. As is often the case, these countries then began fighting for Indian trade on land and sea. For centuries, the trade in India had been peacefully carried out by Arabs but now, these new countries, with the support of their governments, came armed with guns and soldiers on their ships.

The East India Company got a charter to trade in India in 1600 CE from Queen Elizabeth I of England, while Emperor Akbar was ruling in India. The first English embassy under Sir Thomas Roe was sent by King James I and arrived at the court of Emperor Jahangir in 1615 CE, bearing gifts and begging to be allowed to set up trading posts along the western coast. Jahangir magnanimously gave his permission and the first English trading centre was established at Surat, in 1612 CE. Soon, the Company had set up factories in Madras, Bombay and Calcutta and gradually these factories became the nucleus of small towns.

Anglo-French Rivalry

In the mid-eighteenth century, England and France went to war in Europe and that conflict spilled over in India and led to the three Carnatic wars between 1744 CE and 1763 CE. It was during these wars that these two trading companies began to emerge as regional powers. Initially, they had built fortified settlements guarded by soldiers mainly for safety, and to protect their goods, but now these garrisons, usually made up of Indian soldiers, marched out and fought battles. The English blockaded Pondicherry, the French retaliated by attacking Madras and then they both went seeking allies among the Indian rulers of the region. The English appealed to the nawab of Carnatic and the French won the nizam of Hyderabad as an ally, thus leading to

Factories

Although the trading posts of the European companies were called factories, unlike the factories of today, nothing was manufactured there. They were walled enclosures, often guarded by soldiers, with stores, offices and traders' residences within. Gradually, these factories were turned into fortresses, like Fort William in Calcutta. The English set up such factories in Calcutta, Bombay, Madras and Surat; the French in Pondicherry, Chandernagore and Mahe; the Portuguese in Goa, Daman and Diu; the Dutch in Serampore and Nagapattinam and the Danes in Tranquebar (modern Tharangambadi, in Tamil Nadu).

Indian kings becoming a part of the conflict.

These wars were a revelation to the Europeans, who realized that a much smaller but better trained and better armed European army could easily defeat the undisciplined and badly trained soldiers of the Indian states. The first to realize the possibilities of exploiting this weakness of the Indian kings was Marquis Dupleix, the French governor of Pondicherry. So when two Indian states went to war, he offered them the services of the French army in return for trading rights in that region. However, he could not carry out this policy for long as he was recalled to France soon afterwards. This was a great advantage for the English.

The French were defeated by the English in 1756 CE and by the treaty they signed they could no longer fortify their settlements. This left the field wide open for the Company.

The English in Bengal

For the trading companies, all that mattered was finding newer ways to make a profit. Dupleix had originally devised the plan by which he would help Indian rulers with European military and then take control of the trade in the region. However, the man who used this strategy to brilliant effect was the Englishman Robert Clive, whose clever strategy ultimately led to the East India Company taking over Bengal. At that time, Bengal was the richest province of the Mughal empire, producing rice and textiles, with busy sea ports and the nawabs earning rich revenues from the land.

As long as Nawab Alivardi Khan was ruling, he kept a strict control over the activities of the Company in Calcutta. He made sure that the English paid their custom duties; they

Robert Clive

were not allowed to fortify their factories with high walls or have cannons and he did not let them interfere in the work of his government.

Alivardi died in 1756 CE, and was succeeded by his grandson Siraj-ud-daulah. He was a hot-headed and inexperienced young man. He did not trust the English, who wanted to control the trade from Bengal and were greedily eyeing the revenue in the nawab's treasury at Murshidabad. They also started to raise high walls around Fort William in

Calcutta in defiance of the nawab's orders. At this, Siraj-ud-daula, fearing that he would lose control of trade in Bengal, gathered his forces and occupied the fort. But this was only the beginning, and both sides began to prepare for war.

Battle of Plassey (1757 CE)

It was at this juncture that Robert Clive arrived in Bengal. He decided that it would be more prudent to replace Siraj-ud-daula with a more obedient nawab, who would give in to East India Company's demands. He soon found a willing traitor in the nawab's commander-in-chief Mir Jafar.

In 1757 CE, the two armies, Siraj's and the Company's, met at Plassey. Mir Jafar's forces stayed away, leading to the defeat of Siraj-ud-daula, who fled from the battlefield and was later killed. Mir Jafar became the new nawab, but he was a mere puppet in the hands of the English, who began to demand more and more in return for their 'favour' of making him king.

Mir Jafar soon realized that he would be paying dearly for his

Clive's Speech

Robert Clive speaking about Bengal in the British parliament described his experience with Mir Jafar in the following way: 'A great prince was dependent on my pleasure; an opulent city lay at my mercy; its richest bankers bid against one another for my smiles; I walked through vaults which were thrown open to me alone, piled on either side with gold and jewels. Mr Chairman, at this moment, I stand astonished at my own moderation!'

traitorous act. Within a few years, the Company extracted thirty million rupees from Bengal and what followed was a period of open plunder. Soon, the Murshidabad treasury was empty. Finally, when Mir Jafar could not pay any more, he was replaced by Mir Qasim, another puppet ruler, who, in desperation, granted the zamindari of the three districts of Burdwan, Midnapore and Chittagong to the English. This meant that now a trading company from Britain officially became a land owner in Bengal and was given permission to collect revenue. At the same time, the Company officials ran their private businesses, trading in the products of the region. So not only the Company but the officials themselves all became fabulously rich.

Battle of Buxar (1764 CE)

The officials of the Company soon grew so rich through private trade that they began to be called nabobs. For instance, Clive had arrived penniless in India to work as a low paid 'writer' or clerk, but he went back with a personal fortune of 400,000 pounds and a knighthood, becoming Lord Clive!

Indian merchants began to protest as the Company and their officers were not paying any customs duties while *they* still had to. The English also bullied the local craftsmen to sell their goods at cheap rates. Mir Qasim, under pressure from the Indian merchants, finally abolished custom duties for everyone and this made the English very unhappy.

By this time, Mir Qasim had realized that unless the English were curbed, they would eventually bankrupt the treasury and take control over Bengal. So he began to build his own army, but the English retaliated by defeating him in a number of skirmishes. Then Mir Qasim escaped to Lucknow, seeking the support of Shuja-ud-daula, the nawab of Awadh and the Mughal emperor Shah Alam. The combined forces of Awadh, Delhi and Bengal met the English at Buxar in 1764 CE and the Indian allies were defeated.

In the humiliating treaty that followed, Shah Alam granted the diwani of Bengal, Bihar and Orissa to the Company. This meant that the English were now the governors of these regions and could collect revenue, though the administration remained in the hands of the nawab. Shuja-ud-daulah had to pay 50 lakh rupees as indemnity and ceded the districts of Allahabad and Kora to the English. After Buxar, the Company, as governors of a province, became the Company Bahadur, a regional power like Awadh or Hyderabad, owing a formal allegiance to the Mughals but, in fact, operating independently.

The Company now collected revenue, controlled trade and maintained an army, all at the cost of the nawab. Gradually, this led to the annexation of not just Bengal, Bihar and Orissa but also Madras and Bombay. The English occupied Delhi in 1803 CE and Shah Alam became a pensioner of the Company. India was on its way to becoming a colony of Britain.

John Company

The Indians called the East India Company 'Jehan Company' or powerful company, which became John Company in the common parlance of the English. Once the Company began to rule in India, it came to be known as 'Company Bahadur', or brave company.

Three cities grew out of the English factories that had been

Siraj-ud-daulah

set up. In 1698 CE, the Company acquired the zamindari of three villages in Bengal, Sutanati, Kalikata and Govindpur. Here, Job Charnock laid the foundations of Fort William and the city of Calcutta. In 1639 CE, the Company got the lease of Madras from a local raja and built Fort St George. The island of Bombay was given in dowry by Portugal when the English king Charles II married Catherine of Braganza in 1662 CE, and the Company got it at a rent of ten pounds a year.

Wars with Mysore

In the mid-eighteenth century, a new power rose in Mysore when the commander-in-chief Haidar Ali usurped the throne from the Wodeyar kings and declared himself as the nawab. The Company in nearby Madras viewed him as a threat to their plans to control the trade in the region because Haider Ali allied himself with the French. Since Mysore controlled a number of ports along the coast and dominated the spice trade, the English coveted control over the kingdom.

This led to two wars, called the first and second Anglo Mysore wars, and in both of them, Haider Ali defeated the Company. His seventeen-year-old son Tipu even led a raid into Madras and went galloping down its streets!

Tipu succeeded his father in 1783 CE and his brilliant military leadership earned him the title of the 'Tiger of Mysore'. He fought four wars against the English but, unfortunately, he fought alone, as none of the other Indian powers in the region, like the nizam of Hyderabad or the Marathas supported him in his struggle.

Both Haider Ali and Tipu Sultan were very suspicious of the English and Tipu was probably the only Indian ruler who understood the dangers of trusting them. The English, led by the then governor general Lord Cornwallis, allied with the nizam of Hyderabad and the Marathas to defeat him. Tipu lost the third Anglo Mysore war in 1792 CE and was forced to cede territories and leave his sons as hostages till he paid an indemnity. Then, in 1799 CE, the English deliberately provoked the fourth Mysore war and Tipu was killed defending his fortress Srirangapatnam. A member of the old royal family of Wodeyars was placed on the throne as a puppet king and Mysore finally became a vassal of the Company.

The Maratha Challenge

As we've discussed earlier, the people who had the best opportunity and the military ability to replace the Mughals in India were the Marathas. They were a group of brilliant generals under the leadership of the Peshwa; they had already reached Delhi towards the end of the Mughal rule, and had become a centre of power. They did lose some of their power and prestige after their defeat at the hands of Ahmad Shah Abdali at the Third Battle of Panipat in 1761 CE, but they were still a force to reckon with.

After the death of Shivaji, the Marathas had become a loose confederacy of military generals. Each of them had his own army and a base of power—the Peshwa ruled from Poona, Holkar was in Indore, Sindhia in Gwalior, Bhonsla in Nagpur and Gaekwad in Gwalior. The Peshwa headed this confederacy of generals and they fought three wars with the Company. Unfortunately, the generals were much too independent to work well together; they conspired against each other and did not unite against the common enemy.

As usual, the East India Company began to interfere in the internal affairs of the Marathas. For instance, they took sides

Tipu Sultan

Tipu was a far-sighted and enlightened king. He was interested in new technologies and began to modernize his army. He had an economic plan for his kingdom; he improved agriculture, set up factories for sugar, paper and artillery, and introduced sericulture by getting silk worms from Persia. He also sent a diplomatic embassy to the court of Louis XVI of France in the 1790s. A ship flying the flag of Mysore docked at the French port of Toulon to a grand welcome. In the Victoria & Albert Museum in London there is a mechanical toy once owned by Tipu. It has a tiger attacking a European man and when you wind up the toy, the man cries and the tiger roars. Interestingly, Wellesley (later Duke of Wellington) who defeated Tipu would also defeat Napoleon at the Battle of Waterloo in 1815 CE.

between two claimants to the Peshwa's throne. This constant interference in the Maratha matters led to two wars. But it was not till the English won the third Maratha war in 1817 CE that they finally ended the Maratha challenge. The Marathas had to sign humiliating treaties by which the Peshwa was exiled to North India and the other Maratha chieftains were also forced to cede land and were no longer allowed to maintain an army. The once-great Marathas now became docile vassals of the English. One of the reasons for their failure was that unlike Shivaji, the later Maratha chieftains lacked the vision to build an empire and somehow remained more interested in plunder than in governing the land.

Ahalya Bai Holkar

One remarkable Maratha ruler was a woman. Ahalya Bai Holkar was married to the son of Malhar Rao Holkar, who had founded a kingdom at Indore. She was widowed young and at the death of her father-in-law, Malhar Rao, in 1766 CE, she ruled Indore for nearly thirty years with sagacity. Ahalya Bai was loved by her subjects and is worshipped as a saint even today. She did not trust the English and warned fellow Maratha leaders to stay away from the East India Company.

Taking over Punjab

Punjab had been fortunate to get a brilliant king in Ranjit Singh, who had united the Sikhs in 1792 CE and gradually built up an independent kingdom. He had his capital in

Lahore and gradually expanded his kingdom until he came up against the English near the Sutlej River. His kingdom included parts of Afghanistan, Peshawar, Kangra and Kashmir and he ruled with great efficiency, successfully thwarting the English challenge. However, at Ranjit Singh's death in 1839 CE, Punjab went through a period of instability as there were many claimants to the throne. Finally, his youngest son, Dalip Singh, came to the throne under the regency of Ranjit Singh's queen Rani Jindan. This was, of course, the opportunity that the British were waiting for. Sensing the weakness of the Sikhs, the British attacked. There were two Sikh wars in 1845 CE and 1848 CE; in both wars, the Sikh Khalsa army was defeated. The British annexed Punjab and set up Gulab Singh as the king of Kashmir.

The Kohinoor Is Lost

As mentioned earlier, the Kohinoor diamond had been in Ranjit Singh's possession. When the British annexed Punjab, Dalip Singh was forced to hand it over to the British and it was sent as a gift to Queen Victoria. Today, it resides in the Tower of London, with the other crown jewels of the British.

Why Did the Company Succeed?

In the early years, the main aim of the East India Company was to protect their highly profitable trade in India. They maintained small garrisons of soldiers in their factories to protect their warehouses but soon, they began to use these soldiers to help their Indian allies. It was at this juncture that they realized that their well-trained soldiers armed with the latest guns were far superior to the Indian armies. So they could interfere, and take sides in the affairs of Indian regional powers. After their victory at Plassey, it dawned on the Company that what would be even more profitable than trade was to become revenue collectors through the grant of *diwani* of the region. It began in Bengal and soon led to the colonization of much of the country, turning Indian rulers into obedient allies of the Company.

Another factor that led to the growth of British power in India was that no Indian ruler had the vision or ability to replace the Mughals. After the Mughals, only the Marathas had the military power to build an empire but the numerous chieftains never united under one man. Each of them operated independently and was more interested in building their own kingdoms. Also the Marathas were not state builders and had the habit of sweeping across the land only to plunder; they had no interest in taking up the responsibility of building a government. Their constant plundering meant they were feared and hated in areas like Bengal, Hyderabad and Awadh and the rulers of these regions never supported Maratha attempts to gain power.

It was not that there was no talent among the ruling classes. There were a number of highly capable leaders during the eighteenth century, like Alivardi Khan of Bengal, Asaf Jah of Hyderabad, Baji Rao, the Peshwa, and even some noblemen in the Mughal court like Safdar Jung, but somehow none of them had the vision to build an empire to replace the Mughals. Also none of the Indian kingdoms, not even the Mughals, had a navy at a time when they needed the income from trade by sea. So they were dependent on the people who controlled the seas—first the Portuguese and then the English.

Another crucial factor was the superiority of the European armies. Their soldiers, most of them Indians, were better trained, disciplined and armed with the latest muskets and cannons. The Indian kings, who were always at war with each other, welcomed the support of these highly-trained armies, never realizing that this would ultimately lead to the colonization of their land. They were also unaware of how Europeans were already colonizing Africa and South America.

Elsewhere in the World

In the mid-eighteenth century, the Industrial Revolution began in Britain. While this led to the establishment of factories, and the growth of new technologies, the poor were forced to work in terrible conditions and with low wages. It ruined the village economy as it took away the work of traditional craftsmen like weavers and metal workers.

Revolutions were also starting worldwide at this time: the thirteen British colonies of North America became independent in 1776 and the French Revolution began in 1789. Both these revolutions would introduce the concept of democracy and give more power to the people, rather than to hereditary rulers.

Museum Visit

If you are in Kolkata visit the museum inside the Victoria Memorial building. Here you can see many paintings that depict India and the life of the English in the eighteenth century.

2
THE COMPANY BAHADUR
(1770 CE–1857 CE)

~ Administration ~ The Civil Service ~ The Army ~ The Police ~ The Judiciary ~ Exploiting the Villages ~ Ruining Industry and Trade ~ Wellesley and the Subsidiary Alliance ~

After the Battle of Buxar, when the East India Company became the diwan of Bengal, they began to look for newer ways to squeeze every penny from the nawab. This period is known as the dual government in Bengal's history, since this is when the Company collected the revenue and traded extensively, but did not have to worry about the administration, which remained the job of the nawab. It was the perfect arrangement—all the power and profit but none of the responsibility!

The Indian rulers had never been too interested in the welfare of the farmers or the common people, but under the Company rule, it was much worse. Now, there was brazen exploitation by Company men who bullied the farmers and forced Indian craftsmen and traders to sell their goods at ridiculously cheap rates—which led to the eventual ruin of Bengal's economy.

During the same time, criticism of the Company was

growing in Britain as other merchants began to question the trade monopoly of the Company in India and wanted trade to be opened up to everyone. Then, to everyone's surprise, the Company asked the British government for a loan claiming that it had incurred huge expenses fighting wars in India. The British parliament and press was in an uproar at the fact that the Company was claiming to be bankrupt while its men were coming back to England with huge fortunes!

It was clear to the British parliament that it was time to end the Company's trade monopoly in India. The government laid down the condition that to get the loan it had requested, the Company's Indian settlements had to be administered under the supervision of the British parliament. So the dual governance system in Bengal was ended by the Regulating Act passed in 1773 CE. Then other acts, such as the Pitt's India Act and two Charter Acts followed, which gradually shifted control of the Indian territories to the British parliament.

From now on, the government in India was to be headed by a governor general, who reported to the British parliament and the Company Board of Directors. Warren Hastings was appointed as the first governor general of India. He was followed by Lord Cornwallis and between them they laid the foundations of a centralized British administration in India comprising the civil service, the judicial system, the revenue system, the police and the army.

The fourth governor general was Lord Wellesley, who was an unapologetic imperialist. His only aim was to extend British territories in India. He went to war with Indian rulers whom he considered a threat to his imperialist plans, like Tipu Sultan and the Marathas, and he also found new and ingenious ways to exploit the lack of unity among Indian kings. So the exploitation of the Indian economy and the colonization of its people continued, only now it had the backing of the British parliament.

Administration

Warren Hastings effectively ended the nawabi of Bengal. He was aware that Bengal had to be run under a proper administrative system if the British government had to make any profits. Also the Company wanted to extend its power to more territories and so it needed a well-organised army and that required money. The system he and his successor, Lord

Chronology of Governor Generals

Warren Hastings (1773 CE-1784 CE)
Lord Cornwallis (1786 CE-1793 CE)
John Shore (1793 CE-1798 CE)
Lord Wellesley (1798 CE-1805 CE)
Lord Cornwallis (1805 CE-1806 CE)
Lord Minto (1807 CE-1813 CE)
Earl of Moira (1813 CE-1823 CE)
Lord Amherst (1823 CE-1828 CE)
Lord Bentinck (1828 CE-1835 CE)
Lord Auckland (1836 CE-1842 CE)
Lord Ellenborough (1842 CE-1844 CE)
Sir Henry Hardinge (1844 CE-1848 CE)
Lord Dalhousie (1848 CE-1856 CE)
Lord Canning (1856 CE-1858 CE)

Cornwallis, established would be very effective in maintaining law and order, improving trade, and colonizing more territories, but it was certainly not meant for the welfare of the Indian people.

Warren Hastings

At this time, the British-ruled territories were mainly around the cities of Calcutta, Madras and Bombay. These were now made into provinces, which were called presidencies. Madras and Bombay had their own governors and the whole administration was headed by Warren Hastings as the governor general, based in the capital city of Calcutta. Till now the actual job of collecting revenue had been in the hands of Indian tax collectors but now, it was given to British officers of the civil service.

Each presidency was divided into districts under a collector who supervised the collection of taxes. Company officials were no longer allowed to trade privately, instead they were given a regular salary and became a professional bureaucracy. This led to the formation of the Indian Civil Service (ICS) and, with the army and police, they would anchor the British empire in India for the next two centuries.

The administration was divided into four departments: the civil service for general administration; the army to protect the territories; the police to maintain law and order;

and the judiciary for running the law courts. Each of these departments was headed by Britishers.

The Civil Service

Lord Cornwallis created the civil service with strict rules and regulations to prevent private trading and consequent corruption. These officials were paid a salary, unlike the old Company man who was allowed to run his own business, and therefore, they became more efficient. The performance of the civil servants was reviewed regularly and promotions were linked to seniority. In the beginning, these officials were appointed by the Company directors but from 1853 CE, the applicants were selected by a competitive examination held in Britain. Lord Wellesley established a training college for the recruits at Fort William in Calcutta.

During Mughal times, both Hindus and Muslims were part of the bureaucracy but now, Indians were deliberately kept out of high posts and were only employed in low-paid jobs such as clerks and peons. Since the civil service entrance examination was held in London, few Indians could afford to take it. Also, the medium of the examination was in English while the Indian

Steel Frame

The Indian Civil Service was the highest paid civil service in the world! In the 1780s, a collector got a salary of ₹1,500 per month, plus a one per cent commission on the revenue he collected. They were efficient and very powerful and were called the 'steel frame' of the British empire.

education system was in Sanskrit and Persian. The maximum age for the examination was also kept very low. So there was virtually no opportunity for the educated Indian to work in the bureaucracy and this led to great resentment among the upper classes.

The Army

The British were an occupying power and so a well-trained army was essential. Like the civil services, here, too, discrimination against Indians was rampant. Indians were only recruited as common soldiers, called sepoys, the anglicized version of the Hindi word sipahi. Most of the sepoys came from the northern regions of Uttar Pradesh, Bihar and Punjab. For the poor farmers of these regions, a job with a regular salary was very attractive and they made loyal soldiers. However all the senior posts in the army were held by the British and the highest an Indian could go was till the rank of a subedar. The army was well-trained and armed with the latest guns and cannons and was used to conquer new territories, protect the trading interests of the Company, to help

First Indian ICS

In 1863 CE, the first Indian to join the Indian Civil Service (ICS) was Satyendranath Tagore, the elder brother of poet Rabindranath Tagore. He went to Britain to give the entrance examination and his first posting was in the Bombay presidency. He was an author, music composer and linguist, and served in the ICS for over thirty years.

A sepoy of the English army.

suppress revolts and also to keep Indian rulers obedient to the Company.

Why did Indians join the army of a foreign power? The most important reason was the absence of a national identity among the people. There was no idea of nationalism and no sense of belonging to a nation. The people identified themselves as belonging to a caste, tribe or their village. For instance, a man would say he was a thakur from a village in Awadh. No one thought of himself as an Indian, since the concept of a whole and unified India was yet to emerge. Also, at a time of great social unrest and poverty, when Indian rulers were busy fighting with each other and neglecting the work of governance, the army offered a regular job and salary to a poor villager.

The Police

Years of unrest and wars among various regional powers had led to a breakdown of law and order in the country. Trade had become impossible because the highways were highly unsafe and robbers waited for unwary travellers at every turn. So an efficient police force was essential for maintaining administration and Lord Cornwallis created a permanent police force in India by modernizing the old, existing system. Now, each district had a police station (thana) under an officer (daroga); towns and villages had regular police inspectors (kotwals) and watchmen (chowkidar). Later, the post of District Superintendent of Police was also created. Like in the army, Indians were only appointed to the lower positions of the police.

Although the police were able to establish peace and order, they were often oppressive and corrupt and were greatly feared by common people. But one of the major achievements of the police was the catching of criminals called pindaris and dacoits called thugees who regularly robbed and murdered travellers on the highways, often disguising themselves as fellow travellers.

The Judiciary

The Mughal legal system had been a confusing mix of Hindu shastras and the Islamic sharia laws and none of these laws was properly codified. This led to a lot of confusion. So it was decided that a codified system of law was required to better administer justice and a Law Commission was set up which compiled the laws into the Indian Penal Code. Unlike during Mughal times, when people were often judged according to caste, class or religion (the Brahmin often getting a lighter sentence than a lower caste person), now, every person was considered equal in the eyes of the law. Well, almost equal, since Europeans were still tried in separate courts by European judges.

A proper system of courts was also established. The judiciary was headed by a Supreme Court with law courts in every district. In the districts, there were the civil courts (diwani adalat) and criminal courts (faujdari adalat).

Exploiting the Villages

In Mughal times the farmer owned the land he tilled and he paid a fixed amount as revenue to the government. During droughts or floods, taxes were often reduced or written off. Most importantly, since the farmer owned the land, he could not be evicted. The Mughal zamindars were just tax collectors who were stationed in the villages, they did not own the land and could be transferred to other areas.

The British changed this system as they wanted to extract the maximum taxes from the farmers without the bother of having to collect the taxes themselves. They now appointed agents to collect the revenue and these agents, also called zamindars, were made the landowners. This meant that the farmers lost the rights to their land and were also open to the exploitation by the zamindars. They became tenants who could be evicted from their land in case of failure to pay taxes. With the new revenue system began the ruin of Indian rural economy, which continued till India's independence.

The British introduced three new systems of revenue collection: the Permanent Settlement, the Mahalwari and the Ryotwari systems.

The Permanent Settlement was introduced by Lord Cornwallis in 1793 CE. The land revenue in Bengal and Bihar was fixed permanently. The zamindar had to pay this fixed tax and he could keep whatever was left over. However, if he failed to pay, he lost his right to the land and it was auctioned off to another zamindar. So the work of collection was now left to the zamindar and the Company did not have to deal with the farmers. Since these zamindars were dependent on the Company for their livelihood they were loyal to it, often at the expense of the farmers.

There were zamindars even in Mughal times but they lived in the villages, knew the farmers and were involved in village life. Now they were replaced by businessmen and money lenders who bought land rights from the Company at auctions and were only interested in profits. They extracted the maximum they could from the farmers and were not interested in improving agriculture. Most of them were absentee landowners living off their profits in Calcutta, utterly indifferent to the condition of the villagers.

The Mahalwari System was introduced in western Uttar Pradesh, parts of Madhya Pradesh and Punjab. Here, land was owned by a group of villages called mahals and the headman of each mahal was appointed to collect the revenue. Unlike the Permanent Settlement, here, the revenue was not fixed.

The Ryotwari System was introduced in parts of Madras and Bombay presidencies. Here, the revenue settlement was made directly with the farmer or ryot and so the farmer was given rights to the land. Also, the tax was calculated according to the quality of the soil.

In the Mahalwari and Ryotwari systems, the farmers paid high taxes but at least they did not lose their rights to the land. Also they were not at the mercy of the zamindars and moneylenders. As the revenue was not fixed, they were also better able to face natural disasters as taxes could be reduced when droughts or floods ruined crops. However, the taxes in these systems were very high indeed, going up to half of the produce, and it could be raised even further at any time by the government.

The new revenue system created rural poverty on a massive scale. Farmers were always in debt to moneylenders and often lost their land and became landless labourers. Neither the government nor the zamindars were interested in improving agriculture: no irrigation canals or dams were built and farmers were completely dependent on the monsoons. So, year after

Zamindars

Most of the zamindars introduced by the new system of revenue collection were moneylenders and traders who never visited the villages except to extract money. They lived in palatial houses in Calcutta and lived idle, self-indulgent lives.

year, crop yields kept reducing, and yet, taxes were not waived. The tragedy was unimaginable, for example in the Great Famine of 1770 CE, a quarter of the population of Bengal died of starvation.

Ruining Industry and Trade

During Mughal times, India had a flourishing trade in textiles and spices and weavers were an important part of the rural economy. In fact, Indian textile industry was the biggest in the world. This was deeply resented by British merchants and now there was a deliberate plan to ruin it.

By the mid-eighteenth century, the Industrial Revolution in Britain was in full swing, with factories producing textiles in Lancashire and Manchester. Since the markets in Britain itself were already being saturated, these textiles needed newer, and more extensive markets, namely, the British colonies.

In order to ruin the indigenous market of the Indian textile industry, the British bought raw cotton at the cheapest rates from India and shipped it to Britain. Then, cheap mill cloth, produced in Britain's factories, imported and sold in Indian markets. Meanwhile, Indian weavers had to buy raw cotton at high prices and the textiles that were

> **Killing Indian Trade**
>
> *In 1824 CE, the duty on Indian calico cotton was as high as 67.5 per cent and on muslin, it was 37.5 per cent. Indian sugar was taxed at thrice its cost price! British goods imported into India, of course, paid no taxes at all.*

exported to Britain were heavily taxed, making them very expensive. They were, therefore, no competition to the factory-produced, cheap foreign cloth that was flooding the Indian markets. Thus, many Indian weavers lost their livelihood and were forced to either switch to a different trade or work for the British traders at very low wages. Once India had the largest textile industry in the world; now, lakhs of ruined weavers migrated from villages to the cities to live in horrific slums and work as daily wage labourers.

So with the land revenue and trade policies Britain began the economic ruin of India's rural population. It led to some of the worst famines in India's history and poverty at a level that the country had never seen before. For instance, there were twelve major famines between 1770 CE and 1850 CE and little was done to help the farmers. This continued till India became independent.

The government discouraged modern industries from being established in India and therefore, the country did not benefit from

British Wealth

Most of the wealth of the British nobility has a long history of exploitation of human beings. During the Industrial Revolution, villagers in Britain were forced to migrate to cities to work in the factories and live in slums. Their tragedy is described in the novels of Charles Dickens. The upper classes became fabulously rich through the revenue generated by the factories, the colonization of India and China and through the horrific slave trade from Africa; something that British history books often gloss over.

the Industrial Revolution. The few factories that did come up were all owned by Britishers. There were no Indian industrialists and rich Indians were almost always merchants and zamindars, whose fortunes were tied to the Company. No one in the country, the nawabs, the rajas, the Company men or the rich Indian traders had any time to think about the farmers starving in the villages or the weavers dying in the city slums.

Wellesley and the Subsidiary Alliance

One way to increase British territories was through outright wars, but Lord Wellesley came up with a very original plan for taking over Indian kingdoms without firing a single shot. This system came to be called the Subsidiary Alliance because the rulers had to pay a subsidy to the British for the use of their armies. This policy took advantage of the lack of unity among the Indian rulers and ultimately led to all of them becoming obedient puppets in the hands of the British.

The Indian kingdoms were continuing with their self-destructive wars with each other and would often seek the help of the Company army. Now, the rulers were offered the subsidiary treaty, by which the British promised to protect them from not just their enemies but also from internal rebellions. According to the Subsidiary Treaty, the ruler could not have his own army. Instead he would pay for the cost of a British army stationed in his kingdom. A British Resident would be stationed at his court and the ruler had to consult him in all matters of foreign policy, that is, his relations with other rulers.

This subsidy was usually an exorbitant amount and

many rulers were forced to cede territory to meet the British demand. Awadh lost half its kingdom and, as the ruler's army was disbanded, thousands of Indian soldiers lost their jobs. A British writer commenting on the Subsidiary Alliance said, 'It was a system of fattening allies as we fatten oxen till they were worthy of being devoured.'

As one ruler after another agreed to the Subsidiary Alliance, they, in fact, became vassals of the British empire. As they had no armies of their own, they also had no independence. From large kingdoms like Hyderabad, Awadh, the Rajput kings and the Peshwa to small Maratha chieftains and southern rajas and nawabs, one after another, most Indian rulers gave in to the British. In fact, it took less than a century for a trading company from Britain to gain control over almost the whole of India!

It was the perfect way to expand the empire while the Indian rulers paid the cost of maintaining the British army. The British controlled the defence and foreign affairs of the ruler and the Resident also invariably interfered in the internal affairs of the kingdom. If the ruler was not obedient enough, he could always be overthrown, since he had no army to defend himself. This also meant that the rulers never felt any threat to their throne from internal rebellions as long as the British were there to protect them. So they became indifferent to the welfare of their people.

Elsewhere in the World

After the French Revolution, Europe saw the rise of the conqueror Napoleon Bonaparte who came as far as Egypt. Britain feared that he would next move towards India, but Napoleon was defeated at the Battle of Waterloo in 1815 CE. Britain and China also fought the Opium Wars between 1839 CE and 1842 CE.

To Watch

The film Do Bigha Zameen *(1953 CE), directed by Bimal Roy, shows the difficult life the poor farmers led during the days of the zamindars. Try contrasting it with another film,* Shatranj Ke Khilari *(1977 CE), based on a short story by Premchand and directed by Satyajit Ray, which depicts the luxurious, indolent lives of the nawabs of Lucknow.*

3

A TIME OF CHANGE
(1800 CE–1900 CE)

~ Life in India ~ The Orientalists ~ The Spread of Modern Education ~ Rammohun Roy ~ Henry Derozio ~ Ishwarchandra Vidyasagar ~ Other Social Reformers

In Europe, the nineteenth century was an exciting time. There was great intellectual ferment and giant leaps were made in science and technology. The Industrial Revolution in Europe led to economic progress and transformed British society. At the same time, the French and American revolutions introduced new ideas about equality, the rights of people and democracy and these changes opened up new paths of human progress. By the nineteenth century, the West was thinking in revolutionary ways and these new ideas were soon making their way across the seas to India.

This intellectual revolution was led by writers and philosophers like Voltaire, Rousseau, Kant and Charles Dickens. Their work was based on humanism, that spoke of equality and respect towards all human beings and of every person's right to happiness and liberty. At a time when governments supported the colonization of countries and slavery was making Europeans rich, this was a truly revolutionary thought.

There was also a growing opinion among religious conservatives and missionaries that India was a backward country that had to be 'civilized' by the introduction of Western values and the teachings of Christianity. There was much pressure on the British to introduce Western education in India and this was supported by many Indian social reformers such as Rammohun Roy and Ishwar Chandra Vidyasagar.

When it came to its policies towards India, the British government was still highly conservative and unwilling to change. The officials had a superior, paternalistic attitude towards Indians, treating them like children who had to be kept under disciplined control. Modernization through education and technology did not come to India because of any sudden outburst of generosity on the part of the government. It was allowed because education would produce a class of Indians who could be employed cheaply in administration and would be loyal to the foreign rulers. Modern technology like railways, post and telegraphs would open up newer markets for British goods while also making it easier to keep the country under colonial rule and quickly

Missionaries

The first schools in India that taught Western education were opened by Christian missionaries who hoped to convert Indians to Christianity. The positive side of this development was that these schools offered education to children of all classes and castes and soon, even girls' schools were opened.

quell any acts of rebellion. So whatever progress came to India was to help the government make a profit and to run the country cheaply. Colonialism was always about money.

Life in India

What was it like to live in India in the early 1800s? Life was very hard, the country had sunk into the darkness of poverty, superstition and inequality. Education was the monopoly of the upper castes—Brahmins knew well that if they controlled knowledge they could exploit the poor, illiterate people. Most people could not read and their lives were ruled by religious superstitions. People obeyed whatever their priests said quite blindly. The Brahmin or the maulvi was often the only educated person in a village or a town, and he controlled people through his readings of the sacred books and astrological charts and made money through expensive religious rituals.

> ### No Bananas
>
> *People followed Hindu almanacs blindly. And these books, full of astrological instructions, would even tell you what to eat on what day. Imagine losing your caste because you ate a banana on a Thursday!*

For Hindus, their only identity was their caste and they were terrified of losing it, so they obeyed the Brahmins blindly. For example, the Brahmins discouraged people from travelling overseas and declared that crossing the seas would make people lose their caste. So everyone stayed at home and it made them timid, unwilling to take risks. Forget about the world, they knew nothing about their own country—people could live their entire lives without meeting anyone who spoke a different language! Women and Dalits, the lowest caste, were not educated because it was said to be against Hindu religion.

Hindu society was divided by the caste system and its rules were so strict that the upper castes would not allow any freedom to those they considered below them. The condition of the Dalits, or the 'untouchable' caste, was, in particular, pathetic, as they were only allowed to do only menial jobs. They had to stay outside villages and could not enter people's homes as even their shadow was considered unclean! They were barred from temples and could not even draw water from the village well. The Brahmins declared that people would lose their caste if they came in contact with a dalit and the uneducated populace blindly believed them. In fact, the condition of Dalits improved with the colonial government as they finally got a chance to be educated and get jobs in the government. For example, B.R. Ambedkar's father joined the army and then educated his sons.

The status of women was terrible as well—they had no rights at all. They were not allowed to study, were mostly married off as children and could not inherit property. Their lives were an endless drudgery of housework and raising children. They were sometimes even denied adequate food or proper medical treatment, so that, very often, they died young. The brunt of this terrible treatment was meted out to widows, who were not allowed to remarry and lived like servants within their families. Another shocking practice among the higher castes was that of sati. This act of religious murder was primarily done to deprive women of their rights to the family property.

This was a society where more than half the population had no rights and the rich, the zamindars and merchants, were only interested in making money by exploiting the poor and being loyal to their colonial masters. It was this immense inequality in the society that led to the rise of a new intellectual movement, at the helm of which were humanists like Rammohun Roy, Ishwarchandra Vidyasagar and Jyotiba Phule. They realized that a society so unequal and divided could never progress. It was time for India to change and it had to begin with a modern education that was open to everyone.

The Orientalists

Who were the Orientalists? They were British men who came to India as officers of the East India Company and became genuine admirers of Indian culture. These men felt that the British would gain from learning about India and wanted to revive and conserve India's cultural heritage. They wanted the education in India to be in Sanskrit or Persian. On the other hand, there were another group of scholars and reformers called the Anglicists, who felt Indian education was outdated and too full of religious superstition, and they were keen to introduce Western science and the English language in schools and colleges.

One of the earliest Orientalist was Sir William Jones, who came to India as a judge. He was a linguist; he learnt Sanskrit and translated the works of Kalidasa. In 1784 CE, he founded the Asiatic Society of Calcutta, which would go on to pioneer research on Indian history and literature.

Another important Orientalist was Alexander Cunningham. He was an army engineer who stumbled across ancient monuments that would later be identified as the Harrapan civilization. Most of these monuments were in a bad condition, which led him to establish the Archaeological Survey of India to preserve them. James Fergusson, another Orientalist, wrote the first book on Indian architecture. But perhaps the most famous Orientalist of the time was James Prinsep , who worked at the Calcutta mint and took Indology, or the study of Indian culture, to newer heights through careful research. He would be the one to introduce the world to a long-forgotten king named Ashoka of the Mauryan dynasty, and crack the mysterious script that had been found on rocks and pillars built during Ashoka's reign.

Before this, India had no tradition of scholarship through research, and were indifferent to their own history. Whatever knowledge was preserved was jealously guarded by the Brahmins. But even they had no tradition of recording history and only wrote about events that worked in favour of their caste. This biased version of history was often found in the Puranas, which were a confused mass of disorganized information and romantic legends. For instance, it was because of this chaotic record-keeping that India had forgotten one of its greatest philosophers, Gautama Buddha. He had challenged Hindu religious practices, especially the caste system and the Brahmin historians had removed him from their writings.

India's heritage was saved and preserved by British men like Jones, Prinsep and Cunningham, who fell in love with India and laboured tirelessly to preserve its culture. From ancient monuments to literature, painting, sculpture, music and dance, everything was studied with academic rigour at the Asiatic Society and then the knowledge was shared with the world. Soon afterwards, Charles Wilkins started the first printing press and this knowledge was available for anyone willing to buy a book. Sanskrit and Persian books were translated into regional languages, alphabet primers were written for schools and this led to the spread of literacy.

The Spread of Modern Education

By this time, in the West, the sciences were being taught in schools and students were being encouraged to become scientists, engineers, architects and doctors. In India, they were still memorizing Sanskrit shlokas and text from the Quran and schools did not teach subjects like geography, biology or chemistry! Most of the teachers were local priests who were badly educated themselves and there was no curriculum, proper textbooks or a system of examination. When the East India Company, rather reluctantly, decided to invest in education, it was the views of the Anglicists with a more Westernized structure of education through the

> *Prinsep's Ghat*
>
> *Scientist, scholar and linguist James Prinsep soon became the driving force at the Asiatic Society and encouraged men like Alexander Cunningham and Brian Hodgson to collect ancient Indian manuscripts and artefacts. When he died, the Bengalis of Calcutta built Prinsep's Ghat, with its lovely marble arch, by the Ganga, as a tribute to this great scholar. Sadly, Calcutta today has forgotten him and most people call it 'Princes Ghat'!*

medium of English that carried the day.

Thomas Babington Macaulay played the most prominent role in the introduction of English in Indian schools. He had a very low opinion of Indian culture and introduced a resolution that English should be the medium of instruction in schools and colleges instead of Sanskrit or Persian. The plan was to create a class of English-speaking Indians who could be cheaply employed in the government and who would be loyal to the British. Also, the government needed a common language to govern a country with so many vernacular languages and English fitted the bill. Initially, the new class of English-educated Indians were exactly what Macaulay wanted—blindly loyal and anglicized. They discarded Indian clothes for suits, rejected everything Indian and were called 'brown sahibs' or 'Macaulay's children'.

Macaulay's Minute

He was a law member in the governor general's council. In 1835 CE, he suggested that the medium of education and all work in government offices and law courts should to be in English. He wanted to create 'a class of persons Indian in colour and blood but English in taste, in opinions, in morals and in intellect... who may be interpreters between us and the millions we govern.' Surprisingly, he also anticipated what this would lead to, and wrote in his 'Minute on Indian Education': 'Come what may, self-knowledge will lead to self-rule and that would be the proudest day in British history.'

Education departments were set up in all the provinces,

teachers were trained in the new curriculum and universities were established at Calcutta, Madras and Bombay in 1857 CE. However, right from the start, there was little interest in primary education and villages were neglected, so only the rich from urban areas actually benefitted. The level of literacy remained very low and the education of girls did not improve. In 1921 CE, 92 per cent of men and 98 per cent of women were illiterate and there was little opportunity for scientific and technological education. In the late nineteenth century there were only three medical colleges in Calcutta, Madras and Bombay and just one engineering college in Roorkee.

Bankim Chandra Chatterjee

The famous Bengali novelist was the first of two graduates from Calcutta University. He would later go on to write the nationalist novel Anandmath *and the song 'Bande Mataram'.*

But, of course, the introduction of the new curriculum led to some good. It led to the creation of a generation of men who were more aware of the world, who asked some crucial questions—what was wrong with Indian society that it had become so backward? These reformers realized quickly that it was because of three reasons. First, education was limited to the priesthood and the rich. Second, the inequalities of the caste system gave no opportunities to a large part of the population. And finally, there was the oppression of women and the utter disregard for women's education.

Rammohun Roy

One of the earliest advocates of a modern education was Rammohun Roy. He belonged to an orthodox Brahmin family in Bengal but questioned the worship of idols and the many meaningless religious rituals. In 1828 CE, he founded the Brahmo Samaj in Calcutta and through his study of ancient texts like the Vedas and the Upanishads, he preached the worship of one god. He wanted to revive Hinduism in its original purity and rejected the need for priests or rituals by going back to the Vedas.

Rammohun Roy

Roy was also an energetic crusader against social evils like sati, polygamy, child marriage and the caste system. Many young men, who had been influenced by the new liberal thoughts from the West, became his enthusiastic followers and joined the Brahmo Samaj. Their campaign against sati got the support of the governor general, Lord Bentinck, and sati was finally banned in 1829 CE.

Roy was also a linguist; he knew many languages and pioneered printing in India when he began publishing journals in Bengali, Hindi, Persian and English. Through these journals, he shared information about modern education, and wrote about the freedom of the press and the rights of Indians. He was an enthusiastic supporter of Western education as he felt that it was, 'the key to the treasures of scientific and democratic thought of the modern West'.

Henry Derozio

Henry Derozio was a contemporary of Rammohun Roy and, in his short life, was a major influence on a generation of young men who were his students at the Hindu College in Calcutta. His father was Portuguese but he was an Indian in spirit, like his mother. In 1828 CE, he founded the Academic Association, where he encouraged students to question and challenge authority. This started the Young Bengal movement—young, upper-class, educated men began to oppose social evils like the caste system, refused to obey brahminical rules and vehemently supported the education of women. Orthodox society was so alarmed by this movement that they started a campaign against Derozio and had him dismissed from his job. He died soon after at the young age of twenty-two but the rebellious and radical movement he started continued to inspire the youth of Bengal.

Ishwarchandra Vidyasagar

Another man of extraordinary courage was the social reformer Ishwarchandra Vidyasagar, a vigorous opponent of the caste system and a champion for the cause of women. He was a renowned scholar and the principal of the Sanskrit College in Calcutta, where he admitted students of every caste. In 1849 CE, he helped the Englishman Drinkwater Bethune open the first girls' school in Calcutta, which later became Bethune College. As an inspector of schools, Vidyasagar helped open many more educational institutions.

Like Rammohun Roy, Vidyasagar was also a Brahmin and faced the rage of the orthodox society. But his opponents were often afraid of arguing with him because his knowledge of the sacred books was greater than theirs! He even faced threats to his life for trying to help women, especially widows. He began a movement for the remarriage of widows and organized the first one in 1856 CE after a Widow's Remarriage Act was passed by the government. At the same time, he was a passionate educationist who worked tirelessly for literacy—he wrote Bengali alphabet books to help people learn to read.

Other Social Reformers

The social reform movement soon spread all across India. Men and women stood up to challenge superstitious beliefs. Following the Brahmo Samaj, other such associations came

Swami Dayanand Saraswati

up, such as the Veda Samaj in Madras and the Prarthana Samaj in Bombay. Jyotirao Govind Rao Phule (Jyotiba Phule) founded the Satyashodhak Samaj in Pune to fight for equality and against caste rules. Swami Dayanand Saraswati began the Arya Samaj, where he worked towards going back to a simple religious system, rejecting expensive rituals and supporting the rights of women. In the south, there were reformers like Sri Narayana Guru and E.V. Ramaswamy Naicker, who campaigned for the rights of Dalits and fought to get temples to open their doors to everyone.

In many ways, modern India is as much a legacy of Macaulay and other British champions for Western education as it is of Rammohun Roy and Vidyasagar. English as a medium of teaching meant young men looking for employment in the government chose it instead of learning Persian or Sanskrit. This education was also open to all castes. Since the new curriculum was largely

Disobedient Women

One of the myths that the orthodox society of the time tried to popularize was that if a girl became educated, her husband died soon after. They also believed that educated girls became very disobedient. So when girls' schools were opened in Calcutta, groups of men would stand outside, shouting and harassing the little girls studying there.

Pandita Ramabai

Born in 1858 CE, Pandita Ramabai was from a Brahmin family. Her father faced social rejection because he educated his wife and daughter. Ramabai was a Sanskrit scholar, who travelled across the country, championing the need to educate women. She married a man belonging to a lower caste in a civil marriage. She also founded girls' schools and set up hostels for widows in Maharashtra.

secular, students now learnt to go beyond religious beliefs and seek answers to societal questions.

Soon a new middle class appeared in the cities. This class was English-educated and progressive in attitude, and questioned old social structures like the caste system or the oppression of women. They embraced Western thought and learning and it was from among them that the leaders of the freedom movement would rise in the following decades.

Elsewhere in the World

This was the time of great scientific progress in the West. In 1800 CE, the first electric battery was invented by Alessandro Volta in Rome. In 1829 CE, Louise Braille, a blind teacher at the National Institute for Blind Children in Paris, invented the Braille system of writing. In 1892 CE, Wilhelm Rontgen discovered the x-ray and won the first Nobel Prize for physics.

To Visit

If you're in Kolkata, drop by at the Asiatic Society or the National Library to see the displays of books, paintings and photographs from this period.

4

THE GREAT UPRISING
(1857 CE–1858 CE)

~ Many Revolts ~ Tribal Rebellions ~ Princely States ~ Growing Discontent ~ Rural Resentments ~ A Sepoy's Life ~ The Immediate Cause ~ The Uprising Spreads ~ Why the Revolt Failed ~ Changes After 1858 CE ~

The revolt that shook India in 1857 CE has been given many names by historians—the Sepoy Mutiny, India's First War of Independence, the Great Revolt and the Great Uprising. For the common people, it was simply a 'gadar', a rebellion, and a time of trouble. They had faced many like it before. However, no rebellion, before or after, has lit such a conflagration of chaos, violence and rage as the one of 1857 CE.

Contemporary British historians chose to call it the Sepoy Mutiny, trying to dismiss it as a mere revolt by the Indian soldiers in the Company army. In fact, it was a much more significant historical event. It may have begun with the sepoys but ultimately, it became a widespread uprising involving all the people who had suffered at the hands of the British —from royal families, the nobility and feudal zamindars to priests, farmers, traders and craftsmen.

Some Indian historians call it, rather grandly, India's First

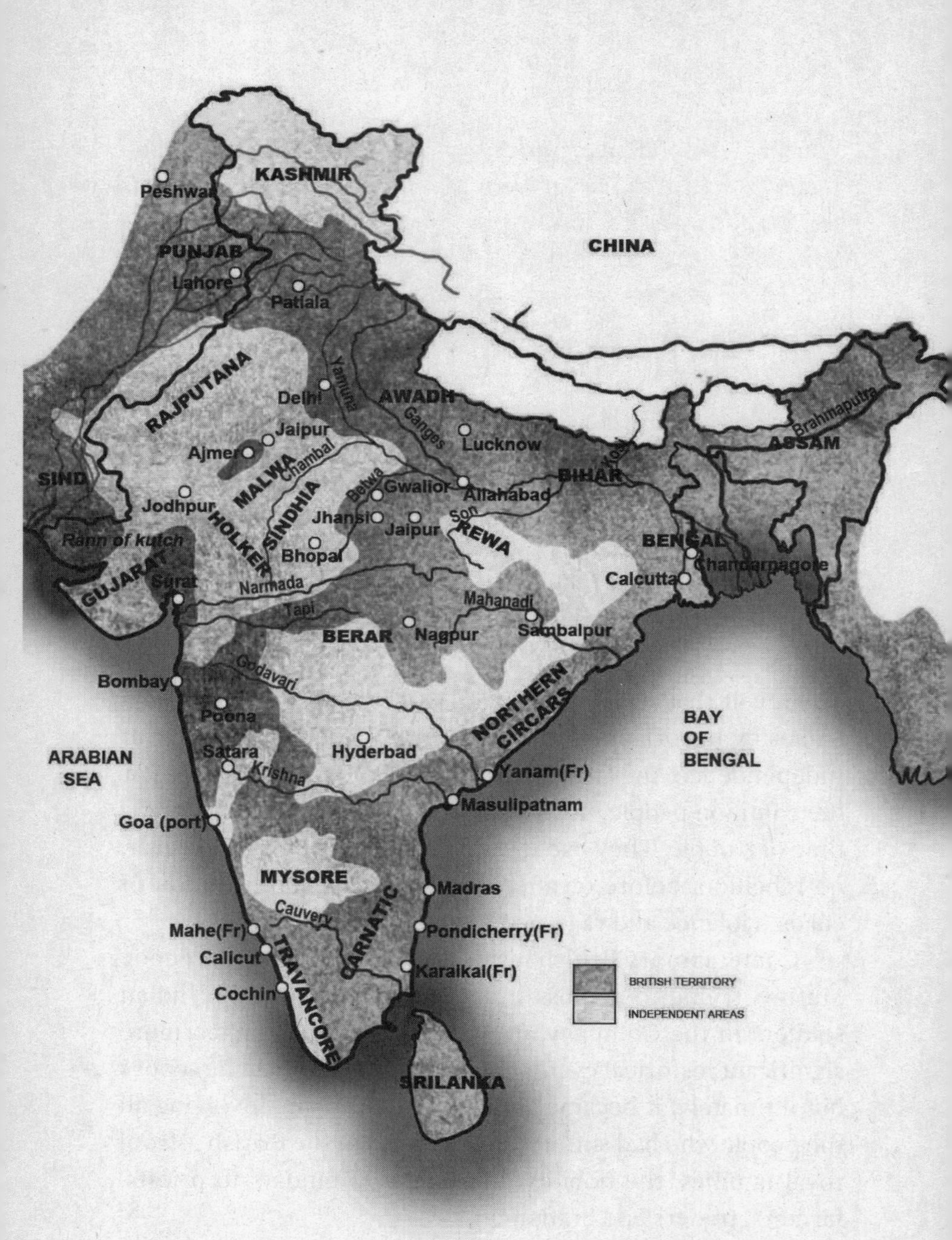

India before the uprising of 1857 CE.

War of Independence, but this entails giving it a pan-Indian and nationalist character that it did not have. The regions south of the Narmada River and north, towards Punjab, remained peaceful and so did Bengal. The uprising was limited to mainly modern Uttar Pradesh, Madhya Pradesh and parts of Bihar. Furthermore, most of the Indian princely states remained loyal to the British. Also, the revolt lacked a true national character as there was no sense of a common identity; everyone was fighting for their own motives, not for a nation called India.

But the gadar of 1857 CE had a fierceness that shook British imperialism to its core and led to many significant changes in the colonial structure. What made the Company Bahadur sit up and take notice was the extraordinary courage and passion with which the common people rose in protest after a century of British exploitation—soldiers, farmers, craftsmen, traders—ordinary people who had suffered enough. Every time the rebelling sepoys occupied a town, ignoring local authorities, the cry that rang out went, '*Khalq khuda ki; mulk badshah ka; hukm subahdar sipahi bahadur ka.*' It meant, 'The people belong to God; the country belongs to the emperor and authority rests with the sepoy commander.'

Many Revolts

A century after the battle at Plassey in 1757 CE, India was seething with resentment. There had been several small and localized revolts before, mainly led by dispossessed landowners, tribals and religious groups. In the south, land owners called poligars who had lost their land revolted under the leadership of Veerapandya Kattabommam and the Maruthu Pandyan brothers. Then there was the Kittur uprising in Karnataka and revolts in Saurashtra, Aligarh, Jabalpur, Bilaspur and Travancore. The army was often rising up in protest against the bad treatment and low pay. All these revolts were ruthlessly suppressed and many of the rebels were hanged.

Tribal Rebellions

The British had also begun an organized exploitation of tribals like the Mundas, the Santhals and the Bhils. These simple people did not possess any legal proof of land ownership in the forests where they lived. Now, they were deprived of their land as it was taken over for the cultivation of cash crops like indigo and jute and they were reduced to being low-paid labourers. Other tribal groups were forced to pay high taxes which led to them falling into the clutches of moneylenders. Plus, Christian missionaries moved in, interfering with their way of life, criticizing the social customs and religious beliefs they had followed for centuries.

The Kols rebelled in 1831 CE and the Santhals in 1855 CE. The Oraons, too, rose in revolt under the leadership of Jatra Oraon. One of the biggest rebellions was of the Mundas, led by Birsa Munda, which took place in the 1890s. The tribal warriors faced the British guns with bows and arrows and fought bravely but all of these rebellions were ruthlessly suppressed.

Princely States

The British were always looking for ways to annexe Indian kingdoms, sometimes through conquest and, at other times, through various clever subterfuges. One of these was, of course, the Subsidiary Alliance, which we've discussed earlier. Most of the princely kingdoms had to bow to the rules of the Subsidiary Alliance, by which they became obedient puppets controlled by the British Resident stationed at their courts. A huge amount of money was extracted from them to pay for the British army stationed in their kingdom and the Resident interfered constantly in their internal affairs.

In 1850 CE, a new policy was introduced to annexe even more territories. It was Lord Dalhousie's idea, and came to be called the Doctrine of Lapse. According to this new policy, when a ruler died without a natural heir, their kingdom could be inherited by an adopted heir only if the adoption was approved by the British. Otherwise, the kingdom was to be annexed to the British dominion. In this way, Dalhousie took over the kingdoms of Satara, Nagpur and Jhansi. Nana Sahib, the adopted son of the last Peshwa, Baji Rao II, lost his pension and was forced to live in exile in Kanpur.

Another provocation was that the Mughal king, Bahadur Shah II, was informed that after him, his descendants would no longer have the title of 'emperor'. He was already living on a pension paid by the Company and on his death his family would have to vacate the Red Fort and move to cheaper accommodation in Mehrauli, in the outskirts of Delhi.

Whenever the British annexed a kingdom, the common people suffered. The kingdom's army was disbanded, the officials lost their jobs, landowners lost their land and people who made a living from the patronage of the royal family, such as craftsmen, palace servants, priests, musicians and dancers, also lost their livelihoods.

The final straw was the dethroning of Nawab Wajid Ali

Shah in 1856 CE and the annexation of the kingdom of Awadh. The Awadh nawabs had been steadfastly loyal supporters of the Company, often meeting exorbitant demands for money and even ceding land to keep the Company Bahadur happy. As a matter of fact, one of the Anglo-Afghan wars was fought on the money extracted from Awadh. In spite of their docility, Dalhousie accused Wajid Ali of misrule, banished him to Calcutta and annexed the kingdom. This led to a huge sense of betrayal among the people of Awadh and also among many of the sepoys in the Company army, as a large section of them came from the Awadh region.

Growing Discontent

Indian society at the time was deeply conservative. People were full of religious superstitions and very suspicious of British attempts to reform their social and religious practices. Social reforms like the banning of sati or legalizing the marriage of widows made orthodox people angry. With the introduction of English, the status of Sanskrit and Persian became secondary and this threatened the existence of the old ruling class. It also heralded the appearance of a new educated middle class, who questioned the authority of the age-old aristocracy and religious leaders. These English-speaking young men got jobs in the new government and were in favour of social change.

Anything new always makes people nervous, and things were no different back in the 1800s. New technology like the railways and the postal system and telegraphs was looked at with suspicion and the activities of Christian missionaries added fuel to the fire. It didn't help that they were often insensitive to common people's feelings, and were often aggressively critical of Indian religions. Even the promotion of education of women by the government was believed by many to be a conspiracy to create social unrest. When the income from temples and mosques was taxed, both priests and mullahs promptly raised the cry that their religion was being endangered by the British. As historian Percival Spear writes, the uprising was 'a last convulsive movement of protest against the coming of the West on the part of traditional India'.

Rural Resentments

After a century of Company rule, there was much resentment bubbling away under the surface of villages. High taxes had impoverished farmers and craftsmen. The old landlords had been replaced by absentee owners who lived in cities and did not care for their welfare. During Mughal times, the farmers had been the owners of the land they cultivated but now, they became tenants who could be evicted at any time. The

> **Trains**
>
> *The first railway line was laid between Bombay and Thane in 1853 CE. Soon afterwards, a network of steel was laid across the Indian landscape, connecting remote towns along the length and breadth of the country. Initially, trains created panic among the common people, who had never seen anything like it before. Villagers even ran away at the approach of these rattling and smoking monsters!*

old zamindars were connected to the land and the Mughals often took measures to help farmers during drought or other natural calamities, but the British were only concerned with revenue collection. Some of the worst famines took place during the British period and killed millions of poor people.

The weavers also lost work because they had to buy cotton at high rates and their handlooms were taxed while the Indian market was flooded with cheap British factory cloth. When a kingdom was annexed by the British, the landowning class lost their source of income and their traditional role in the bureaucracy of the kings. In Awadh, for instance, thousands of landowners, called taluqdars, were deprived of their land and their government positions. When the sepoys finally rose in protest, the taluqdars, farmers, weavers and small traders in rural society also rose with them and thus transformed a soldier's mutiny into a much wider uprising of the people of the land.

A Sepoy's Life

A peasant joined the gora paltan to become a sipahi or a sawar (cavalry) since it meant a regular salary and more respect in his village. However the lives of the sepoys, as the British called them, were hardly easy. They were paid less than their British counterparts and could not be promoted beyond the rank of a subedar. There was open racism among the officers, who treated Indian soldiers with cruelty and contempt, which had led to a number of small mutinies before: Vellore in 1806 CE and Barrackpore in 1828 CE. In the words of a British writer, 'The sepoy is regarded as an inferior creature. He is sworn at. He is treated roughly. He is spoken of as nigger.

He is addressed as suar or pig...the younger men seem to regard it as an excellent joke, as an evidence of spirit and praiseworthy sense of superiority over the sepoy to treat him as an inferior animal.'

At Dum Dum

In January 1857 CE, at an army camp in Bengal, a khalasi (labourer) asked a high-caste sepoy for some drinking water and was refused. The khalasi, who worked at the ordnance factory at Dum Dum, laughed and said that soon the sepoy would have to bite into cartridges covered in animal fat. Where would his caste be then? This news spread like wildfire and soon all the sepoys began to protest.

There was also enormous ignorance about the religious beliefs of the sepoys among the European officers. For example, Brahmin sepoys insisted on living and eating separately from the others, but they could not do so when on a campaign. They were also afraid of travel because they feared they would lose their caste but, regardless, these soldiers were sent off to fight in Afghanistan and Burma. When they came back, they were ostracized in their villages because they had crossed the seas. And additionally, these sepoys were often refused additional pay, called 'bhatta', for their duties outside their provinces. There was a growing feeling among the sepoys that their officers did not respect them or their religious beliefs. Also, a large section of the soldiers came from Awadh and in 1856 CE, they were angry at the way Nawab Wajid Ali had been dethroned and exiled by Lord Dalhousie under the Doctrine of Lapse.

Wajid Ali Shah of Awadh

The Immediate Cause

With all the internal resentment waiting to bubble out, all that was needed was a spark for the revolt to start. And it came with the introduction of a new rifle. The Enfield rifle used a cartridge which was covered in a greased paper wrapper. The soldier had to bite off the wrapper before loading the cartridge into the rifle. News spread that the grease being used was cow or pig fat. Since cows were sacred to Hindus and pigs are considered unclean by Muslims both Hindus and Muslims felt their religions were being disrespected. The cartridges were soon withdrawn but, by then, the damage had been done.

In May 1857 CE, soldiers in the Meerut Regiment refused to use the new rifles and ninety soldiers were arrested, court martialled, and sentenced to ten years of imprisonment. On 10 May, the other soldiers mutinied, killed the British officers and their families, released their imprisoned colleagues and then rode off towards Delhi. They crossed the Yamuna River and then surged into the Red Fort, where the aged Mughal king Bahadur Shah II lived a retired life as a pensioner of the British. A reluctant Bahadur Shah II was declared the emperor of Hindustan and the sepoys spread into the city killing any European or Christian convert they could find. The small British contingent withdrew in disarray and Delhi was soon occupied by the rebels.

> *Mangal Pandey*
>
> *The first protest against the greased cartridges was by Mangal Pandey, a sepoy in the 34th Native Infantry Regiment stationed in Barrackpore, Bengal. He fired at his superior officer and asked other sepoys to join him. However, he was soon arrested and executed on 7 April 1857 CE.*

The Uprising Spreads

As the British watched in horror, the uprising spread like wildfire, ultimately reaching Kanpur, where the retired Nana Sahib, the heir of the last Peshwa, was living. Like Bahadur

Shah II, he was swept away by the events and joined the revolt, supported by his retainer Tantia Tope, who led an armed uprising. Next, it spread to Lucknow, where Begum Hazrat Mahal, the wife of Nawab Wajid Ali, came out in support of the rebels as she wanted her young son Birjis Qadar to be restored to the throne of Awadh. In Jhansi, Rani Laxmi Bai, who had been prevented by the British from placing her adopted son on the throne, personally led her army to battle against British troops.

Laxmi Bai and Hazrat Mahal

Two women stand out for their exemplary courage during the uprising. Laxmi Bai, rani of Jhansi, wore armour like a soldier, rode a horse and led her troops herself. She died fighting at Gwalior. One English general described her as, 'the only man among the rebels.' Hazrat Mahal, too, met the sepoys who were laying siege on the Lucknow Residency herself. She later escaped to Nepal and died there. She lies in a nameless grave at the Jama Masjid in Kathmandu.

The rebellion was particularly strong in Kanpur, Jhansi, Bareilly, Arrah, Gwalior and Faizabad. The main leaders were Bakht Khan in Delhi, Nana Sahib and Tantia Tope in Kanpur, Begum Hazrat Mahal in Lucknow, Rani Laxmi Bai in Jhansi, Khan Bahadur Khan in Bareilly and Kunwar Singh in Arrah. In these regions, the British lost control for a while and, in many rural areas, the administration was managed by local zamindars.

After the first shock, when British soldiers and civilians

were massacred in Kanpur and the Lucknow Residency was put under siege, the British quickly rallied. Extra troops were brought in from China and, within a year, the revolt was over. Delhi was occupied again by the British by September 1857 CE and the siege of the Lucknow Residency was raised after five months.

The British reprisals were brutal to make sure no such uprising happened again. Villages were burnt and thousands were summarily executed across the region. Tantia Tope was captured and hanged. Nana Sahib probably escaped to Nepal and was never heard of again. As a matter of fact, for decades, rumours would fly that Nana Sahib had returned to lead another rebellion.

The saddest fate was reserved for the poet-king Bahadur Shah II, in whose name the sepoys had marched out in revolt. Two of his sons and a grandson were captured and summarily shot. The old and helpless king was exiled to Burma, where he died two years later lamenting his fate. As historian Surendranath Sen says, he died 'a plaything of fortune, in a foreign land, far from the country of his ancestors, un-honoured and unsung, but maybe not altogether unwept.'

Lucknow Residency

The British government did not repair the badly damaged Lucknow Residency. It stood, its walls broken and pock-marked by bullet holes, as a reminder to the people of the futility of rebelling against the angrez sarkar. The Union Jack flew over it night and day.

Why the Revolt Failed

If the uprising of 1857 failed within a year, it was because it was not a planned revolution. For a revolution to succeed it needs a centralized leadership that coordinates its efforts but in 1857 CE, there was no single leader who could meet the challenge of a disciplined British response. Bahadur Shah II was old and reluctant, and his sons had no military experience. The sepoys fought with great bravery but there were no experienced generals to guide them. Local leaders rose in sporadic revolt, not knowing how to coordinate their efforts with the others. It was all highly disorganized, without any plans, and with no source for funds and so, the revolt eventually lost steam. The sepoys soon ran out of ammunition and were fighting with swords and spears against soldiers armed with guns and cannons.

> ### Mysterious Chapattis
>
> *During the uprising, bundles of chapattis, balls of atta, red lotuses, packets of gur, saffron flags and coconuts were carried from village to village, often by sadhus and fakirs. Many speculate that people with secret messages carried them as a sort of code of identity but in fact no one knows exactly what message these mysterious gifts were supposed to convey.*

Most importantly, the revolt never became a truly Indian movement. The three presidencies of Bengal, Madras and Bombay remained peaceful. Indian princes in Hyderabad, Kashmir, Gwalior, and the Rajputs and the Sikhs were not keen to see the rise of a Mughal king once again, and remained loyal to the British. The Sikhs had been fighting the Mughals for centuries and Sikh soldiers now defended the Lucknow Residency against the sepoys. Also, the British army was much better equipped, and led by experienced officers. They were led by experienced, battle-hardened generals like Henry Lawrence, James Outram, Henry Havelock, Hugh Rose, John Nicholson and Colin Campbell. The uprising was doomed from the start.

The uprising of 1857 CE can be called a rebellion, but certainly not a revolution. It could never become a true Indian movement because the feeling of nationalism was still absent; no one was fighting for a nation. It was the last flicker of protest by the medieval and feudal classes dispossessed by the new order—deposed royalty, old landowners, religious leaders, and these people were only concerned with their own interests. There was no leader with the vision to create a pan-Indian movement for freedom and no one was thinking of the welfare of the common people.

The middle class had gained much from British rule—an efficient administration, peace after years of wars, modern education, social reforms and regular jobs. They did not support the uprising and the Company babus even held meetings in support of the government in Calcutta and Bombay. However, within decades, this feeling of loyalty would change, and the new leaders of the freedom movement would rise from this class.

Changes after 1858 CE

What the uprising did was draw the attention of the British

government to the misrule of the East India Company. The widespread anger was an eye-opener to the people who believed that they were ruling over a peaceful society reconciled to British rule. The British government knew it had to act. By a royal proclamation in 1858 CE, all Indian territories and possessions were taken over from the East India Company by the British government and Queen Victoria was declared the empress of India. The East India Company now lost both its monopoly over trade and its role as the administrator of India and vanished from the scene. The new governor generals, who were appointed solely by the British government, came to be called viceroys and they were answerable to the British parliament.

Queen Victoria

Instead of supporting social reform, now the emphasis was on public works, with the railways being extended; roads, bridges, irrigation canals being built and colleges being opened for modern education. The government now treated the Indian princes as allies and there were no more attempts to annex any kingdom. Instead, the rajas and nawabs were flattered with fancy titles, invitations to durbars and gun salutes.

There were also changes in the army. Recruitment was now focused on what the British called the 'martial races', the people who had remained loyal during the uprising. These included the Sikhs, the Pathans, the Gurkhas, the Jats and the Rajputs. More Europeans were recruited, all higher posts were reserved for them and the artillery divisions were manned only by Europeans.

For Indians, the uprising of 1857 CE had many quiet and long-lasting results. First of all, it was the beginning of a rudimentary sense of national unity. There was also inspiring religious unity among the Hindus and Muslims during the uprising: Kunwar Singh came to the aid of Hazrat Mahal, Azimullah supported the cause of Nana Sahib. Most importantly, Indians realized that the British were not invincible. When a genuine Indian freedom movement began

Viceroys

There were several viceroys in India between 1858 CE and 1947 CE, with Elgin appearing twice. They lived in great pomp and luxury and were the highest paid government officials in the world. For a while a viceroy was even paid more than the prime minister of Britain!

within a few decades, the uprising of 1857 CE inspired the leaders with the hope that their British masters, no matter how intimidating, could, after all, be defeated.

Chronology of Viceroys

Canning 1856 CE–1862 CE
Elgin 1862 CE–1863 CE
Lawrence 1863 CE–1869 CE
Mayo 1869 CE–1872 CE
Northbrook 1872 CE–1876 CE
Lytton 1876 CE–1880 CE
Ripon 1880 CE–1884 CE
Dufferin 1884 CE–1888 CE
Lansdowne 1888 CE–1894 CE
Elgin 1894 CE–1898 CE
Curzon 1898 CE–1905 CE
Minto 1905 CE–1910 CE
Hardinge 1910 CE–1916 CE
Chelmsford 1916 CE–1921 CE
Reading 1921 CE–1926 CE
Irwin 1926 CE–1931 CE
Willingdon 1931 CE-1936 CE
Linlithgow 1936 CE–1943 CE
Wavell 1943 CE–1947 CE
Mountbatten 1947 CE–1948 CE

To Watch

For a dramatized account of the revolt, check out Aamir Khan's film Mangal Pandey: The Rising *(2005 CE).*

To Read

Ruskin Bond's A Flight of Pigeons, *set in 1857 CE, is about British protagonist Ruth Labadoor's attempts to reach her relatives in the midst of the uprising. Also check out the Sherlock Holmes mystery* The Sign of the Four *which refers to the uprising. For Hindi readers, there's poet Subhadra Kumari Chauhan's popular poem about Laxmi Bai called 'Jhansi ki Rani'.*

5

A SLEEPING GIANT AWAKENS (1885 CE–1909 CE)

~ Rise of Nationalism ~ Naoroji and the Drain of Wealth ~ Birth of the Indian National Congress ~ The Moderate Phase ~ The Radical Phase ~ Partition of Bengal ~ Swaraj, Swadeshi and Boycott ~ The Surat Split ~ The Home Rule League ~ The Muslim League ~ The Morley-Minto Reforms ~ The Revolutionaries ~

The last decades of the century saw a remarkable political awakening among the people as India took its first tentative steps towards true nationhood. The country now had an educated middle class that replaced the old monarchs, the landlords and the traditional priesthood, who had led the uprising in 1857 CE. By the 1880s there was a generation of young men who had been educated in modern colleges, had read the history and political philosophy of the West, and had learnt about the rights of man and about democracy. They had a modern outlook to life and became bureaucrats, doctor, lawyers and academics.

This educated, urban, middle class began to question what the priestly class had been teaching them for centuries. How could India have become colonized when the Brahmins had always claimed the superiority of the Indian civilization? According to the Brahmins, Europeans were supposed to be unclean beings, to be dismissed as mlechhas. Then how could a bunch of mlechha traders come and conquer this supposedly perfect land?

These young men came to the conclusion that the common people had been let down by the ruling class, kings, nawabs and landowners, and misled by its religious leaders. Now they began to seek an answer for themselves and, instead of harking back to the glories of the past, they looked towards progress and a modern future. The historian Percival Spear wrote about late nineteenth century India, 'Beneath the burnished cover of the British administration, the mind of India was actually in ferment.'

Rise of Nationalism

One of the most important results of British rule was that it offered thoughtful, educated Indians another option to the traditional way of life that was dictated by kings and religious leaders. When they began to speak in English, people from different parts of India could easily communicate with each other for the first time. Along with this, modern forms of transport introduced by the British, like the railways and communications by posts and the telegraph, brought people together and slowly, this led to a sense of nationhood.

Travelling by trains had a social impact that few could have anticipated. People began to travel for work and discovered that the gods did not, in fact, curse them when they travelled beyond their villages, and it did not make them lose their caste. Then, in the trains and at their new work places they met people from other regions and could talk to them in English. People soon discovered that they shared many things like festivals, clothes and even food habits. So sharing a samosa and an earthen cup of sweet, milky chai on a train played its part in uniting the country.

This new generation of English-educated, middle-class youth looked around with very critical eyes. First, they felt that Indian society needed to change and then they looked critically at the activities of the government and discovered the many faults of colonialism. Finally, they decided to take their future into their own hands and one of the most exciting phases of the history of modern India began.

Naoroji and the Drain of Wealth

At this time, Dadabhai Naoroji, a social reformer, wrote about how the wealth of the country was being drained away by the British, leading to ever-deepening poverty. The British always projected themselves as 'saviours' of an uncivilized society. Dadabhai Naoroji's book, *Poverty and Un-British Rule in India* created a furore as he showed, with facts and figures, how the Indian economy was being drained of its wealth. He said that the Indian government was the 'lordliest and costliest administration in the world'. Huge amounts, running to millions of pounds, were being sent to Britain as 'home charges' that paid for the salaries and pensions of retired ICS officers.

Around this time, many people were seething in anger at the attitude of superiority and racism among the British. The angrez bahadur lived in separate cantonments, they had their own law courts, clubs, schools and hospitals and even separate train carriages. So, in spite of what the government so piously declared, Indians were an enslaved people and there was no true equality in the country.

There was also a cultural awakening as people began rediscovering India's ancient heritage. As education spread among people, newspapers began to be published in both English and vernacular languages and people started reading articles that were often critical of the government. Gradually, political associations began to be formed. The British Indian Association was the first to be founded in Calcutta in 1851 CE by Surendranath Banerjea. Dadabhai Naoroji began the East India Association; Gopal Krishna Gokhale and Bal Gangadhar Tilak were active in the Poona Sarvajanik Sabha and there were also the Bombay Association and the Madras Native Association.

Indians now began to organize themselves. Banerjea toured the country to protest the government trying to discourage Indians from joining the ICS. Then during the tenure of Viceroy Lord Ripon, the Home Secretary Courtney Ilbert introduced a bill to modify the criminal code and permit Indian judges to try Europeans. There was a huge furore by the Europeans, who started a campaign against it, and the bill was finally taken back. This taught Indians some valuable lessons about the power of political protest and how to organize it.

Birth of the Indian National Congress

Interestingly, the Indian National Congress (INC), which is one of the oldest democratic organizations in the world, was formed at the initiative of the retired British civil servant Allan Octavian

Allan Octavian Hume

Hume. He imagined a political organization that would be a platform for educated Indians to communicate with the government. It was going to be what he called a 'safety valve' for Indian discontent because the last thing the government wanted was another popular uprising like that of 1857 CE. The INC was to be an organization that could be observed and supervised by representatives of the government. It is doubtful that Hume could have foreseen that one day the Congress would lead the struggle to free India from colonial rule.

The Indian National Congress met for the first time at the Gokuldas Tejpal Sanskrit College in Bombay on 28 December 1885 CE, with seventy-two delegates. It chose Womesh Chandra Bonnerjea as its president. Among the delegates were Dadabhai Naoroji, Subramania Iyer, Pherozeshah Mehta, Badruddin Tyebji, Dinshaw Wacha, K.T. Telang, G.G. Agarkar, M. Veeraraghavachariar, N.G. Chandavarkar, Rahmatullah Sayani, M.G. Ranade, P. Ananda Charlu, B. G. Tilak and G.K. Gokhale.

The members of the Congress were very different from the rajas, nawabs and zamindars who had led the uprising of 1857 CE. In spite of the turbans and caps they wore, these were members of the rising middle class. There were thirty-nine lawyers, fourteen journalists and one doctor.

Within a year, the number of delegates had gone up to 436 and it kept rising steadily till a time came when giant tents had to be erected for the meetings.

Dadabhai Naoroji

It was a very modest beginning. The Congress met once a year in different parts of the country. British officials would also attend the sessions and some even got elected as presidents. It also had very modest aims. It began as a platform where leaders from different parts of the country would gather and discuss the problems being faced by Indians. Then they would petition the government, very politely, to help solve the problems, with a long list of demands, and the government would just as politely ignore their requests.

> **Women Delegates**
>
> *There were six women delegates at the 1889 CE session of the Congress. One of them was Kadambini Ganguly, India's first female graduate and a practising doctor, and she addressed the gathering.*

The Moderate Phase

During the first few decades, the Congress was a very moderate organization, which did not question the right of the British to rule India. They were only interested in a greater involvement of Indians in the government, especially in its economic policies, and more Indians being allowed into the ICS. At the same time, they dutifully declared that they had great faith in the justice and magnanimity of the British Raj. They did not think India was ready for independence and no one even dreamt of organizing any protests. As a matter of fact, they usually began their sessions by loyally singing 'God Save the Queen'!

In the beginning, the British were quite favourably inclined to the Congress. This moderate phase, led by visionaries like Gokhale, may not have been very dramatic but it laid the foundations of the freedom movement by slowly building awareness among the people. The core principles of the party were established: equality, secularism, political and social reform and democracy. One day, these principles would be enshrined in the Constitution of India.

In the early years, the Congress consisted of only educated, English-speaking Indians who lived in cities. Its members had very little personal knowledge of rural regions and villages and even small towns were, by and large, unaware of the activities of the Congress. India was very poor, a majority of its people were illiterate, society was divided by caste and the lower castes and women had no rights. The leaders therefore believed

Caste

Initially the Congress was as caste ridden as the rest of the country. At the early sessions, Brahmin members came with their own cooks and lived and ate in separate tents. This was firmly stopped by Gandhiji.

that Indians were not ready for democracy and had to be first educated about human rights. Thus the Congress pushed first for more economic, social and educational reforms.

The Radical Phase

The moderate phase began to wane because despite all their efforts, the Congress failed to get the government to listen to its petitions. In the early years of the twentieth century, the Congress began to move away from its ivory tower years and there was change in the air. Now a new group of leaders rose who began to be called the 'radicals'. They were growing impatient with older leaders who wanted to negotiate with the government. They wanted action, for things to get done. Younger members like Aurobindo Ghose wrote articles in his newspaper *Bande Mataram* calling for action.

The new leadership was led by three dynamic men: Bal Gangadhar Tilak, Bipin Chandra Pal and Lala Lajpat Rai, affectionately called Lal-Bal-Pal by their followers. Tilak was the first Indian leader to realize that no freedom movement could succeed without the support of the masses. So he called for political agitation like strikes and boycotts and mass demonstrations, which would spread awareness of the freedom movement among people. For the first time, the idea of freedom floated in the air as Tilak talked about swaraj or self-rule and said firmly, 'Swaraj is my birthright and I shall have it.'

Tilak and Gokhale were contemporaries and colleagues in Poona but had very different views on the national movement. Gokhale felt that Indians were not ready for self-government while Tilak spoke passionately about swaraj. They became, respectively, the faces of the moderate and radical factions of the Congress.

Partition of Bengal

The radicals soon found their cause. In 1905 CE, Viceroy Lord Curzon issued an order dividing the province of Bengal into two parts—East and West Bengal. On one level, this was a practical decision as the Bengal province was just too big to be administered properly. It included the present areas of Bengal, Bihar, Jharkhand, Orissa, Assam and Bangladesh. Now there were to be two provinces: East Bengal and Assam, with Dacca as its capital, and West Bengal with its capital at Calcutta.

What made it so contentious was that Bengal had been divided along religious lines. East Bengal had a majority of Muslims while the west had more Hindus. The Bengalis, always volatile and vociferous, had been at the helm of the national movement and this was seen as a divide and rule tactic to weaken them, and to attempt to divide them through religion. As Viceroy Curzon said, with his usual arrogance, he planned to 'dethrone Calcutta' and was keen to see the 'peaceful demise' of the Congress. When the province erupted in angry protests against the Partition, he treated it with imperial disdain.

If the government had intended to divide the people, it had the opposite effect. There were demonstrations and public meetings all across the province and the day of the Partition was observed as a day of mourning. The nation observed a hartal, and everything remained closed. In Calcutta, people fasted all day and went out in the streets singing patriotic songs. Hindus and Muslims exchanged rakhis as a symbol of brotherhood.

The 1905 CE protests taught Indians some valuable lessons about how to organize political agitations. The

Songs of Protest

As popular protests and mass demonstrations became common, many poets composed songs that began to be sung by people. Bankim Chandra Chatterjee wrote his anthem to the motherland, 'Bande Mataram'. Subramania Bharati wrote in Tamil, 'The conch shall blow the song of victory. The world shall know that we are free.' Kazi Nazrul Islam, called bidrohi kobi (rebel poet), sang out in Bengali, 'Open your heart—within you dwells all the religions... your heart is the universal temple.'

Rabindranath Tagore wrote the immortal poem that began, 'Where the mind is without fear, and the head is held high.' It was during the 1905 CE protests that he composed the song, 'Amar Shonar Bangla', which is today the national anthem of Bangladesh. With the Indian national anthem 'Jana Gana Mana' to his credit as well, Tagore is the only poet in the world to have written the national anthems of two countries.

Ramprasad Bismil wrote passionately in Urdu, 'Sarfaroshi ki tamanna ab hamare dil mein hai...' (*'Our hearts are filled with the fervour of rebellion...'*) *Subhadra Kumari Chauhan praised Rani Laxmi Bai and wrote in Hindi,* 'khub ladi mardani woh to Jhansi wali rani thi...' (*'She fought so well, our queen of Jhansi...'*)

national movement now became better organized and the involvement of the masses became an integral and essential part of it. The Partition was finally retracted in 1911 CE.

Swaraj, Swadeshi and Boycott

New words now entered India's nationalist vocabulary—swaraj, hartal, swadeshi and boycott. Swaraj was the right to self-rule; for the first time, Indians were talking of a rule by the people and for the people, of a democracy instead of an oppressive colonial rule. Hartal meant strike, where people stopped their daily jobs and life came to a standstill. Swadeshi literally means 'belonging to one's own country'; during this time, it came to mean the campaign against the economic policy of the government that was ruining Indian handlooms, handicrafts and industry. So people were encouraged to use Indian products, wear khadi, or homespun cotton clothes and revive India's economy by boycotting factory-made British goods. Boycott meant rejecting all goods and products that were foreign.

The twin ideas of swadeshi and boycott caught on immediately. The movement spread from Bengal to the rest of the country. Huge bonfires were lit to burn British factory cloth, shops selling British goods were picketed (that is, groups of people would stand outside these shops, protesting) and washermen and cobblers refused to clean foreign clothes or polish imported shoes. Even women began to take part in the protests. The use of khadi clothes became symbolic of nationalism and soon it would become the uniform of the freedom fighter.

The call for swadeshi also encouraged the start of Indian

industries—steel works were founded by Jamshedji Tata, chemical factories were started by P.C. Ray and a steam navigation company was started by V.O. Chidambaram Pillai. Schools and colleges were started by Indians, where a nationalist curriculum was taught, aimed at developing pride in India's civilization. The Bengal National College was started in Calcutta for students who had been expelled from various colleges for joining the Partition protests of 1905 CE. Aurobindo Ghose was its first principal and today, it is the Jadavpur University.

The Surat Split

In 1907 CE, the differences between the moderate and radical factions of the Congress finally came to a pass at the Surat session. Realizing the danger of a split, Tilak and Gokhale tried their best to keep the peace but the hot-headed young members refused to listen. Both factions put up their candidates for the post of the president and the situation soon deteriorated into chairs being thrown around and a shoe being flung at the stage, which hit Surendranath Banerjea. To the delight of the government, the police had to be called in and the session ended in shambles.

This gave the government the opportunity to arrest the radical leaders with the excuse that their writings were seditious, or anti-state. Tilak was sent off to a jail in Burma, Aurobindo Ghose escaped to the French settlement of Pondicherry, gave up politics and became a spiritual teacher. Lala Lajpat Rai and Bipin Chandra Pal withdrew from politics for the time being. Chidambaram Pillai was arrested and faced years of imprisonment and Gokhale, struggling on alone, died a few years later. After the popular protests against the partition of Bengal, suddenly the movement led by the Congress lost all its momentum.

In 1914 CE, the First World War began and the government included India in the war effort without consulting any Indian leaders. As thousands of Indian soldiers fought in the battlefields of Europe and Africa, they realized that the British claims of military superiority were quite hollow. Also, in India, there were widespread shortages and rising prices because of the war, and that led to rising dissatisfaction. But the Congress could not take advantage of this situation due to lack of leadership.

The Home Rule League

When Tilak was released in 1914 CE, he was inspired by the Home Rule movement of Ireland and started the Home Rule League in India. The purpose was to advance India towards self government by educating people about democracy. At the same time, another league was started by a very unusual Englishwoman named Annie Besant. She had come to India to work for the Theosophical Society, an organization that spread the message of Indian religions worldwide. She soon joined politics and eventually became the first woman president of the Congress.

Tilak and Besant merged their activities and soon, the offices of the Home Rule League were operating all across the country. For a while, they were even more active than the Congress. Leaders like Chittaranjan Das and Motilal Nehru joined the League and began to demand that India be given dominion status, like the British colonies of Canada, Australia and South Africa. Dominion status would give more political rights to Indians; they would be autonomous and only nominally under the British crown. But the government was not interested—in fact, Besant was put under house arrest and only released after wide protests. The activities of the Home Rule League soon merged with that of the Congress.

Annie Besant

The Muslim League

Since the defeat of 1857 CE, Muslims had withdrawn from public life as without a Mughal emperor, the Muslim leaders felt they had lost their power. The All Indian Muslim League was founded in 1906 CE by a religious leader Aga Khan, the leader of the Khoja Ismaili community and Nawab Salimullah of Dacca with the aim of petitioning the government in the interest of the Muslims. The League was a very feudal organization, made up mainly of rich landlords and the former nobility and they were very loyal to the government. The government was already feeling threatened by the activities of the Congress, and now welcomed the new organization and offered support.

The Muslim League grew from the fear that if India became independent, Muslims would become a minority in a

Hindu nation. However, many Muslim leaders like Abul Kalam Azad and Mazharul Haque, remained within the Congress. The British were quick to take advantage of this feeling of insecurity and, after years of ignoring the Muslims, suddenly discovered them as allies. Now the government had a weapon to create disunity between Hindus and Muslims in the growing freedom movement. This policy of divide-and-rule would be used till the country was divided into India and Pakistan in 1947 CE.

The Morley-Minto Reforms

In 1909 CE, the government announced the Indian Council Act that came to be known by the names of the then Viceroy Lord Minto and the Secretary of State Lord Morley. By this Act, more Indians were inducted into the legislative councils but they only had an advisory role, and thus, no real power. It was a lukewarm attempt to keep the moderates happy. Continuing with their policy of trying to create a religious divide among Indians, for the first time, Muslims were given separate constituencies where only Muslim

Dominion Status

Dominion status was the political status that had been granted to some of the British colonies like Australia, Canada and South Africa. By this the people of the region ran their own internal affairs. India had asked for dominion status as early as 1908 CE but was always refused as it was only given to countries dominated by the whites.

candidates could stand for elections.

The Revolutionaries

Maulana Abul Kalam Azad

After the swadeshi protests of 1905 CE, new groups of freedom fighters began to be formed, who chose the path of active revolution. Many of the young radical members of the Congress were inspired by the Russian Revolution, which overthrew the autocratic regime of the Tsars and brought power to the people. They believed that only violent protests, and not negotiations, would force the British to leave India. These freedom fighters, often called the 'revolutionaries', were most active in Bengal, Punjab and Maharashtra and started secret societies like the Abhinava Bharat Society that was founded by Savarkar in 1904 CE in Maharashtra and the Anushilan Samiti that was started in 1902 CE in Bengal.

In these societies, members were taught the use of firearms and explosives and their targets were unpopular British officials. Random acts of violent protest had started even earlier when in 1897 CE, the Chapekar brothers assassinated two British officers in Poona and Vanchi Aiyer shot the collector who had sentenced Chidambaram Pillai. In Bengal, Khudiram Bose and Prafulla Chaki threw a bomb at a judge and Jyotindranath Banerjee, or 'Bagha Jatin', died during a gun battle with the police. In 1912 CE, there was an attempt on the life of Viceroy Lord Hardinge when a bomb was thrown at a procession in Delhi.

Revolutionaries were also active abroad. Lala Hardayal started the Ghadar Party in the United States. Rashbehari Bose was active in Japan. Among the others working abroad were Madame Bhikaiji Cama, Shyamaji Krishnavarma, Muhammad Barkatullah and V.D. Savarkar.

These revolutionaries became heroes to the people, although many older Congress members did not agree with their politics. They created a greater awareness about the freedom movement, and taught people to fight back against the British, even with violence if necessary. However, these were individual acts of bravery that failed to start a popular uprising. As it usually happens with militant revolutions, their actions just led to even harsher violence by the government. Most of the revolutionaries were caught, over 200 of them were killed and others were sent to prison.

For a freedom movement to succeed, it has to mobilize the masses. For that, India needed a very unusual leader with a truly unique political strategy. And this leader was about to arrive from South Africa.

The Press

By the early twentieth century there were many nationalist newspapers in circulation, like the Kesari *and the* Mahratta *in Marathi, edited by Tilak; the* Bande Mataram *and the* Amrita Bazaar Patrika *in Bengali; and English language papers like* The Hindu, The Tribune *and Subramania Bharati's* Weekly India.

Elsewhere in the World

The Russian Revolution inspired many freedom movements across the world. It began in 1917 CE and overthrew the regime of Tsar Nicholas II. The revolution was primarily led by workers and peasants. After the revolution, Bolsheviks, led by Vladimir Lenin, formed the Union of Soviet Socialist Republic (USSR).

On the Net

Check out the story of Bhikaiji Cama, who designed the first Indian flag. In fact, the story of how the Indian flag evolved to its modern shape and form, is worth a read.

6

TALKING OF SATYAGRAHA (1915 CE–1930 CE)

~ Gandhiji in South Africa ~ Sabarmati Ashram ~ The Beginnings of Satyagraha in India ~ The Montagu-Chelmsford Reforms ~ Changing the Party ~ Jallianwala Bagh ~ The Khilafat Movement ~ The Non-Cooperation Movement ~ Chauri Chaura ~ The Aftermath ~ The Simon Commission ~ The Purna Swaraj Resolution ~ The Revolutionaries ~ Rise of Communalism ~ Ambedkar and Periyar ~

When the First World War ended in 1919 CE, the public mood in India was a very unhappy one. Indians had loyally supported the British and thousands of Indian soldiers had died in Europe but things had not changed in India. Many promises were made before the war like the Indians were to be given self-rule after the war ended, but, as usual, the government did nothing to honour them. At the same time, people were suffering from shortage of goods and the consequent high prices of food, and many areas were facing a drought. Many of the Congress leaders, like Tilak and Lajpat Rai, were in prison and the dream of freedom seemed very far away. But this was all about to change with the coming of a man from South Africa in 1915 CE.

Mohandas Karamchand Gandhi was forty-six and a successful lawyer when he arrived in India. He had already garnered a reputation as a fighter for civil rights and a political leader. He had led a fight against the apartheid government in South Africa for the civil rights of non-white people. He had been away from India for two decades and now travelled in third class train compartments on a journey of discovery. With his arrival, the history of the Indian freedom movement was about to take a very different turn. Jawaharlal Nehru wrote about Gandhiji's arrival in his book *The Discovery of India:* '[His arrival was] like a whirlwind that upset many things but most of all the working of people's minds.'

Gandhiji in South Africa

By the time Gandhiji arrived news of his very original form of protesting had already travelled to India. He attended Congress sessions and he received a warm welcome especially from Gokhale, who became his friend and mentor. He spoke about the strategy of protest that he used in South Africa, that he called satyagraha. Gandhiji described satyagraha as a struggle for truth through non-violent non-cooperation. After swaraj and swadeshi, now two new words entered the vocabulary of the freedom fighters—ahimsa, or non-violence, and satyagraha. But people were also a bit puzzled. They all believed that a freedom struggle meant facing the police and army of the oppressor. How could such a movement be non-violent?

As a young lawyer in South Africa, Gandhiji had got a taste of the racist policy of the government in the country, where white rulers kept the non-white people separate and

Mahatma Gandhi and his wife Kasturba.

did not give them any rights. They were not allowed to enter many areas like schools, colleges, hospitals, and even drinking water taps were closed to them. They found it hard to be educated or get jobs. This system of racial segregation was known as apartheid. Gandhiji led a non-violent movement in South Africa to give the people their rights as citizens, faced police batons and once, even a lynch mob nearly killed him. He was jailed and made to break stones but that did not break his spirit. General Smuts, the governor of South Africa said to Gandhiji, 'As it is I have put you in prison and tried to subdue you and your people in every way. But how long can I go on like this when you do not retaliate?' Finally, the South African government had to give in to the demands of the protesters.

Now, back in India, Gandhiji decided to use the same system of non-violent resistance, satyagraha, against the British oppressors. Satyagraha was the fight for truth and justice and the weapon of that fight was ahimsa or non-violence. So during a political demonstration, you did not protest by picking up stones, guns or bombs, you did it peacefully. You faced the batons and guns of the police and yet you did not fight back. As Gandhiji kept saying, satyagraha and ahimsa needed immense courage from ordinary people. For it to succeed against a colonial power, the whole nation has to rise up in protest, so that the country comes to a standstill and makes it impossible for the government to function.

Sabarmati Ashram

Gandhiji was both a political leader and a social reformer. He founded the Sabarmati Ashram near Ahmedabad, where he established a commune where everyone was equal. People of all castes and religions, rich and poor, lived together. Everyone had to work, cook, clean, grow vegetables, milk the cows and spin thread on charkhas, which were woven into khadi cloth. Everyone, from Brahmins to the 'untouchables', ate together.

Since he was young boy, Gandhiji had rejected the absurd rules of the caste system. He prayed every day but did not visit temples or perform religious rituals. According to him, every religion had good things to teach us and at his prayer meetings there were readings from the holy books of all religions.

> **Gandhiji's Religion**
>
> *When asked if he was a Hindu Gandhiji replied, 'Yes I am. I am also a Christian, a Muslim, a Buddhist and a Jew.'*

The Beginnings of Satyagraha in India

Gandhiji started with a small satyagraha at Champaran in Bihar. Here he led the farmers to protest against the exploitation by the British owners of indigo plantations. The farmers were forced to grow indigo that was used to dye cloth, over any other more profitable crop and then paid very little. They worked in terrible conditions and were often beaten and thrown out of their homes.

When Gandhiji arrived at Champaran, he was arrested. But when he was taken to court in Motihari, hundreds of farmers gathered outside in protest and a nervous magistrate let him go. Gandhiji surveyed the area and presented a report that forced the government to rule in favour of the farmers. It was here that he gathered his first group of loyal followers—J.B. Kripalani, Mazharul Haque, Rajendra Prasad, Narhari Parekh and Mahadev Desai, who became his secretary. Gandhiji's popularity soared after the Champaran satyagraha. He was the first Congress leader who had actually visited villages and taken up the cause of the poor and it made him a true mass leader.

At the same time, Gandhiji was also taking up social issues. Aside from leading the freedom movement, he was involved in building better relations between Hindus and Muslims. He was also fighting against the caste system and for the emancipation of women. He spoke endlessly for secularism and amity among religions and he also helped Indian crafts people immensely through his support of khadi.

The Montagu-Chelmsford Reforms

In 1919 CE, an act was passed that came to be known after the Secretary of State E.S. Montagu and Viceroy Lord Chelmsford. In the provinces, a few unimportant departments were handed over to Indian ministers but once again, the Congress was disappointed as the real power was still vested in the viceroy and the governors. There was no offer of dominion status or any sharing of governance with Indians. What made the Congress even more worried was an attempt to divide Indians through religion, by offering separate seats not just to Muslims but also Christians and Sikhs. In fact, parties based on religion, like the Muslim League and the Hindu Mahasabha, were supported by the government and encouraged to oppose the Congress.

Changing the Party

Gandhiji understood that unless the Congress became a party of the common people, instead of only the educated elite's, it could not achieve anything. So he brought some radical changes in the Congress. So far it had been a gathering of urban, English-speaking sahibs talking vaguely of reforms, who had no real contact with the rural masses. But Gandhiji travelled the length and breadth of the country constantly, addressing rallies and inviting people to join the party. He was also a master organizer, worrying about everything from budgets to the putting up of tents at meetings. Then he opened the doors of the Congress to everyone by reducing the membership fee to a small amount and soon people from small towns and villages began to join.

Gradually, people began to address rallies in regional languages and national gatherings were held in Hindustani. Finally the Indian National Congress was becoming a people's party and the British government could not ignore it any longer.

Jallianwala Bagh

The political scene changed when the government passed the Rowlatt Act in 1919 CE, which gave the police unlimited powers to suppress protests. Indians were shocked to discover that people could be arrested without warrants and jailed without trial for as long as the police wanted. The Congress announced a hartal and some of the demonstrations turned violent in Amritsar. The army was called in and the military commander, Brigadier General Reginald Dyer, banned all public gatherings.

On 13 April 1919 CE, Baisakhi day, people from nearby villages came to Amritsar to pray at the Harmandir Sahib and visit Baisakhi fairs. Most of them were unaware of Dyer's order. A large, peaceful crowd, including women and children, had gathered in a park called Jallianwala Bagh. Dyer marched in with his soldiers, closing the only exit to the park and ordered his troops to open fire. The obedient troops went on firing till their ammunition ran out. What followed was a horrific massacre where at least 400 people were killed and over a thousand injured. No action was taken against Dyer and for the rest of his life he never uttered a word of regret.

Dyer thought he was saving the Raj by ending political protests forever when in fact he opened the eyes of Indians to the reality of British imperialism. Indians had been told that the British Raj was this benign government, ruling for their benefit, but now they understood they were a colonised nation and that the British had no mercy for Indians. What shocked people even more was that this happened in Punjab, from where thousands of Sikh soldiers had been conscripted and had died during World War I, fighting for Britain. The freedom movement was galvanized, hartals paralysed the country and an indignant Rabindranath Tagore returned his knighthood.

Rabindranath Tagore

The Khilafat Movement

There was anger among Indian Muslims for another reason as well. The Sultan of Turkey was also their Caliph, the spiritual leader of all Muslims. Turkey had supported Germany and had been defeated in World War I. The Sultan had to sign a humiliating treaty

> **Gurudev and Mahatma**
>
> *It was Tagore who began calling Gandhiji a mahatma, a great soul. Bapu returned the compliment and addressed him as gurudev. But Gandhiji was always very uncomfortable with the title of mahatma.*

and lost much of his empire. Two Muslim political leaders in India, the brothers Shaukat Ali and Muhammad Ali began a protest called the Khilafat Movement and the Congress gave its support to the cause, with Gandhiji addressing many meetings. Some Khilafat leaders like Abul Kalam Azad, Ajmal Khan and M.A. Ansari later joined the Congress Party.

The Non-cooperation Movement

On 4 September 1920 CE, the Congress called on India to join a satyagraha as Gandhiji felt that the country was ready for it. Some leaders like Madan Mohan Malaviya and M.A. Jinnah disagreed as they felt that the party was not capable of organizing an India-wide agitation and keep it non-violent. But at the Congress session, Gandhiji's plan got the vote and when Jinnah stood up to speak he was booed off the stage. A furious Jinnah walked out, resigned from the Congress and soon became the president of the Muslim League.

How did satyagraha work on the ground? First the country came to a halt as there was a mass boycott of offices, law courts, banks, schools and colleges. Bazaars shut down, no one bought British-made goods and people stopped paying taxes. Gandhiji's hard work of creating a nationwide network of party offices meant that there were trained Congress workers in towns and villages who organized and led the hartal. The message in all these protests was that India was no longer willing to cooperate with the government and so this came to be called the Non-cooperation movement.

The most dramatic events of this period were the bonfires. Swadeshis encouraged people to wear khadi and all across India foreign cloth went up in flames in giant bonfires. Shops selling foreign goods and liquor were picketed, often by very angry women. The Swadeshi movement was so successful that the sale of Lancashire cloth went down by *half* in one year. When Gandhiji travelled around by train to spread the message of non-cooperation, at railway stations piles of jackets, caps, trousers and shirts would be set alight on the platforms. Often the railway staff would halt the train just to get a darshan of Gandhiji!

For the first time, the Congress had organized a mass agitation across the country and, for the most part, it had remained peaceful. Ordinary, unarmed people showed amazing courage facing police batons, guns and men riding horses carrying spears. Thousands of people were injured or arrested, some only for wearing khadi or singing a patriotic song, and for the first time, women came out and joined the marches. The advantage of satyagraha was that it was a form of protest that everyone could join and they did so by the thousands—farmers, traders, tribals, tea plantation workers and the coolies of Howrah station, who refused to carry goods from trains. C. F. Andrews, a British scholar devoted to Gandhiji wrote about the Non-cooperation movement, 'It is good to be alive these days. The whole of India is aflame.'

Bapu's Fashion

Some students in Madurai complained to Bapu that it was expensive to wear khadi kurtas. So he simplified his fashion ensemble even further to just a dhoti and a shawl: the chhoti si dhoti and the khaddar ka chaddar that is iconic today.

What Gandhiji understood was that imperialism cannot work if people did not cooperate with their rulers. After all, the British were ruling India to make money. Now the government began to feel the effects as no taxes were being paid and people were not buying foreign goods. At the same time, the jails were full of protesters and daily life was paralysed. In November 1921 CE, the Prince of Wales arrived on a tour hoping to revive the spirit of loyalty among Indians. In Bombay, he drove through empty roads and closed bazaars as everyone had gone off to listen to Gandhiji!

A British Gandhian

Charles Freer Andrews (1871 CE-1940 CE) came to India in 1904 CE to teach at St Stephen's College in Delhi. Soon he became a passionate supporter of India's freedom struggle. His friendship with Gandhiji began when he visited Gandhiji in South Africa. Andrews wrote and spoke publicly in support of independence for India.

Chauri Chaura

On 4 February 1922 CE, in the village of Chauri Chaura in the Gorakhpur district of Uttar Pradesh, the people were holding a torchlight procession when they were fired at by the police. An angry mob chased the policemen back to the station and set it on fire, killing twenty-two policemen. Gandhiji, who had insisted on non-violence throughout the movement, was deeply shocked and immediately suspended the satyagraha.

This made many younger leaders like Jawaharlal Nehru very angry as the satyagraha was going very well but Gandhiji was firm in his resolve. He said that satyagraha had to be non-violent and people needed to understand that.

After the Non-cooperation movement ended, Gandhiji was arrested and put on trial. He calmly admitted that he was guilty of breaking the law and agreed that he should be punished severely. He said it was his moral duty to protest against injustice and it was his right to fight for freedom. Also, as his movement had been largely peaceful, the government could not claim that he was leading an armed rebellion. To everyone's surprise, the British judge trying him called him a 'great patriot and a great leader' and said he regretted giving Gandhiji a sentence of six years imprisonment. A smiling Gandhiji left the court an even bigger hero.

The Aftermath

During Gandhiji's imprisonment, some Congress leaders led by C.R. Das formed the Swaraj Party to fight the elections to the provincial assemblies but the party faded away after Das's death. The Khilafat movement also died after the Sultan of Turkey was deposed by Kemal Ataturk and Turkey became a secular, democratic state.

Gandhiji had, rather optimistically, promised swaraj in one year but that did not happen. The greatest achievement of the Non-cooperation movement was that it had created a political awakening among people and united India. It created awareness about the freedom movement even in the smallest of villages and proved to the doubters that a mass movement was possible. Indians lost their fear of authority with ordinary people defying the police peacefully; they forgot their differences of caste and religion and marched together. Swaraj had not come but India was going to fight on.

The Simon Commission

In 1928 CE, the government appointed a commission under Sir John Simon to suggest further action. Both the Congress and the Muslim League immediately rejected this commission as it had no Indian member. When Simon arrived, he was welcomed by black flags and banners saying 'Simon Go Back!' The commission failed and the Congress once again demanded dominion status within a year. It also said that if this demand was not granted, it would start a movement demanding full independence. The government, however, still ignored their demands.

Marching in Pride

There were many attempts to design a flag for India. In 1907 CE, the freedom fighter Bhikaiji Cama, a Parsi lady, presented a flag at a conference in Europe that had green, yellow and red bands with a lotus, the words 'Bande Mataram', and a moon and a sun. The Congress protesters carried a tricolour of saffron, white and green with a charkha in the middle. During the Non-cooperation movement, at a march in Nashik, when their flags were snatched by the police, a band of boys got shirts stitched in the tricolour and marched out in triumph.

Protests against the Simon Commission.

The Purna Swaraj Resolution

When Gandhiji and other Congress leaders were released from prison, the freedom movement began to come alive again. In December 1929 CE, at the Lahore session, Jawaharlal Nehru was elected president and the Congress declared that its goal was Purna Swaraj, or complete independence. By the banks of the Ravi, the tricolour flag of saffron, white and green was unfurled for the first time and 26 January 1930 CE was declared as Purna Swaraj Day. One day we would celebrate it as our Republic Day, when the Constitution of India was unveiled.

The Revolutionaries

As the Non-cooperation movement was suddenly halted

Bhagat Singh

after the events at Chauri Chaura, many passionate young men felt disappointed and turned to revolution. In 1925 CE, Ramprasad Bismil, Jogesh Chatterjee and Sachindranath Sanyal carried out a daring robbery at Kakori railway station in Uttar Pradesh, looting a train that was carrying the railway treasury. During a demonstration against the Simon Commission, Lajpat Rai was hit by a lathi, which left him badly injured and later he died. Bhagat Singh, Shivaram Rajguru and Sukhdev Thapar shot and killed Saunders, the police officer who had ordered the police action. In Bengal, Surya Sen led a daring raid on the police arms depot in Chittagong. Most of the revolutionaries were caught and executed or imprisoned and others, like Chandrashekhar Azad, died fighting.

The revolutionaries became heroes and inspired many people to join the freedom movement. However, like their predecessors, they failed to lead an India-wide uprising.

Rise of Communalism

This was the time when, for the first time, religion began to play a crucial role in politics; parties based on religion, like the Muslim League, the Hindu Mahasabha and the Rashtriya Swayam Sevak Sangh, began to come up in full force. As these parties only cared for the benefit of their own communities, it was to their advantage if they could divide the country around religion. The government now had a new way to sow disunity within the freedom movement and encouraged these parties to spread hatred and fear among people. The plan was to declare that India could only survive as a country under the benign umbrella of the British Raj. Of course, most of these parties were not interesting in the sacrifices of fighting for freedom; they only wanted the power afterwards.

Jinnah

Trained as a lawyer, Mohammad Ali Jinnah worked with Dadabhai Naoroji and began his public life as a nationalist, a liberal and secular man. When he was a member of the Congress, he was hailed as a champion of Hindu-Muslim unity and even defended Tilak against the charge of sedition. When he left the Congress, he was elected the president of the Muslim League and became a passionate Muslim. He was transformed into a demagogue who declared that the two communities could never live together and demanded a separate nation on the basis of religion alone.

Ambedkar and Periyar

The freedom movement also led to a revolution within Indian society. The Congress had always known that a freedom struggle could only succeed in a society that was equal and democratic. That meant that there could be no inequality of gender or caste. From the time of the Non-cooperation movement, women had begun to come out of purdah to join the struggle. At the same time, leaders were speaking out against the disgraceful caste system.

Gandhiji began his campaign against the caste system and 'untouchability' at his Sabarmati Ashram, where people of all castes lived together. He called the lower castes harijans, or the people of God, and led satyagrahas at temples that barred the lower castes from entering. In South India, E.V. Ramaswamy Naicker, popularly called Periyar, started the Self-respect Movement, which encouraged a society where the backward classes could gain equal rights and self-respect.

Another towering social reformer was the extraordinary B.R. Ambedkar, who championed the cause of the Dalits. He himself had faced discrimination all his life. He travelled abroad, got degrees in economics and law, and learnt Sanskrit to prove that nothing in our ancient books said that people should be treated as 'untouchable'. He led satyagrahas at places where Dalits were not allowed, started schools and colleges, published journals and travelled across the land educating people. Ambedkar made Dalits conscious of their rights, and gave them the courage to fight for equality.

Elsewhere in the World

The Ottoman empire ended in 1923 CE and the Turkish Republic was established under Mustafa Kemal Ataturk. In 1924 CE, a new government was formed in China under Sun Yat Sen.

On the Net

Read about the Europeans who supported our freedom struggle and were devoted to Gandhiji. Check out the lives of C.F. Andrews, Hermann Kallenbach and Madeleine Slade, who was called Mira Behn by Gandhiji.

7

A LONG MARCH TO DANDI
(1930 CE–1942 CE)

~ Civil Disobedience ~ Why Salt? ~ The Dandi March ~ At Dharasana ~ The Gandhi-Irwin Pact ~ Round Table Conferences ~ Gandhiji in London ~ The Government of India Act 1935 CE ~ Did the Civil Disobedience Movement Succeed? ~

With the resolution for Purna Swaraj in December 1929 CE, the Congress made it clear that it now wanted independence and nothing else. The time to wait for the British government to offer dominion status was long gone and the two acts of 1909 CE and 1919 CE had disappointed Indians and delivered little. The feeling within the party was that it was time to revive the rebellious spirit of the Non-cooperation movement again and organize a country-wide protest to tell the government that India was no longer ready to wait.

A mass campaign meant it had to be planned very carefully. So the first few weeks of 1930 CE, everyone waited for Gandhiji to guide them towards the new phase of the freedom struggle. The only way to make the government listen was if a majority of Indians came out in a peaceful satyagraha and brought the country to a standstill. The Congress knew it was going to be a mammoth task to make all of India demonstrate at the same time and they also had to make sure that the people kept their satyagraha peaceful.

All through the January of 1930 CE, Gandhiji wandered around Sabarmati Ashram trying to come up with a strategy for the mass satyagraha. He wrote to Rabindranath Tagore, 'I am furiously thinking day and night. And I do not see any light coming out of the surrounding darkness.'

Civil Disobedience

Gandhiji was of the view that the movement that came to be called Civil Disobedience had to go beyond just a rejection of the government and a withdrawal of support. Now the plan was to actively break the law, although in a peaceful manner. Not only was India going to go on a hartal but Indians would also provoke the police into arresting them.

Like in the Non-cooperation movement, schools, colleges, offices, law courts and markets would close, people would refuse to pay taxes or buy foreign goods. Those working in the government, police and army would quit their jobs and then there would be peaceful demonstrations during which an unfair law would be broken. The question was: which law?

It was a time when there were very few telephones, no mobiles, and definitely no email or Facebook; only snail mail—telegrams, postcards and inland letters. So it was not easy to organize a satyagraha. Congress leaders travelled across the country to address people and explain their plans. Local Congress leaders were given precise instructions on how to organize the demonstrations and they had to make sure that the protests were peaceful.

The challenge before Gandhiji was to find a law that could

be broken easily and peacefully by everyone. It had to be a satyagraha that left no scope for violence while, at the same time, involving the maximum number of people. What he finally decided was this: they would break the salt law and refuse to pay the salt tax.

Why Salt?

The idea of breaking the salt law came about from the government's imposition of the salt tax. The production of salt was made a monopoly of the government, which meant no one else could make or sell salt, not even for their personal use. Everyone had to pay a tax to the government when they bought a packet of salt and the government made a neat profit as the tax was eighty times the cost of producing salt!

Gandhiji's plan to break the salt law was logical, since everyone, from the poorest to the richest, needed salt and was therefore affected by the tax. Also, it was a law that would be easy to break. Anyone could make packets of salt and sell them. As Gandhiji explained, 'There is no article like salt outside water by taxing which the state can reach even the starving millions, the sick, the maimed and the utterly helpless. The tax constitutes therefore the most inhuman poll tax the ingenuity of man can devise.'

Gandhiji's plan was that he would walk from Sabarmati Ashram to the beach at Dandi, a coastal village, and pick up salt from the sea shore. Simultaneously, across India, people would break the same law. However, many of the leaders were not sure it would work. After all, the tax formed a very small part of the government's revenue and it would not affect the country's economy. But Gandhiji, with his impeccable political instinct, knew that this tax touched the life of every Indian and therefore, this symbolic act of defiance could mobilize the nation into action. As his friend and comrade C. Rajagopalchari observed shrewdly, 'It is not salt but disobedience you are manufacturing.'

The march from Sabarmati Ashram to Dandi was the finest hour of Gandhiji's efforts to galvanize a nation and inform the world about India's freedom struggle. In today's world of sophisticated communications, it would be considered a brilliant media event. When the world heard of the satyagraha, it was puzzled: why was a man walking for days just to make salt? Reporters began flying in from everywhere to cover the event and it made headlines across the world. Suddenly, people became aware of India's freedom struggle. The British government had not anticipated such an impact. The Muslim League led by Jinnah, however, refused to join, even though they were invited, and so the movement became a Congress show.

> ### *The Plan*
>
> *Gandhiji explained how the salt satyagraha would work: 'Supposing ten men in each of the 7,00,000 villages in India came forward to manufacture salt and to disobey the Salt Act, what do you think this government can do?'*

Gandhiji began the campaign by writing a long letter to the then viceroy, Lord Irwin, that began with a courteous, 'My Dear Friend' and went on to make a list of demands. He wanted the government to reduce land tax by half, prohibit the sale of liquor, protect India's textile industry against factory-made cloth, abolish the salt tax and release political prisoners. Then he very kindly gave the details of what would happen if the government did not cooperate. Irwin, convinced the satyagraha would fail, did not bother to reply.

The Dandi March

At dawn on 12 March 1930 CE, Gandhiji and seventy-eight members of the Sabarmati Ashram marched out to the serenade of bhajans. They could have taken a bus or a train to Dandi, instead they walked for twenty-five days covering 400 kilometres. They would start marching at dawn, stop at one village for the afternoon, start walking in the evening again and spend the night at the next one. Since they had no idea how the government would react to their protest, when they began their march they all said their goodbyes to their families as they were not sure they would come back alive.

The marchers represented a cross-section of Indian society—students, teachers, weavers, mill workers, leather workers, businessmen,

Be Not Afraid

Jawaharlal Nehru wrote about what Gandhji achieved through the satyagraha, 'The essence of his teaching was fearlessness...not merely body courage but the absence of fear from the mind... The dominant impulse in India under British rule was that of fear, pervasive, oppressing, strangling fear; fear of the army, the police...against this, Gandhiji's quiet and determined voice was raised: Be not afraid.'

Mahatma Gandhi walking to Dandi.

Food for the Marchers

Gandhiji's instructions went to every village on the way by postcard: 'Morning before departure—rab and dhebra; the rab should be left to the party itself to prepare. Midday—bhakri, vegetables and milk or buttermilk. Night—kichadi with vegetables and buttermilk or milk.' (Rab is a sweet soup made of wheat flour, jaggery and ginger. Dhebra is a chapati of mixed flour flavoured with fenugreek. Bhakri is also a chapati flavoured with cumin seeds and ghee). Gandhiji himself had only goat's milk, raisins, dates and three lemons.

scientists, medical students, a postman, a bhajan singer, Gandhiji's son Manilal and grandson Kantilal. The youngest marcher was a sixteen-year-old student called Vitthal Thakkar and the oldest was sixty-year-old Gandhiji. In fact, he walked faster and with greater stamina than many of the other marchers. The irony was that he had not taken salt in his food for years!

Every detail of the march had been planned through innumerable postcards to the villages on the route. In these postcards, there were detailed instructions on the food to be prepared, the shelters to be built and the times of arrivals and departures. At every village, Gandhiji addressed the people talking of social issues like the importance of hygiene, Hindu-Muslim amity, the education of girls and the equality of Dalits, besides the satyagraha.

In the growing summer heat Gandhiji walked on, carrying his tall walking stick along dusty village tracks where people sprinkled water and laid leaves on the rough ground. They built arches with the tricolour flag to welcome him and women sat by the road spinning at charkhas and singing bhajans. The crowd following them grew and grew until it was like a river of white weaving its way across the Gujarat landscape. And they were followed by reporters and photographers from the world press—the Dandi March had now become a world event.

The government could only wait and watch, they could not arrest Gandhiji as during the march no laws had been broken. Irwin had optimistically hoped that a sixty-year-old Gandhiji would fall ill and abandon the march instead he was as fit and energetic as ever. As he said with a laugh, 'Less than twelve miles a day, in two stages with not much luggage—child's play!'

The marchers arrived at the sea shore at Dandi on 6 April 1930 CE. Gandhiji picked up a handful of sea salt from the shore and the salt satyagraha was on. The government had tried to remove all the salt from the seashore at Dandi, but it didn't matter. When the sandy salt had to be sold, in all the commotion no one could hear the soft-spoken Gandhiji so it was auctioned off for ₹1,600 by his secretary Mahadev Desai, who had a very loud voice.

All across India, people who lived by the sea walked to the seashore to produce salt, and others sold packets of salt. People picketed shops selling foreign goods and liquor shops. All educational institutions, offices and bazaars remained closed. Gandhiji was, of course, arrested and soon the prisons were filled by almost 90,000 freedom fighters. Life came to a standstill as the movement spread across the Indian subcontinent. In the mountains of the North-west Frontier Province, the Pathans who were called Khudai Khitmadgar, or servants of God, were led by Khan Abdul Gaffar Khan, popularly called 'Frontier Gandhi'. In Nagaland, a thirteen-year-old princess Rani Gaidinliu led the protests. She was

Nehru on the March

'Many pictures rise in my mind of this man, whose eyes were often full of laughter and yet were pools of infinite sadness. But the picture that is dominant and most significant is as I saw him marching, staff in hand, to Dandi... Here was the pilgrim on his quest of truth; quiet, peaceful, determined and fearless, who could continue that quest and pilgrimage regardless of consequences.'

jailed in 1932 CE and Jawaharlal Nehru went to meet her. She was only released in 1947 CE, when India became independent.

The government responded with rage. Freedom fighters were beaten with batons, fired at with guns and tortured in prison; villagers had to abandon their homes; nationalist newspapers were banned and even women and children were beaten and arrested. What was extraordinary was that, in spite of the police brutality, at most places the satyagraha remained peaceful. For Indians, the image of the British being a mai-baap government, that took care of its poor, uncivilized, brown subjects like a parent, was finally and irrevocably shattered. But this time the world was watching. Reports and photographs of the brutality of the government against peaceful, unarmed protestors were published in newspapers across the world and this ruined the British government's self-proclaimed image of being the kind and benign rulers of India.

The Civil Disobedience movement achieved two very important things. First, it gave Indians the confidence that they could defy the British and succeed. Second, it was a moral victory for Indians because now the world knew the reality of the colonization of India.

At Dharasana

The satyagraha at the Dharasana Salt Works in Gujarat was the perfect example of a peaceful non-violent protest. By then Gandhiji had been arrested, so the demonstration was led by Sarojini Naidu. The factory was surrounded by barbed wire and guarded by policemen carrying rifles and steel-tipped sticks. As groups of satyagrahis calmly walked up to the barricades to enter the factory, the police came down on them with violence. As men fell bleeding to the ground, women ran up to help them away to a first-aid station and another group took their place. All that could be heard was the thud of sticks landing on bodies and the cries of pain but *no one* picked up a stone or hit back.

Sarojini Naidu

This horrific scene of brutality was reported by American reporter Webb Miller who wrote, 'Not one of the marchers even raised an arm to fend off the blows... In eighteen years of my reporting, in twenty countries, during which I have witnessed innumerable civil disturbances, riots, street fights and rebellions, I have never witnessed such harrowing scenes as at Dharasana.' As Gandhiji had always said, satyagraha was not for the coward, it needed endless courage.

The Gandhi-Irwin Pact

Even after many of the primary leaders, like Sardar Patel, Gandhiji and Nehru, had been arrested, the protests did not stop. What made the government nervous was that the movement had spread to villages and the government feared that it would also affect the bureaucracy, army and the police. Finally, in early 1931 CE, Lord Irwin invited Gandhiji for talks. Gandhiji travelled straight from Yerwada Jail to walk up the

Jawaharlal Nehru

steps of the brand new Viceregal Palace in New Delhi. All Indians realized the significance of the scene: this was the first time that the Congress, representing a colonized people, and the British Raj were meeting as equals.

The agreement that followed is called the Gandhi-Irwin Pact. The government now bent a little and allowed peaceful picketing, the manufacture of salt for personal use and promised to release all political prisoners. Meanwhile in 1930 CE, a Round Table Conference had been held at London, which the parties representing various communities such as the Muslim League, Hindu Mahasabha and the heads of the princely states, had attended. It had failed as the Congress, who truly represented Indians as a whole, was missing. In this meeting, Gandhiji agreed to attend the second conference to be held for further discussions.

Round Table Conferences

There were three Round Table Conferences held in London between the British government and the Indian leaders. Most of the delegates went there as representatives of their own communities—Muslims, Sikhs, Christians, Dalits, and so on. There were also the maharajas and nawabs and even tea planters and Anglo-Indians. In these conferences, the government was not even interested in discussing dominion status and it did not help that the other Indians leaders spent their time squabbling about the benefits to their own communities, such as reserving seats in the legislatures. None of them was interested in the hard task of winning freedom; they just wanted a share of the spoils. As for the Indian princes, all they wanted was to hold on to their kingdoms and none of them had the courage to defy the government. The only positive result that came out of these conferences was the passing of the Government of India Act of 1935.

Sardar Vallabhbhai Patel

Gandhiji in London

In 1931 CE, Gandhiji travelled by ship to attend the second Round Table Conference at London. In Britain, as soon as he landed, he was followed by reporters everywhere, further proofs of how the Civil Disobedience movement had captured the attention of the world. He addressed many meetings but the most interesting was the one to the workers at the textile mills of Lancashire. These workers were facing a difficult time because the khadi campaign had led to a huge fall in the sale of factory cloth in India. However, despite this, Gandhiji's persuasive speech was welcomed with applause.

Gandhiji was invited to tea by King George V and, to the horror of the British, he went to Buckingham Palace in his usual ensemble of dhoti, chappals and shawl. When he was asked if he was inappropriately dressed to meet a king, he replied with his toothy grin, 'The king had enough [clothes] on for both of us.' There was a subtle message being conveyed through these words; he was not an obedient subject meeting his king. He was the representative of a colonized country fighting for freedom and he was not going to bow down to anyone.

At every opportunity, Gandhiji used the press to get his message across to the people. On another occasion, one reporter asked him, 'Mr Gandhi, what do you think of Western civilization?' Gandhiji nodded solemnly and replied, 'That would be a good idea.' For centuries, Western countries had treated Asians as barbarians and Gandhiji was reminding them gently that our civilizations were much older.

As nothing of substance was achieved at the Second Round Table Conference, Gandhiji came back and the satyagraha was resumed. He was arrested again soon afterwards, along with most of the other leaders, and because of police terror, gradually the protests began to slow down. The satyagraha was finally withdrawn in 1934 CE.

The Government of India Act of 1935 CE

By the Act of 1935 CE, now the people of each province would elect their own government. Each province would have its own legislature, like the vidhan sabhas we have now, and the political party which won the largest number of seats would form the government. However, this was not true democracy as very few people got the right to vote; in fact, just 14 per cent of the people could do so.

Also, the real power still remained in the hands of the viceroy and his all-British Executive Council, who controlled 90 per cent of the budget. In the beginning, the Congress rejected the Act, but later they decided to fight the elections. In the 1937 CE elections, the Congress swept the polls, forming governments in seven out of eleven provinces and coalition ministries in two more. The Muslim League, which claimed to represent all Muslims, contested 482 seats and won only 109, doing badly even in Muslim majority areas of Punjab and Bengal.

First-time Ministers

The Congress ministers were entitled to ₹2,000 but took only ₹500 as their salary. They travelled third class in trains. In spite of having very little power, many of them worked hard to start education and health-care programmes and tried to help poor farmers and factory workers.

Did the Civil Disobedience Movement Succeed?

The Civil Disobedience movement did not win independence for India but it did achieve a lot. First of all, it made the British realize how powerful the freedom movement had become and how it had now reached every corner of the country. There was also growing anger among the government servants, the army and the police. For instance, the soldiers of the Royal

Garhwal regiment refused to fire at a peaceful demonstration in Peshawar. The soldiers faced court martial and went to jail for their courage. That was why Lord Irwin invited Gandhiji for talks and even the Buckingham Palace opened its doors to him.

Till now, the Western press had not taken the Congress seriously and the British press seldom covered protests in India. However, when reporters came to India to cover the Dandi March, they realized that this was a genuine mass movement and the possibility that Indians would one day win freedom was very real. And if they did, they would be the first colonized Asian country to do so. In the United States, which had also fought for freedom against the British, there was a growing popular support for India's freedom fighters.

What made the world sit up was that India's freedom struggle was such an unusual one. It was non-violent when most successful revolutions, like the ones in France, United States and Russia, had been violent. The world was amazed at the courage and discipline shown by ordinary people against the terrorism of the government. It proved that satyagraha was an effective tool of protest. Also, it finally destroyed the colonial myth that the British ruled India with kindness and generosity for the welfare of Indians.

The two satyagrahas of 1920 CE and 1930 CE gave India courage and people no longer feared the police and the army. Men, women and children, the rich and poor, people from towns and villages were now part of the movement. Even more importantly, Indians once again became proud of their own culture and civilization. Taking to the streets, carrying the tricolour, singing patriotic songs and bravely facing police lathis gave them back their self-respect. They were not afraid anymore and they were not going to give up.

Indians finally realized that Western civilization was not superior, that imperialism was morally wrong and that they had the right to demand freedom. The Civil Disobedience movement had been a mental battle as well as a physical movement, between the powerful Raj and ordinary, unarmed people. To the amazement of the world, the people made the Raj step back and listen to them. After 1930 CE, Indians knew with certainty that one day they would be free.

Elsewhere in the World

Europe was still recovering from the First World War when, with the rise of the Nazi Party in Germany led by Adolf Hitler, the clouds of war gathered again. The Second World War would start in 1939 CE and this time, the conflict would spread to Asia.

To Watch

Watch Richard Attenborough's film Gandhi *(1982 CE) for a beautiful depiction of the Civil Disobedience movement. Also check out Shyam Benegal's* The Making of the Mahatma *(1996 CE) about Gandhiji's years in South Africa. And, of course, watch Sanjay Dutt-starrer* Lage Raho Munna Bhai *(2006 CE) for a hilarious depiction of 'Gandhigiri' in real life!*

8

THE FINAL MARCH TO FREEDOM

(1942 CE–1947 CE)

~ The Idea of Pakistan ~ The Princely States ~ World War II and the Cripps Mission ~ The Quit India Movement ~ The Azad Hind Fauj ~ The Cabinet Mission ~ Independence and Partition ~

The British had always tried to prove that India was not a nation; that it was divided by religion, caste, warring rulers, and even language and culture; and that the Raj was the glue that held it all together. The message was that if the British left, it would all fall apart. With the start of the Second World War, as the British faced challenges at home and abroad, their policy of creating dissensions among Indians continued and the sad fact is that many Indians joined them in this divisive political game.

The rajas and nawabs, for example, were not interested in an independent India and the communal parties were busy trying to get their narrow demands met, playing into the government's hands. Gandhiji once described the freedom struggle as a battle between 'three mighty conflicting forces

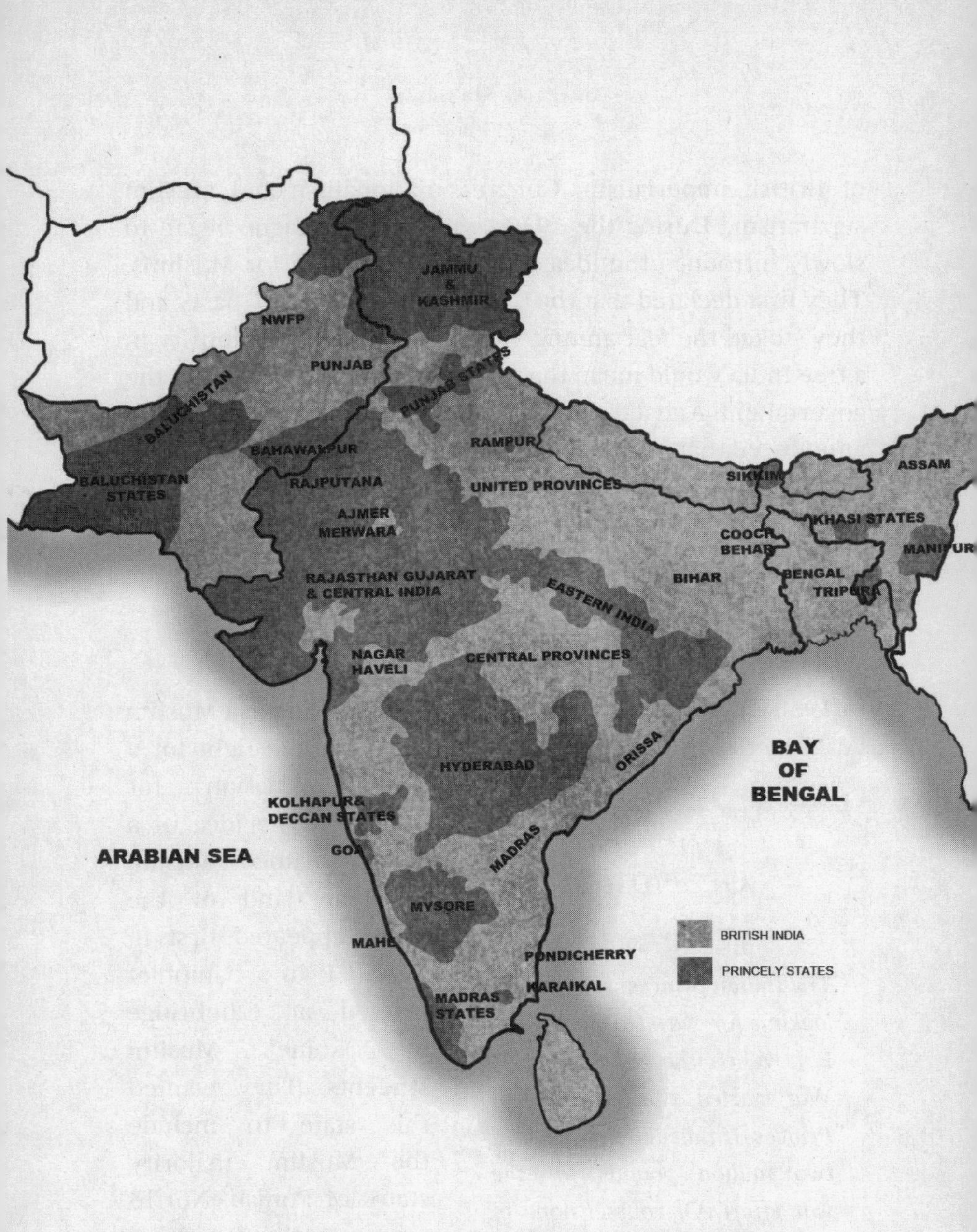

A map of India with the princely states in 1947 CE.

of British imperialism, Congress nationalism and Muslim separatism.' During the 1930s, the Muslim League began to slowly introduce the idea of a separate nation for Muslims. They first declared that the Congress was a 'Hindu' party and they stoked the fear among Muslims that being a minority in a free India would mean that they would not have a say in the government. And it didn't help when Hindu communal parties announced that in an independent India, Muslims would have to live like second class citizens. They only reinforced the fear among Muslims and made Jinnah's message even more effective.

The Idea of Pakistan

In 1930 CE, the poet Muhammad Iqbal, speaking at a Muslim League session, suggested that the party should fight for a separate nation for Muslims. The idea of a country named Pakistan (or, the land of the pure) appeared first in 1932 CE in a pamphlet printed at Cambridge by some Muslim students. They wanted this state to include the Muslim majority states of Punjab, North-west Frontier Province, Kashmir, Baluchistan and Sind. However,

> **Princely Generosity**
>
> *The Indian princes were always looking for ways to please the Raj. When the Second World War started, the Assembly of Princes immediately pledged two million pounds for the war effort. Of course, none of them supported the freedom movement.*

Bengal and Hyderabad, both of which had large Muslim populations, were not included.

Mohammed Ali Jinnah

Jinnah was initially quiet on the demand for a separate Muslim state. Then in the elections of 1937 CE, the Muslim League fared very badly. Jinnah was keen to form coalition governments with the Congress in some of the provinces but the Congress, which had won majorities, did not show much interest. This was the point at which Jinnah embraced the idea of a separate Muslim nation and suddenly, 'Pakistan' entered into the vocabulary of Indians. Then Jinnah began to campaign aggressively, banking on the Muslim fear of being the minority to make them feel insecure about living in a free India. This campaign was very successful. He was, after all, a brilliant speaker and political organizer, and he now declared that not just Muslims but Islam itself was in danger and called on all Muslims to unite behind the Muslim League.

During his Congress days, Jinnah had been hailed as a champion of Hindu-Muslim amity. At political meetings, he used to be heckled by mullahs because of his views. But when he quit the Congress (because the party supported Gandhiji instead of him) and became the president of the Muslim League, there was a complete reversal of his views. Jinnah suddenly became a devout Muslim, changed his natty suits for a sherwani and fur cap, and soon he was the master of divisive politics.

Jinnah now unveiled his 'two-nation theory' and, tapping into the faith of Muslims, he declared that 'a vote for the League and Pakistan was a vote for Islam'. It is India's tragedy that many Muslims believed him and the campaign was successful. When Iqbal had introduced the idea of Pakistan in 1930 CE at Lucknow, there were seventy people in the audience. In the Lahore session in 1940 CE, over a lakh people applauded Jinnah as he declared that the Muslim League would only be satisfied with a separate nation. By the next elections, in 1946 CE, the League had a much larger share of the Muslim vote. When respected leaders like Maulana Azad and Khan Abdul Ghaffar Khan rejected the idea, Jinnah declared that they were traitors to the Muslim cause.

The Princely States

At the time, British India was divided into the eleven provinces that were ruled by the viceroy and 562 princely states, ruled by rajas, maharajas, nawabs and a nizam. Some of these princely states were very large, like Kashmir and Hyderabad, and some were so small that they were really zamindaris of a few villages. Of course, these kings were all powerless puppets who only ruled at the pleasure of the Raj, offering their allegiance to Britain.

At one time, kings took greater care of their subjects because if they did not, the subjects would rise in rebellion. But now, as the rulers were protected by the British army, they had no fear of losing power. So they spent extravagant lives while their subjects lived in abject poverty. In many ways, the living conditions of people were better in British India, as there was an efficient administration as well as the rule of law and proper education and health-care systems.

The princes did their best to stop the Congress from spreading nationalistic ideas in their kingdoms. Younger Congress leaders like Subhas Chandra Bose and Jawaharlal Nehru were keen to enter the political arena of the princely kingdoms as they were outraged by how the princes had supported the government during the Round Table Conferences and sabotaged their efforts to gain self-rule. The people in these kingdoms were also keen to get involved in the freedom movement despite the attempts from their kings to keep them away, and soon political organizations began to spring up here.

World War II and the Cripps Mission

If the Congress believed that the government in any way respected the wishes of the Indian people, this illusion was broken when the Second World War began in 1939 CE. In this war, Britain and France were fighting Germany led by Adolf Hitler, allied with Italy. As they had done in 1914 CE, the Indian government immediately joined the war. Again, no Indian

> **Gaekwad**
>
> *A rare enlightened ruler was Sayajirao Gaekwad, the maharaja of Baroda who set up schools and colleges and granted scholarships. Among the students given scholarships was the young B.R. Ambedkar, who used it to go abroad to study.*

political party was consulted. The irony was that India was fighting in a war that was supposedly in defence of freedom and democracy while it still remained a colony.

The Congress ministers in the provinces and members of the provincial assemblies resigned in protest of India's involvement in the war, but the Muslim League did not do so. In fact, the day the Congress ministers resigned, the League gleefully celebrated it as the 'Day of Deliverance'. This immediately made Jinnah a loyal ally of the government and from then on, the government did all it could to appease the Muslim League. Meanwhile, Congress leaders went on individual satyagrahas by giving anti-war speeches and many of the leaders were arrested.

By 1942 CE, the war scenario had changed and it was not going in Britain's favour. Japan had joined Germany and had swept through the British colonies of Singapore and Burma and reached the borders of India. After American troops were attacked by Japan at Pearl Harbour, the US had also joined the war on the side of the Allies, that is, the British and the French. This helped the freedom struggle because the Americans supported India and urged the government to end the stalemate with the Congress.

In March 1942 CE, Sir Stafford Cripps led a mission to India to decide India's future. However negotiations broke down as the British only offered India dominion status after the war. By then, the Congress was only interested in an immediate and complete transfer of power to Indians. Also, the Cripps offer left it to the provinces and the princely states to decide whether they wanted to join the Indian union or not. This would have inevitably led to the princes and the Muslim League staying away, and the Congress rejected the offer.

The Quit India Movement

The Cripps Mission had raised a lot of hopes and the Congress was deeply disappointed at its failure. On 8 August 1942 CE, at the session in Bombay, the Congress passed a resolution asking the British to leave India immediately. Gandhiji, speaking from the podium, declared, 'I am not going to be satisfied with anything short of complete freedom... Here is a mantra, a short one that I give you. You may imprint it on your hearts and let every breath of yours give expression to it. The mantra is, do or die. We shall either free India or die in the attempt.'

Next morning, all the Congress leaders were promptly arrested and the Congress was banned. The government thought it had nipped the problem in the bud but what followed was an unprecedented popular uprising across India. There were no leaders to guide the people but they spontaneously poured out into the streets in protest. Every symbol of British rule, from offices to railway and police stations, were attacked. In some areas, the locals took over the administration and the government lost control. A new group of young leaders now came forward to lead the protests.

> *People Power*
>
> *Local governments led by people called jatiya sarkars ran places like Ballia (Uttar Pradesh), Darbhanga (Bihar), Satara (Maharashtra), Dharwar (Karnataka), Balasore (Orissa) and Nandigram (Bengal).*

Though initially taken by surprise, the government

responded swiftly with ruthless and violent repression, with the police and army firing at the demonstrators. There are no official records, but thousands were injured or killed. Viceroy Lord Linlithgow later admitted that it was 'the most serious rebellion since 1857 CE, the gravity and extent of which we have so far concealed from the world for reasons of military security.' The protests were unplanned and leaderless and faced such brutal repression that it began to slow down. By September 1942 CE, the movement had waned but the government was shaken at how widespread the upsurge had been.

The Azad Hind Fauj

At this time, Indians were also breathlessly watching the adventures of Subhas Chandra Bose. Once among the young leaders of the Congress Party, he had left the Congress in 1939 CE after a disagreement with Gandhiji and had formed a new party called the All India Forward Bloc to follow a more radical policy. As he was planning protests in Bengal, he was arrested, first imprisoned and then put under house arrest. In 1941 CE, he had escaped from house arrest in Calcutta and managed to reach Germany, where he planned to take the help of the axis powers (Germany, Italy and Japan) against the British. Meanwhile, Rashbehari Bose and Captain Mohan Singh had formed

> **Rani Jhansi Battalion**
>
> *In the INA, there was a women's battalion called 'Rani Jhansi', led by Captain Lakshmi Swaminathan (later Sehgal).*

the Azad Hind Fauj or the Indian National Army (INA) to fight for India's freedom. The INA had been formed with the Indian soldiers who had been prisoners of war captured by the Japanese army and they invited Bose to lead it.

Bose arrived in Japan in 1943 CE and declared the formation of the Azad Hind (Free India) government and gave the battle cry of 'Dilli Chalo!' The INA fought the British army in Burma and reached as far as Kohima in north-east India. Then in 1945 CE, the fortunes of war changed as Germany surrendered in Europe. The Japanese began to withdraw and soon afterwards, surrendered when the United States dropped atom bombs on the cities of Hiroshima and Nagasaki. It is believed that Bose died in a plane crash on his way from Bangkok to Tokyo and the INA soldiers had to surrender as well.

In 1945 CE, three of the INA officers—Gurbaksh Singh Dhillon, Shah Nawaz Khan and Prem Sehgal—were put on trial for treason and the country erupted in anger. They were defended by a team of lawyers led by Bhulabhai Desai, Tej Bahadur Sapru and Jawaharlal Nehru and even though they were found guilty, because of the popular mood, their sentences were remitted the following year.

The Cabinet Mission

By 1946 CE, the war was over and there was growing unrest in India, which was now spreading into the armed forces and government departments. Sailors of the Indian navy mutinied in February and there were strikes in the army and air force. Labour protests shook the railways, the post and the telegraph departments. Then, to everyone's surprise, the conservative party led by Winston Churchill, who had always vehemently resisted all attempts to give India independence, lost the elections in Britain. The new Labour government, led by Clement Attlee, was much more open to the idea of independence for India.

The Cabinet Mission, led by Lord Pethick-Lawrence arrived in India in March 1946 CE. Its objective was to discuss the transfer of power from the British government to the Indian leaders. One of its proposals was the formation of a Constituent Assembly to draft a constitution for India. An interim government was to run the country while the constitution was being drafted. When the Congress agreed to form the interim government, the Muslim League began to protest and announced Direct Action Day on 16 August 1946 CE, which led to widespread communal violence, especially in Calcutta.

Jinnah was still adamant on his demand for a separate nation for Muslims. The Indian princes were not interested in joining the Indian union. As the country watched with bated breath, Gandhiji held a series of talks with Jinnah trying to convince him that a division of the country would be a mistake but failed. Whatever proposals were made by the government or the Congress were rejected by Jinnah, who kept up the threat of a civil war, and further communal violence, if his demands were not met.

A deeply disappointed Gandhiji withdrew from the talks and left the negotiations to leaders like Azad, Nehru and Patel. Instead, he went to Noakhali in Bengal, which had been the worst affected by the Direct Action Day riots, walking from village to village, urging people to be peaceful. Finally the Congress had to agree to a division of the country. In July

1946 CE, elections were held for the Constituent Assembly. The Congress swept the polls while the League did well in the reserved Muslim seats. Jinnah once again refused to cooperate with the Assembly.

Independence and Partition

The process of Independence and Partition was, by no means, smooth. Jinnah kept using the threat of violence and civil war to get what he wanted and the British no longer cared as they were leaving the country anyway. The Muslim League turned communal riots into a very effective political weapon and Hindu communal parties were quick to join in. As the country watched helplessly, there were horrific riots in Calcutta, where over 5,000 people were mercilessly slaughtered. Then the violence spread to Bihar and criminals joined, looting and plundering during the riots. Although the riots were encouraged by the Muslim League government of Bengal, Jinnah blamed it on 'Gandhi, the viceroy and the British', and threatened that 'India will be divided or destroyed.'

Finally on 20 February 1947 CE, Attlee announced

> **Radcliffe**
>
> *The difficult task of drawing the boundaries of India and Pakistan was given to a boundary commission led by Sir Cyril Radcliffe. In just five weeks, he drew the boundary across detailed maps of Punjab and Bengal. But, of course, he did not visit any of the regions that he was dividing between two countries; for him it was only a line on the map.*

Lord Mountbatten

in the British parliament that the British government would transfer power into Indian hands by June 1948 CE. At the same time, Lord Mountbatten arrived as the last viceroy of India. But when he arrived in a country that was devastated by communal violence, he decided that power would be transferred to India and the new nation of Pakistan as quickly as 15 August 1947 CE. Pakistan would include provinces with a Muslim majority, such as Baluchistan, Sind and the North-west Frontier Province, and the two provinces of Punjab and Bengal were to be divided. So the new country would have provinces at two ends of the subcontinent, making the perpetually dissatisfied Jinnah complain that he had been given a 'moth-eaten' state.

Historian B.R. Nanda writes about Jinnah's stubborn and destructive ambitions: 'He does not seem to have foreseen the long-term consequences of his campaign. The result was that he managed to achieve just the opposite of his professed aims. He had stressed the need for Muslim unity when, in fact, he was destined to split Indian Muslims. The partition did not solve the communal problem, it only internationalized it. What had been a political debate between rival communities and political parties became an issue between two 'sovereign' states.'

India became free, yes, but under a cloud of unimaginable tragedy. The Congress leaders had hoped to avoid a civil war by agreeing to the Partition but instead, the violence got worse. People living in Punjab and Bengal were forced to move because of the Partition, and, as millions crossed the newly-drawn borders, violence erupted with great ferocity. By some estimates, one million people lost their lives. Not only that, people's lives were uprooted as they moved between countries to start all over again, and it created a bitterness that still effects the relations between the two countries. It has led to three wars and further poisoned the relationship between Hindus and Muslims for generations.

At the midnight hour on 15 August 1947 CE, Nehru was sworn in as the first prime minister of the Republic of India in the central hall of Parliament, which is now our Lok Sabha. This poet-balladeer of the freedom struggle sang an unforgettable paean to his land and its people and said, 'Long ago we made a tryst with destiny and now the time comes when we shall redeem our pledge, not wholly or in full measure, but substantially. At the stroke of midnight hour, when the world sleeps, India shall awake to life and freedom.' He ended his historic speech with these soaring words of

Division of Goods

All the property of the government, including tables, chairs, cars, and even the musical instruments of the army bands, had to be divided equally between India and Pakistan! The problem was that there was only one Viceroy's buggy and so, a coin was tossed and India won. On 26 January 1950 CE, the first Indian President, Rajendra Prasad, rode the horse-drawn carriage on the first Republic Day.

hope and promise: 'To the nations and peoples of the world we send greetings and pledge ourselves to cooperate with them in furthering peace, freedom and democracy. And to India, our much-loved motherland, the ancient, the eternal and the ever-new, we pay our reverent homage and we bind ourselves afresh to her service.'

On the evening of 15 August 1947 CE, crowds surged on the Rajpath as the tricolour was raised for the first time on top of the India Gate. As people watched with delight and excitement, the flag went slowly up the flag pole and then there was a gasp of surprise as suddenly across the monsoon sky, a shining rainbow curved behind the flag like a message of joy. India, free and democratic, a rainbow nation of people, was now on a new journey.

The India Gate at New Delhi.

Elsewhere in the World

India was the first colonized nation to win its freedom in the twentieth century. Soon, one by one, the colonized peoples of Asia, Africa and the Americas would throw out their colonial masters. And our non-violent struggle, Gandhiji's satyagraha, would inspire leaders like Martin Luther King of the United States, Nelson Mandela of South Africa and Aung San Suu Ki of Burma. Time *magazine referred to them as 'Gandhi's children'.*

Monument Visit

If you live in Delhi, go visit the India Gate once again and check out the Amar Jawan Jyoti, or the flame of the immortal soldier, which commemorates all the unknown soldiers who have died fighting for our nation. Then visit the serene lawns of Raj Ghat and stand a moment beside the samadhi of Gandhiji and remember all the leaders of our amazing freedom struggle. Today we are a democratic nation because of them.

9
LIVING IN BRITISH TIMES

~ Changing Indian Society ~ Life of the Sahibs ~ Maharajas, Nawabs and a Nizam ~ Stepping out into the World ~ Three-piece Suits and Mulligatawny Soup ~

To the Indians, the English, or the angrez, were white-skinned, brown- or yellow-haired strangers from a faraway land, and they they were often bemused by the English. Many of the angrez wandered around India, their sweaty faces going red in the sun, asking questions and poking around broken down buildings full of bats and spiders. Many of them learnt Sanskrit and Persian, enjoyed smoking a hookah, chewing paan and riding elephants.

Soon they began to rule Indians and became their mai-baap sarkar, coming to towns and villages as magistrates, judges and policemen. Then the missionaries arrived, and they built not only churches but also schools and hospitals, printed books and helped the poor. For the poor, especially the Dalits, they often seemed kinder than the upper classes and the Brahmin priests. They offered the lower classes a chance for better lives. As a matter of fact, for the common people, the angrez were not always hated colonial masters and, at times, the English magistrates and judges were less corrupt than the erstwhile Mughal officials.

Three centuries of European presence in India, especially that of the British, changed Indian society in many ways. Similarly, India also influenced its colonial masters. However, unlike the invaders of the past such as the Mughals, the British did not merge into Indian society. They lived very separate and segregated lives, mixed little with Indians and ultimately, most of them went back home. The last Mughal emperor, Bahadur Shah II, lived in Delhi, Queen Victoria, who was the imperial head of the British Raj, lived in London and never visited her empire. Many of the British bureaucrats and judges genuinely cared for Indians and did help them but somehow, most of the British men and women who came to India remained distant strangers in the land till the end.

Changing Indian Society

Modern education, the latest technology, the railways, telephones, telegraphs, factories with machines, schools and colleges with a secular curriculum, trained teachers and a system of examination were all a result of British rule. Indian society, which had become mired in superstition and illiteracy, was dragged into the modern world by the British and it led to many changes. There was a gradual weakening of the caste system too—the Dalits now had the opportunity to be educated. Modern education, and later the freedom movement, led to women stepping out from behind the purdah.

The life of the poor—the farmer, the weaver and the labourer—remained full of struggle. The textile industry was ruined, as we've discussed earlier, and weavers were forced to work as farm labourers or as daily wage-earners in cities, living in slums. The rich Indians were not interested in helping the poor and very often, it was the zamindars and the moneylenders who exploited them. As a matter of fact, the people who *did* try to help were British district collectors, who were efficient and mostly honest. After independence, the villagers missed these men who visited them in their sola topis and sat on charpais, listening to the complaints of the farmers. It was because of these men that, in spite of all the angry talk of the freedom movement, the British left India with a surprising amount of goodwill.

Life of the Sahibs

Just as the Indians were changed by their interactions with the British, so were the sahibs and memsahibs influenced by their experiences in India. Although the British lived in India for over two centuries, they led segregated lives and the racial discrimination was open and unapologetic. Every small town had a cantonment area, a gated community where the only Indians were the servants. There were separate schools, hospitals, clubs and restaurants for the white-skinned, and trains had carriages marked 'For Europeans Only'. Even the mixed race of Anglo-

> **Sports Exchange**
>
> *Indians taught the British a Mughal game played on horses using long sticks and a ball called chaugan and the British named it polo. The British, on the other hand, introduced cricket and football to India.*

A game of polo.

Indians had train compartments reserved for them.

The women and children only interacted with their Indian servants and never ventured into the bazaars or invited Indians to their homes. So, in their memoirs, the women would fondly remember the khansama and the mali, and the children, the ayahs, but they never had Indian friends. Life was comfortable but boring for the memsahib, as she had very little to do all day. Then when the summer arrived, they packed up and left for the hills. It was the British who developed hill stations like Darjeeling and Shimla, that were designed like miniature English towns with cottages, shopping arcades, theatres and clubs.

Maharajas, Nawabs and a Nizam

The rulers of the Indian princely states were, in many ways, much worse than their British counterparts. They led self-indulgent lives of luxury and decadence and cared little for the welfare of their subjects. Their time was spent in palaces and trips to Europe, buying expensive cars, jewellery and gambling in casinos. All their efforts were to please their colonial masters. The newspapers in Europe were full of stories of their extravagant lives and huge harems. One Nizam of Hyderabad had four official queens, forty-two begums and forty-four khannazads or 'palace women'.

These rulers were safe on their thrones as long as the Raj survived, so they were fiercely opposed to the freedom movement. For example, during the Round Table Conferences, they did their best to spoil the efforts of the Congress. Gandhiji called the Indian princes 'the greatest blot on British rule in India'.

Army of Servants

One book lists thirty-six types of servants employed in a sahib's household. It included khansama (head bearer), mali (gardener), bawarchi (cook), ayah (maid), dhobi (washerman), harakara (messenger), hajjam (barber), farash (furniture keeper), syce (stable hand) and duria (dog keeper).

Stepping Out into the World

In the nineteenth century, most Indian women never stepped out of their homes. Only poor women went out because they had to earn a living. Most of the women were not educated and spent their lives running their homes, cooking and bringing up children. Women's education began in Bengal

Aruna Asaf Ali

with missionaries opening schools and social reformers like Ishwarchandra Vidyasagar and institutions like the Brahmo Samaj, who encouraged women to study. Then, with the freedom movement, women gathered courage and stepped out to join demonstrations. They have not looked back since then.

Bhikaiji Cama travelled to Europe, worked with Dadabhai Naoroji and designed the first Indian flag. Sarojini Naidu became the president of the Indian National Congress, led protests during the Dandi March and was also a popular poet. Fiery women like Pritilata Wadedar, Bina Das and Kalpana Joshi joined the revolutionaries, threw bombs and shot at unpopular officials. Laxmi Swaminathan joined the Indian National Army of Subhas Chandra Bose and led a battalion; Aruna Asaf Ali led the protests during the Quit India agitation. After independence, Indian women also got the right to vote.

Three-piece Suits and Mulligatawny Soup

The arrival of the Europeans brought about changes in the daily lives of Indians, especially in what they wore and ate. Men who worked in the government offices and British companies began to wear trousers and shirts instead of the traditional dhoti, and the higher officials wore natty three piece suits in imitation of their British masters. As women came out of purdah, although they didn't wear European dresses, they changed the way they wore their saris. The ladies of the Tagore family of Jorasanko were the first to wear the sari with pleats in front and the pallu thrown across the left shoulder, which made it easier to walk. They also introduced the blouse, in the beginning with full sleeves and a high neck, and later with shorter, puffed sleeves. Sarojini Naidu was quite a fashion icon, swishing up on stage in gorgeous Kanjeevaram sarees that proudly declared her love for Indian textiles.

Can you imagine Indians cooking without the green chilly? Well, till the Portuguese brought the chilly to India, we used pepper. The Portuguese had colonies in Mexico and South America and introduced many fruits and vegetables to India that are now part of our daily menus, like corn, potato, tomato, sweet potato, tapioca, peanuts, capsicums, papaya, pineapple and cashew nuts. At the same time, Indians taught Europeans to use spices in their food, and dishes like kedgeree and Mulligatawny soup, mango chutney and curry, are India's gift to British cuisine.

The Memsahib's Table

The British had many courses at meals and the bawarchi had a lot of cooking to do. One book lists a typical breakfast with mutton chops, chicken cutlets, devilled kidneys, egg dishes, duck stew, prawn dopiaza, breads and kedgeree (an English version of our khichdi)!

WHAT HAPPENED AND WHEN

1802 CE–Government House built in Calcutta
1857 CE–The Great Uprising
1885 CE–Founding of the Indian National Congress
1905 CE–The Partition of Bengal
1906 CE–Formation of the Muslim League
1907 CE–Split in the Congress between the Moderates and the Extremists
1909 CE–Morley-Minto Reforms
1911 CE–Coronation Durbar in Delhi, when King George V and Queen Mary visited India and were feted with a grand ceremony at the Red Fort
1913 CE–Gandhiji starts Satyagraha in South Africa
1914 CE–First World War
1915 CE–Gandhiji arrives in India
1915 CE–Annie Besant forms the Home Rule League
1917 CE–Champaran Satyagraha
1919 CE–Government passes the Rowlatt Act
1919 CE–Massacre at Jallianwalla Bagh
1919 CE–Montagu Chelmsford Reforms
1922 CE–Non-cooperation movement begins
1928 CE–Simon Commission arrives
1930 CE–Civil Disobedience and the Dandi March
1931 CE–Gandhi-Irwin talks
1935 CE–The Government of India Act

1937 CE–Elections in provinces
1939 CE–Second World War
1940 CE–Jinnah proposes his plan for two nations
1941 CE–Subhas Chandra Bose escapes from Calcutta
1942 CE–Cripps Mission arrives in India
1942 CE–Quit India Movement
1942 CE–Subhas Bose forms the Indian National Army
1944 CE–Gandhi-Jinnah talks
1946 CE–The Cabinet Mission arrives
1946 CE–Direct Action Day call by Muslim League, riots in Calcutta
1946 CE–Constituent Assembly meets
1947 CE–Lord Mountbatten sworn in as last viceroy of India
1947 CE–House of Commons in Britain passes the Indian Independence Bill
1947 CE–14 August, 1947–Pakistan celebrates independence day
15 August 1947–India becomes independent with Jawaharlal Nehru as prime minister

Section Four

INDEPENDENT INDIA

1
BUILDING A NATION

~ India in 1947 CE ~ Death of the Mahatma ~ Writing the Constitution ~ The First Elections ~ Making the Princely States Join India ~ The Settlement of Refugees ~

On 15 August 1947 CE, Indians celebrated their hard-won freedom with the joyous bursting of crackers, the radio playing patriotic songs and the tricolour flag flying triumphantly from every rooftop. But there were many pessimists around the world who dolefully shook their heads and predicted that it would not last. How could an Asian country of poor, illiterate brown people become an independent democracy, especially one that was so divided by religion, language and caste? They pointed out the many economic and social problems that India faced and the monumental tragedy of the Partition that was still playing out and saw only doom in the future.

We *did* face what looked like insurmountable problems. Over two centuries of colonial occupation had ruined the economy. We had no modern industries and we exported very little. During medieval times, our biggest source of income had been the textile industry and that lay in tatters post the British rule. There was unimaginable poverty and the government could not even provide enough food for the people. Most of the people were illiterate and there was no system of health-care.

Along with that, our society was still a highly unequal one, with the divisions of caste and religion always leading to conflict. The riots before Partition had made it much worse, creating a great divide between the Hindus and the Muslims. The condition of women was also no better—most of them were illiterate and many still lived in purdah. The freedom movement had given some liberties to city women but it had not reached the villages. The lower castes were still exploited, and lived without any hope, doomed to poverty by a cruel society. So the pessimists and the sceptics did have a point.

It was a bleak picture, true. However we also had some hidden strengths. First was the hope and optimism in the air and the determination of our people to face and defeat every challenge. If we could win freedom, we could defeat poverty as well. We were also fortunate to have a group of extraordinary leaders who had the wisdom and foresight to lay the foundations of Indian democracy. They worked with extraordinary passion, unity and a sense of purpose.

These leaders came from different parties, and at times, they held opposing views, but at their core they were patriots and the welfare of the nation always came first. We, both the people and the leaders, were all ready for our tryst with destiny.

India in 1947 CE

What was the country like at the dawn of 15 August in 1947 CE?

Let's start with the villages that had suffered the most

from the exploitation of the imperial government, the landlords and the moneylenders. Agricultural production, especially of food crops, was falling and people had less food available per person. Then there were the famines that devastated the countryside, the worst being the one in Bengal in 1942 CE, which killed three million people. What was even more shocking was that while the poor peasants were taxed, the bureaucrats, the landholders and the merchants were not. As taxes were high, most farmers had to borrow from moneylenders to pay them and often lost their land in the process.

Choosing Ambedkar

When selecting the chairman of the drafting committee for the Constitution, Nehru and Patel could have easily chosen a fellow Congressman, but instead, they chose the man most qualified for the post—B. R. Ambedkar, a man who had often opposed Gandhiji and was no admirer of Congress politics.

The colonial government did little to help farmers. There were few irrigation projects, no modern farming methods were introduced and there was hardly any use of improved seeds or fertilizers. Most farmers still used primitive wooden ploughs and not iron ones and no one had

B.R. Ambedkar

even heard of tractors or harvesters. So the land produced less and less every year. Nearly 82 per cent of the population lived in villages and they were poor and starving. Another source of income in villages used to be weaving and handicrafts but by now, the textile industry had collapsed because of high taxes and the cheap factory cloth in the market.

For the colonial government, India had been only a market for their factory goods so they had actively discouraged the growth of industries. The few industries that were in India were mostly owned by the British. There were factories for cotton, jute and tea, but very few for machinery. India was making sewing machines, lamps and bicycles, but no cars or trucks. In fact, India was importing not just machinery and cars but even small things like biscuits and shoes. So when the British government built roads and laid railway tracks, no one owned a car and only seven train locomotives were produced in a year.

Harvest

In the last fifty years of British rule, the production of food crops went down every year. After independence, with the support of the government, it began to grow at 3 per cent per year.

Between 1940 CE and 1951 CE, the average Indian could expect to live to the age of only thirty-two years. This was because there were no health services in the villages and often people died because of epidemics like cholera and malaria. Most of the towns had no proper sanitation systems and regular water supply was often limited to the areas where the Europeans and the rich lived. Most towns had no electricity and in villages, they had never even seen an electric bulb. No one went to school as there was none in a village and very few in towns. So in 1951 CE, 84 per cent of the population could not read or write and 92 per cent of the women were illiterate.

When India finally became free, our leaders had quite a task ahead of them. They had to improve agriculture or a large part of the population would starve; they had to start industries from scratch so that people could find employment. The older industries like handlooms and handicrafts had to be revived. Schools and colleges had to be opened and girls had to be encouraged to study. Hospitals and health centres needed to be built and doctors and nurses needed to be trained to run them. The Dalits and other lower castes had to be given equal rights, not just by law, but also by giving them a way to fight centuries of exploitation. There was also the problem of refugees, communal violence and the immense task of writing a new constitution.

A Poet's Fear

Rabindranath Tagore died before we became independent but he feared what India will be like when the British left. He wrote, 'What kind of India will they leave behind? What stark misery?'

Now compare this India with the country you live in now and you'll realize how much we have achieved. But we still have a long way to go.

Death of the Mahatma

Gandhiji's death was a tragedy that Indians were unprepared for. Gandhiji was heart-broken by the decision to divide India and so, on 15 August, he was far away from the celebrations in Delhi. He stayed in Calcutta, spending his day in silence and prayers. Then, as people began to cross the borders—Hindus and Sikhs into India and Muslims into Pakistan—communal violence reared its ugly head once again and the army struggled to control it. At Nehru's request, Gandhiji returned to Delhi and he went on a fast and the violence went down.

He was staying at Birla House in New Delhi where, frail, tired and heart-broken, he nearly starved to death. Here, every morning and evening, he held his prayer meetings, where a large crowd gathered. On 30 January 1948 CE, he walked to the prayers leaning on his two 'walking sticks'—his grandnieces, Abha and Manu. A man in khaki clothes came up to him, bent as if to touch his feet and then pulled out a gun and shot him thrice in the chest. With a prayer on his lips, Gandhiji died soon after and life came to a standstill across the country.

The killer was Nathuram Godse, who had been a member of the Rashtriya Swayam Sevak Sangh and the Hindu Mahasabha. He was a Hindu bigot who believed that Gandhiji was against Hindus because he supported equal rights for Muslims. Godse thought he was upholding the cause of the Hindus. What he did was silence the man the country needed desperately at its time of need. The only man who could have taught India to live in religious harmony and may be helped us avoid the six decades of religious strife that has followed.

Sarojini Naidu on Gandhiji

One of the finest words about Gandhiji came from the poet and freedom fighter Sarojini Naidu: 'Who is this Gandhi and why is it that today he represents the supreme moral force in the world... [He is] a tiny man, a fragile man, a man of no worldly importance, of no earthly possessions, and yet a man greater than emperors...this man with his crooked bones, his toothless mouth, his square yard of clothing... He overthrows emperors, he conquerors death, but what is it in him that had given him this power, this magic, this authority, this prestige, this almost God-like quality of swaying the hearts of men?'

Writing the Constitution

What is a constitution and why did we need it so urgently in 1947 CE?

A constitution is the document that establishes not just what kind of government a country will have but also spells out what kind of society it will have. Soon after Independence Day, the Constituent Assembly began to meet to debate and write the Indian Constitution. It had a tough challenge before it. It was working at a time when riots were raging outside and refugees were flooding the cities. And then, to add to the catastrophe, Gandhiji was assassinated.

The Assembly began with one absolute premise—India was going to be a democracy where power would be vested in the hands of the people. The inspiration for this was our freedom struggle which had also been a movement for equality and social reform. The Assembly studied the constitutions of various countries like the United States, the United Kingdom, France and Ireland. But they also had to consider the special challenges that faced India.

The Indian Constitution is a social, political and legal document that states how a government is to be formed. It lays down the structure of our democracy and establishes a parliamentary form of government. It gives us an independent judiciary, an elected legislature and an executive to carry out the will of the people. It lays down the fundamental rights and duties of the people. It states the duties of the executive, the legislative and the judiciary bodies of the government. It also bans social evils like untouchability and bonded labour. And most importantly, it gives every adult citizen the right to vote.

With the adoption of the Constitution, India became the largest democracy in the world. The Preamble of the Constitution says it all: a free democratic India which promotes liberty, equality and fraternity.

The new constitution was adopted on 26 January 1950 CE and we still celebrate it as Republic Day, with a parade of marching soldiers, dancing children, horses, camels and elephants that turns the Rajpath in Delhi into a colourful portrait of our vibrant land each year.

The First Elections

'One citizen, one vote' was the greatest gift of our Constitution. Today, every Indian of eighteen years and above—man or woman, rich or poor, literate or illiterate, of every region, social class or religion—gets one vote. Every Indian going to vote during an election holds on to this right with great

Preamble of Our Constitution

***We, The People of India** having solemnly resolved to constitute India into a **Sovereign, Socialist, Secular, Democratic Republic** and to secure to all citizens:*
***Justice**, social, economic and political;*
***Liberty**, of thought, expression, belief, faith and worship;*
***Equality**, of status and opportunity;*
And to promote among them all,
***Fraternity**, assuring the dignity of the individual and the unity and integrity of the Nation;*
***In Our Constituent Assembly**, this twenty-sixth day of November 1949, do **Hereby Adopt, Enact And Give Ourselves This Constitution**.*

passion as the vote gives power to the people. The elected government is therefore of the people, by the people and for the people.

Our first elections took place in 1952 CE, led by our first Chief Election Commissioner, an ICS officer and mathematician named Sukumar Sen. With 17 crore and 30 lakh voters, this first election was held for both the Lok Sabha and all the state assemblies. A voter's list had to be prepared and, as most of the voters were illiterate, election symbols had to be designed. Even in 1952 CE, there were many political parties—14 national parties and 63 regional parties contesting 489 Lok Sabha and 3,283 state assembly seats.

It was a mammoth task for a poor country—224,000 polling booths had to be built and, as each party was given a separate ballot box, 2 million steel ballot boxes were made. And since this was a time before computers or email and a very small telephone network, 16,500 clerks typed out the electoral rolls and 380,000 reams of paper were used to print them.

Before the elections, Nehru travelled all across the country, covering over 40,000 kilometres, addressing the people, educating them about how to vote and about their voting rights. He did not only promote the Congress; in fact, he emphasized that the people were free to vote for anyone they wanted, that they were all equal and should vote without fear. The Congress won an overwhelming majority in the Lok Sabha and all the state assemblies. Nehru took office as the first elected prime minister of the Republic of India.

> **Voting Cows**
>
> *The election symbol of the Congress was a pair of bullocks and so, in Calcutta, stray cows wandering around on the road had their backs painted with the words 'Vote Congress' in Bangla. One voting booth in Orissa was visited by two leopards and an elephant but no voter!*

Making the Princely States Join India

Although many challenges had been surmounted, there was still a major task remaining. India could not be a nation if the princely states remained independent. The people of these

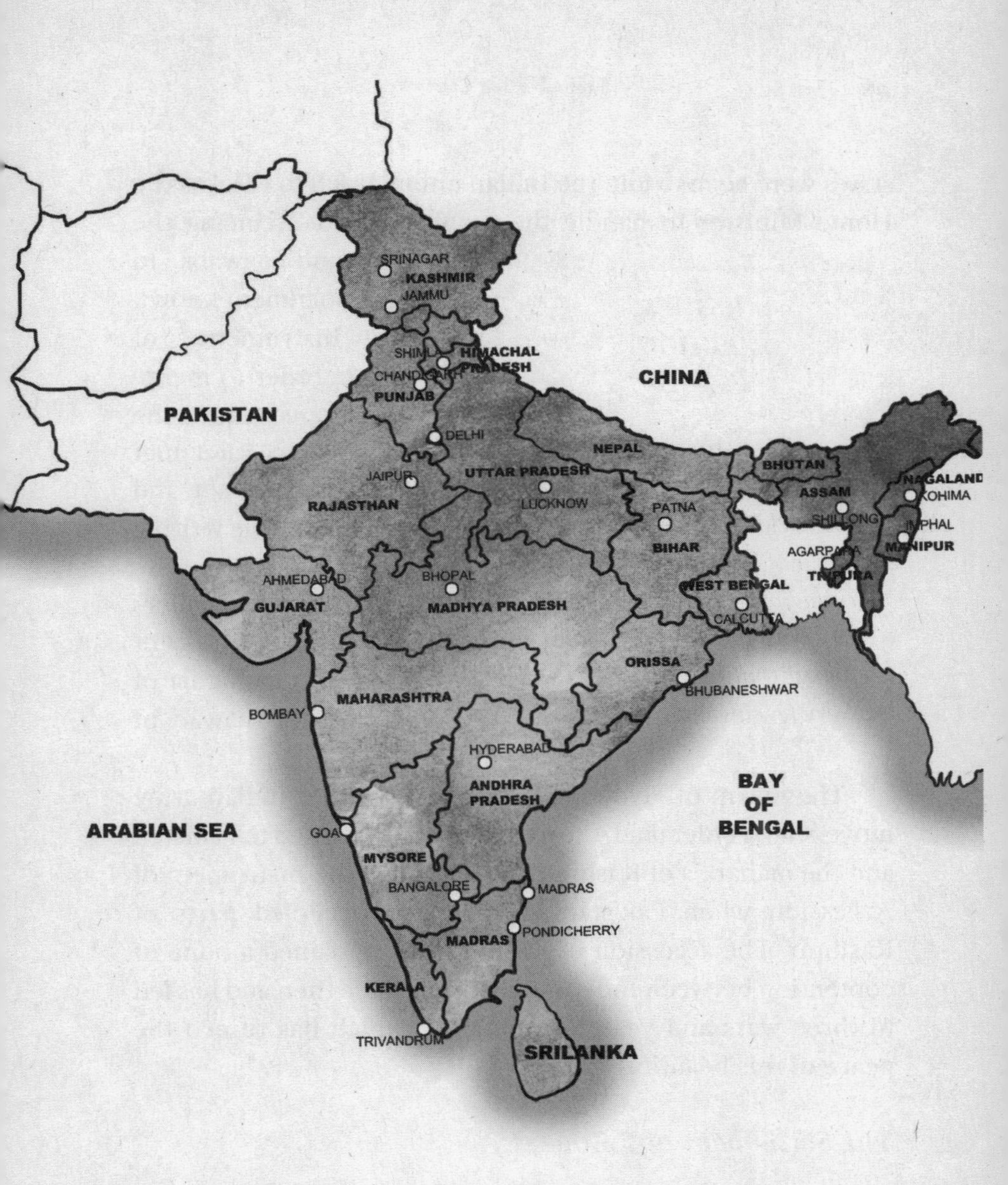

India in 1960 CE with the states.

states were keen to join the Indian union. It fell to Patel as the Home Minister to handle the tough job of convincing the maharajas and nawabs to sign a legal document known as the Instrument of Accession in order to merge their kingdoms into the Indian union. So Patel met one ruler after another and most of them saw the writing on the wall and gave in. However three rulers resisted—the nizam of Hyderabad, the maharaja of Kashmir and the nawab of Junagadh.

The First Election

In that first election, Indians went to vote in their finest clothes and there was an air of celebration. Simple rural folk surprised critics by voting carefully and thoughtfully and there were very few invalid votes.

The nizam of Hyderabad gave in when the Indian army moved into Hyderabad, the nawab of Junagadh fled to Pakistan and the maharaja of Kashmir finally signed the Instrument of Accession when Pakistan invaded and occupied parts of Kashmir. The accession of Kashmir has remained a bone of contention between India and Pakistan since then and has led to three wars and years of militancy, which has ruined the peace of this beautiful valley.

The Settlement of Refugees

At a time when the coffers of the government were empty, six million penniless refugees poured into Punjab and Delhi in the north and into West Bengal in the east, post the Partition. They came with nothing and needed food, shelter and occupation. In Punjab, the refugees were often settled in lands and homes that had been abandoned by Muslims. But in the east, where few Muslims had moved and the refugees kept coming for a long time, the job was much harder. A ministry was set up for refugee rehabilitation and it helped the refugees build new lives in India.

Mad Nawab

The eccentric nawab of Junagadh, whose kingdom was in the middle of Gujarat, wanted to join Pakistan even though a majority of his subjects were Hindus. His greatest passion was cars and dogs and he spent millions on them.

Elsewhere in the World

After India's independence, European colonies in Africa and Asia began to win freedom. In the 1950s and 1960s, Ghana, Zaire, Nigeria, Tanzania, Algeria, Uganda, Kenya, Zimbabwe, Malawi and Egypt in Africa and Malaysia in Asia became independent.

On the Net

Do a Google Image search and check out the pictures from the first ever elections in India—from leaders canvassing for votes to the early polling booths and the tamper-proof steel ballot boxes. Plus, the entire Constitution of India is available to read on the net! You can find it on sites like www.constitution.org.

2

THE CONSTITUTION OF INDIA

~ The Voice of the People ~ Fundamental Rights ~ The Legislature ~ The Executive ~ The Judiciary ~ Symbols of Our Republic ~

You may think that the Constitution sounds like a difficult and boring document full of big words that even many adults find it hard to understand. Preamble...fundamental rights...directive principles...legislature...judiciary...your head begins to spin! You might also think: how is the Constitution useful in my life? After all, it's just a document. But the truth is, the Constitution affects the life of every Indian, and that includes you!

Our founding fathers worked for three years to write this Constitution, keeping us, the citizens of India, in mind. It is this document that tells us what kind of society we will have, what kind of government we should form and our rights and duties as citizens. It talks of not just the India of the past or the present but also of the India of the future. And who does the future belong to? To you, the children, of course!

Actually, if you read it patiently, the Constitution is not that hard to understand, especially the preamble and the section on Fundamental Rights. So let's see if we can make this simpler.

The Voice of the People

The Preamble is the first page of the Constitution and it establishes its guiding principles. It begins with these simple but very important words, 'We, the people of India'. With these words we declare with pride and confidence that this is the voice of the people of an independent, democratic nation. A nation where people are free, equal and have clearly stated rights and duties. At the same time, the role of the government is spelled out.

> ### *The Longest in the World*
>
> *The Indian Constitution is the longest in the world. That's because India is a pretty complicated country with many challenges. Our Constitution has 395 Articles, divided into 22 Parts and 12 Schedules. The original document had 117,369 words. So it is the size of a fat novel!*

The Preamble puts down in clear terms what the Constitution plans to achieve. With simplicity and courage, it states what the future of India and its citizens will be. It represents the hopes and dreams of a people rising from centuries of colonialism, but still reaching for the stars. Originally, the Preamble said that India was going to be a 'sovereign, democratic republic'. The words 'socialist' and 'secular' were added by the 42nd Amendment in 1976 CE.

The Preamble is the final word on any ambiguities in the Constitution and it is the guiding spirit of our laws. It makes a pledge to the people of India, promising all its citizens a democratic country governed by justice, liberty and equality. Also it states very clearly that the power is now vested in the people of India.

The Constitution created three arms of the government—the legislature, the executive and the judiciary. They serve as checks and balances to each other so that no one arm can become too powerful.

The Draft Committee

A dozen members of the Constituent Assembly played a crucial role in the drafting of the Constitution, of whom three were women. The members include Jawaharlal Nehru, Vallabhbhai Patel, B.R. Ambedkar, Rajendra Prasad, Abul Kalam Azad, Durgabai Deshmukh, Rajkumari Amrit Kaur, Hansa Mehta, K.M. Munshi, Pattabhi Sitaramayya, Satyanarayan Sinha and Govind Ballabh Pant.

Fundamental Rights

The most important section of the Constitution, that affects all our lives, are the articles that spell out our Fundamental Rights. The historian Granville Austin calls it the 'conscience of the Constitution'. It was influenced by the Bill of Rights of the United States, the Irish Bill of Rights and the Declaration of Human Rights of the United Nations. And of course, it was also inspired by our experience during the freedom struggle.

The Fundamental Rights are stated in seven main parts: The Right to Equality; the Right to Freedom; the Right against

Exploitation; the Right to Freedom of Religion; Cultural and Educational Rights; the Right to Property and finally the Right to Constitutional Remedies. They also abolish untouchability and prohibit forced labour. Today the Right to Education has also become a Fundamental Right and it is the duty of the state to provide free education to every child till the age of fourteen.

How do Fundamental Rights affect the lives of common people? It gives us the privilege of living anywhere we want; do any work we choose to do; follow any religion we like. We have freedom of speech and that means a free press, which can also criticize the government if it wishes. Discrimination on the basis of caste is illegal and no one can force another to work as a bonded labour. Anyone discriminating against another on the basis of religion or caste can be put in jail. We are all equal before the law. Finally, if our Fundamental Rights are threatened by anyone, even the government, we can appeal to the judiciary to protect them.

There is another section in the Constitution called Directive Principles that lays down guidelines on what the government should do for its citizens. It spells out how the promises made in the Preamble are to be carried out by the government. However, unlike the Fundamental Rights, these are only instructions and a citizen cannot take the government to court about them. The Directive Principles advise the government to provide adequate means of livelihood for people, with equal pay for men and women and humane working conditions. The government also has to make sure that all the wealth is not concentrated in the hands of a few powerful people. All workers should receive a fair wage and the government should ensure a minimum salary.

The Directive Principles are essentially guidelines for the government and cover many subjects, such as providing health-care; improving agriculture; protecting the environment and wildlife; preserving historical monuments; organizing village panchayats and encouraging them to improve the economic condition of villages.

The Legislature

The process of formation of our government begins when we go out and vote to elect an MP, or Member of Parliament. The Indian Parliament has two houses—the Upper House called the Rajya Sabha and the Lower House called Lok Sabha. We vote for the members of the Lok Sabha. The states have their Vidhan Sabhas to which we vote MLAs or Members of the Legislative Assembly.

The Lok Sabha has 543 members and the Rajya Sabha 250 members. Members of the Rajya Sabha are nominated by political parties, state governments or the central government. That is how people from various fields—like the cricketer Sachin Tendulkar, the singer Lata Mangeshkar and the late writer Khushwant Singh—have become Rajya Sabha members.

At each general election, political parties contest for seats. Each state is allotted a number of seats in the Lok

Duties of the Government

The Directive Principles were inspired by the duties of the government as spelled out by Mahatma Gandhi and also by the Directive Principles included in the Irish Constitution.

Sabha depending on its population. After the election results are declared, the political party that has the maximum number of seats in the Lok Sabha forms the government and also selects the prime minister. All bills, which are to be made into laws, have to be passed by both Houses and then sent to the president for his assent. The president can send a bill back for reconsideration but if it is passed again by both Houses, then he has to sign it. Once it is signed, the bill becomes a law.

The Executive

The executive is the arm of the government that runs the country and it is headed by the prime minister, who works with his council of ministers. This is similar to the British parliamentary system except for one crucial difference—in Great Britain, the government is headed by Queen Elizabeth a hereditary monarchy, but in India we elect a president who is the head of state. B.R. Ambedkar explained the role of the president in the following words: 'He is the head of the State but not the Executive. 'He represents the nation but does not rule the nation.'

The leader of the party that wins a majority of seats in the Lok Sabha is invited by

> ### *Nehru in a Hurry*
>
> *While signing the first copy of the Constitution, Nehru got so excited that he did not leave any space for Rajendra Prasad, who was the President of the Constituent Assembly, to sign. So Prasad had to squeeze in his signature at an angle.*

Rajendra Prasad

the president to form the government. The prime minister, as the leader of the majority party in the Lok Sabha, chooses a team including cabinet ministers, ministers of state and deputy ministers. If a minister who is not a Member of Parliament is selected, he has to win an election to the Lok Sabha or get nominated to the Rajya Sabha within six months of his appointment.

President's Rule

According to the Constitution, President's Rule may be imposed on the states in case of a failure in the constitutional machinery of a state. During this time the bureaucracy reports directly to the Governor. But the Constitution does not allow President's Rule at the centre. This is aimed at protecting the country from becoming a dictatorship.

The Judiciary

The judiciary, headed by the Supreme Court, is the guardian of the Constitution. It is the duty of the judiciary to make sure that the government functions within the Constitution and that is why our founders made sure that the judiciary was an independent body.

The judiciary is headed by the Chief Justice of India, who is appointed by the president and is usually the senior-most judge of the Supreme Court. Below the Supreme Court are the High Courts, in each state, and the subordinate courts. What is interesting is that the Constitution gives Indian citizens the right to appeal directly to the Supreme Court if they feel that their Fundamental Rights have been threatened in any manner, without having to go through the lower courts. The Supreme Court also decides all matters of conflict between the states and the centre.

> *PIL by Postcard*
>
> *Anyone can make a Public Interest Litigation (PIL) appeal to the Supreme Court, which means that anyone can take legal measures for the protection of public interest. A PIL appeal can be sent to the Supreme Court by a simple postcard and the court will take it into consideration as a writ petition.*

Symbols of Our Republic

Every independent nation has symbols for their country. The Constituent Assembly approved of a flag, a national anthem, a national song and an icon as symbols for the new Republic of India.

The Indian flag is a tricolour with three stripes of saffron, white and green. In the central white band is the 24-spoke

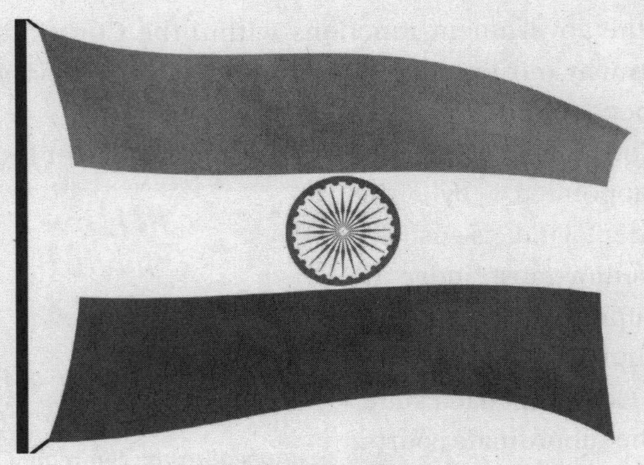

The national flag of India.

Ashoka Chakra in dark blue. The flag is made of hand-spun cotton, or khadi.

> ## The Tricolour
>
> *Our first Vice President, S. Radhakrishnan, a scholar and philosopher, explained the significance of the three colours of our flag. Saffron stands for sacrifice and the spirit of renunciation. The white represents the path of truth and green is our connection to plants and our soil. The Ashoka Chakra symbolizes the law of dharma, and ethical and moral living.*

Our national anthem is 'Jana Gana Mana', written by poet and Nobel laureate Rabindranath Tagore. It was first sung at the Calcutta session of the Indian National Congress in 1911 CE. Our national song is 'Vande Mataram', written by Bankim Chandra Chatterjee, which first appears in his Bengali novel *Anandamath*, published in 1882 CE.

The Lion Capital, or the symbol of four lions standing back to back, that we see on all official Government of India papers and on currency notes, was taken from the Lion Capital symbol of Emperor Ashoka, found at Sarnath. It has the words 'Satyameva Jayate' inscribed on it, which means 'Truth Alone Triumphs'. The first postage stamp of Independent India shows our national flag, the date 15 August 1947 and the words 'Jai Hind'. It was priced at three-and-a-half annas. The second stamp showed the Lion Capital.

S. Radhakrishnan

School Trip

If you live in Delhi or are visiting it, try and attend a session at the parliament, either the Lok Sabha or the Rajya Sabha; if not, maybe you can attend a session at the Vidhan Sabha of a state capital. It is the best way to understand how our parliamentary system works. It is often very noisy, full of action and great fun to watch!

3
MAKING A DIFFERENCE

~ Green Revolution ~ Operation Flood ~ Bhoodan ~

A scientist in the United States develops a new type of wheat that yielded more grain. An engineer from Kerala comes to Gujarat and meets the milkmen of Anand to run a cooperative. A Gandhian begins to walk from village to village begging for land. Sometimes momentous events begin so quietly, no one even notices them. But they end up transforming the lives of millions of people.

It is done with selfless generosity by men and women who only aim to do good, and that is often a greater achievement than winning elections or conquering land. Often history is written as a list of tragedies. The early years of India's independence were indeed full of sadness—the Partition and communal violence, the influx of refugees and the death of Gandhiji. However, through it all, people struggled on—we wrote a Constitution, we settled the refugees as best as we could, and we went out and voted in a true act of optimism.

So instead of focusing on the tragedies, in this chapter we'll read about two success stories that were the first to tell the world that India was not going to remain a under-developed nation for long—the Green Revolution and the

Celebrating a harvest in Punjab.

Operation Flood. And most amazingly, these stories do not begin in our cities but among the farmers in the countryside, the poorest of Indians. They are also the legacy of our second prime minister, Lal Bahadur Shastri, who started the work on the Green Revolution and Operation Flood.

Green Revolution

In the 1960s, Indians knew all about standing in a long queue at ration shops to get some grain and sugar. The country suffered from chronic food shortages as the population kept rising and there were many cases of starvation during droughts. India was often dependent on food aid from the West.

Around this time, the government, led by Prime Minister Lal Bahadur Shastri, decided to focus on improving agriculture.

The government started agricultural research institutes to produce better seeds and introduced high-yield varieties of seeds, chemical fertilizers and pesticides. It also improved irrigation and encouraged the use of farm equipment like tractors and pump sets by giving easy loans to farmers.

A scientist in America called Norman Borlaug had developed a variety of high-yielding Mexican dwarf wheat. This was introduced in Punjab and it started what is now called the Green Revolution. The results surprised everyone. Between 1967 CE and 1971 CE, foodgrain production rose by 35 per cent! This meant that India now had enough food to feed itself. It also brought prosperity to rural areas. Soon surplus stocks began to build up a buffer of grain, to be used during droughts. The Indian economy also got a boost as we no longer had to import grain or depend on food aid.

Operation Flood

Another revolution brought us something that we now have sitting on all our breakfast tables—that slab of golden Amul butter. This story began in the town of Anand in the Kaira district of Gujarat, where in 1946 CE, Sardar Patel had established a small cooperative—the Kaira District Cooperative Milk Producers' Union. In those days, milk dealers would buy milk at cheap prices in the villages and sell them for a huge profit in the towns. The milkmen who supplied milk to Bombay went to Patel for help and he decided that the farmers should run the business themselves.

Under Verghese Kurien's inspired leadership, by 1962 CE, the Kaira Union had grown to a network of cooperatives sending milk directly to cities, so that all the profits remained with the farmers. From 250 litres of milk, the business soon began handling nearly a million litres a day and grew from 100 members to 5 lakhs! These cooperatives then used their profits to build schools, roads and wells. Best of all, in many villages, it was the women who took care of the cows and buffaloes and collected the milk, so now they began to earn and used the money to improve their lives.

Verghese Kurien

Later the 'Amul' brand was launched, with factories producing butter, ghee, cheese, baby food and ice cream. It competed successfully against powerful international companies. In 1964 CE, Lal Bahadur Shastri wrote to chief ministers to start milk cooperatives in the

Verghese Kurien

Verghese Kurien was an Indian social entrepreneur, who was at the helm of the 'White Revolution' by setting up milk cooperatives all across Gujarat. Then the cooperative movement spread all across the country. He started factories to make Amul products and began the Institute of Rural Management at Anand for professional managers to work in the rural areas. He also made sure that at the milk cooperatives, everyone queued up together—men and women of all castes and religions.

A packet of Amul butter.

states and the Anand business model was then extended across the country through the National Dairy Development Board's highly successful programme called Operation Flood. The Mother Dairy milk booths in your locality are part of that movement. The initiative was extended to oil seeds, fruits and vegetables, as a result of which we now have the popular brand of Dhara cooking oil and the Safal fruit and vegetable stores.

> ### Women's Show
>
> *As part of the Operation Flood, an NGO called the Self-Employed Women's Association (SEWA) established over 6,000 women's dairy cooperatives, where women ran the whole show.*

The White Revolution meant that millions of landless farmers, who individually owned a couple of buffaloes, could join a cooperative, get a good price for their milk and also get loans to buy more cattle, make a good living and increase their business without middlemen taking their profits.

A Mother Dairy milk booth.

Bhoodan

Another post-independence success story is that of Vinoba Bhave, who was taking a Gandhian path towards helping farmers through land reform. At that time, most of the land was owned by big landowners and the government was passing laws to limit the amount of land that could be owned by one person. The land that was confiscated in this way was distributed among the farmers who actually tilled the land.

Vinoba Bhave joined Gandhiji in 1916 CE and took part in several satyagrahas, and was arrested many times. He felt that landowners should be asked to donate their excess land to farmers—this idea sparked the movement called Bhoodan. He and his group walked from village to village, talking to landowners, appealing to their sense of fair play and charity and begged them to donate one sixth of their property as a

Vinoba Bhave

gift to society.

The first donation was at Pochampalli in Andhra Pradesh in 1951 CE and by 1967 CE, 4 million acres of land had been donated. Vinoba Bhabe also had a programme called Gramdaan, where the land was collectively owned by the village. In cities, there was Sampattidaan, or donation of wealth; Buddhidaan or the gift of knowledge; and Jivandaan or people dedicating their whole life to the welfare of others.

Vinobha Bhave died in 1982 CE; he never sought political office or public recognition. His movement was about people helping themselves and not waiting for the government, and, in thought, it was pretty similar to Kurien's Operation Flood. It was all about self-reliance and believing in the values of equality and charity. He was, as he said, trying for 'a change

The Gandhi Look

Vinobha Bhave reminded everyone of Gandhiji. As he walked the dusty paths of villages, he wore a khadi dhoti, a chadar and chappals, and carried a stick. Many called him the spiritual successor of Gandhiji.

in heart, a change in values'. He was one of the first to start an organized welfare movement that was led by the people, what we today call an NGO (a non-governmental organization).

To Watch

Watch the story of Verghese Kurien and Operation Flood in the film Manthan *(1976) directed by Shyam Benegal, starring Smita Patil, Girish Karnad and Naseeruddin Shah. It was financed by the farmers of Anand, who all paid one rupee each!*

4
GROWING UP IN A FREE INDIA

~ Join the Queue! ~ Going to School ~ Shopping, Entertainment and Eating Out ~ At Home ~

The 1950s and the 1960s seem like a long time ago but there are still many people around who grew up then. This was the first generation that was born in Independent India. Let's take a look at their childhood years, what their daily lives were like. Compare it to your life today and you will get a pretty good idea of how the country has changed. Also how, surprisingly, it really hasn't changed in some ways. There are still class tests and board exams, summer holidays and trips to your grandparents', and the same old relationships with your siblings and best friends.

Join the Queue!

One of the strongest memories of a middle class 1960s child would be of standing in a queue and waiting! Most people's day began with standing at the milk booth to get a glass bottle of watery milk. Then there was the horror called the ration shop where you had to wait in line, nervously clutching your ration card, hoping to get some subsidized rice or wheat, sugar, cooking oil and kerosene. The ration shop owner would often sell the goods to others at higher prices and after an endless wait, you would come away with very little. For many kids, these shops were their first experience of the corruption they would see spread gradually all through the government.

No kid, except for the very rich, owned a watch. Fathers and uncles would apply to a government company called Hindustan Machine Tools (HMT) and then wait and wait till finally, after months, a clunky watch would arrive and there would be a celebration in the family like the kind you might have when your father buys a new car.

Of cars there were just two models: the Ambassador and the Fiat, and their design remained unchanged for decades. Most people travelled by bus and even the Prime Minster was stuck with a white Ambassador that had an engine that could be heard from miles away. The good thing about there being so few cars was that there was no such thing as a traffic jam. You could stroll across Chandni Chowk, probably the most congested road in Delhi, with only cycle rickshaws and the trams rattling down the road, ringing their bells.

Nowadays, we are all so used to having so many choices when we go shopping. Take shoes and clothes, for instance. In the 1960s, kids wore shoes from Bata, whether they liked it or not, and the company did not have much of a variety back then. So if you went looking for party shoes, you came back with a boring black or brown or white. And no one made pink or purple strappy sandals with glitter on them. Designer clothes? No one had even heard of the term. You went to the tailor in the market and begged him to stitch one something, carrying a photo torn from a magazine perhaps, but of course, the end product would often be nothing like what you had dreamed about.

Ambassador car

Of course, no ordinary household had air conditioners, or even refrigerators. People slept on charpoys on the terrace in summer, under the stars. There was always water in the taps and the rivers were broad spreads of sparkling, clear water. Words like 'pollution' and 'climate change' that are so relevant today, did not exist in common vocabulary.

Going to School

In those days, there was only eleven years of school with one board exam at the end. Then there were three years of college for graduation and two more years for a master's degree. However, there were fewer subjects to study, which meant fewer tests and much more free time. So in the evenings, the local parks would be full of kids playing and being noisy.

Children were not encouraged to argue with their parents or teachers and concepts like 'peer pressure' or 'generation gap' were non-existent. And, of course, since there were no computers, and no Internet, when you had a class project, you had to slog in the library, looking up books and making your own notes the old-fashioned way.

Shopping, Entertainment and Eating Out

There were no supermarkets or shopping malls and markets were small, single-storey shops with cluttered shelves. Shopping would be packed in flimsy brown paper bags that would split on the way home. (You may have noticed that many grandmothers have a habit of folding and saving plastic bags because when they were growing up plastic bags were very precious!)

Eating out was a very rare treat because most families could not afford it and also options were limited. There were no pizza parlours, burger joints or coffee shops and most restaurants served Indian or 'continental' cuisine, which mostly consisted of something vaguely European, with gluey soups and hard breads. Indian food usually meant Mughlai or Punjabi and when restaurants began serving up dosas and idlis—the first of those being the Udupi restaurants that popped up in many cities—people would queue up to get in. Anything with noodles was called 'Chinese' and even the cooks had no idea that Hakka and Szechuan were different cuisines.

There was exactly one television channel: the national channel, Doordarshan, and initially, it was broadcasted for just a couple of hours every day. Many television sets were in schools and the kids of the locality would go there in the evening to crouch inside the dark auditorium, watching the grainy black-and-white images, mesmerized. Since there was only one channel, you pretty much had to watch everything, from the news to Krishi Darshan, a show about farming, from

The logo of Doordarshan.

hockey and kabbadi matches to endless folk dances. But Doordarshan did not cover the five-day-long cricket test matches, for which people had to depend on the radio for updates!

But the great movies of the time made up for the lack of channels on the television! Films had wonderful stories, good acting and absolutely lovely songs. When Dilip Kumar and Madhubala lip synced to Majrooh Sultanpuri's lyrics and Naushad's music the whole auditorium sighed with joy. They were often about real issues facing India at the time instead of being only about Bollywood romances. But filmy fashion was as much of a rage as it is today—of particular note was the Sadhana kurta (named after the actress Sadhana) that was so tight that girls had to move sideways to climb into buses since it was too tight for them to move forward in it!

At Home

Most families were large, with at least three generations living together. The term 'nuclear family' had still not become popular in India. It meant space was tight at home but it had two great benefits—grandparents and cousins. Grandpas had all the time in the world to answer your crazy questions, take you on morning walks and teach you to recognize trees and birds and, on summer nights, show you the constellations of stars. Grandmas were the ones you told your deepest secrets to, the ones you were too scared to tell your mom, and many of them were wonderful storytellers.

An old-fashioned telephone.

Most women did not work, so you came back from school to hot meals served by mothers. Of course, it also meant that they had more time to brood over your report card, and lectured you about the importance of a good education! Living with cousins meant that summer holidays were spent blissfully poring over books, fighting over film magazines, listening to the radio and singing along to Muhammad Rafi and Lata Mangeshkar. The growing popularity of The Beatles and The Rolling Stones in the West also began to make a mark in India and soon, the walls of every teenager's room would be covered with the cheeky face of Paul McCartney and the brooding visage of Mick Jagger.

On those sleepy summer afternoons there were board games and everyone honed their skills at cheating at cards. You walked more—to the market, to school, and it was good for you. You did not sit before a television stuffing your face with chips but went out to play and made real friends, not virtual ones.

Of course, growing up in the first two decades of Independent India had its problems but it also had its good times. Life was slower and simpler, there was less of an economic gap between the rich and poor. Your leaders were often people you genuinely admired, as many of the founding fathers were still around. Their public behaviour was courteous and civilized and a lot of faith was placed on their judgement. For instance, when Nehru inaugurated the Bhakra-Nangal dam in Punjab, the whole country celebrated.

What was unique in these years was the unflagging optimism for the future. Parents and grandparents of this first post-independence generation remembered how bad it used to be as a colonized people, and taught children their history well. After years of struggle, India was finally free and had embarked on an adventure full of optimism. The spirit of independence was infectious: We were a nation, we would survive the initial hardships and we were going to decide our future. This optimism was the strongest fragrance in the air.

They were not bad, those times.

5

WHAT HAPPENED AND WHEN

The first thirty years of independent India were eventful times. In this chapter is a chronology of the important events of this period, to give you an idea of how India fared during those years. It was during these times that, slowly but surely, the institutions of our country were being established. Industries began and Indians began to achieve excellence in many fields of sports and arts. We also fought three wars with Pakistan during this period, and one with China. We faced an Emergency declared by the government, which took away our Fundamental Rights, after which the people responded with anger by throwing out the government in the next elections.

In these three decades, we were still trying to find our way and often making mistakes. In spite of the challenges we faced—rising prices, lack of jobs, a corrupt leadership, bad public services—we still held on to our faith in democracy.

The greatest achievements in these times were by ordinary Indians doing extraordinary things. Indians excelled in science, sports, social work, arts, films, music and dance. They began movements for social welfare to help the poor improve their lives. They won international awards and proved to the world that India was a great nation. The story of India after independence is the story of the achievements of ordinary Indians who fought all odds and won, and who never gave up hope, going to vote year after year, demanding a leadership and a government they deserved. They were often disappointed but their fight still went on.

1947 CE

- Clement Atlee, the British prime minister, announces that Britain would leave India by June 1948 CE.
- Lord Mountbatten arrives as the last Viceroy of India.
- Cyril Radcliffe is made chairman of the Boundary Commission to demarcate the boundaries between India and Pakistan.
- India becomes independent on 15 August 1947 CE. Gandhiji spends the day in Calcutta in prayer to stop communal riots.
- India's First Cabinet is formed:

  Jawaharlal Nehru (Prime Minister, External Affairs)
  Vallabhbhai Patel (Deputy Prime Minister, Home, Information and Broadcasting)
  Rajendra Prasad (Food and Agriculture)
  Abul Kalam Azad (Education)
  John Mathai (Railways and Transport)
  Baldev Singh (Defence)
  Jagjivan Ram (Labour)
  C.H. Bhabha (Commerce)
  Rafi Ahmed Kidwai (Communications)
  Rajkumari Amrit Kaur (Health)
  B.R. Ambedkar (Law)
  R.K. Shanmukham Chetty (Finance)
  Shyama Prasad Mukherjee (Industries and Supplies)

N.V. Gadgil (Works, Mines, Power)
Kshitish Chandra Neogy (Relief and Rehabilitation)
Narasimha Gopalaswami (Minister without portfolio)

- Kashmir seeks help after Pakistan invades. India sends troops.
- C.N. Annadurai forms India's first regional party the Dravida Munnetra Kazhagam (DMK) in Madras.
- Sarojini Naidu becomes the Governor of Uttar Pradesh: the first woman governor in the country.
- Vijayalakshmi Pandit becomes the first woman ambassador of India, to the USSR. Later, in 1953 CE, she is elected the president of the General Assembly of the United Nations.
- The National Physical Laboratory (NPL) of India is founded.

1948 CE

- Gandhiji is assassinated on 30 January.
- Indian troops enter Hyderabad. The army of the nizam surrenders.
- C. Rajagopalachari takes over as the governor general of India from Lord Mountbatten.
- Ambedkar presents the draft of the Indian Constitution to the Constituent Assembly.
- India's first ice cream company, Joy Ice Cream, is opened.
- India wins the hockey gold at London Olympics.
- Highest tank battle in the world at Zoji La Pass as Indian tanks beat back Pakistan's. This pass had been seized by Pakistani troops in an attempt to capture the Ladakh region.

- Air India starts flights from Bombay to London.
- M.A. Jinnah dies in Pakistan.

1949 CE

- India decides to stay in the Commonwealth, an organization of countries that were once British colonies.
- The National Defence Academy at Khadakwasla is founded.
- General K.M. Cariappa becomes the first Indian chief-of-staff in the Indian Army.
- The National Museum is founded, and starts operating inside the Rashtrapati Bhawan.
- Muthamma Chohivia Beliappa becomes the first woman to clear the Indian Administrative Services (IAS) examination and joins the Indian Foreign Service.

1950 CE

- India is declared a sovereign democratic republic on January 26.
- Rajendra Prasad becomes India's first president.
- The Supreme Court is inaugurated. Justice Harilal J. Kania is India's first Chief Justice.
- Vallabhbhai Patel passes away.
- Sukumar Sen is appointed India's first Chief Election Commissioner.
- Anna Rajam George of Tamil Nadu becomes the first woman IAS officer.
- New coins are issued—one rupee, half-rupee, quarter-rupee, two anna, one anna, half anna and one pice. For the

first time, they show the Lion Capital instead of the head of a British monarch.

1951 CE

- Shyama Prasad Mukherjee starts the political party Bharatiya Jan Sangh.
- India's first elections are fought by fourteen national parties and sixty regional parties.
- India's first census begins.
- The Murugappa Chettiar Group begins manufacturing the 'Hercules' bicycles.
- Prem Mathur becomes the world's first woman pilot in a commercial airlines when she joins Deccan Airways and flies a DC-3 plane.
- The First Asian Games opens in Delhi.

1952 CE

- The first elections take place in independent India. The first session of the elected parliament in free India begins. G.V. Mavalankar is the Speaker of the Lok Sabha. Finance Minister C.D. Deshmukh presents his first budget.
- India launches the world's first family planning programme.
- The construction of Chandigarh begins.
- In cricket, India defeats England in its first ever test victory at Madras. Then it wins a series against Pakistan.
- India's first radio telescope is established in Calcutta.
- Jehangir Art Gallery, the first in India, opens its doors in Bombay.

- At the Helsinki Olympics, India wins the hockey gold. K.D. Jadhav wins the bronze in bantam weight wrestling.

1953 CE

- The National Film Awards are started. The first Best Feature Film Award goes to the Marathi film *Shyamchi Aai* directed by P.K. Atre.
- Edmund Hillary and Tenzing Norgay become the first to climb Mt Everest.

1954 CE

- India and China sign a treaty called the Panchsheel Treaty, or the Five Principles of Peaceful Coexistence.
- French colonies in India at Pondicherry, Mahe, Karaikal and Yanam join the Indian Union.
- The Bhakra-Nangal Dam is inaugurated.
- The world's largest fertilizer demonstration project, where experts went to villages to demonstrate how to use chemical fertilizers to farmers, begins. It would cover two lakh plots of land.
- The Harappan port of Lothal is discovered by archaeologists in Gujarat.
- The Sahitya Akademi, the Sangeet Natak Akademi and the Lalit Kala Akademi are established.

1955 CE

- Satyagrahas for liberation intensify in the Portuguese colony of Goa.

- The HEC-2M, the first computer in India, is installed in Calcutta.
- Satyajit Ray's first film in Bengali *Pather Panchali* wins the National Film Award. It will go on to win the Best Picture award at the San Francisco Festival. His second film, *Aparajito*, will go on to win at the Venice Film Festival.
- Dharamvir Bharati writes the Hindi play *Andha Yug* in verse.
- The Hindu Marriage Act makes monogamy a law and allows divorce.
- The Imperial Bank is nationalized and named the State Bank of India.

1956 CE

- B.R. Ambedkar converts to Buddhism. He dies a few months later.
- The Hindu Succession Act gives the right to inherit property to women.
- The Ashok Hotel, India's first five-star luxury hotel, opens.
- Hero Cycles starts by producing twenty-five cycles a day. It will go on to become the biggest cycle company in the world.
- The first plant of the Bharat Heavy Electricals Ltd. (BHEL) is set up in Bhopal.
- Automobile Products of India launches India's first scooter, the Lambretta.

1957 CE

- The decimal coinage system begins, with one rupee divided into one hundred naya paisa. Coins of 10, 5, 2 and 1 paisa are issued.
- Vividh Bharati, a programme made up of short skits, interviews, music and plays, begins to broadcast from All India Radio.
- The Bhabha Atomic Research Centre opens in Trombay.
- Archaeologist V.S. Wankaner discovers the world's largest collection of rock art at Bhimbetka.

1958 CE

- The first Indian Institute of Technology (IIT) is established at Bombay.
- R.K. Narayan publishes *The Guide.*
- Mohan Rakesh writes the Hindi play *Ashadh Ka Ek Din.*
- Wilson Jones is the first Indian to win the World Amateur Billiards Championship.
- Mihir Sen is the first Indian to swim the English Channel.
- Nek Chand, the artist, starts his rock garden in Chandigarh.
- Vinobha Bhave is awarded the Ramon Magsaysay Award for community leadership.
- The new Supreme Court building is inaugurated.

1959 CE

- The Dalai Lama of Tibet and one lakh followers are given sanctuary in India, after they are forced to leave Tibet due to Chinese oppression.

- Television starts in India, with two programmes a week for a single hour.
- Dr Sambhu Nath De of the Bose Institute, Calcutta discovers the cholera toxin.
- Dr N. Gopinath and Dr R.H. Betts perform the first successful open heart surgery at the Christian Medical College, Vellore.
- The Indian Institute of Technology, Kanpur, is established.
- Ramanathan Krishnan wins the Singles title at the London Lawn Tennis Championship.
- Arati Saha is the first Indian woman to swim the English channel.

1960 CE

- The government announces that English will continue as an additional or associate national language for India.
- Air India buys its first jet, the Boeing 707.
- Milkha Singh finishes fourth in the 400m final at the Olympics.
- The Nagarjuna Sagar Dam is built over the Krishna River.
- The first Subscriber Trunk Dialling (STD) telephone service starts between Lucknow and Kanpur.

1961 CE

- Goa, Daman and Diu are liberated from the Portuguese.
- India participates in the Non-Aligned Summit at Belgrade.
- Indian Navy's first aircraft carrier INS *Vikrant* is launched.
- Britannia starts manufacturing bread in Delhi and Bombay.

- Hindustan Machine Tools (HMT) produces its first batch of watches.
- The Indian Institute of Technology, Delhi is established.
- Manuel Aaron becomes the first Indian Grandmaster in chess.
- The Arjuna Award in sports is started.

1962 CE

- At the third general elections, ballot papers and indelible ink is used for the first time. Earlier, each candidate had a separate ballot box. The Congress wins a majority and Nehru heads the Cabinet as prime minister.
- S. Radhakrishnan becomes the second president of India and Zakir Hussain the vice president.
- Oil India commissions Asia's first and longest fully automated cross-country pipeline system that is over 1,400 km long.
- In September, Chinese troops invade India in the north-east and occupy Tawang, Walong and Bomdila. As war begins, a state of Emergency is declared. A ceasefire is signed in November.
- The second largest planetarium in the world is built in Calcutta.
- The state of Nagaland is formed.

1963 CE

- Sucheta Kripalani becomes the first woman Chief Minister of Uttar Pradesh.
- Chittaranjan Locomotive Works builds passenger locomotives.

1964 CE

- Jawaharal Nehru passes away on 27 May. Lal Bahadur Shastri becomes the second prime minister of India.

1965 CE

- Pakistan troops attack Indian posts in Gujarat and Kashmir in March, leading to a full scale war. The Indian army nearly reaches Lahore. A UN mediated ceasefire is negotiated in September.
- Hindi becomes the official language. Anti-Hindi riots occur in Madras.
- The first Indian expedition led by Commander M.S. Kohli conquers Mt Everest.
- Jayaprakash Narayan wins the Ramon Magsaysay Award for public service.

1966 CE

- Lal Bahadur Shastri and Ayub Khan of Pakistan sign the Tashkent Agreement for peaceful relations after the war.
- Shastri dies at Tashkent on January 11. Indira Gandhi is sworn in as the prime minister.
- The Shiv Sena is founded by Bal Thackeray in Bombay.
- The Indian rupee is devalued by 36.5 per cent.
- Reita Faria becomes the first Indian to be crowned Miss World.

1967 CE

- In the fourth general elections, the Congress wins majority. Indira Gandhi is elected prime minister.
- Advertisements are introduced on the radio, on the Vividh Bharati channel.
- J.V. Narlikar is awarded the Adams prize by Cambridge University for his work on gravitation and cosmology.
- Scientist C.N.R. Rao wins the Marlow medal from the Faraday Society, London.

1968 CE

- First heart transplant surgery in Asia is performed at the KEM Hospital, Bombay.
- Dara Singh is declared World Professional Wrestling Champion.

1969 CE

- Kanu Sanyal, a Communist Naxalite leader from West Bengal, forms a new party of Maoists: The Communist Party of India (Marxist-Leninist) [CPI (ML)].
- The state of Meghalaya is formed.
- The Madras State is officially renamed Tamil Nadu.
- India's first nuclear power plant at Tarapur becomes operational.
- The superfast train, the Delhi-Howrah Rajdhani, is introduced, which runs at 130 km per hour.
- The first Dada Saheb Phalke award is given to actress Devika Rani.

- The Jawaharlal Nehru University is inaugurated in Delhi.

1970 CE

- The government nationalizes fourteen banks.
- Haryana brings electricity to all its villages.
- India's first off-shore oil well starts at Cambay.
- The National Dairy Development Board begins Operation Flood to increase milk production. Soon Mother Dairy booths appear in all major cities.

1971 CE

- India's first mid-term elections takes place. The Congress wins the majority and Indira Gandhi becomes prime minister.
- India protests as refugees from East Pakistan begin to flood into West Bengal after atrocities by the Pakistani army. By October, 10 million refugees come into India.
- India recognizes Bangladesh as a separate nation. War is declared between India and Pakistan.
- Indian forces enter East Pakistan to support the Bangladeshi freedom fighters, called the Mukti Bahini. In the western front, they occupy parts of Sialkot and Sind.
- General Niazi and his troops surrender in East Pakistan to Lt. General J.S. Arora. Ceasefire follows on the western front and the war ends.
- By an amendment of the Constitution, the government withdraws recognition of the former rulers of the princely houses and abolishes their privy purses.

- The Indian cricket team led by Ajit Wadekar wins the first series in England.

1972 CE

- A new party, Anna Dravida Munetra Kazhagam (AIADMK) is formed in Tamil Nadu by actor M.G. Ramachandran.
- Prime Ministers Indira Gandhi of India and Z.A Bhutto of Pakistan sign the Shimla Agreement to avoid force and resolve differences through diplomacy.
- India and Bangladesh, led by Mujibur Rehman, sign the Indo-Bangladeshi Treaty of Friendship, Cooperation and Peace.
- The census estimates India's population at 54.97 crores.
- Kiran Bedi becomes the first woman to join the Indian Police Service (IPS).
- The Postal Index Number (PIN) is introduced.
- Ela Bhatt launches the Self-Employed Women's Association (SEWA) to help women get loans in Gujarat.

1973 CE

- The Foreign Exchange Regulation Act (FERA) is introduced. It controls the amount of foreign exchange to be held by companies and individuals and greatly hampers international business.
- General Sam Maneckshaw, who led India during the conflict with Pakistan, is the first Indian to be made Field Marshal.
- The State of Mysore is renamed Karnataka.

1974 CE

- India explodes a nuclear device at Pokhran, Rajasthan.
- Gaura Devi of Reni village in Garhwal leads women to protest the cutting of trees by contractors. The women cling to the trees and start the Chipko Movement, which spreads through the region.

1975 CE

- Jayaprakash Narayan leads a protest movement against Indira Gandhi after an Allahabad High Court judgement declares her election illegal.
- At the suggestion of the government, President Fakhruddin Ali Ahmed proclaims an Internal Emergency citing threat to India's democracy. This means that people no longer have their Fundamental Rights and many opposition leaders are jailed without trial.
- Press censorship is imposed and some newspapers carry blank columns in protest.
- Small pox is eradicated from India.
- India's first satellite, Aryabhata, is launched.
- The Hindi film *Sholay* is released and is a smash hit.
- The fortnightly magazine *India Today* is launched.
- Farokh Engineer becomes the first Indian to win a Man of the Match at the World Cup.

1976 CE

- The 42nd Amendment of the Constitution makes India a 'socialist secular republic'. It also gives precedence to the Directive Principles of State Policy (the duties and the power of the Union) over Fundamental Rights. It becomes a very controversial amendment.

- Doordarshan is separated from Akashvani (previously, All India Radio) and starts showing commercial advertisements.
- The Bengali writer Ashapurna Devi is the first woman to win the Jnanpith Award for her novel *Pratham Pratisruti*.

1977 CE

- General elections are declared and opposition parties come together to form the Janata Party. Jagjivan Ram, a Congress Dalit leader, resigns and joins the Janata Party.
- The Janata Party gets absolute majority.
- Indira Gandhi is defeated at Rae Bareli, Uttar Pradesh, and resigns as prime minister. The Emergency is withdrawn.
- Morarji Desai becomes the first non-Congress prime minister of India. At eighty-one, he also becomes the oldest prime minister in the world.
- Justice J.C. Shah heads the Shah Commission to enquire into the excesses committed during the Emergency.
- The CBI arrests Indira Gandhi on charges of corruption. She is released unconditionally the next day.
- External Affairs Minister Atal Bihari Vajpayee addresses the United Nations General Assembly in Hindi. The language is used there for the first time.
- The Union Planning Minister admits that 50 per cent of the country's population still lived below the poverty line.
- Ela Bhatt wins the Ramon Magasaysay Award for community leadership for her work among unemployed women vendors in Gujarat.

A NOTE FROM THE AUTHOR

(And More Books You Can Read!)

If this book has got you interested in history (and we hope it has!), here are some books you may dip into for further reading. History books are usually rather fat and scary, but the trick is to only read what interests you.

The best way to discover books is, of course, to wander around the school library and experiment with new titles. This list is also for school librarians.

There is a lot of information on the Internet but it is not always correct. Wikipedia can usually be trusted and the information on the websites of universities and museums are usually accurate, but it's best to cross-check with your teacher or look up a few books.

Also, if you have any questions about Indian history you can always write to me at subhadrasg@gmail.com. I promise to reply. Cross my heart and all that...

List of books:

- *India: A History* by John Keay.
- *A Brief History of the Great Moghuls* by Bamber Gascoigne.
- *We, The Children of India* by Leila Seth.
- The Puffin Lives series of biographies of important Indians (of which I have written two: the ones on Ashoka

and Mahatma Gandhi).

- *The Wonder That Was India*, volumes one and two, by A.L. Basham and S.A.A. Rizvi.
- Books by Abraham Eraly, my favourite historian. Try *Emperor of the Peacock Throne: The Saga of the Great Mughals* and *The Mughal World* to know more about the Mughals. *Gem in the Lotus: The Seeding of Indian Civilisation* is about the time of the Buddha and *The First Spring* (volumes one and two) is about the Gupta period. The *Age of Wrath* about the Sultanate period.
- Books by Percival Spear, especially his history of modern India.
- Books by K.T. Achaya on Indian food provide for a mouth-watering read, especially *Indian Food: A Historical Companion*.
- *Daily Life in Ancient India: From 200 BC to 700 AD* by Jeannine Auboyer.
- *A History of Ancient and Early Medieval India* by Upinder Singh—full of weird and fascinating information and lovely photographs.
- The Rupa Charitavali Series for biographies (of which I have written the one on King Akbar).
- And as for my own books, if you liked this one, you could try *A Flag, A Song and A Pinch of Salt: Freedom Fighters of India*; *Saffron, White and Green*, about the freedom movement, or the fun *Let's Go Time Travelling*, about how people lived in the past.

Happy Reading!

Subhadra Sen Gupta

ACKNOWLEDGEMENTS

When you work on a book that takes forever to finish, you need a lot of help; from family, friends and editors. And for this book I also have to thank an army of historians who did all the real work. I just peered over their shoulders and took notes.

It is of course very risky thanking family and friends because then they want to be taken out to lunch. Still, here goes: My sister Sushmita who understands my need for solitude and is supremely stoic when I am being irritable. My friend Tapas Guha whose dedication to brewing coffee has always brightened my days. Also Vidya Mani and Devika Rangachari who understand the craft of writing history.

Without editors I am sunk. They find my mistakes, hold my hand and are very adult about my tantrums. So a thank you to Sudeshna Shome Ghosh who asked me to write this book, not knowing I'll be late by a couple of years. A big shukriya to Sohini Pal who tried her best to cross-check everything, made brilliant suggestions and probably knows the book better than I do. Finally my thanks to Priyankar Gupta who had the courage to tackle a giant manuscript and brighten its pages with beautiful illustrations.